Amber Medland read En[...] Cambridge and has an [...] University. She lives in London.

Further praise for *Wild Pets*:

'Smart and funny . . . tosses out picture-perfect descriptions with casual brilliance . . . *Wild Pets* is an instant set text of the emerging canon of millennial fiction.'
Anthony Cummins, *Guardian*

'A wickedly funny and emotionally complex novel that skates along the dazzling surface of life then takes a deep, chilling drop into the waters below.'
Jenny Offill, author of *Weather* and *Dept. of Speculation*

'Captures the Millennial experience sharply and sympathetically . . . The influence of Sally Rooney's *Normal People* is palpable . . . [but] Medland's book takes a turn for the darker. With hints of Gwendoline Riley and Ottessa Moshfegh . . . this is an impressive, cumulatively powerful first outing.'
Stephanie Cross, *Daily Mail*

'A ripe and excellent debut . . . funny and smart and human and true.'
Andrew O'Hagan, author of *Mayflies*

Wild Pets
Amber Medland

faber

First published in 2021
by Faber & Faber Ltd
Bloomsbury House
74–77 Great Russell Street
London WC1B 3DA

This paperback edition first published in 2022

Typeset by Faber & Faber Ltd
Printed and bound by CPI Group (UK) Ltd, Croydon, CR0 4YY

A CIP record for this book
is available from the British Library

ISBN 978–0–571–35871–7

2 4 6 8 10 9 7 5 3 1

If one follows Blake's mind through the several stages of his poetic development it is impossible to regard him as a naïf, a wild man, a wild pet for the supercultivated.

T. S. Eliot

I
Before Prozac, There Was You

August–December 2016

1

Every man I meet thinks that they can make me understand the grid system. They do this by repeating, *Look, it's a grid*. Sometimes, they draw a square in the air, or outline a grid on the sidewalk, toeing the lines between paving stones.

On that first ride into the city, Ray – who has skipped a meeting to fetch me from JFK – points out the Manhattan skyline, as if he's arranged a private view. I nod, though the dark mass of the city is not one I recognise from any movie. On the plane, I watched *Ghost* three times and ignored the woman sitting next to me. She was wearing a pink T-shirt with a Care Bears logo. Her name was Sadie, she told me, and she was looking forward to the duty-free trolley. When I got up to go to the toilet, she said that she was on her way to visit her pregnant daughter in New York. I put my headphones back on. My choice of film and its repetition seemed to annoy her, almost as much as my sobbing through 'Unchained Melody' had irritated Ezra. Last night, I tried to watch *Ghost* with him. He switched it off before the end.

At 32,000 feet, I found myself going back, again and again, to the scene with the clay, the one where Patrick Swayze is still alive. I asked the stewardess for another gin and tonic. They were out of ice, but I took it anyway. All the lights were off except pinpricks above readers and the dull glow of screens playing movies. I looked out of the window, imagining him somewhere, millions of miles below, working maybe, or smoking. I remember looking at Sadie. The foil on her aeroplane meal was torn.

The box looked like she'd licked it out. If the plane crashed, that would be the last thing I'd see. Ezra might not find out for hours. Days, even. Here lies Iris, died beside Sadie.

ƚ

Ray indicates, then swears at the driver in front. You'll need a proper coat, proper shoes, he says.

I hate it when Ray pretends to be a father. He calls when the conversion rate swings in my favour. He sends reviews of the US adaptor plugs available at Heathrow.

The radio presenter sucks in her breath like Billy Joel is foreplay. *Wasn't that just the best?*

Does she say that every time?

And not some J.Lo fashion parka, Ray says. There are real seasons here.

We have seen each other twice a year since I was eight, so Ray sometimes feels compelled to deal out these pearls of wisdom.

He starts talking about winters in Chicago, which he refers to as base camp. They have a house in River North but he travels a lot. He works in private equity. The apartment in Manhattan is usually rented out. In return for *borrowing* it, I have to water the plants. I have to make an effort with his fiancée, Lindsey. Decorating the flat was one of her projects. When I got my acceptance from Columbia, she texted me to ask How do you feel about fabrics?

As soon as we arrive, a doorman springs up from his chair, his shoes squeaking on the marble floor. A transistor radio, hidden from view, shouts soccer scores in Russian. Ray salutes and carries my hand luggage past, leaving the suitcases in the back.

2

✗

I stare into the darkness, replaying last night in my mind. I flick through scene by scene. Ezra is staying over. I pick him up from Battersea Park Station. On the way home, he has an air of quiet resolve which makes me nervous. He kisses me once, properly, and then barely talks to me. I try to kiss him. He tells me to wait.

I talk too quickly about things that do not matter and he answers in monosyllables. He keeps smiling to himself, as if at a private joke.

When I unlock the front door, he produces an aeroplane sleep mask and I fight the urge to run. I pretend not to have seen it.

Inside, I turn on the television and flick through news channels until I find *Bringing Up Baby*. I sit on the bed, hugging my knees, while he unpacks.

Katharine Hepburn tries to catch an imaginary tiger and swooshes her net over Cary Grant's head. Katharine Hepburn topples a vase and Cary Grant dives to catch it.

You've got that look you used to have, of being the hunter and the hunted, I say, keeping my eyes on the screen. My heart is beating very fast.

Television, Ezra says. I switch it off and sit back on my heels.

He turns on the Kronos Quartet and says, Clothes.

He admires me. Now, ask for it, he says.

2

I hadn't lived alone before I came to New York, and if there are other people in the building, I can't hear them. I don't want to call Ray because all I have to say to him is How do you turn off the air conditioning.

I turn on the TV. Hillary Clinton's face fills the screen. The system stays rigged against Americans, the borders are open to 65,000 Syrian refugees. The image turns sharp and bright – a luxury cruise ship appears. A helicopter patrols the skyline. Donald Trump's America is secure.

I change channels. A woman in a tight T-shirt presses a button and a mist of atomised petals devours a pair of sports socks. Because you have better things to do than pick up after him.

The window doesn't open far, but if I press my face into the gap, I can see a slice of Broadway. I decide to go for a run. The window frame leaves an angry weal across my forehead.

120 days until I see Ezra again. I record birds on my phone. They sound like car alarms. I send him the most alien. He calls and I get back into bed with the phone pressed against my pillow.

That, he says, playing me the sound I have just sent. What is it?

Angel song, I say.

We said we wouldn't do this.

It sounds like he is talking from inside a steel drum. He is wired and tetchy. The band don't go on until 3 am, he has told me that already.

I imagine him backstage, crouching behind speakers to talk to me.

I miss you, I say.

I feel sick, he says. I don't know what's wrong with me.

Maybe because you miss me, I say.

I listen to his breathing. I can hear the soundcheck going on. *Testing testing*.

☖

A few days later, Ray and Lindsey come by the apartment to check I'm settling in. We have a dinner reservation at Nick and Toni's. Ray takes a work call in the elevator. I smirk at our reflection: I, six foot, Lindsey five foot, Ray, halfway in between, power-posing. When I showed Ezra a photo of Lindsey, he said, She looks like Lady Penelope from *Thunderbirds!*

Outside, the magnolias are in full bloom. The doorman picks petals from the sidewalk with a frown, as if he has been remiss in letting them fall. When he recognises me, he smiles.

So, if you want take-out, this is where we go for pizza, Lindsey says, pointing at a neon sign.

This is one of her favourite games. This is where we go for coffee.

Here, you can get juice, but if you want a really great juice, you should head down to the Village.

Every ten days or so, Lindsey checks that I haven't trashed the place. She snacks while I talk to her, on saltines, or sticks of celery dipped in ranch dressing made with 0 per cent Greek yoghurt. She puts hot sauce on tuna. In the beginning, I try and draw out a hidden streak of brilliance or malice. She can never tell when I am joking, which makes her question whether

5

I am *genuine*, whether I am being *sincere*. She acts like she is the only one affected by this predicament. After a few weeks, I ask her to call ahead and say I'll leave the keys with Nikolai.

⚸

The second-last movie I watched with Ezra was *Bullets over Broadway*. We ate magic mushrooms from a damp box he had ordered online, and lay on my bed, head to toe. I like to hold on to his feet when I'm tripping. I watched the ceiling shimmer. Spirals of light everywhere, like I was watching the DNA of the air unwind.

On screen, a man asked, Which is more important, to be a good man or a good artist?

Ezra snorted from somewhere near my toes.

Stupid question, he said.

Yeah, I said, then, Wait, which?

A good man, obviously, he said, just as I said, A good artist, duh.

I've been in New York for two weeks and I am running out of movies set in Manhattan. I watch *Sleepless in Seattle*. I watch *When Harry Met Sally* twice. I order pad thai from Thai 72. I cannot remember the address of Ray's flat. I use Find My Friends to find myself and explain the delay to the voice on the phone.

What do you want?

Pad thai, I say again. Pad thai.

3

I dress for induction day carefully: overalls and a tight T-shirt, no bra. I'm going for Demi Moore in *Ghost*. I check my email before I brush my teeth.

24.08.16 10:04
From: ezramunroe@gmail.com
To: irisirisiris@gmail.com

Hey,

I know I wasn't sure about sharing a Spotify account initially, but it's good. One thing: please don't rearrange my playlists. I've put a lot of time into figuring them out. Each one is its own biosphere.

In terms of staying in each other's imaginative mind-spaces, I'm very much inside the Velvet Underground's first album right now. It's the one with a banana.

On missing you: You could be right. It could also be a comedown.

Do you mean my 5 pm or your 5 pm?

Don't hit shuffle. It's better in this order:

Little Dragon	Ritual union
Grimes	Infinite love without fulfilment
Air	Ce matin-là
M.I.A.	Paper planes
Billy Joel	The longest time
Nick Drake	From the morning
The Smiths	This charming man

I rename some of Ezra's playlists and then play mine on loop.

I take a photo of the brick tower behind the 72nd subway. Halfway up, there's an advertisement saying YOU ARE NOT ALONE with a 1-800 number.

I sit in the back row. I try to channel that girl on *America's Next Top Model* who says, I'm not here to make friends, I'm here to win.

Let's get one thing straight from the beginning: There are no stars on this program.

The director is witchy and glamorous. None of you are special, she says. If you have other options, take them. If you're looking for money, or fame, or attention, or validation: there's the door.

Fliers are handed out: an extra induction day for international students, another for students of colour.

Patronising much, I mutter.

Some of us are trying to listen, says a white girl in a turban. And if you find it patronising then it probably isn't for you.

She is not wrong. So far I have been mistaken for: Spanish, Portuguese, Egyptian, Jewish, Turkish, Cypriot. I don't sound American and I don't look English. As soon as I open my mouth, I confirm that I'm not from here.

One of our early days in bed: Say something in Indian, Ezra said.

I put one hand either side of his face and said *Sadak se nikal jao* (get out of the road).

Nance hasn't forgiven me for leaving yet. We both know she'll have to eventually because she doesn't like most people. I send her messages to soothe her pride.

Iris:	I'll send you macarons and roses if we start talking again. If you don't then soon you'll hear of me in the news: girl, 21, asked to be spoken of in passing as *girl*, eats herself to death in hideous but spacious apartment. I'm taking a tour of the world via a website called Seamless. You're speaking to an immigrant with a broken heart. Take pity.	**09:27**
Nance:	I'm jealous of your feasts and money. I see Joan Didion lives across the park from you. Have you stalked her yet.	**12:35**

I am tired of not having an answer to questions about my weekend. I resolve to go to the Met. Entrance is free for students and it is scorching out. I tell Ezra I am going to the Met and he sends back a ninja emoji. I found his emoji use amusing at first, but now I think it is lazy. I will withhold my replies until he gets the message and starts using words again. It is a straight walk across the Park. I am wearing a blue sundress and Keds. In my sunglasses, I feel like a tourist and more free. I will be in at least five couples' photographs today and there is nothing they can do about it. A bride and her fiancé are posing by the lake. She wears cream lace brocade and carries pink roses. He is a few inches shorter than her and the photographer encourages him to kiss her for the photos, presumably so that one side of his face is hidden. He must be very rich. I listen to Lorde, 'Royals'.

28.08.16 23:34
From: ezramunroe@gmail.com
To: irisirisiris@gmail.com

Hallo,

Life thing: Went to Notting Hill carnival. It was very loud and aggressive and there were lots of drunk people. I suppose it was worth going to although I never really understand the point of these things. Maybe useful though in terms of not feeling guilty about sitting at home. Steve is back from his travels which is good. He's here for two months. He broke up with his girlfriend – they were going out for four years. You wouldn't have liked her. She talks a lot about marketing in terms of transport metaphors. Getting stuck on the hard shoulder, that sort of thing. So anyway, he's back.

The gig was shit. The acoustics were shit. Dolly was there. Not much else to say about that.

I'm rereading *The Art of War*.

Sun Tzu says: The supreme art of war is to subdue the enemy without fighting.

Interesting thing: I know you thought I was high when I was talking about fractals but look! The largest salt flat in the world: Salar de Uyuni. It's in southern Bolivia. See the way it's consistent but random – that's fractals. A never-ending pattern. Wiki says: Fractals are infinitely complex patterns . . . They are created by repeating a simple process over and over in an ongoing feedback loop. Nature is full of fractals. For instance: trees, rivers, coastlines, mountains, clouds, seashells, hurricanes, etc.

I got in on a proposal for a book on the history of salt and a few of Nance's poems. We were drunk when I pressed send and I'm not sure she remembers. It was the proposal that did it. I have always had potential. Nance has a horror of plot and can only write first sentences. She is doing a doctorate on radical women and epistolary forms. She tells me the romantic fragments, like: Mary Shelley learned to write by tracing the letters on her mother's grave.

Nance and I met in Freshers' Week at Oxford. She disliked me. I didn't notice her. I was busy making Ezra fall in love with me and I used her as bait. Ez can never resist the opportunity to give a definitive opinion, and neither can she. Nance throws in Kristeva, or Marx, and Ezra brings in the *New Scientist*, which Nance reads occasionally, to spite him.

I have never known what I think or what I want. Nance says I am repressed.

To which I say, I am more of a prism than a beam of light.

Which, she says, is the essence of repression.

They justify my lack of conviction differently. Nance says I'm a writer and talks about Keats and negative capability, Ezra praises my emotional intelligence. Sometimes I think they should have ended up together.

We were lying in the shade behind college when I first mentioned this to Ez. He wrinkled his nose, as if Nance's proximity could damage his erotic capital.

I don't even find her attractive, he said.

That's not the point, I said. I crawled into the sun and kissed him. I did not say that Nance and I had slept in each other's beds every night for the past week – that I knew the whiteness of her thighs and how vulnerable Nance felt that I'd noticed it. His mouth tasted of frozen berries, which he had been eating from a plastic cup.

Nobody else has eyes like Nance. Like blue lagoons, the kind of deep blueness you could drown in. Turquoise, one iris split, starry at the centre. They are full of light. That Nance is also going blind is the world's cruellest joke. She has macular degeneration. On nights out, strangers say, Are your eyes real? What brand are your contacts? But Nance can fend for herself and I leave her to it. I watch her eviscerate people. *My sight is fucked.* I watch her make people cry. I pull her off when they're bloody.

When we met, I said it too. She told me to piss off. I backed away, and she said, Not literally, Jesus. We do not talk about her sight unless we have to. I remind her to make doctors' appointments. She tells me that she won't pay good money to hear what she already knows. I turn on lights when she is reading. She wears skyscraper heels, and if she notices that I am slowing down to cross the road with her, she hangs from my arm like a grizzling toddler.

Nance has porcelain skin and only wears black clothes. When people comment on this she says, I'll stop wearing black when they make a different colour. She has inspired three essays, a short story and a few poems. She has a cameo appearance in each. That more than one boy has rhymed Nance with Romance is, to her, unforgivable. The lines about her are the ones that people remember. Nance delights in this and thrusts open books into my hands.

I actually said that, she says.

Nance is a hypocrite and scoffs at my long-held fantasies of being a muse.

Subject not object, remember? You would get bored if you actually had to do it. All of that studied ephemerality, day in, day out.

Do you know me at all?

Edie Sedgwick, Marianne Faithfull, Courtney Love. How did it turn out for them, she says.

Maybe they weren't good enough.

At what? she says. At what?

When Max, the drummer, started calling me Yoko, I was thrilled. He has always found me unconvincing.

Tell Ezra what you just said, I said. He'll think it's hil – ar – ious.

Ezra had just started wearing contacts then and squinted into the sun.

Yoko was an artist, he said.

London

You're insane, man, Ndulu says, shoving strawberries into his mouth. You are sick in the head if you think they've got worse since signing with Warp. Screws loose, I'm telling you. Those men are *artists*. Those men are *prophets*.

You know who was properly sick, Lucas says: Ben Wao. I don't know what he was on last night, but we need to get some. He was gurning his face off.

Ah, whatever man, you're just griping because you got greedy.

I thought your guy was reliable, that's all I'm saying. *Best guy in Camberwell*, you said.

He's not my guy, he's *a* guy. If it was such shit why isn't there any left, boy? Tell me that.

It is August, late morning, and Lucas and Ndulu haven't slept. They were out all night grieving the imminent closure of Fabric. Paying their respects, Ndulu calls it. He jumps to touch the beam in Max's kitchen.

Lucas is muttering, scraping the carbon off the toast which he has just burnt. Max has been silent since Lucas called the kids who overdosed and got Fabric shut down, trailer trash. A few weeks back, Max said this phrase was offensive and Lucas has been throwing it around like confetti since. The cat next door, Lucas says, is trailer trash. Björk is trailer trash. Beyoncé: trailer trash.

That argument happened at noon, when practice was meant to have started.

Yeah, but we only got in at, what, eleven? Lucas said. Chill the fuck out.

Ezra stretched to show it was all fine with him, mentally rubbing a mark off his tally chart of hours spent working. He put a thumb between the pages of *Songs of Innocence and Experience* and joined in, squabbling over who introduced who to Aphex Twin.

It was definitely me, Ezra says, affecting a combatant attitude.

He joins in conscientiously for a few minutes, then goes back to reading. On the floor, Max is holding his drumsticks tight in one hand, as if someone might try and take them. At their last party, which Max swore was his last time high, he had an epiphany, and sat looking slowly between them – Let me get this straight, he said. Ezra has the voice. Lucas is the best producer. Everyone loves Ndulu.

The others haven't brought it up since, but Max has started taking GarageBand tutorials.

Max tilts his head to read the spine of Ezra's book and says, Any good?

Ezra glances over at Lucas and Ndulu – he doesn't like to bring ideas to practice until they are so developed as to be irrefutable – but they are absorbed in firing Skittles across the table.

Own goal! Ndulu yells and punches the air. Orange orange orange orange. How does it feel, bitch?

I've been wondering about this whole existential-mythic idea—

– Sorry, Ez baby, Lucas says, cupping a hand to his ear. What was that?

Ndulu, watching, clicks his neck and grins. Ezra makes his expression neutral.

Are you guys ready then, he says, standing up.

Existential, c'mon, don't leave us hanging—

Max, you?

Ndulu and Lucas glance at each other then rush him: Just tell us, what's the secret. What's the big news – Hey E*zra*. Hey Mr *Front*-man. Aw c'mon, just tell us – what's the secret whatsthesecret—

Ezra sighs and puts down his book.

So, given that William Blake was reimagining Milton's original existential-mythic conception—

Wait, Lucas says. What?

Ezra repeats himself in full three times before realising the joke. He puts his earphones back in. Lucas makes a noise like *ooo* and flounces an imaginary skirt until Ndulu punches his arm. Ezra turns up the volume on *Rumours*.

They are his best friends, but for the last few months, Ndulu has been the only one Ezra likes consistently. At least, Ndulu doesn't depend on him for anything. Max has endless questions, which Ezra is increasingly sure he only asks so that he can voice pre-prepared counterarguments. When he couldn't find words for the new Alt-J track at a party, Max lapsed into French, and Ezra was embarrassed for him, but more so for knowing him.

After the Republican primary debate, Max said, Obviously Trump is a terrible guy, really awful, but look at the alternative. He shrugged like it was a no-brainer, and Ezra wondered whether any drummer, even a childhood friend whose dad is head of A&R at Infectious, is irreplaceable.

Just give us five, Ez, Ndulu says.

When they come back in, Ezra tells them about the email, casually. He doesn't mention that it was only addressed to him. When Lucas snatches his laptop, Ezra tenses, but Lucas just Googles the blogger who sent it. She's looking for young

London-based talent. She has 64,760 followers on Instagram and a septum piercing.

She is *smoking*, Ndulu says. Did Luke-ass tell you about his new friend?

Ndulu tells them, adjusting the bass on his guitar as he speaks, while Lucas plugs in amps.

She was hungry, man. It was *savage*. And Lucas is like—

Ndulu dashes across the room and hides in the curtains, whimpering, making the tassels quiver.

The others laugh. Ezra returns to his book, making notes in the margin, until Lucas pulls out his earphones.

We're all ready, Lucas says. Let's go.

Practice begins. It is almost 4.30 pm. Ezra has been awake for twelve hours.

⚑

He is running, running, running. Every day, Ezra has to push himself a little further in order to function in the afternoon. When summer began, mothers out with their children started greeting him, as if they were friends, so Ezra started leaving his glasses at home. He wants to keep his brain guessing. Since graduating, he worries that he is getting lazy. He wonders when the cognitive decline began, and if he should have persevered with A-level German. He reads articles online about neuroplasticity, about how by the mid-twenties, *pruning* of the neurons in the brain occurs, and it gets much harder to forge new neural pathways. He makes himself brush his teeth with his left hand.

Ezra is still replaying his last conversation with Iris's mother. He'd been running interference all day, distracting Iris when he knew she was about to lose it, pulling ridiculous faces behind

Tess's back. He helped with dinner while Iris packed. On the news: a clip of the Foals playing Glastonbury. The camera zoomed in on Yannis Philippakis's T-shirt: Abuse of power comes as no surprise.

There was a piece in the paper this morning about how Brexit will affect tour schedules, Tess said. But things are going well for you?

Yeah, they are, Ezra said, yeah.

As he grasped for detail, Ezra told himself that it was a question of chronology. There is a time in the future when what he was saying will be true – Dolly has agreed to be their manager, they have fifty thousand streams, they have started getting mentioned on blogs. They don't have to do the 4 am slot any more.

Getting going has never been the problem, Ezra thinks, waiting for the traffic to subside, the problem is other people getting in the way. He gets a text from Ndulu saying he needs to get his bike fixed, another from Lucas saying he'll be late.

It has been a year since the members of Idle Blades moved back home, set up a studio in Max's garage, and committed to band full-time. Their first track was a result of what Ezra, on a bad day, described as a by-product of Lucas's rank opportunism. He would never have done it himself, which Lucas knows. Ezra hadn't even wanted to sing until Lucas goaded him into it. He knows how good his voice is, but he didn't want to look like he was showing off.

They spent a summer in the Lake District as teenagers; listening to Red Hot Chili Peppers and Radiohead, reading *On the Road*, rolling joints, spearing crayfish, jumping into shallow water. Lucas and Ndulu had guitars, Max improvised drumsticks, Ezra sang and snorted delicate lines of ketamine until he

K-holed and they threw a duvet over him. When he came to the surface, Lucas was the only one still awake, tinkering on Garage-Band. His face was grey and flinty. Holy fuck, he said, laughing at what he could hear pulsing through his headphones, which he pulled off and handed to Ezra. Ezra listened to Lucas clatter around the tiny kitchen, and pressed play, again.

He forgot about it until Lucas used one of their recordings in a DJ set. Lucas only told them about the Soundcloud once they reached five thousand hits. The others were thrilled. Ezra was used to classical musicians, used to precision, and the track was a mess. He found it humiliating and started learning to hide that then.

He stops to retie his shoelaces. He has spent a year playing gigs in pubs full of kids he recognises from school and sloping off to open mics to play protest songs about Trump which he knows aren't very good, but which he feels are important.

You know Dylan was twenty-one when he wrote 'Blowin' in the Wind'? *Twenty-one.*

That evening, Lucas sends a message on the band's WhatsApp:
7 pm, Hermit's Cave.

Ezra writes a message to Iris.

Here is the list of pubs he could have chosen. Equidistant. But he's Lucas and so he chooses the one three minutes from his house.

When can we talk?

Ezra holds down the backspace key. He doesn't want to sound petty. He checks his pulse with two fingers. Impending sense of doom. He has read about the symptoms on Reddit, where he checks the interactions between various drugs. He logs what he takes on his phone, on a Sticky called Grave Matter. Iris says this is like Sherlock Holmes keeping a list of drugs in his pocket for Mycroft to find. Ezra doesn't discourage this version of the more shameful truth; he needs some way to hold himself accountable – but then, so does Sherlock Holmes.

At the pub, Lucas is fizzing with energy. He skipped his sister's birthday party to go to a gig in Bristol.

Ma was pissed but it was worth it, he says. I can't think of anything worse than spending an afternoon in a room full of teenage girls into Taylor Swift.

There were only three of them, he says. Geeky, but in a trippy way. Those guys who watch *Blue Planet*: Pink Floyd, acid, anime, paisley. When I saw them, I thought *you are having a laugh*. But when they start playing, people lose their minds. They're more electronic but their equipment is no better than ours. According to their bass player, they've worked out how to use multiple loopers inside their laptops. They can record audio that they're playing live, add and subtract different loops at any time, trigger synchronised midi clips, and route all that through a bunch of different channels to the mixing deck.

Ndulu snaps his fingers in recognition – So then—

Exactly. They can stack another loop on top of it and start playing on top of that loop. The sound is more complex than anything I've heard.

Lucas expects the others to have the same reaction, and when Max asks if anyone fancies a burger, an argument breaks out. Ezra pulls out his phone. He hates timing when to say he can't afford it. He's spent his money for the month on sound equipment.

Ndulu elbows him in the ribs. Who are you sexting?

Ezra shrugs. He opens Soundcloud and pulls up the page of the night. He knew it was happening, but he couldn't justify the train fare in his head. Lucas doesn't seem to need to justify anything, he just acts. Ezra waves away Ndulu's chips. He has enough for bus fare and a pint. His mother leaves him casseroles to keep warm in the oven. Ezra understands that it's kindness on her part, but resents it. She suggests that he join her at Mass, but he hasn't been back since Iris left. Ezra remembers how nervous it made her.

Will I have to kneel? she asked. Do I have to take the – biscuit?

As far as Ezra is concerned the host might as well be a Hobnob. Even so he finds the question irritating.

It's not complicated. Do what everyone else does. Stand when they stand, sit when they sit.

Afterwards, Iris clutched Ezra's hand. She'd been mesmerised for the entire service and couldn't understand his ambivalence.

You must have liked it when you were a kid, right, all the rituals—

– You're thinking of *Brideshead*. All I remember is trying to make out the shape of the choir girls under their robes. And flirting across the vestibule.

When Ezra gets home he turns off the overhead lights, switches on his Mac, puts in his earphones and starts working. He does not move for six hours.

He has never hated a sound more than the Skype ringtone. He keeps thinking Iris has picked up, and then, when he speaks, Skype rings again. He uses the time to throw heaps of laundry behind the screen. Iris picks up, breathless, like she's just come home from something. Her voice causes some kind of chemical response in Ezra's body.

Are you sure you're okay? You seem tense, she says.

Lucas still can't get the bridge. Max could do it. My *mother* could do it.

You must be exhausted.

He's had lessons for two years. He's just more interested in fucking around with sounds on his laptop than he is in music.

Ezra knows he is repeating himself, but as he talks things seem to be less terrible, or at least more proportionately so. Just as he starts to feel better, her image starts strobing.

Have you moved?

No, she says.

Because something is different.

It's fine. Keep going.

Ezra tries, but her speech starts stretching out in a slow-motion stutter, like tired gunfire. Ezra watches her flicker and wonders at the futility of communicating in this way.

Why do you keep ringing and hanging up, she says. Her irritation makes him want to bite her.

Then his laptop dies. He's left his charger in the studio. He starts picking objects from his childhood bookshelf at random and chucking them in the bin. Model aeroplanes, his christening socks, a copy of *Swallows and Amazons* – he needs none of it. His phone pings, WhatsApp.

Iris:	Why did you hang up?	18:03
Ezra:	I've been right here. Did you hang up?	18:03
Iris:	Yeah.	18:03

Ezra:	Oh. Why?	18:04
Iris:	For kicks.	18:04
Ezra:	*. . . typing . . .*	18:04
Iris:	I know Skype was rubbish but I got most of what you were saying.	18:05

Ezra can see that she's typing, so he stops. Iris finds it easier to talk to people than he does. Ezra gets caught up in contemplating the absurdity of most social situations. She does too, but she knows how to incorporate it into her talking.

Iris:	I'd find collaborating on lyrics really hard. I'd hate it actually.	18:09
Iris:	Maybe it's difficult to relinquish control to Lucas?	18:09
Ezra:	He's not taking it seriously.	18:11
Iris:	It makes sense that you're driving each other crazy. You're spending all your time together. Maybe you could mention it to Ndulu & see if he's finding it hard too?	18:11
Iris:	Realistically, hanging out with a group of men isn't your forte.	18:12
Iris:	*pointedly not mentioning women, either in groups or individually*.	18:12
Ezra:	I'm so tired. Yesterday was bad. I ended up going to bed in the afternoon.	18:15
Iris:	The chrysalis effect, remember? Think of the people we admire. How many of them had fantastic early twenties?	18:15
Ezra:	I've been doing this for a year though. I'm tired of waiting.	18:17

4

Before I left, Ezra set up Gmail accounts for us both and told me not to check mine more than once a day. I set a timer for one hour on my phone, then half an hour, then twenty minutes.

02.09.16 12:32
From: ezramunroe@gmail.com
To: irisirisiris@gmail.com

Interesting thing: Hey, so today I started trying to layer up harmonics in the background of Pendant. (Harmonics are silver tones btw.) But yeah, the layering is when you touch the string, gently, at a point which is mathematically proportionate to the length, e.g. 1/3 or 1/5, and the string vibrates on either side of where you rest your finger . . . making a much higher, glassier sound, which can only be at a perfect interval from the root pitch of the string (if your finger's not in exactly the right place, the note won't sound).

I read a study about lab rats kept in cages with food, water and cocaine. Some rats go for the coke, even if they're starving to death, even if it gives them an electric shock. But when the scientists introduce other rats, and an exercise wheel, most rats lose interest in the coke. When I tell Ezra this, on Skype, he looks disturbed. His hair is sticking up where his headphones have been pushing it forward.

So, in this analogy, he says, am I the rat or the coke?

⚐

I go to the Hungarian Pastry Shop on 111th and Amsterdam. There is a mural like stained glass on the wall. The place is full of people reading or writing things down. A man with dirty blond hair smiles at me. He pushes out the chair opposite him with his foot. I barely have room to set down my books, let alone the warm weight of marzipan which I didn't want to buy, but I shake my head and pretend to read. When he leaves, he comes over to say goodbye.

I have a boyfriend, I say.

Okay, he says, but I'm in your workshop.

Sorry, there are so many new faces—

Sam, he continues, thirty-one, from Austin, finding New York pretty goddamn miserable. There's no proper Mexican food. No political affiliations, no criminal record.

He grins, raising an eyebrow to indicate that I should respond in turn.

Iris, I mutter.

He bows his head like he's taking his leave. M'lady, he says, ironically.

I open my laptop like it's urgent. I read an article written by an anthropologist, about a rock he bought in Spanish Catalonia for $15. It is a pink trapezoid with a strange translucence. It looks like a blend between rose quartz and soap. He puts it on his windowsill. After a day or so, salt crystals start appearing on the rock. Not wanting to ruin it, he rinses the crystals off. By the next day, the rock is sitting in a pool of brine. He tries moving the rock, baking it in an oven, keeping it on a copper tray. Nothing works. Those who think a fascination with salt is a bizarre obsession, he writes, have never been in possession of a rock like this.

I WhatsApp Nance to tell her that proposing a book about a mineral was stupid:

You should have stopped me.   15:03

Nance replies:

You shouldn't trust a word I say. I went to formal last night   15:47
and told somebody I missed the craic in Dublin, and a girl
said, I'm sorry . . . do you mean crack, like, *crack*?

Another for your list: Wollstonecraft and her husband lived
in separate houses.

MW said: I wish you, from my soul, to be riveted in my heart;
but I do not desire to have you always at my elbow.

I get another coffee. I get a new email from Ezra. I try to save reading it until I've finished the article, but soon I'm marking every line to tell him anyway, so I give in.

02.09.16 14:45
From: ezramunroe@gmail.com
To: irisirisiris@gmail.com
Hello,
One problem with this system is that it relies on an interesting thing and a life thing having occurred.

Life thing: Lucas and I spent the last two weeks mixing the new tracks without the others. The guy we're renting the studio from isn't bad. He was stoned most of the time, so he didn't get in our way. I've never seen an adult male eat so much Turkish delight.

It's easier without the others there. Max tends to go with my ideas if I can explain them in a way that makes him feel involved. It's tricky because if he doesn't feel autonomous, he pouts. He's got a chip on his shoulder about his dad, but he never misses the chance to remind us how much of this wouldn't have been possible without Infectious. There's a lot of ego management. If Lucas is late, Max gets shirty, but if Lucas is there, he and Max bicker, which takes time too. Thank God Ndulu is happy taking a back seat.

I'm not sure what's going on at the moment. I keep flying off the handle at things that wouldn't normally bother me. The first track is done though.

Interesting thing: I've worked out the trick is to do the work and then pretend I don't care about it – it's like you said, Lucas's cultivated indifference. I'm taking the path of active passive resistance. Or covert resistance. Sun Tzu would approve.

⚔

Lexi says, Meet me at the Angelika. They're reshowing *The Master*.

We have known each other since school. We were the only two on the athletics team with no natural ability, but we worked hard and bonded over that. Lexi said it was immigrant grit. After practice, she would walk around the changing rooms naked. I had to stop myself from staring. Back then, Tess still said shaving your legs above the knee was slutty.

Tess runs all the time. She doesn't say I should, but she expects it. The idea of not exercising is anathema to her, closely followed by lie-ins, obesity, letting oneself go. She keeps those who succumb at a sympathetic distance. I used to think she looked like a Rajasthani princess, like Gayatri Devi. Nani used to put small pieces of Sellotape on her forehead to stop her frowning.

Unacceptable, Tess says, blithely, as if she's remarking on a bad haircut she once had. By way of compromise, she punctuates our conversations by saying *frown* automatically, in such a neutral tone that sometimes I think I've imagined it. *You'll thank me later.* When she mixes gram flour and water into a paste, for face masks, she makes enough for me too, and leaves it out, covered in tin foil. She wears oversized cashmere jumpers, fur coats and tiny skirts. In kindergarten we had to write down what our mothers ate and drank. I wrote dry martinis and white wine. Tess found this hilarious. It was my only school assignment that ever made the fridge.

Lexi approves of all of this and says, knowledgeably, that my mother *knows her worth.*

Lexi moved to London from Slovenia when she was nine and her accent slides between countries. Today, she is Parisian. We check the showing times in the lobby of the Angelika.

But so, you and Ezra have a plan, Lexi says. You have strategies to maintain your primal connection. I point out the trays of candy with the plastic scoop and Lexi wrinkles her nose.

You have talked about it? Given his track record?

Have you ever had a Sour Patch Kid? Or what is it, Cracker Jack?

Lexi rolls her eyes and gets us two Diet Cokes. Her rule is that food has to be either delicious, beautiful or health-enhancing. Otherwise, she does not eat. I watch the man behind the till gaze at her. She has loose blonde curls, which I have accepted I will never have, and a button nose.

Lexi knows what she's talking about. She used to send her ex-boyfriend dirty videos on Snapchat. Ever since he recorded those videos with another phone and cut them with clips of

28

himself masturbating, Lexi is evangelical about the importance of leaving no digital paper trail.

I don't know which is more disturbing, that he took the time to do that, or that he thought his presence was *necessary*. My video was sensual. Very Coco de Mer. And there he is—

She makes a pumping gesture, then wipes her hand on a napkin.

Our erotic lives are composed of so much more than the visual. Make him a one-minute clip, or an audio file: you, talking about your day, what you're feeling, touching, tasting. Make it *sexy*. Keep it light.

I choke on my Diet Coke.

You are not taking this seriously, she says sternly. We all have needs.

5

I have class three times a week. My workshop is full of men who read *Moby Dick* at twenty-six and think that they could have written it. Sasha is teaching the workshop. She's published two novels about anti-heroines. When she critiques the men's work, they say, No, you misunderstood what I was trying to do.

She has an auburn pixie crop so close you can see her skull. She wears Doc Martens. I want to say something she has never heard before.

The end of land was the landscape of Sylvia Plath's childhood – the cold, salt, running hills of the Atlantic. Her vision of the ocean was the clearest thing she owned.

All I can say is: It is the history of salt.

I suffer from salt cravings, Lisa says. Doritos especially. Do you have Doritos in England?

Different flavours, I say. The class looks interested in this. I want to list them.

Craving salt is not the same as wanting it, or needing it even, I say.

I look at my phone under the table while my face cools down. Ezra tweets a photo of a heap of onion, gleaming white on a chopping board. He is wearing odd socks, one grey, one blue. There is a hole in the blue toe.

The caption reads: Is this enough for dahl?

I sign up for the non-fiction class because Nance keeps saying

I need to confront reality. In return, she promises to make an effort with Ezra.

I email Nance lists of the people I am meeting: Bassey, who tells me how to make a negroni the New Orleans way: gin, vermouth, Campari and orange peel, a whisper, he says, a *murmur* of orange.

Finn, from LA, who declares himself done with the American novel in the first class.

Lisa, who says you have to have guys here on crop rotation.

The girl from Mumbai who laughs at my Hindi. The fleet of literary bros.

The thirty-year-old with the abusive ex-lover who retells the Persephone myth every week. She is from Kansas and moved to Mexico to be with him.

Huevón, she says. *Cabrón*.

I do not tell Nance I have seen Lexi because she hates her, though they have never met.

07.09.16 16:56
From: nancyomalley@magd.ox.ac.uk
To: irisirisiris@gmail.com

So hungover. Sick as a bus to Lourdes.

Dinner after the seminar did not go well. (Did I tell you I'm convening it now?)

I got into an argument with the speaker. He said that epistolary space can't exist online. I said that conceptual space runs alongside material space anyway, connecting and resonating with it at times but not contained within it, so the erotics of epistolary space doesn't rely on the physical distance, the letter travels on the intermediary, the post office, etc.

Does your *email* have an *email office*, he said.

I pointed out that time is a kind of distance and any distance between writer and reader creates a structure of delayed gratification. Patronising smiles all round. Dr Postman wasn't having it.

Of course, you millennials are too busy shouting about yourselves on Twitter and photographing your lunches to care about forging real connections . . .

Professor Kennedy has us compare the introductions which he has written to several anthologies of short stories. He wears stiff jeans and a thick belt. I have never seen a man tuck his shirt into his jeans before.

Never teach, Kennedy says. Choose a partner who will support you. My wife, my sweetheart, said, Darlin', don't take the big corporate job. Your work is all that matters.

Paul shifts pleasurably in his chair. Paul was the first to volunteer his story in workshop. In his stories, a woman cooks dinner and serves it to the protagonist – also called Paul – on a tray. Then a neighbour-lady brings over a peach cobbler. Sasha encourages us to read this as satire of suburban America, but Paul resists this interpretation.

Kennedy tells us that place matters only so much as we imbue it with significance. My feelings about India are sentimental and have little to do with India itself.

I try to argue, but what I remember does not help my case:

1. my mother's voice
2. peacocks
3. bougainvillea, spilling down white walls
4. warm orange-yellow heaps of mangoes buzzing with flies

5. a beggar girl holding out her arm hung with tinsel and emblems
   of the gods for car windshields.

An Arundhati Roy fan then, Kennedy says, and moves on to
the next: The act of writing is about forcing the reader to submit
to your reality. Make it so they have no choice.

After class, Sam and I exchange feedback. He is writing a
dystopian novel about two men on an oil rig at the end of the
world. I give him a printout of Grant Wood's *American Gothic*.

I thought it might be helpful, I say.

Sam studies the page, then shoves it in his pocket. Not many
puritans around come the apocalypse, he says. But thanks.

In the computer room, Lisa slams her locker. Do you think
what Kennedy says is weird?

Cut the fat, Paul says. He is sitting with his back to us, looking at cribs online. That's Hemingway. What Kennedy is saying
is that once you tap off the sap – the sentiment you're attached
to – the tremendous will of the writer comes through.

He says *will* like he is thrusting.

Over time, I realise that there are few windows you can throw
yourself out of in New York and there are nets under all of the
bridges.

᛭

On Saturday, I try to go to Brooklyn. I stay near the doors of
the 1 downtown, reading *Just Kids*. I am wearing a black velvet
dress that kicks out, like an ice-skater's dress. At Times Square, a
man gets on and stands behind me, his back against the doors,
his erection pressed against my hip. There's no room to move. I
take a step to the left, but he does too. I wish I had not moved,

then he would not have followed, or I wouldn't have known that he would. Does he consider this a shared erotic experience? It's as if this thought makes blood rush to his prick, and then we get to Penn Station and he is gone.

I smooth my skirt down at the back. At 14th Street, I cross the platform and get the 1 uptown. I think of how I will tell Nance, which bits to omit, which to amplify. The most awful bastard, I will say. He was wearing a wetsuit. He was wearing assless chaps. I will say whatever I need to.

Apparently, if someone flashes you, you're meant to take out your phone, film them and post it online. Twitter will do the rest, the experts say. But I couldn't even look at him. I never can.

That evening, I paste the line from Borges which I have saved to my desktop into an email: Being with you and not being with you is the only way I have to measure time.

A few hours later Ezra replies:

Sundials, hourglasses, moon, stars, water-clocks, church bells (though maybe that's cheating as they're clock-dependent?). Plants. Menses. Obelisks, cigarettes, candles.

Life thing: Max turned up with four massive watermelons this morning, so I tried to make the watermelon cooler you made last summer. It tastes like rum and watermelon pips.

Good line. Can I steal it? It doesn't scan though so I'd have to cut it down.

Interesting thing: I've been reading about transcendental meditation. Apparently, David Lynch was really into it. There are

34

these great interviews where he talks about how it helped him make films.

I had to take down my Twitter account. You can still keep yours if you want. Some randoms started following me and Dolly says it's not good for our image if all of my tweets are to you.

I do not tell him that it is Borges. I like that he thinks I could write that.

6

We had to write about our summer holidays for the first day of sixth form. By the time I woke up, Tess had already gone to work. My bus fare was on the counter. There was a note, *back by 7, cook whatever*, under the old-fashioned cereal dispenser I bought on Amazon after we watched *Thelma and Louise*. It was full of Fruity Pebbles. *Nutritionally abject.* Tess only eats brightly coloured cereal when she feels bad about something or is having sex. She'd scrawled *D* on my essay, which still lay on the kitchen table where I'd finished it the night before. Later, in a different colour, she'd amended the grade: *C-. Imprecise (limited?) vocabulary.* Phrases like emotional labour make Tess wince. Intersectional feminism gets the shudder.

Mumbai was never a holiday. *Do you see me drinking a piña colada?* But there was never any question of not going. On the return flight, she'd be hysterical with relief, giggling, not herself. During take-off, she made me swear to stop her booking tickets. *It's a sickness. If I had a gambling addiction, you'd report me to – I don't know – child services. Refuse to board the plane. Say you're being smuggled, incur an injury . . .*

Our annual visits took weeks of preparation; gathering report cards, getting vaccinations and haircuts. Tess turning on my bedroom light to remind me of something that had occurred to her in the night, another thing I mustn't mention. Tess staring into the cupboard where she kept our Indian clothes, frowning as she does when she's thinking in Hindi. *Not everything is a costume, Iris.* Me sitting on the floor counting malaria tablets.

Tess stuffing cashmere socks, Nairn's oatcakes and M&S ginger biscuits into our suitcases, then taking them out again, keeping up a fervent diatribe as she stalked between the rooms of the house. *Why do I bother. No really. Tell me. Survivor's guilt?* Her questions are always rhetorical. The prickly silence on the way to Gatwick, the Johnnie Walker bought in duty-free. Tess's scorn when the trolley served coronation chicken. Her refusal to accept that the stewardess was not responsible for a *botched attempt at cultural appropriation which smells, by the way, disgusting.* Tess, pulling out my earphones, five hours in. *Go to sleep.* The first hotel room dismissed as draughty, the second accepted with vague derision, the flowers picked up on the way to the flat in Malabar Hill, Tess smelling the buckets of water for chemicals, choosing the freshest from each. Nani calling the cut flowers *dying things.* Tess, refusing to wear a seat belt in the taxi, throwing her arm across my chest whenever the driver braked. Tess, glaring out of the window. The pollution clotting my lungs.

5 July 2007

In the hotel, Tess opened all the windows. I could taste the air outside; savoury and dark and throbbing with crickets. She turned off the air conditioning and asked them to send up fans. We were already late for dinner. Nani would be watching for us from the balcony.

Tess arranged her hair at the dressing table while I paced our twin-bedded room.

I'd asked if we could get a double. I'll sleep better.

Inhabiting my womb wasn't enough for you?

My face was hot. I closed my eyes for a moment and pretended to be her niece. Tess would have made a fabulous aunt, the kind of aunt you beg to go and stay with.

Upstairs, I watched her try on identical gold earrings with a sangfroid that felt antagonistic. She put on red lipstick then blotted her lips, delicately, on a tissue.

What do you think?

Whore of Babylon.

She blew me a kiss in the mirror.

An hour later, the car turned abruptly into the driveway. The gatekeepers touched their hands together. Tess returned their greeting, then rearranged her pashmina despite the eighty-degree heat. We walked up the stairs in silence. She rang the doorbell, then thrust the dripping flowers into my arms. I could feel her tensing up. I wanted to swap bodies. Hurriedly, she pulled a tissue from her bag and scrubbed her lips. *They don't need any more ammunition*, she muttered.

My god, is she starving you, Beti? Nishta, the child is skin and bones.

Hi Mum. Tess walked past and slid the bag of gifts under the side table.

Last time, Nani returned the Crème de la Mer products that Tess had given her the previous summer. They were still in the same bag. *What, you'd rather I waste these things? These beauty things? Everything has a price and now you are single-income. Anyway, what good are they to an old woman like me?*

The flat smelt of Odomos and Lysol laced with sandalwood. Tess called for a nimbu soda and stooped to hug Nana in his chair.

Samir, nimbu soda!
I already told him, Mom.
He doesn't understand you.

I hugged Nana too. *I have put aside some books. Later, you must come up to my study. It is so light up there, so spacious. Most wonderfully, my wife cannot go up there any longer because her legs cannot carry her up!*

I grimaced.

They used to mark my height on a wall upstairs before the damp got to it. They live in two bedrooms and the living room. For exercise, Nana walks up and down the drive. Nani watches him through the curtains.

Taller than a eucalyptus, Nana said.

Nahin, she has her father's height. Those dimples, Nani said, pinching my cheek.

She took a boiled sweet from a dish and sat down in her chair, sucking it noisily. I sat down next to the glass table in the middle of the room. It was scattered with boxes, one that smelt of tamarind, another full of stale sugar-coated fennel. I took a handful, which got stuck between my teeth.

Iris, those'll be full of dust. They've been there for decades.

Look at those bony knees, Nani said.

Tess retrieved the flowers from the hallway and fetched the usual vase.

Nani fussed as she filled it with water. *Nu, Samir can do that. The child needs to eat.*

Look at that red one, Iris. Gorgeous.

They're a bit gaudy, aren't they, Nani said, winking at me.

In her strange provocative way, I thought she was trying to engage. When I posed this theory to Tess, she didn't talk to me for several days.

10 August 2011

Tess wouldn't let me go to Nana's funeral because of the open pyre. I sat in the flat and played Solitaire. At dinner, the only sound was the fan whirling slowly above the table. Nani refused to eat, then snatched pieces of roti from Tess's plate. She kept badgering Tess about Ray.

What kind of example are you setting the child? Nani grew plaintive. A look flickered between them.

Mum, he's been gone for six years.

All I am asking is what will you do?

Oh, you know. Scratch cards. Rake leaves. Smoke until the air turns blue. Drink apricot brandy in the bath and watch my toes prune.

I stared at a dish of mango pickle, where a mosquito was in its death throes. When playing golf, the British employed some local boys as caddies, others as jam-boys, so that the mosquitos would bite them instead. They got to take the jam home to their families. I never knew how they got the jam off. Did they stop feeling the bites after the fifth or sixth? Did each bite make them anticipate the sweetness instead?

Tess fixed her gaze on the mosquito. Nani coughed mucus into a handkerchief, which turned into a coughing fit. Tess squished the mosquito in her napkin and screwed it into a ball. I looked at a teaspoon where the dim light of the room hung like a moon.

7

We are still in the first cycle of stories, still sizing each other up. We pick the characters from novels that we'd most like to be. I pick the mannequin in Jean Rhys.

By the time the sign-up sheet reaches me, the only slot left is next week. When I write my name down, the left side of my face goes numb.

I text Nance to say that I am having a stroke.

Nance texts back: Did you smell toast burning? Because I've had that myself and often it is actual toast.

When I call Ray, he says he wanted to get me into the US medical system anyway.

You can say what you want about the healthcare here, but it's like Switzerland; fantastic if you can pay for it.

On Monday, Lexi comes with me to the MRI. I have to wear a paper gown. Lexi averts her eyes, then sits next to the tube reading *Vogue*. The doctor gave me earplugs, but nobody warned me how loud and pulsing it would be inside.

Ten minutes in, Lexi remarks dispassionately, Your thighs look quite thin from this angle.

I laugh in a shrill, untethered way. An electronic voice says: Please remain as still as possible.

Ray emails a few days later. Subject: Spoke to Dr because you're on my insurance. All tests negative. Let's explore other avenues.

In the body of the email, there's a link to an article on the connection between creativity and mental illness. I test the phrase mental illness on Ezra, who laughs.

Sorry, he says, about that. Wasn't expecting it. So. Do you have a mental illness?

I resent the question. He should know that I do not.

You don't have to live in my head, I say.

Ezra wipes a speck of dust off my face on screen – It's the same head it was a few weeks ago.

⚰

We go to Tom's Diner after workshop. My left arm has gone to sleep. I cradle it in my lap, my fingers prickling. I order a veggie burger and a glass of tap water and listen to the others talk about the murder of Keith L. Scott and the protests in North Carolina.

He was holding a *book*, Conrad says. Bassey starts reciting the names of unarmed black men who have been killed by police. There's a lump of something solid in my throat, and I tap at it, like it might dissipate. When I ask for water, again, the waitress glances helplessly at the others.

Sam says, Can we get a jug of tap water.

She looks relieved. Oh, *water*, she says.

I look at Sam gratefully. It's tough to be a foreigner.

It's not the accent, Sam says. It's because you mutter.

On days that I have class, I work in the computer room. Sam spends a lot of time there too because his roommate is a bona fide lunatic. He brings me paper cones of chlorine-tasting water from the cooler in the hall. When he goes out to smoke, he says, Can I get you anything? Oreos? Reese's? He sends me links to the American short stories that everyone else read in high school.

42

He forwards me an email thread called ALWAYS RELEVANT & UP-TO-DATE. Bassey works out the MFA is costing us $167 per hour. That morning, I spend two hours lying on the floor trying to convince myself to get up and open the blinds. Tess would say this was laziness. Those two hours cost $334. Conrad posts articles from the *New Yorker* and *The Atlantic*, and a YouTube clip of the Clinton ad where teenage girls look in the mirror with Trump's voiceover. Remi updates his Process Notes daily. Sleep: Six hours. Exercise: One hour. Meat, sex, caffeine, alcohol, porn: Nil.

I want to forward the thread to Ezra but there's too much that won't make sense. I open Spotify and Ezra is listening to Nick Cave, so I do too. I reread his email.

28.09.16 21:04

From: ezramunroe@gmail.com

To: irisirisiris@gmail.com

Transcendental meditation, what a let-down. It turns out you have to pay your own guru to get your own mantra. And if you tell people the word it loses its . . . charge? It's utterly ridiculous. I'm not paying a bozo for a word like pizza, I'm going to choose my own.

It's normal to drop having a boyfriend into conversation. You're a girl with a British accent on a course full of men, so it's functional. I wasn't suggesting that you wear a sign.

I'm not surprised that people are sceptical about the band. Maybe don't mention it?

Wait until we're famous. Or say I'm a cage fighter instead.

On Skype, when the camera fails, Nance talks to her fish about me. They are raggedy golden things, like they have been fighting each other.

Did ye hear that, lads, she says.

I think that she can't hear me, then realise she can, but I turn off my microphone and play along. It's comforting, and now she doesn't know whether I can hear her either.

One of our games: mid-rant, Nance stops talking, but her lips keep moving. And you would not believe what he said next, the bastard, I lip-read.

Nance, I can't hear you, I say. I think Skype is broken.

At school, we used to play a game with the security cameras. There was a tunnel between the school and the sports fields. It went under the road so that students would not have to cross it. A few of us would start off at the top of the slope, and walk in slow-motion formation towards the camera. I used to imagine myself suspended in a solution. A creature in a jar; thorax, abdomen. Then the school would send a man to fix it. It was the only game I ever won. Someone would start giggling and then the others would dissolve. I learnt that I can self-hypnotise. I moved in a trance for the rest of the day. I tried it by myself, but they never sent the man to fix the camera.

We are talking about the games we played as children. Nance went to convent school. She was the best at *going into the nuns* – they were in a separate building, on the other side of a field, strictly off limits. The boldest children used to run out of school and jump up at their window without being seen. You could get thrown out of school if you were caught, but Nance never was.

The man Nance is seeing is called Piers. He likes to take her to Minamoto, the Japanese sweet shop. He buys her sugary things:

kingyo, goldfish swimming in mounds of muscat grape jelly, mochi; pink and apple-green. He is writing a book on forms of epistolary address in nineteenth-century literature. She met him at a conference. He gave the plenary address on Edward Lear's letters. On the final day, he introduced her as his girlfriend. He is forty-seven. His full name is Piers Talby-Browne. I Google him as soon as she tells me.

I don't trust people who only have black-and-white photos of themselves online. Piers has the lacquered look of men who moisturise. His hair is blond and pushed back from his face. His thin lips are slightly parted, humorously.

Presumably this is the best photo of him, I say.

Oh, because your taste is stellar, she says.

I shrug. Nance and I have different criteria. She has the advantage of falling in love with men's minds.

I tell her what Kennedy said about his wife and she snorts.

Your man Kennedy is notorious for the women, she says. He was riding the box off everything at Trinity – Trinity Dublin, I mean. He was over there for the semester. My friend Niamh from home says he came on to her in Doyle's one night.

You didn't hear how he spoke about his wife, I say.

Why would Niamh make that up?

I refuse to argue with Nance on this. She doesn't have a romantic bone in her body.

Dr Postman told Nance's Director of Studies that her manner was aggressive at high table.

They like my direct way of talking when it's on the page, Nance complains, God forbid I open my mouth.

She's nervous about sleeping with Piers. I tell her to buy new underwear. I send her links to Agent Provocateur.

Nance scowls, clicking through them. It's alright for you, she says, you've got no tits.

I tell her about the gold pendant Mary gave me before I left for New York. (You don't have to wear it, Ezra said.)

Show, Nance demands. I move close to the screen so it dangles in front of the camera lens. Nance clucks. That's a miraculous medal. I can't believe your man didn't mention Our Lady of Grace is now watching over you. I mean the choir is one thing. But Ezra wasn't even an altar boy. You know we've a holy water font inside our front door?

We watch the first half of *Withnail and I* and drink VitaminWater spiked with vodka. Nance saw me drinking raspberry and apple flavour on Skype and got jealous. She went to three different supermarkets to find some. Lindsey left a crate behind the fridge. I have started a Post-it note of things to thank her for because I do not want to be gracious more than once.

I stare at Richard E. Grant's contours.

You're so gross, Nance says.

What?

He's a cadaver. His hip bones would leave dents in you.

I cast around for sturdier men. Robert Downey Junior.

You and the manics.

Magnets, ha. At Nance's expression, I add, I'd never be bored. Anyway, I'd way rather be manic than depressed. I reach for another VitaminWater. Electrolytes, I say.

Do you know, Nance interrupts, Rihanna has an IV drip for her hangovers.

It is easier to watch things in parallel with Nance than it is with Ezra. Nance doesn't care whether we're laughing at the same thing. When I leave the room, I leave the film running, and she

46

fills me in on what's happened when I come back. Sometimes I turn off the volume and listen. Nance is noisy in everything she does. I can hear the ice cubes in the glass, the sound she makes when picking sweetcorn from her teeth.

London

You need to indicate, man, Ndulu says, urgently, tapping at the window. It's *that* one. All the celebs stop there.

They've been in the van for three hours and there are four to go before they hit Newcastle. For Ezra, it's a minute-by-minute effort not to throw up. He can't risk opening his mouth, because he'll be sick all over the dashboard.

All the celebs go to a *service station on the M1*, Max repeats, witheringly.

Until a few days ago, they had planned to get the train. Ezra pointed out to Max that they'd only save three hours and it would cost five hundred quid. He reminded Ndulu how much fun they'd had last time. In the rear-view mirror, Ezra watches, resentfully, as Lucas stuffs his duvet under the seat in front. Lucas bitched about the van more than anyone, but he's been asleep on the backseat since 5 am. The column of their sound equipment on the seat between Max and Ndulu is so wide that Ndulu can't see around it. Max has downloaded a six-hour course in Japanese on Audible, and alternates between sounding out vowels and reading aloud from marketing blogs. He has put himself in charge of the band's social media.

No such thing as wasted time, Max says.

Scout out Grindr you mean, Ndulu grins. Really? Local service stations? You're filthy.

Max's neck goes blotchy. He came out a few years ago, and although his boyfriend Haruto has been to a few parties, Max doesn't talk about him much.

48

Lucas pulls out his earplugs and bellows, Oi, pull over.

The driver glares at him, then swerves abruptly. His wife is on speakerphone, and for the last twenty minutes they have been arguing in Polish. He turns on the radio.

The UK will begin the formal Brexit negotiation process by the end of March 2017, PM Theresa May has said.

When they get out, Ezra sticks his head back in the van. Can we get you anything?

The driver gives him a long hard look and then says, Cornish pasty.

They cross the car park in silence. Miserable-looking families tug children along on wheelie suitcases, which Ezra disapproves of. He also disapproves of the truckers eating burgers behind the wheel. It's about to rain. The McDonald's arches are garishly yellow against the grey sky. Ezra is about to ask why this place is famous when Ndulu bursts between them, putting his arms round their necks, so that his feet leave the ground.

We've got to treat Lucinda like a *queen*, he says.

Ezra chokes a bit and pushes Ndulu off. Who?

Who, Ndulu says, throwing up his hands. He's all *who?!*

You can't name a rental, Lucas grumbles.

Shhhh man, she'll hear you, Ndulu says, looking scandalised.

Max lists bands who named their rentals.

Lucas interrupts, Does it have to be Lucinda.

You worried people will think she's named after you? Ndulu grins.

Bad luck not to name a van maybe, Max says, sceptically. Like a pirate ship.

Pfff, none of you have a clue. If Lucinda gives up on us before we hit Newcastle, you've got yourselves to blame. Ndulu turns

49

and walks backwards, facing them – now, Lucas's got his Percy Pigs, Max has got his executive neck pillow – he punches Max's arm – hey, give it to Ezra, man, get him some of that sweet REM cycle action.

Ezra scowls. He has been talking a lot about sleep cycles recently. But he's relieved that Ndulu has forgiven him. Ezra missed his birthday party. Iris had to submit to workshop before midnight. Her hands were shaking so much that she couldn't type. Ezra sent her a YouTube video on how to make origami cranes. Tell me the story, he said. Set it somewhere cold. Talking slowly, Iris made a fleet of deformed birds, mauling them as he typed. Ndulu kept ringing until Ezra turned off his phone and put it in a drawer. See? We're in our own time zone. Our own space-time continuum.

The van smells worse when they get back in, like cherryade, piss and unwashed feet. Last time she was in a rental, Iris identified the last element as nail-polish remover and Lucas said, It's meth.

Iris rolled her eyes, then wrote a note on Ezra's hand. *Since when has Lucas done meth?!?!*

Ezra rolls down his window. At least in the front, he feels in control. He pretends he's driving; he could grab the wheel if he needed to. But the passing cars give him vertigo. He doesn't like the idea of someone who dislikes them driving them around, so he tries to be friendly.

So, do you like being a van driver?

A blue Volvo in the next lane swerves. The driver holds down the horn.

He yells, In your country you have donkeys on the road still?

Ezra clocks Max's frozen smile in the rear-view mirror and

for a moment he misses Iris so much that his stomach hurts. He wouldn't be able to catch her eye now without laughing. Grudgingly, the driver opens his pasty, which smells stale and meaty. Ezra realises he is hungry. He turns to see if there's food in the back, and Lucas glowers at him. Lucas has been spoiling for a fight for days.

It started a few weeks ago, at 3 am, with Ndulu picking out a chord progression. Then Max worked on a percussion line until his arms ached. Lucas spliced in ambient sounds he had recorded walking around London – he has 400GB on his laptop which no one else is allowed to see. Lucas and Ezra pulled two all-nighters in a row, tinkering with the transitions, building up layers of sound.

Ezra found it easier to record vocal lines when it was just the two of them, like they were both listening out for the same sound. They went home to sleep, and in the days that followed sent hundreds of messages back and forth. It was their first shared creative frenzy and the first time they had worked synergistically, like an organism – normally Ezra handed them a *fait accompli*. Then, Ezra vanished for what Lucas keeps calling *seventy-two hours*. Ezra turned his phone off, finished the song and sent it to Dolly, who replied: *love* it!!!

The next day, Ezra forwarded them the email and pretended to update his Mac in the long pause after they opened it. A few minutes later, he heard the buzz of the speakers turning on. Ndulu sat down with his head bowed to listen. Out of the corner of Ezra's eye, Max shot everyone his politician's smile, though no one was looking at him. Lucas was white and pinched. Ezra heard how he had gutted the song for parts, but he also heard how good it sounded. He couldn't keep the pride off his face. Lucas flinched at the massive drop before the chorus, but he didn't say anything until the track finished. He stood, reshaping his headphones for a moment, shaking his head, as if both appalled and impressed at his bandmate's audacity.

What the fuck, Ezra.

Oh, come on, Ezra said, trying to seem casual. Look at Ndulu!

Ndulu was playing air guitar. Lucas turned on him, and Ndulu sat up and reached for his real one. Ezra knew he had already won, so he tried to keep his voice neutral.

Do you not like it then?

That's not the point, Lucas snapped.

Well, Max said . . . if this is our hit.

It's not up to you, Lucas said. We've all clocked fifty, sixty hours on this.

They have been circling this topic for months, in different guises. Whenever it comes up Ndulu gets distracted and Max absorbs himself in a practical task. Sometimes Max will call Ndulu over to look at an amp or Ndulu will suddenly need to show him something on YouTube. If pushed, Max says he's just happy to be part of it, that it beats being a lawyer, and Ndulu says, Come on, boys, these are the *times*, the *times of our lives*. If the diversion works, either Lucas or Ezra will get so annoyed with one or both of them that the row dissipates. Otherwise, Max and Ndulu melt away, and Ezra and Lucas are left scowling at each other.

Ndulu? Lucas said pointedly, as if he was referring to an earlier conversation.

Ezra saw Ndulu shake his head at Lucas, minutely, and felt a lurch in his stomach – they outnumbered him. He held his breath, but after a moment, Ndulu started picking out the bassline on his guitar.

It's good, Ndulu said, finally. You know it is.

Max clapped his hands together. Ezra wished Max wouldn't stand up for him.

Tea anyone? Max said. Squash?

I need a cigarette, Lucas said, bitterly, and went outside.

That evening, when he was walking home, Ezra called Iris to vent. He needs to feel normal by the time he gets back. He doesn't want his mother to twig that anything is wrong.

She keeps getting out old boxes of Leonard Cohen and Dylan LPs.

Why don't you tell Lucas that you need him, that you couldn't do it without him, Iris said. Ezra pretended to think she was joking, though it wasn't the first time she'd suggested this.

How is admitting you need him ridiculous? You've told it to me hundreds of times.

I've never said that, specifically, Ezra scoffed. Anyway, I'm sorry I'm boring you.

Iris sighed. That isn't what I meant. She paused for a moment. Fun fact, she said, changing tack: When Keith Richards said Mick Jagger had a tiny todger in his autobiography, Jagger demanded a public apology before he went on tour again.

Ezra laughed, almost against his will, feeling better in spite of himself. That's great, he said. Helpful. Thanks.

In the van, Ezra joins in the talk over what they would be like on *Pimp My Ride*. Ndulu wants a Chevy Express. Lucas wants fuel

53

efficiency. Max starts talking about Burning Man. He's never been, but he has read about it.

Bullet-proof windows, Ndulu says, laser tag.

Beds, Lucas interjects. We need beds.

They argue about who would get which bunk.

I'm not going underneath Max, Ndulu says, you *reek*, man.

Ezra watches Ndulu play around. He knows Ndulu is worrying about his sister, but it doesn't show. Ndulu has never been explicit about what is wrong with Raya, who is twelve, but Ezra has Googled the time frames and thinks it's leukaemia. Ndulu updates Ezra on the hospital trips like he's reporting on a football team they both follow. He brings it up when they're walking, or on the bus, never when they're making eye contact. Ezra assumes that Ndulu shares this with him and not the others because of Jess. Ezra was five when she died. She was born prematurely. Ezra remembers her raw and purple, grub-like. The first time Ezra saw her, Ezra said she was maggoty, and he still remembers his mother's face. He brought it up in confession once, but the priest said it wasn't a sin. Jess spent most of her short life wired up to a machine which Ezra still thinks of as a mechanical heart.

Ezra volunteered this information when Ndulu first mentioned Raya was sick, then worried that he was implying that Raya would die too, and faltered, but Ndulu just nodded.

Ezra didn't tell Iris about Jess until the first time he brought her home to meet his parents.

It hadn't come up, he said.

Iris was quiet for a moment, then said, You haven't mentioned her before.

Ezra likes that Iris said *her*. He is used to people referring to

Jess as a tragedy that befell the family, which is how his mother talks about her, like a hurricane.

After he told Iris, he felt empty. She squeezed his hand and said, Do you want to work for a few hours?

So they did. Ezra at his desk, Iris cross-legged on his bed, switching places, getting up to get water, to make tea. Ezra padded over a few times to put an earbud in her ear, and watched as she listened, and smiled, or screwed up her face. As dusk fell, Ezra pushed back his chair and stood next to her. He placed a hand on the small of her back and she sat up very straight and very still.

Arms, he said. She raised them and he pulled her dress over her head. She unbuttoned his shirt. They worked like that, half naked, frustrated, distracted, until the room grew dark around them.

Later, slightly drunk, Ezra hid Iris's bag in the airing cupboard, so, even if she wanted to, she wouldn't be able to leave.

You know, Max muses, if we're doing well on time, I wouldn't mind driving past the Angel of the North.

Everyone groans. Ezra opens the latest work Iris has sent him on his phone and tries to get lost in it. Working together has been different lately. They have always treated each other's work as another dimension. It is the third person in the relationship. Their work merges into *work*, no singular. But now he likes things that she doesn't, and finds himself keeping quiet about them, because when Iris's expression is blank his excitement dims too. When he played her his latest obsession, a piece of Scandinavian electro, a mixture of coins falling into water and synths, Iris looked panicky.

You don't like it, he said.

It's not that. I don't know how to talk about it.

Ezra looks at the photos from the last press shoot. They had to ditch the first lot.

What's with the serial killer chic, Dolly said, drily.

Iris was there for the first shoot, which Ezra realised later was the problem. Her certainty about him curtails who he can pretend to be. He's used to church choirs; used to hours of practice with no applause. He isn't a natural performer, and he can't fake it in front of her. He can't try out new phrases. When he said, Allow it, he could see her lip twitching, which tipped the others off to how self-conscious he was, and led to an hour of ridicule.

At this photo shoot, they give Ezra a baseball cap, which helps. It sits strangely on his curls, which always look dirty. The set has three cubes which they're meant to pose on. Dolly makes Ndulu sit on one of the blocks so that Ezra looks taller. She puts Max behind his drums.

It's because my body is like Yogi Bear's, isn't it, Max says, dolefully.

Ndulu made this joke first and Max has been repeating it since, trying to reclaim it.

Lucas laughs and chokes on his gum. Ndulu thumps him on the back.

Time to get serious, guys, Dolly says, sharply. Her hair is in a top knot and she isn't wearing any make-up. Move forward, Lucas. Yup. That's it.

In the photos, Ezra looks younger than he feels. His expression says he doesn't care about anything. Ndulu is lanky, but the photographer has made the muscles in his arms more defined.

56

Lucas's dark red hair is bolder, and the flecks of gold which Iris swears are in Ezra's eyes, in this photo, show.

The only other photo Ezra has on his phone is of him and Iris. Lucas took it last time they went to Dover. Max's grandmother passed away the week before, and Max's mother gave him the key to her cottage for a week, on the condition that they cleaned it out. The sand around them is marked with lines of dirt where the tide has come in and dragged out kelp and bits of driftwood. Ezra shields his eyes from the sun, irritated at the camera's intrusion, but expecting it. Wind blows his curls forward, and makes Iris's hair like an animal, wild, and dirty, glinting coppery in the sun. She wears a half-smile, he a grimace. They both have a wry expression, like they're playing along, and neither will remember the photo being taken.

It took them most of the day to get to Dover. Lucas drove. Max and Ndulu sat in the back, and in the middle row of seats, Ezra slept on Iris. She worked with her notebook on his back, rubbing his head occasionally. When he woke up, he didn't recognise Lucas's voice at first. He was speaking quietly from the front seat.

It's only an issue because I'm still living at home, Lucas is saying. They think they need to give me the play-by-play.

Hmmm, Iris says. It's probably better to have a father who likes women too much than one who doesn't like them at all.

He's such a cliché, Lucas says. But the more she tells me, I just think – you were the one who married the shagger. You know he told me – Lucas hesitates, lowering his voice even further – that they haven't had *relations* – he even said it like that, *relations*, for ten years. Like I can go to her and say, Ma, Dad says you're not putting out.

Iris is quiet for a moment. She draws small circles with her finger on the back of Ezra's neck. Then she says, I find it helps to think of both parents like Alka Seltzer. You don't have to absorb it exactly. You just have to become liquid enough to hold them.

Ezra cringes, thinking Lucas will be scornful. When he opens his eyes, Iris is looking out of the window, and in the rear-view mirror, Lucas looks thoughtful.

They stop at a beach, half an hour's drive from the bungalow. As they get out of the car, Ezra mutters to Iris, How do you do that.

Act like a mascot, you mean?

It's more than that.

Mmmm, she says, kicking a stone. I didn't say anything for the best part of five hours there.

Really? he says. Oh.

They walk up a small hill to look at the sea, which is dark and blue-grey like beaten steel, with frills of white rushing towards them.

When they get back, Max has set up his cello on a rock near the edge of the water. He is wearing an aqua polo shirt which looks strange against the lichen.

Who brings a cello to a beach, Ezra says in disgust, and Lucas mutters something.

Iris glances at them. Cut him some slack, she says, lightly. He wanted to play at his gran's funeral but his grandfather said he couldn't bring Haruto, so he's not going.

How do you know that? Ezra says, bewildered, then to Lucas, Did you know that?

Lucas nods and stoops to pick up a pebble. He starts skimming stones and they go bouncing across the water. Iris is shivering – it's freezing, but she stands clicking pebbles together in her hand.

Ezra feels stupid. Why is he still practising then, he says, lamely.

Iris's first stone lands with a splash at the edge of the water.

Maybe he's hoping he'll change his mind, she says.

Lucas and Ndulu start looking for cowrie shells. Lucas's mother has hundreds of them at home. They look like milk teeth.

They used to be traded as currency, Ezra says. They were also used as dice.

Is this one? Iris says, picking up a stone and showing it to Lucas. Is this?

After half an hour, Ezra gets bored. Time to go, he says. I'll tell Max.

Leave it, Lucas says. We can take a few hours. We're almost there. He sees Ezra's impatience and sighs. Fine, I'll drive the rest of the way.

He pulls a baggie from his pocket and shakes out four pinkish capsules. Ezra accepts his greedily. Ndulu gulps one down, hands one to Iris, and carries the last towards the rock where Max is sitting. Max opens his mouth and continues playing, seamlessly. The music swells from the water, and Ezra feels bad for being the only one not to know. For a moment, Ezra wants to sit at Max's feet. He is playing the same Bach cello suite over and over. Ndulu drops the capsule into Max's mouth, then, carefully, pours water from a bottle into his mouth.

Iris sits down to read by a puddle of dirty water further down the beach. After half an hour, she's calling it a rock pool and appears mesmerised by its contents. There's slimy lichen in it and algae and a bright yellow piece of worn-down surfboard, which she calls yellow thing. She rescues it and holds it with great affection. Ezra squats down next to her, nodding as she points out seahorses, starfish. On the rocks, Max seems a magnificent figure, like the strokes of his cello are conducting the ocean. Ndulu is trying to make friends with a black Labrador, seemingly without an owner, which barks at him and the ocean in turn.

Iris can't stop laughing and liquid streams from her nose and into her mouth. Ezra hands her a tissue. He realises Lucas is sitting on the rocks, doing nothing, and tells Iris he'll be back in a second. The walk over is uncomfortable, like moving between different worlds. He stands awkwardly beside Lucas, and they both watch Iris, who appears to be replanting strands of seaweed.

What do you two even talk about? Lucas says.

It catches Ezra off guard, but he feels lucid, emboldened – explaining the world to each other, mostly. Sometimes it feels like between the two of us we might have something close to objective reality, like drawing arcs with a compass.

Ezra realises he has said none of this out loud, and Lucas is still looking at him, expectantly. Ndulu is by the rock pool now, poking something. Ezra gets up and runs across the rocks, and straight through the pool, spraying Iris.

She yells, *Why* would you do that.

Ndulu laughs until his eyes are streaming with water too. He wipes his eyes and sits back on a rock, watching Ezra picking seaweed, gingerly, from his shoe.

Stone cold maniac, I'm telling you, Ndulu says.

Iris looks at the ruined rock pool, shaking her head. She retrieves yellow thing and puts him in her pocket, then glares at Ezra, who is standing at the water's edge.

Whenever he does something like that, something that doesn't suit him, I can't assimilate it, she says, grumpily. I don't believe in it. And then it's like it didn't happen at all.

Ndulu cackles and flicks water at her.

Chill out, man, he says. You're playing in a dirty puddle innit. It's the pills.

Iris shrugs and pulls herself up, picking her way, barefoot, across the cold rocks.

Ezra sees her approaching and bends down to pick up a stone. He feels foolish and unable to explain his impulses.

Ezra counts the first time they took hallucinogens in Dover, three years ago, as the day they started going out, though Iris insists it was months before. It was the first time Iris had been to a beach in England. It was also her first trip and she got stuck halfway up the steps cut into the cliff. Ezra was sitting on the beach, stacking pebbles into towers. He recognised the symptoms of not remembering how to walk. He had never seen someone try to disappear so conspicuously. It was partly because she was so tall and partly because she was dressed so inappropriately and the wind kept catching up her skirt, a problem she seemed aware of, amazed by and totally unable to solve. When Ezra appeared on the step below, Iris gazed at him wide-eyed.

Look at this place, she said.

Ezra turned and saw how strange it was to be eighteen and tripping on a beach in winter. He took both of Iris's hands in his and walked her down the steps.

Watching Iris crossing the beach, Ezra finds himself nostalgic for that time, when it took him almost an hour to coax her down.

In the evening, Iris sits in between Ezra's legs on the floor. He tries to untangle her hair, which is crispy with salt, and pretends to watch the football. Max and Lucas argue over the commentary. Iris goes through Ezra's new lyrics, crossing out anachronisms and asking what pitch this would be sung at, whether he really needs that adjective. Ezra gets impatient and cuts out the knot he can't undo with a knife. She is irritated when he hands her the chunk of hair.

I could have done *that* myself, she says.

They go to bed straight after dinner. They've slept here a few times, but Ezra always forgets how small the room is. He stumbles on the way in and she catches him. He kisses her and thinks how alive her mouth is. He wonders if he's still high, but the ceiling is not shimmering. Her neck and arms and breasts taste of salt. He bites her stomach. He watches her sucking on his fingers and all the blood rushes to his head. Outside, someone turns Alt-J on, and turns the volume up. Ezra is grateful for the privacy.

He arranges pillows and she belly-flops over them.

8

In the first week of October, the trees drop their leaves overnight. I feel guilty. I've missed Kennedy's class again. I could have gone. I realise there was a moment when it almost felt possible. I could have walked there and sat through Kennedy talking about why meta-fiction was all a ruse. But I would not have taken anything in, and that effort, those ninety minutes, would have cost me two days on the floor.

I call Tess. She wants to get T-shirts made saying CITIZEN OF NOWHERE and LIBERAL METROPOLITAN ELITE.

I'm not wearing one of those.

Did I ask you to? Did you see the interview with your future president?

He won't win.

Have you asked your father which way he's voting?

I haven't spoken to him since he made me a doctor's appointment three weeks ago.

What's wrong with you this time?

I tell her an abridged version. Tess thinks therapists are for weak-willed narcissists looking for someone to blame.

And if your face stops going numb, Tess says, then what's next, your arm?

I didn't talk much as a child. I didn't have anything to say. My mother filled up the world, and I swam in it. I had to see a specialist after the school pointed out I was late developing. Tess was furious. *When will these idiots learn to drive.* While we were in a traffic jam, she left a message with the headmaster's secretary

63

expressing gratitude for his feedback. According to the specialist the curriculum had been simplified to such an extent that I had been struck dumb with boredom and subsequently she would be sending the school the bill. In the doctor's office though, Tess's mood shifted. She kept scrutinising various pamphlets detailing neurological disorders, but her eyes were narrowed. I answered the doctor's questions easily and Tess beamed, then rolled her eyes to the doctor.

My daughter prefers to have an audience.

But after that, I never stopped chattering. Tess listened, interrupting with the occasional wry observation.

I scroll through possible causes. Aneurysm. Charcot-Marie-Tooth disease. Diabetes. Lyme disease. For forty minutes, I scan my body for ticks, obsessing over a small lump behind my left ear. I read an article about a woman who went to the doctor in agony. They told her it was period pain. A few days later, she was rushed into hospital. When they sliced her open, they found a tumour nestled in her gut, like a 3lb tick.

There's no shame in talking to someone, Ray had said. Lindsey and I were both in analysis for years.

When I mentioned the referral to Lisa, she said, Let me know if you can scam some Adderall, and when I told Ezra this, his eyes lit up.

✗

Would it be any different if I was in London and he was in Barcelona? Would it get easier?

These are questions I ask myself often. Barcelona was one of our happiest separations. Idle Blades were moving around, listening to local bands. Ezra sent postcards about the Basilica de

Santa Maria del Mar, the winding paths of Gaudí's Park Güell, the hot blue tiles.

Whenever we talk, I put the blinds down, turn off the overhead lights and put a lamp behind my laptop. I pretend that Ezra is still in Barcelona, and six hours ahead of me.

I shift the computer slightly so that Ezra will not see the plates stacked up behind me. It makes sense, I have decided, to do washing up in batches.

I tell him about Sasha yelling at Finn in workshop. He refuses to do any of the reading. He *doesn't want to pollute his natural voice*, like he feels under attack from all these other voices. I don't get it, because as soon as I hear a voice like mine, I wrap myself in it.

Ezra is on GarageBand. I can hear him clicking.

If he stops working every time I call then he will get nothing done. We aren't, he points out, talking about anything particularly interesting. School gives my life a structure and he is vigilant about protecting his. I try to convince him that I am not the enemy.

At 3 am, I spill Diet Coke into my laptop and call Ezra. He is waiting for a DJ and leaves the venue because I am hyperventilating. He tells me to put my laptop in rice to draw the liquid out.

The next day, I call, just as he's dragged himself to his desk. He's had a fight with Lucas.

I don't know what his problem is, Ezra says. He wanted the track finished; I finished the track. I did what I have to do.

We talk for a while, and Ezra asks if I could ask the doctor for some Valium. It might make the van more bearable.

His sleep paralysis is back. My heart sinks when he mentions it. We both know it is a precursor to one of his lows.

✦

On Friday, I get the cross-town bus to Dr Liderman's office, near the Waldorf Astoria.

The waiting room is bright, fluorescent lit. There are back copies of *Oprah Magazine* on the table.

I go to the bathroom because the lights hurt my head. There is a packet of floss hidden on top of the mirror and bloody floss in the bin.

I don't trust people who floss at work. They tend to be evangelicals.

When I go back, Liderman's door is open. She's wearing a black skirt and a powder-blue blouse. I imagine she has a wardrobe full of pastels; the kind of woman who says *I really shouldn't* and then orders dessert. Her office feels like a room in a doll's house. I glance at the walls, but there aren't any pictures, only three diplomas with red wax seals. There is a bookshelf with an empty fish tank on top, and a black leather sofa, which I sit on.

On the table in between us, a framed card says:

Life always offers you a second chance. It's called tomorrow.

So, Iris, Liderman says. Why are you here.

I smooth my hair, nervously. I feel like I'm in a job interview. How soon is too soon to throw in an Adderall request? What about benzos?

You come highly recommended, I say.

You moved to New York two months ago?

Yes.

Boyfriend?

He's on tour.

Her phone vibrates and she frowns, texting for a moment. So, he left you to go on tour?

He's working.

My ladies do love the musicians, she says.

The room is warm. Looking around, I realise there aren't any windows. I scan the bookshelf: *Put Down the Drink and Find Your Man*, *Co-dependency Schmodependency*.

She asks what I want to get out of our sessions.

It's covered by my father's insurance. He's trying to fix me, I say, sourly.

She smiles and writes something down, then asks how I'm finding New York. I talk more than I mean to, and as I do, Dr Liderman winces, as if at a recent painful memory.

God, you couldn't pay me to be twenty-one again, she says.

She asks if I'm on any medication. I say that I was on SSRIs as a teenager, but only for a few weeks.

This is a *physical* problem, I say. It's like there's something wrong with my circulation. It's like pins and needles, but pricklier, and it keeps moving around. It feels like my body is trying to warn me.

Liderman mentions, casually, that antidepressants can be beneficial in treating neurological abnormalities.

I don't need them. I have a nice life. As long as I sleep properly, and exercise, I'm fine.

Liderman nods, earnestly, like I have just shared valuable information. Do you play a sport?

I run every day.

My gosh, running is *hard*, she says. Good for you.

67

I get lost so often that I have developed a system: I only run in L shapes, so that Manhattan is as simple as Tetris pieces. I run up and along and up and along and down and back.

And are you getting enough sleep?

Not really.

What do you do when you can't sleep?

Netflix. Work. Sometimes I have a drink.

Liderman nods and writes something down, then she underlines it.

⁂

I have forgotten my headphones and outside the street is loud. I have started attracting crazy people. An old woman shuffles along in flannel slippers, pushing a shopping trolley. There are windmills stuck through the bars, blades whirring: metallic purple, pink, gold, slicing the air. I don't know what I will do if she talks to me, and her lips are already moving. *You*, she says. *You*.

I keep my watch set to London time. It's noon. Ezra will be in the studio. Nance will be at the library, but I call her anyway. Nance has never been to the right specialists, which makes me uncomfortable, because she needs them more than I do.

Liderman asked me if I found the sound of ice cubes tumbling into a glass exciting, I say.

Are you allowed to find it exciting if it's tonic water?

Nance will not drink gin and tonics without ice and lemon. We have left hundreds of Wetherspoons because of this. Before I left, we argued because she said that her stipend meant she couldn't afford to go anywhere else. I flattened the Brexit paraphernalia on the tables and slipped it into her bag.

I'll ask next time, I say.

9

When Nance does not want to acknowledge the content of her conversations with Piers, she forwards them to me with no message. At first, I look up the references, and the books he recommends, but there are too many.

Piers says that their conversations are less Robert Browning and Elizabeth Barrett Browning than Voltaire and Diderot.

Nance says that she won't forward any more unless I stop calling Piers the Love Doctor.

What a loss, I say.

We're on Skype. I'm trying to scrape the sriracha from one of Lindsey's china plates. I left it for a few days, and it has formed a sheen of a swirl, like bacteria. Nance holds up her laptop, proudly, to show me the four lines about Idle Blades from the *Guardian* taped to her wall. There are books stacked up on the windowsill. I can always tell how much work Nance is getting done by the state of her bedroom. When all the objects are lined up at right angles, then not a word has been written.

The need to expose Dr Postman's stupidity got me to the library, Nance says. Thoreau was that way too. Emerson's obituary said that he did not feel himself except in opposition.

I edge my feedback from workshop off the desk. Beneath my note: According to Tacitus, Germanic tribes thought prayers uttered in salt mines were heard most clearly, listened to most attentively, by the gods, Finn has written: Why should I care.

I tell Nance that Lisa said Finn's stories should have been

included on the handout with excerpts from the Bad Sex Awards. She said he had no interest in female interiority.

Oh, I got internal all right, Finn said, leering.

Lisa hissed, Why don't you just buy a doll.

The way men talk about sex here is all tits and ass. I find it relaxing because it has nothing to do with me.

At this, Nance looks indignant. Feminism is a collective—

I cast around for things to distract her. If Piers were Irish, you wouldn't look at him twice.

That's a terrible thing to say, Nance says.

You call the Irish men I fancy knackers.

Well, they are, the most of them, and through no fault of my own.

Nance lists the men I have liked since we have known each other. I do not say that, unlike her, I know plenty of men like Piers.

⚲

Ezra gets back from a string of gigs in industrial towns on Sunday night and does not call me until Wednesday evening. He sends me a playlist:

Leonard Cohen	Suzanne
Bob Dylan	Don't think twice, it's alright
Johnny Cash	I walk the line
Gnarls Barkley	Who's gonna save my soul
Nick Drake	Time has told me
The Smiths	There is a light that never goes out

He sends me a link to a blog. The band's genesis tale has changed. They grew up in Birmingham. Apparently, Ezra wakes up with lyrics fully formed in his head.

On Skype, I tell him that I would rather not communicate via press release.

Talking to Nance all the time makes you meaner, he says.

Whose fault is that?

I have been lying on the floor for an hour, and when I look closely at the screen, I can see the impression of the rug on my cheek. Ezra hasn't noticed. He is taking apart a drum pedal. Last time we spoke, he was putting it together. I know where screw A goes, where screw B. He is doing it wrong. I saw him get muddled earlier. I am planning on telling him, but not yet. He screws up his face to focus on the screwdriver, which keeps slipping.

U2 rent a hotel when they get back from tour, he says. It takes time to acclimatise to normal life.

Like astronauts.

Exactly, he says.

Later, on WhatsApp, I tell Nance that Ezra seems to find our separation useful for his work. I type it again and again until I pass as casual. I delete exclamation marks, add semi-colons.

He made the valid point, I say, that he has more time these days.

Nance writes back the next morning:

Will I ring him for you? He could bring me gifts as penance.   21:37
Last time we spoke he told me that he thinks of me as a
confession box. I laughed at the time, but I was thinking

71

about it, and whenever he needs to justify himself, he plays the Catholic card. The confession box licenses trans-gression.

ps. Watch the election debate tomorrow. Learn something about your new home.   **21:39**

10

I have not been able to get up for two days. I keep the blinds down, the air conditioning on and the duvet up to my ears. I have a new policy: containment. I have run out of tissues, and toilet paper, and I keep wiping my nose on the duvet. The crying comes in bouts. When I close my eyes, it is as though I am leaking tears. I press the space key when my laptop falls asleep. At least on Netflix, I am God; no breaking news. I stop crying for the duration of one episode of *Friends*. When Netflix starts the automatic roll-over, I want to kiss the executive who has released me from that six-second tyranny. How long would I stay in the room if it kept on playing?

Conrad invites me to dinner with his girlfriend. I don't know how to explain that I cannot leave the flat, so I don't show up. I send exhaustive updates to my friends at home and they reply too quickly.

Ezra calls these my hibernation days. He says they balance out the fact that I'm so present the rest of the time. I say that I am a bacterium. I say that I have isolated the bacterium. I text him a photo of bacteria in a petri dish.

On your bacteria feeling: It's your way of naming that's   **06:00**
problematic. Actually, it's a very reasonable instinct which
has evolved from the survival mode known as the static-
existence-biological-flux-bubble-sea-anemone impulse,
which is buried deep within each and every one of our
human psyches, from back in the day when we were all

like sea anemones, rolling around on the ocean floor and
absorbing whatever was in reach of our tentacles . . . so
don't worry about it.

At home, when I feel this way, Ezra reads to me, or works
next to me with headphones. We have learnt to take it like a
storm, full on. Batten down the hatches. He knows when I
need him to stay. He gets into bed and holds me, balancing
the laptop on his chest. We watch old children's TV shows
on YouTube; *The Magic Roundabout* and *The Herbs*. He is
Zebedee and I am Florence. He is Constable Knapweed and
I am Dill.

I call him at 2 pm. He asks if I have been for a run. I say the
leaves are too slippery. He asks whether I am eating properly.

You know only thirty-one states in the US let inmates on
death row request last suppers? I have been scrolling through
images of canteen trays loaded with fried chicken, cherry Kool-
Aid. One man, who was hanged for murder, asked for a single
olive, which still had the stone.

Ezra has been reading a book about mindfulness. He tells me
this is as effective as antidepressants.

I cannot make him vertical on Skype. Whichever way I turn
my phone, his head rotates.

He is leafing through the *Diagnostic and Statistical Manual*
and reading out the diagnoses that might apply to him.

The good news is that my case is pretty black and white. Mild
to moderate social paranoia, situational anxiety, alcohol-induced
sexual dysfunction; don't laugh, if we're doing this, we're going
to take it seriously. Okay? Good. Also: nicotine withdrawal,
potential alcoholism?

I move the tequila soda I am drinking behind the laptop screen.

What's the similarity between me and a bat, he says.

Wings?

We can both identify sounds at long distances. Sonar, he says, calmly.

He keeps turning pages. I try for defiance and drink it in two gulps. I knock my tooth on the ice and clutch my cheek while I listen to him trying so hard for me.

Cocaine withdrawal, thank God not permanent. Can you imagine that. Caffeine-induced sleep disorder. Bipolar, we'll get to that. Major depressive disorder – apparently a single episode constitutes a diagnosis? Fine. That too then. Panic disorder without agoraphobia. Oooh, dissociative fugue – I like the sound of that one, hang on a sec.

He IMs me the definition:

Patients with this Dissociative Disorder may suddenly and unexpectedly travel away from home and experience impaired recall of their past. They may be confused about their former identity and even assume a new one.

He examines my face. He covers one eye then the other on screen – Everything seems to be in order. As I was saying, in my case, we're going to coast past narcissistic personality disorder, exhibitionism, fetishism, sexual sadism, pyromania, all of which are apparently diseases. He snaps the book shut – what I'm trying to say is that these definitions are the problem, and even if some of the terms feel relevant, it's just a new way of explaining. He looks away as he always does in the moments I want him

75

to look at me forever. And it isn't how I see you, he says. It isn't who you are.

⚉

Nance and I keep lists of the things we will buy once we are rich. She gets obsessed with the money diaries published by anonymous women online. I send her links to Valentino dresses and crystal-encrusted leotards. I pick out pendant necklaces from Tiffany's that can only be worn with backless dresses. I send her links to wedding dresses from Vera Wang. When she mutters about the patriarchy, I say, We could just wear them around.

We both want the Veuve Clicquot fridge. I want to fill mine with canapés. Nance wants to take the shelf in the middle out and fill hers with Veuve Clicquot. Magnums, she says.

⚉

Ezra is experimenting with lucid dreaming. He thinks it might cure his sleep paralysis.

Ezra:	It's ridiculous. I have been following the instructions I found online to the letter.	**19:46**
Iris:	. . . *typing* . . .	**19:46**
Ezra:	It's the first thing I do every morning.	**19:47**
Iris:	. . . *typing* . . .	**19:47**
Ezra:	But nothing in these dreams has anything to do with me.	**19:48**
Iris:	Do you think it's like a lifeline ending on your palm?	**19:52**
Ezra:	Lifelines are irrational and meaningless.	**20:20**
Iris:	Dreaming of cul-de-sacs sounds a lot like a lifeline ending to me.	**20:20**

76

Ezra:	The two things are not remotely similar. Palm-reading is nonsense. Hokum. Whereas a dream journal is a way of articulating the feedback loop between the subconscious and unconscious. Having a gap there doesn't seem healthy.	20:30
Iris:	Lucid dreaming is up there with tarot cards.	20:32
Iris:	Don't you want to explain the difference to me?	21:14

We talk for a while after that. Hearing Ezra's voice makes me feel less far away, but after we talk the flat is even quieter. He texts me a few hours later, when I am calculating the hours I have left to sleep if I go to sleep now.

| | I found my diagnosis. Moderate social paranoia combined with selective amnesia and the projection of negative attributes (often with roots in own innately selfish desires) onto people who cause insecurity. Is there a remedy to this? Zen? Zanax? Zopiclone? | 23:37 |

At the Lion's Head, nobody bothers me, and I can read through Breitbart forums on my own. When I read for too long, a high-pitched ringing starts in my ears. I try to watch the second presidential debate. Trump seems on the brink of assaulting her. Muting it makes it worse. At least Trump's words distract me from his circling, his glowering; the stink of violence coming off him, grasping the podium with both hands. I tell Sam that watching Hillary hold her space is painful.

I wish we could run a beta version of what happens if he gets elected, I say.

Politics here is practically entertainment. Power moves. Like

WWF, you know? Anyway, what about you guys? I mean, don't get me wrong, I love an imaginary monarchy as much as the next guy . . .

Later, he sends me a YouTube clip of the debate set to an ominous Danny Elfman soundtrack. It's like a horror movie. But I heard the menace of that music the first time round.

At school, in the corridors, people argue over who's funding the political documentaries flooding Netflix. There's a constant exchange of articles and tweets. Lisa stops watching the news and calls it self-care. Finn snorts: Every time I hear 'self-care' I think about masturbation. A guy from the film MFA becomes known as the Republican from Venezuela. Nobody is saying anything new. He won't get past the pussy grabbing. He won't really build a wall. This is what happens when you ignore a section of the population. If I try to join in, someone inevitably says, Come on, you have Nigel Farage. And I don't know what to say to that.

The sidewalk smells of frying peanut oil and trash. If Ezra were here, he'd button me into his coat. My fingers ache with cold but I message him.

The more I read, the less I understand. When I try, my brain **21:58**
vibrates and then blows a fuse. It just shuts down, like it's
short-circuited.

How is everyone else so sure about their opinions?

Voicenote recording. I squint at my screen. It's 5 am in London and Ezra finds recordings of his speaking voice excruciating. I've tried to convince him to sing instead but he mutters that voicenotes are unnatural. *Think of the ambient noise pollution!* We

78

both know the real reason. As soon as he lets me hear his voice there's no distance. In written messages, he can always claim *that isn't what he meant*. But the green bar fills and my heart lurches. I press the phone to my ear. He sounds sleepy and rumpled.

I know what you're thinking, so don't go getting ideas. I don't like this at all . . . and we've used up most of my phone memory as it is . . . so voicenotes are still strictly out of bounds but these are extenuating circumstances because I need the intonation to make my point . . . really you're taking advantage of me being this tired . . . why aren't you here to make me coffee? I miss you. There, I said it. Anyway . . . .There's no correlation . . . or no necessary correlation . . . between knowing what you're talking about and doing so with confidence – Trump – *Oh, it's too early for Trump*. My point is: if those guys in your workshop are grandstanding again, remember: most of the time all we're looking for is a chance to say *that's preposterous*.

I message Nance about Ezra's theory of Zen and Zanax and she points out that Xanax is spelt with an X.

| Nancy: | So maybe he isn't as clever as he thinks. | 22:30 |
| Iris: | English proverb: Give neither counsel nor salt till you are asked for it. | 22:32 |

I miss my books. I buy a battered copy of Pablo Neruda's love poems on the way home. It doesn't have the ode I'm looking for. *I know you won't believe me, but it sings, salt sings.*

11

There is a Halloween disco and I arrive expecting a ball. Earlier, I tested various outfits on Ezra.

I'm thinking Grace Kelly in *Rear Window*. Or late 1990s Carrie Bradshaw.

Those are two completely different women and neither of them is Indian, he said. Hey, what about M.I.A.?

She's Sri Lankan, but perfect.

Just as I'm about to head out, Nance turns up on Skype. She's wrapped fairy lights over her cardigan and up around her head like a crown. Happy Diwali!

Last Diwali, Ezra bought me the Kama Sutra. I wasn't impressed. We'd agreed to work together but he left the library mid-afternoon with no explanation. I hadn't eaten all day. I walked back blowing on my hands, freezing. I wanted to get straight into bed, but when I opened my door, he was there, grinning, holding a plate of French toast. There were tealights flickering on every surface and plates of them on the floor. He'd turned my bedroom into a dark lake of floating lights. He fed me French toast before he undressed me. Sorry, it's a bit burnt, he said. Caramelised, I said, licking maple syrup from his hands. That's how we do it in Mumbai. He was dripping hot wax on my stomach when the smoke detector went off. He pulled a sheet over us, but the porters came. All of the buildings around the quad were evacuated, and we stood, shivering in towels. Ezra, giggling; I, mortified.

If those are from Poundland then that really isn't safe, I snap at Nance.

Do you know how long this getup took? Nance demands.

Ezra didn't remember. But then neither did I.

Can't believe I nearly electrocuted myself for this, Nance grumbles, untangling herself.

Sasha is wearing red lipstick and spiked heels, so she's my height. Last week, she asked what I was reading and I reeled off Sam's syllabus with pride.

Iris, she said, grimacing. Did you notice anything about those names? Write this down. Toni Morrison, Lorrie Moore, Joy Williams, Jennifer Egan, Jamaica Kincaid, Ann Beattie, Flannery O'Connor, Karen Russell, Aimee Bender. That should be enough to get you started.

I spent the rest of the day in the library.

Urgh, who is she kidding, like she was one of the first people in Greenwich Village, Lisa says.

I am wearing emerald silk. I feel like a river and look naked. The corridor is full of flappers and men who have come dressed as themselves. I am woozy with being around people.

Who are you meant to be?

She's Sylvia Plath, Lisa says, in her *Mademoiselle* days.

It is the kindest thing an American girl has said to me. I don't expect much from Lisa. She taught me about claiming space but prefers that I not occupy it. She doesn't like the attention I get from men and doesn't understand that it is because I don't expect anything from them. I'm not a threat. Lisa has four-year plan tattooed on her forehead.

Uh-oh, she says, here comes trouble.

Sam is wearing a builder's hat with cans of PBR taped around the sides. When I came in, he held up a straw and I pretended not to see.

Too good for the cans then, m'lady?

Even you are too good for the cans.

Ouch, he says, clutching his chest. I like your hair this way.

I roll my eyes.

Can't blame a guy for trying.

☧

In the second week of November, it rains every day. Trump is elected. I spend most of the weekend lying in bed, with my forehead pressed against the wall. In the evening, the messages start flooding in on WhatsApp.

Lexi: I just left the flat for the first time today and I had   **19:04**
to come back again because I kept looking at
people and thinking was it you? Did you vote
him in?

Lexi: It's not that I expect everyone's opinions to align   **19:24**
with mine. Obviously, I don't. But I thought there
were some fundamental things we agreed on.

Ezra is on an Airbnb bender. He sends me links to houses which cost millions of pounds to rent. Windmills, converted chapels. In this one, we could both have studies. You could write in the turret! We've been furnishing our imaginary house for years. It has been an attic, a lighthouse. For a while Ezra wanted to deck out a shipping container. I froze that one out. We've been in the same place long enough now to know each creak on the stairs. Stacks of books, sheet music, wooden floors, a fireplace, a blue front door. He adds a soundproof studio. I insist on a bathtub in a greenhouse, heated all year round. The four-poster

82

bedroom, right at the top, where nobody else is allowed. Ezra
sends a link to a green velvet sofa on Ebay.

Iris:	We're running out of space!	22:06
Ezra:	You'll have to get rid of some books then.	22:06
Iris:	Nobody needs three pianos.	22:07

On Monday, I coax myself out of the flat. I am wearing two
heavy Indian skirts and I am still shivering. On the subway, my
metro card doesn't work and a woman with grey frazzled hair insists on swiping me through with hers. I thank her and she shrugs,
helplessly. Sam is in the computer lab on Buzzfeed, eating dis-
counted Haribo. When he sees me, he grins and opens his browser.

You know he only got 10 per cent of the vote in Manhattan?
Have you seen the latest *SNL*?

Is that all you're watching now?

Sam laughs and says, Nah, I'm on the pulse.

At Halloween, Lisa brought Sam up when we were in the
bathroom.

Don't take this the wrong way, but isn't your whole little girl
lost thing a bit degrading? You act so dumb around him. It's like
you want a certain kind of attention from guys, like you need
rescuing.

I have a boyfriend, Lisa.

Who you only ever mention as a trophy or an alibi. Lisa
pursed her lips. I'm just saying. There are only a few eligible
guys on the program.

At 5 pm, Sam and I leave together. Earlier, I admitted that
I've never seen a Marvel film.

You *have* to see *Doctor Strange*, he says. I'll come with you.

He starts telling me why the superhero franchise is so important, but when he pushes the revolving door, it jams, and he kicks at it half-heartedly.

That douchebag is a virus. He's slavery and smallpox and deep-fried Oreos rolled into one. Ma just sent an email round banning *political talk* at Thanksgiving. She says it'll get too emotional once you factor in the liquor, but that's bullshit.

Outside, it's dark, and I can taste blood from where the cold has split my lip. A Varsity team pushes past, and I hold on to Sam's coat, to steady myself.

Let's get you out of here, he says.

He puts one hand on each of my shoulders and steers me through the crowd. Once we're off campus, I can breathe. He stares down Amsterdam.

I know just the place, he says.

I have to jog every few steps to keep up. It's easier to focus on staying close to him than getting out of everyone's way.

Most of the tables in the Hamilton are empty. The waitress brings over a bucket full of ice and Coronas. I take a handful of free popcorn, then another, hungrily.

You're easily pleased, Sam says, watching me. He opens two Coronas and pushes limes in. I read him a few of my proverbs.

Ugandan proverb: The lucky eagle kills a mouse that has eaten salt.

Turkish proverb: What is salt to tasteless food what is a word to a foolish head.

Danish proverb: Better a salt herring on your own table than a fresh pike on another man's.

Russian proverb: Eternity makes room for a salty cucumber.

It's okay, Sam says. The worse your art is the easier it is to talk about.

Ashbery?

Sam high-fives me. He is telling me about his agent when the woman at the next table catches my eye. Her hair is glossy, white, curled in a way I didn't know they curled hair any more. She's staring at me. I wonder if my nose is running, and sniff. I try to focus on Sam, but she is mouthing something.

Sam turns to see what I'm looking at and his face darkens. He goes over to her table. The woman looks defensive, then juts her chin towards me. Sam moves to block her view. I look at my phone until Sam returns, shaking his head – New Yorkers. They are *not* happy people.

What was she saying?

She's running low on vodka.

The waitress is ushering the woman out. As she passes she hisses, Muslim bitch.

Sam looks at me as if I'm about to break. I take a swig of Corona and avoid his eyes. My face is hot. Well. That was weird – I hold the Corona to my forehead – Not that it matters, but I'm not even Muslim. Probably just as well it was me.

When I finally glance at Sam, he looks so overwhelmed that I laugh. Is it the skirt do you think?

Iris, Sam says, shaking his head. You are not having a good week.

He starts telling me about the racist shit that happens in Austin. There's a dumb rivalry between us and the Mexicans. It's not a proper – he gestures to the empty table – it's not like that. We take our food seriously, that's all.

I pick the plastic sign from the table, twirl it between my

fingers. Sam takes it, impatiently, and puts it back where it was. You made me lose my thread.

I read the sign. What's a pickleback?

What's a pickleback? he says, smiling again.

After the first pickleback, I tell him that there is nobody like Ezra in the world.

Goddamn adorable, he says.

He is only ten years older than me but there's a lifetime between us. He has a money clip and bartends and sleeps around. I have only been with Ezra. I feel seventeen around Sam.

When you get to my age – and don't get me wrong here, I'm sure your boyfriend is aces, but you're what, twenty-one? How many people have you even met outside of university? He snorts and drains his beer. There's a whole cornucopia out there, he says.

A cornucopia?

That's right. I went there. A corn – you – cope – ee – ah.

London

Dolly has bleached her hair white, and Ezra can't tell whether the mixture of youth and age is arousing or scary. She sweeps back her bob to show the two new piercings in the top of her ear.

Rose gold hoops, Dolly says. *So* infected.

Sick, Ndulu says.

The car stinks of Happy Meals, which Ndulu insisted they pick up at 7 am. Ezra couldn't face his. They played a corporate event in Shoreditch last night. Ezra ate cold cheese puffs and drank too much free wine. Ndulu groans. He gave himself Lemsip poisoning, staying up, watching the election.

Man, when I threw up, I thought my insides had gone radioactive.

Jackub turns to Ezra and grins, flashing a silver filling. Since they started booking him on consecutive days, Jackub has decided they're okay. He's driving them to Liverpool tomorrow. When they set off, he typed The Leadmill into the GPS and clapped Ezra on the shoulder, like they were bonding.

London to Sheffield: Three hour, three hour thirty.

No rush, Ezra said, hastily.

Lucas booed. Ndulu threw pick-and-mix.

Boys, boys, Dolly said, smirking.

At the first service station, Ndulu thrust the *Guardian* review of Idle Blades under Jackub's nose. Jackub sucked his teeth, approvingly.

Ndulu drums on the ceiling, reciting the names of all the

bands who have played the Leadmill: Arctic Monkeys, the Stone Roses, the Strokes, the White Stripes, Oasis, Muse, Kings of Leon, Manic Street Preachers, Bloc Party.

Ezra gets closer to vomiting with every beat. He tries to distract himself by assembling his Happy Meal toy, but the propeller is missing. Jackub turns on Radio 1 and Ndulu starts crooning along.

Ezra frowns, trying to hear Dolly and Lucas, who are deep in conversation on the back seat.

Dolly talks to Lucas like he's an insider. They savour the same artists – artists they discard when the industry discovers them. A few times, Ezra accidentally professed his love for Blondie, or Woody Guthrie, and Dolly's smile left Ezra with the distinct impression that she was humouring him.

This is like terrible spoken-word poetry, Max complains.

Ndulu raises his right hand, like he's swearing an oath. I'm an artist, man, we have to *create*.

He pulls out his phone and starts uploading their photos onto an app which exaggerates their features. Max posts a photo of Ezra at fifteen, earnest and wearing a fleece, on the group WhatsApp. Ndulu blends this image with Ezra's twenty-one-year-old serial killer stare. They pass the phone around the car, howling with laughter. When Jackub sees it, he pretends to shrink away from the passenger seat.

Jezu Chryste, he says.

Ezra tries to stop scowling. He is wary of moving his face; Ndulu keeps making him into memes and posting them on Instagram. Max holds on to the phone for a moment. He likes the app because it makes his hair less floppy and sharpens his bone structure.

There's a bit of Hugh Grant in this one, Max says, showing the photo around.

Ndulu snatches it back. Contacts, he says, attaching the photo to a draft and swiping dramatically – Haruto – sent.

Max protests, but he looks pleased. Ndulu smiles, like he's flirting.

So, when is the bf gonna join us?

He's getting the train after work, Max says, glancing at Dolly. I said that he could probably come along for the drinks after.

More the merrier, Dolly says.

Dolly doesn't have much time for Max. Iris says she once described him as *part of a package deal*, but Ezra doesn't know whether he believes that. He tries to focus on what Dolly is saying. She's just out of a relationship with *the original fuckboy*.

Lucas frowns. Has he called you since Leeds?

In the rear-view mirror, Ezra watches Lucas fold his hoodie into a pillow for Dolly. He isn't sure whether Lucas's concern for her is empathy or a tactical manoeuvre, but it makes him feel like he's watching a car crash in slow motion. This morning, he lay in bed ruminating over what their closeness could mean for the band, then Skyped Iris. She seemed irritable. When he asked if she was okay, she picked up her laptop and showed him how dark it was outside.

It's 2 am, she said.

It's like that here too, he said. Shall I call later?

She sighed. I think you're being paranoid. Lucas isn't staging a coup.

Dolly confides in him, Ezra said, stubbornly. And he encourages it.

Maybe he fancies her? Iris said. Ezra looked stricken, so she moved on, hastily. Have you ever asked Dolly *anything* about her life?

Dolly hands around schedules for the week. As she's explaining them, Ezra peers at the swollen tissue around the piercing in her ear.

You know, forty-six thousand people die from sepsis every year, he says. And that's just in the UK.

Ndulu shakes his head and then mimes shooting himself.

It's probably a blown-up statistic, Ezra adds, hastily. Tea tree is good.

He wishes he could cover the rear-view mirror. He gets out his phone to see if Iris is still up –it's 5 am in New York. Iris is offline but she's sent him an email:

11.11.16 04:58
From: irisirisiris@gmail.com
To: ezramunroe@gmail.com
Sorry for being moody. Still can't sleep.

On the subway: a girl was complaining to her friend about how stuffy the train was, and this woman started yelling. Go home if you don't like it, etc.

She looked like someone's Las Vegas grandma; white curls, a visor.

I was watching her face and she *hated* the girl. It seemed personal, like she hated *her* specifically – that girl on that train – not as a symbol. She really did feel like the girl was trying to displace her. Maybe the most dangerous people are the ones who don't realise how powerful they are.

What I should have said on the phone: Dolly might be nervous about talking to you too. You're her big break.

1. Simon & Garfunkel: They couldn't agree on the 12th track of *Bridge over Troubled Water*, so there are only 11. When Garfunkel praised Simon for his songwriting, he replied, Arthur and I agree about almost nothing, but it's true, I have enriched his life quite a bit.

2. Pink Floyd: When the bass player left, he said the others couldn't use the name Pink Floyd, or his inflatable pig, so they sued him.

3. The Libertines: Pete Doherty kept taking more and more drugs, until Carl Barat kicked him out of the band. When they went on tour, Doherty robbed his flat.

4. The Kinks: Did you know they were brothers? In 1996, at the older one's 50th birthday, the younger one leapt on his birthday cake and declared himself a genius.

5. The Beach Boys: Mike Love has fired the whole band and now tours with a substitute band i.e. he is the only Beach Boy.

What I mean is that: If things weren't tense, you'd be doing something wrong x x x

Ezra can tell that she's shaken. He checks Spotify, then starts typing Is listening to grey noise at 5 am a good idea and deletes it. Spotify has become their default mode of tuning into what the other is feeling; sometimes when Iris says she's fine and she isn't, it's the only way Ezra knows. He starts to type what's the worst that can happen which normally works when she's catastrophising. Recently though, Iris can't put her fear into words, which scares him. Instead, he starts writing a list of things he knows she loves to send her later:

Goldberg Variations BWV 988, Peter Pan, Reese's Pieces, sour gummies, SWAN matches, *National Geographic*, flannel shirts, champagne, roses, manga, knee socks.

But these things aren't enough without being near to him, she's told him that. He thinks for a moment and types:

There are five bays full of natural bioluminescence left in the world. One litre of water has within it hundreds of thousands of *Pyrodinium bahamense*, minuscule dinoflagellates that give off an ethereal greenish-blue light when disturbed. When you swim in the water, your skin glitters; you drip light.

So how is Yoko settling into New York, Dolly asks.

Ezra twists too fast in his seat, and a burning pain passes along his shoulder blades. They have been hauling kit around for weeks.

Pretty much, he says, wincing.

He glances at the phone by his side. He writes down lyrics on Notes and the idea of Dolly reading them makes him want to crawl into a hole. He doesn't want the Yoko thing to catch on either.

Dolly has been cool towards Iris since their Camden gig. Iris and Nance hadn't realised that Idle Blades wouldn't be on until midnight and they started drinking at 6 pm. At 11 pm, Nance pointed out the reserved seats in the VIP area, and Iris tore the signs off while Nance kept a look out. Ezra turned up just before the set to find the girls sprawled on the chairs, talking. Iris had her legs over the back of one of the chairs.

Those are for industry people, Ezra said.

They'll just have to slum it like the rest of us then, won't they, Nance said, loudly. They should go down the dole disco.

We'll fix it, Iris said, smearing a label onto the back of the seat as if it would stick there.

When Ezra got backstage, Dolly told him that Iris and her little friend were banned from the dressing room.

They're completely out of control, Dolly said.

When Ezra told Iris this the next morning, she looked hurt. Ezra pointed out that it wasn't Dolly's fault.

She could have told me herself, Iris said, flatly. Look, you're nicer to each other when she's there, so I'm glad she's around, but that doesn't mean I have to like her.

It would be great if you could not alienate the one person I've got in my corner.

Iris's expression hardened. You know, she basically told me that we're going to break up. She said that for the next few years you're going to be a dick, and not everyone can handle that. And that I have to decide whether all of this is worth it.

Ezra crammed a whole piece of toast into his mouth. He didn't want Iris to see how much this bothered him.

☀

Lucas pushes the heaviest equipment off stage and they start breaking down the set. They have half an hour. Ezra's throat is raw and he's not sure how he's going to sing tomorrow. He sets to work on the tiny screws that hold the rig together. The venue is packed with people here to see the headline act, a punk-rock band with blacked-out posters. The speakers are throbbing with high bass versions of their hits. They haven't eaten since lunchtime, when they split a bag of croissants. When Ezra unplugs the keyboards, black spots pop behind his eyes. He can't stop mentally replaying their set, which he feels like he missed, because he spent the whole time chasing the high of their Brighton gig.

That night, it was like all of their rehearsals paid off, distilling themselves into a few brilliant minutes. Everything happened as it was meant to; there were new pockets of time in the tracks, for experimenting, for showing off. Ezra lifted his guitar above his head, and held it reverently against an amp, producing a splintering electric sound. Lucas grinned at him, and then they were playing, building off each other's spontaneity with the kind of intimacy that made Ezra forget they were on stage.

Tonight, it was like playing into a void. Ezra couldn't hear Lucas in the wedges. Max was off by a beat. They keep the studio clean, like a laboratory, and he's got used to hearing their songs' sound captured, smoothed down. The Leadmill is full of aural junk that he can't shut out. Ezra pushes his earplugs further in. He's worried about tinnitus, but the disconnect between the energy he can see out there and the muffled noise feels like diving underwater. So many piercings it looks like a handful of ball bearings has been flung out. A pint goes flying backwards. Max keeps glancing around the curtain. Ezra is about to tell him to bring Haruto backstage when there's a howl of feedback over the speakers.

Idiots, Lucas mutters.

We'll have crew to do this shit one day, Ndulu yells, and we'll be out there like— He puts out his arms like he is flying.

Ezra winds the cables, wrapping them over and under his elbow. Ndulu puts the guitars in the guitar coffins. Lucas carries the keyboards outside, where Max guards the open van. Lucas crawls under the deck where the amps are plugged in to retrieve

94

the guitar pedals, which Max stacks, carefully, in boxes. Ndulu folds the keyboard stands. While Lucas is counting the cable ties, Ezra slips to the bathroom for a line.

Ezra likes picking up without the others. He saves his dealers' first names according to the towns they live in and gives them elements for surnames. Earlier, Sheffield Mercury sent him a pin from outside the Sainsbury's where his silver Prius was parked.

It's yellowish and clumping. There's more than enough for one, but is there enough for two? If he shares with Ndulu he'll have to share with Lucas too. Ezra hesitates, then inserts his key into the bag. It feels like snorting shards of glass. Then he sticks the key in his mouth, rubs his gums, and washes his hands.

He's high when he comes out of the bathroom and disgusted by all the drunk people.

There you are, Max says, looking relieved.

They find Haruto, near the stage. There's a stench of after-shave and mephedrone and men out on a night. Ezra swallows dripback, feeling spry and wiry. When Haruto kisses Max there's a wave of *oi oi* and colour creeps around Max's neck. Ndulu grins at Ezra. Nearby, a group of men keep glancing over. They're holding pints and they all seem to know each other. They look like cats given a mouse to play with. The word *poof* cuts through the music, then *dirty faggot*.

Ezra raises his eyebrows quizzically at Haruto.

Haruto nods, but his expression is strained. His hand keeps moving to Max's waist and then fluttering away again. Ezra checks where the exits are.

One of the men barges into Haruto. Are you giving out blow-jobs?

Haruto doesn't turn around, but Max does.

I think there's been a misunderstanding, he says, firmly.

Do you think there's been a *misunderstanding*, lads.

Dolly is waiting somewhere, Max says gruffly, not looking at Haruto. Let's go.

The lights go down. Lucas says something, angrily. Max pulls at his arm. As they're walking away, one of the men shoves Haruto and he stumbles. Ezra games out the sequences of possible actions. He sees them like beams of light on the floor, blacking out one by one. Lucas pushes the man, hard, in the chest, then hurls himself on top of him. Within moments, the bouncers are pulling them apart and dragging all five of them to the exit.

Ezra expects the men to be thrown out after them and keeps a wary eye on the door. Max is very pale. He and Haruto step to one side. The bouncer opens the door to push out the rest of their equipment. Wordlessly, Ndulu, Lucas and Ezra haul it into the van. Jackub gets out to help. When he sees the blood on Lucas's face, he grins.

Good night?

Ndulu is exhilarated. He slams the trunk.

I look more gay than you do, he says, cackling, then sees Max's expression. Shit man, sorry. It's the adrenaline. They would have eaten us *alive*.

There's a long pause, then Ezra bursts out, We're screwed if we get blacklisted. People have to want us in their venues—

Lucas's nose is still bleeding. He wipes it on his sleeve and stands, stony-faced.

Ezra checks the trunk. All I'm saying is you shouldn't have—

Right, because you should have, Lucas interrupts. You just stood there.

Ezra's face is burning but he also feels that this isn't fair, that

Lucas is using this to play the hero.

What would it have achieved? Ezra says. It wouldn't have ended well for us.

Lucas rounds on Ezra. What don't you get about being a collective?

Nobody says anything for a moment. Max is still staring at the ground, hands deep in his pockets. Ndulu flaps his T-shirt against himself, like he's cooling a fire.

I've got twenty quid burning a hole in my pocket, he says.

Let's go, Lucas says, and walks off into the night. Ndulu follows him without a word.

♱

Down the steps towards the Green Room, a group of girls are smoking and laughing. Ezra noticed them hanging around the stage door earlier. He diverts his course to the bar. They're meant to be courting press, but he doesn't want to be seen for a few hours. On the walk over, Ezra asked where Haruto had gone, and Max said, Home. He has an early start.

Dolly has left five tequila shots under their name. They don't have salt or lime. Ezra spots Lucas, Max and Ndulu in a corner, talking to a few girls. Dolly wants them to cultivate their fan base. He turns his phone on to check for signal but puts it away before it lights up. He doesn't know whether Iris will reassure him, or whether reassurance is even what he wants. He takes the last two shots and goes to sit on the edge of a small stage where there was live music earlier. He stretches his sinuses out with his thumbs, and inhales, sharply.

You know Freud used to cauterise his patients' nasal passages with cocaine.

Ezra chokes on warm tequila.

No, he says, coughing. I didn't.

Treatment for hysteria, the girl says, evenly. D'you have any spare?

She's sitting further down the stage. Ezra tries to work out how he hadn't seen her, patting his pockets, like there might be some left. She has a boyish, compact figure and she's not wearing a bra.

No luck, Ezra says. Was the treatment effective?

She blows her fringe out of her eyes.

The patient's pulse stopped for thirty seconds, she says. Then a doctor pulled out twenty inches of gauze which Freud left up there.

No *way*, Ezra says.

True story, she says, shaking her head, solemnly.

She starts telling Ezra more about Freud and coke, how he was a massive user. On some level he knows that she's only talking to him because he's in a band. He noticed her at the gig, near the stage, dancing intensely. She doesn't mention it though, and it's a relief not to have to recap the gig.

She exhales, looking around the packed room like it's dismal.

What – a – shitty – night, she says. You look like you're stuck on a bachelor party. I shouldn't even be here. I've an exam tomorrow.

What subject?

Psychology. I gave up revising after this crazy paper of Freud's – 'Masturbation, addiction and obsessional neurosis'.

Ezra turns his laugh into a cough and thumps himself on the chest.

She smiles at him. What?

'Paper Planes' starts playing. Ezra hadn't noticed the music.

This one's for all of M.I.A.'s bad girls, the DJ says.

Ezra stands up abruptly, aware of how prickly his fingers are, and how sticky the floor is, like it's been coated with Jäger bombs. He looks across the room and sees Max glancing over.

I'll have to Google it, Ezra says. I've just spotted the stag.

Okay, she says, raising her beer. See you.

12

The fish tank in Liderman's office is full of goldfish. They glide around a plastic mermaid. Her tail is stuck in the coral gravel. Seaweed flares around her. When Liderman gets up to feed them, I can see the nail polish she's used to fix the ladder in her tights.

So how much would you say you drink, Iris.

I feel like a cornered dog. Not more than everyone else.

She scatters dull yellow flakes into the tank. They sit on the surface of the water.

Everyone is a tricky word, Iris. Take me, for instance – I don't drink at all. Pinot Grigio? Not interested. Daiquiris? No sirree. Piña colada? Not for me, *thank you*. Let me tell you, those people who say that a glass of wine with dinner is good for you? Delusional. Dangerous and delusional.

I mutter something about being European and she says, Aren't you British? She screws the lid of the fish food on tight. You seem anxious to me.

It's been a rough week, I say.

Tell me about it, she says. I've got clients calling at all hours – the Donald should ask for commission. And what about socially, are you making any friends?

I played beer pong because I saw it on TV. In my mind, I was a sorority girl. Halfway through I realised that there were no sorority girls playing, only man-boys with facial hair. Then I realised that the ping-pong ball was furry with dirt from the floor and people's feet. I went to the bathroom, threw up, splashed my face with water, and went to bed. Yes, I say, yes. I am making friends.

Have you experienced anxiety like this before?

I don't believe in anxiety.

Liderman picks up the piece of paper I put on the table between us. It is a revised version of the one in the bin outside, copied from various bar napkins.

She gives me a long hard look. So that's two small glasses of wine a night, she says.

I nod, primly.

I'll spare you the lecture on what you're risking by drinking to that excess. I could tell you about the danger to your liver, your kidneys, the imbalance of your neurotransmitters, the blood sugar problems, the depressive effects of alcohol – but you're a smart girl. You know all that. Can you show me, with your hand, how big a small glass of wine is?

The feeding frenzy in the tank has claimed its first victim. One fish floats to the top, like a sacrifice. I think of Nance and move my finger and thumb closer together.

†

I get my first piece of mail from Ezra and keep it on my windowsill for a week. When I open it, a blue exercise book slides out. There's no note. Here are Ezra's dreams:

I'm in a forest, and it's familiar, but it's dark. I try and retrace my steps, but whichever way I turn it's the same. The trees are very tall, and the spaces between them are wide and smooth, like avenues. I hear an engine and think, maybe I'll hitch-hike – this is a good sign in terms of my progress in lucid dreaming, which requires the ability to think within the dream – but there's smoke everywhere, and I'm coughing. A plane takes off from between the trees and flies straight at the moon. I wake up.

I'm in a ball pit with children. This is strange because I have never been in a ball pit. The balls are red and yellow. All the children are wearing children-clothes, like dungarees. They start playing. I realise there's no exit, so I'm not just too big, I'm stuck, and I don't know the rules of the game. Then, a mean-looking one with bright green eyes says, Wanna play, and I realise he's the devil. I wake up.

I'm near the cloisters of the Uffizi Gallery, in front of a large replica of the *David*. He has massive hands. The choir are singing the chants of the Benedictine Monks of Santo Domingo de Silos. I ask the Choir Master whether we can sing 'It Ain't Me Babe'. He says no. I ask whether we can sing 'I Walk the Line'. He says no. Someone hands me a guitar. It turns into an octopus. Its tentacles latch on to me. I wake up.

Lexi wants to try a new Indian place downtown. I suggest a few starters. Lexi nods, then asks the Dominican waiter what's good. He suggests a monkfish curry, which is $16.

She watches enviously as I take spoonfuls of crispy sev and dip each in yoghurt, tamarind.

You know dairy really isn't good for you, she says.

Lexi likes to give me advice. To sleep with silk pillow-slips to avoid mussing a blow-out, to start an ISA, to download various apps. I download the apps and never use them.

Lexi prescribes phone sex, but Ezra has no interest. I read the letters of Henry Miller and Anaïs Nin and WhatsApp him a line by way of example: I want to undress you, vulgarise you a bit.

Ezra sends back a link to the Kronos Quartet with no message. On Skype, I slump, deliberately, Quasimodo style. Ezra's lip twitches but he will not correct me. He refuses to say words that he does not mean and will not be goaded into it.

I decide to take Lexi's advice and be proactive. I put on a tracksuit because he will only see me from the waist up anyway. From the waist up, I will be irresistible, like a centaur.

Two hours later, Ezra messages:

Dolly took us to this crazy underground bar and there's no signal! Are you free now?

We FaceTime but he is walking and the image is blurred.

Let's try again tomorrow, I say.

His image is frozen. He looks like a child leaping off a swing.

REALISE REAL LIES

Liderman follows my gaze and nods sagely. Makes you think, doesn't it, she says.

We have been talking for forty minutes. The heating is in overdrive. Liderman is pink as a ham. She gave me an electric fan, but it doesn't help. She asks me, for the third time, how my *sadness* manifests itself. All I want to do is lie on the floor.

Liderman clears her throat. What I'm hearing is that you have several disorders which are what we call *comorbid disorders*. We can rule out bipolar, but I'd say generalised anxiety disorder and major depressive disorder and premenstrual dysmorphic disorder at least. You're high-functioning though and that's something. One of my clients, she leans forwards to confide, *star* clients, like she wants me to guess the celebrity, came to me in a state of nervous collapse, close to mania. Three prescriptions later? She smiles – this is her mic drop – I had her back at work in two weeks.

She has lipstick on her teeth, which is coral, and clashes with her lilac blouse.

I mutter, Before you go on antidepressants, make sure you're not surrounded by assholes. This is what Sam says when I say I've only ever felt this bad for a few days at a time.

Pre-New York? he asks. Or pre-Trump.

Either, I say. Both.

Liderman narrows her eyes. I bet you like old movies, right? You know how there's always that cute doctor with the *To Kill a Mockingbird* glasses and the brown leather bag? And someone gets sick and he rushes in and makes it all better? I stare at her and she smiles, slyly. Remind you of anyone?

I push the soft plastic blades of the fan back against themselves and it drones in alarm. Liderman takes it from me, turns it off and puts it on the table.

Ezra doesn't wear glasses any more, I say.

What happens when Gregory Peck isn't there?

I knew she'd only seen the movie.

What I'm saying, Iris, is that without managing your symptoms – you'll always fall apart again.

The fish tank is covered in a violet scrim today. I wonder if she removed the dead body with a net. I imagine it spiralling down the toilet.

Tess has downloaded Skype on her phone and starts calling every few days. I do not pick up because she will not be impressed with what she sees. I ask if we can schedule a time so I can rev myself up.

She leaves a voice message: Oh, I'm sorry, I didn't realise you were so very important. Is there a secretary I can call?

⚹

I collect the prescription because I am worried that Liderman will know if I don't. I put the bottle in a bathroom drawer. Then I take it out again. I glance at it while I'm plucking my eyebrows, like it might ambush me. I pick it up, pretending my hand is someone else's hand. Nothing to do with me, officer, I was just passing by. I am relieved when I cannot open it.

Reasons to take antidepressants:

I can't get up. I can't work.

I have given up everything to be here and I'm living in my bedroom.

I only feel like myself when I'm talking to Ezra. Why would he want to talk to this.

If I don't take them, am I choosing to be unhappy?

What else to do?

What if Liderman's right and I'm fundamentally broken.

And yet. The weight of choosing between possible selves. It feels like I am being asked to kill a part of myself. Spiritual hara-kiri.

I tell Liderman I will try harder.

I call Lexi to tell her that I'm going to be on my period at Christmas and I *need* to have sex with Ezra.

She clicks her tongue sympathetically. When I was going to Mexico with Matteo, I took this pill, you just take it three times a day – very simple – when you stop, you bleed.

Did you get it from the doctor?

I bought it online. It's the brand name that matters, she says, defensively. This was GSK.

Ezra says he doesn't want me putting chemicals in my body.

We'll put a towel down, he says.

Sasha tells us to try everything now.

It's only going to get harder to change, she says. Do it all before you hit thirty.

So, we start to Do things. Not just write, we do. We do coke in dive bar restrooms. We take acid in Central Park. We pick fights in dive bars. We drink cheap wine at poetry slams in Queens. Lisa offers me Adderall and I take it and it is bitter and blue. I drink myself up to zero, then plus one, plus two—

Whenever I don't know what to say, I tell men about my disappointment in fire escapes. I am stuck in endless conversations about fire escapes. Sam corners me and says that pissing off a fire escape is the male equivalent of having a good cry.

On the subway back, there is a horrible lucidity which makes me notice the foot of someone's tights in the bin and how the roof of a boy's mouth is like a fish belly when he throws his head back, laughing.

I call Nance. Been off carousing the streets without me, Nance says.

There's no carousing to be had without you, I say.

That's right. And don't you forget it.

The next morning, I feel like my brain has been scraped out with a metal spoon. I sit on the edge of the bath and call Ezra.

It will pass, he says. Like a migraine, remember?

People take anti-migraine pills, I say.

He sighs. If you want to take them, you should.

I don't know what I want, I say, listlessly, but I don't want this.

Bear in mind that these drugs can change the chemical structure of your brain. You know how to live with your structure. If you start screwing around with that, you might change how your memories are encoded, which would be permanent. You haven't always felt like this.

I wonder, if I hang up, how many times he will call me.

I want him to tell me to open each capsule and pour the beads down the sink.

Come home, I imagine him saying.

I just need to pull myself together, I say. Do you think everyone needs to pull themselves together?

No, he says, thoughtfully, but then perhaps other people are not so often falling apart.

13

Piers takes Nance to the Members' Room at the Tate. They make up stories about the other diners and the people on the South Bank far below. They eat hot croquettes and sip glasses of fino, which, Piers tells her, he drank every night when he was lecturing in Bilbao. You don't forget nights like those, he says. It can be painful, when all one really wants is to focus on work, but it's a mistake to cloister oneself. He tells Nance about days of reeling between the Deustuko Unibertsitatea and the Guggenheim, which surpasses the Guggenheim in New York by far, and though the Venice Guggenheim has a place in his heart, the one in Bilbao is the best of the lot.

They wander through the Georgia O'Keeffe exhibition and he calls Nance back to look, *really look*, at the delicate hues of the irises, the flamboyant brushstrokes.

People say these paintings are about bodies, but really . . .

He shows her John Opie's portrait of Wollstonecraft – Do you see her expression, how she's glancing up as if someone is interrupting her work and, really, she would rather return to it?

He reads her Chekhov short stories in Russian. They visit the Freud museum and have a picnic on Hampstead Heath. When Nance can't choose between the postcards in the gift shop he buys her one of each – Wolfman's Dream, Eros, Gradiva. He laughs when she picks up an audio guide and takes it, gently, from her hands. The next time they meet, he gives Nance a framed print of Lucian Freud's *Girl in Bed* and says, She reminds me of you, so it only seems fair that you have her.

When Nance says she has never been to Berlin, he says, *Yet*. You haven't been *yet*.

But Nance is out of sorts, and when I start therapy, she decides she wants therapy too. She is entitled to five sessions of CBT through the University Counselling Service.

A woman wearing a scrunchie tells Nance that every time she finds herself procrastinating, she should remember to Only Handle It Once and say, OHIO. After she says this, doing her work will seem preferable to repeating it. It reminds me of YEEHA and I add a cowboy-lasso action which makes Nance laugh.

The therapist suggests affirmations:

I matter.
My work matters.
Interacting with people brings me joy.

I suggest alternatives:

Pain is weakness leaving the body.
My body is a work of art. (Madonna)
Happiness is no excuse for mediocrity.

Nance seems brighter on Skype. I ask her whose affirmations she chose.

She says, So, I was on the bus – one of the scuzzy ones that smells like cat food – and I looked around at all your ones and I thought: I matter more than you. I matter more than you. I matter more than you. And you know what, it did work.

In the weeks after, Nance calls me less and I am not about to chase her. I WhatsApp Ezra to complain that I can't make myself work and he replies have you tried OHIO?

I email Nance saying that I hope business is going well for the Love Doctor and my workshop was fine and I'm glad she's finding time to comfort Ezra.

19.11.16 13:33
From: nancyomalley@magd.ox.ac.uk
To: irisirisiris@gmail.com
Dear Iris,

If you call him the Love Doctor I will actually be sick. And then you'll have to explain to my mother how I drowned on dry land.

In fairness, at this point I thought the asking was implied. Don't be an eejit: All that we have in common is missing you.

xoxo

Ezra is touring Europe. Their gigs are the only blocks of colour in my calendar. We talk on Skype.

I grumble that Nance always gets what she wants.

He says, but does it make her happy?

You tell me, I say.

We're both awake at weird times, he says. And we only ever talk about you.

You answer her questions about the band, I say.

Like what?

Before I can make up an example, Ezra says, Anyway, it's different. Nance asks about objective facts. You tend to ask about my feelings. Do you not want me to be friends with her? He

110

frowns. I'm trying to remember our longest conversation. It was just after you left. She interrupted, so I thought she had urgent advice, but she just looked solemn and said: Even Odysseus wept. Ezra shakes his head – She's so insecure, it's exhausting.

She's the most confident person I know!

For the rest of the conversation, I ask pointedly objective questions about travel arrangements and Ezra is brusque with me. He emails a few hours later.

21.11.16 00:51
From: ezramunroe@gmail.com
To: irisirisiris@gmail.com
I'm sorry I snapped. It's just that I have to be there all the time. There's no way out of it. It has to happen and I have to become the kind of person who can do it. It's like being in a succession of small boxes. I turned my T-shirt inside out every day for the last week. We get up at 6 am. Four to eight hours in a van, into a small dark venue, unload and set everything up in a windowless underground room that smells of beer and sweat, then you're stuck in a tiny box dressing room with five people, play a show in the box, pack up load up go to a small box of a hotel room for sleep. Coke to stay up, drink to knock out. The most interesting thing I've seen is people's room service on trays. I've been dehydrated for two weeks.

I learn to send one in every ten texts I want to send. Perhaps I should get another phone and text myself.

My very own department of dead letters, I tell Nance.

Like Bartleby, she nods. Or Humboldt? You know – Saul Bellow.

14

Lisa starts a WhatsApp group called Outsiders Dinner for people who can't go home for Thanksgiving, or don't want to. She sends a link to an NPR article called How to Talk to Your Trump-Loving Uncle. Then a shrugging emoji. Or you could just, you know, not.

Other than to go to class, I have not left my room for a week. I can't face putting my head out the window so I download an app to tell me what to wear. When I wash my hair, I am surprised by how heavy it is, like a snake.

Ray asks me to have dinner with them. I write a note thanking Lindsey for her kind invitation. Unfortunately, I'm not in the mood to celebrate genocide.

I leave the apartment so rarely that taking cabs seems justified. The only way to face myself down is to reduce the possible outcomes of any situation by narrowing down the decisions I have to make. Remi's flat is up past Morningside Heights in Harlem.

Sam opens the door and hugs me with one arm. He has flour by his ear and I brush it off.

Gravy, he says.

Nice apron, I say. Butch.

There are fairy lights sparkling behind him. Bruce Springsteen is playing, 'Dancing in the Dark'.

I have confessed Springsteen as a guilty secret. I shake my head at Sam and push past. The counter is heaped with food: mini pecan pies, dishes of sweet potatoes. Remi and Conrad are taking turns poking some meat with a skewer.

En garde, Conrad says, running it through. What did I tell you? No blood.

Gross, Lisa says. She is drinking rosé with an ice cube in it. Remi comes up behind her and slips an arm around her waist.

Thank you for inviting me, I say.

No problem, Lisa says. Thank him.

Only three of the seven of us are true blue aliens: me, a Canadian, and a Northern girl. We clashed in a seminar after she said that the class divide is worse in England than it is in America and I snorted accidentally. I meant that more people slip through the net in America, there are more homeless people, but before I could clarify, Finn said, Don't you have like a fuckin' caste system in India and I was too busy hating him to care.

What caste are we? I asked Tess. I was six. The first thing I learnt to say in Hindi was my father is away on business. Which, as Tess remarked, tartly, was true.

Tess smiled a small, cool smile out of the window that meant I should change the subject.

Why do you ask?

Nana said the achuta bhangi came and swept and swept.

We drove on, silent in the blare of horns, and I felt smaller and smaller. When the driver called his wife, Tess said, Never use that word again. As to caste, it is irrelevant, especially to you. It's also illegal. She squinted out the window and then, as if in spite of herself, made a pyramid out of her hands: Shudras; labourers. Vaishyas; artisans, tradesmen. Kshatriyas. Then Brahmin – priests, academics, professors.

I sensed that I had room for one more question before she froze me out. Are we rich?

She laughed. Ask your father.

I am clutching two bottles of wine, one red, one white. Everyone except Lisa is drinking beer and I want to slip one into my bag.

Typical Iris, Lisa says. But I feel charitable towards everyone that night, even Lisa. Things feel charged and possible. I feel comfortable in my skin. I tell stories of my flailing through New York. We aren't in a bar, so everyone can hear me speak. I help with the washing up and push the black beans from Sam's stuffing down the drain while he distracts Remi.

On the walk back, there is scaffolding and metal poles which disrupt the view of the moon. Sam is drunk, but not sloppy. I feel like I am trying not to break into a run. He is going to show me how to flag down an American taxi. I have been having difficulties.

Smart girl like you, no way.

None of his keys work in the front door to his building, and I have a moment of looking at the statue of an angel holding a clock. Then I look away.

Why don't you come up and see the place, he says. It's not the Ritz, but it's not bad for round here either. I have roommates, he adds. I don't know if they're here.

I am very drunk, suddenly. I rest my forehead on the metal pole and see the moon bisected. My heel twists beneath me. Sam catches my arm.

Whoa, hey now, let's get you some water, he says.

We walk up the stairs together, doing the Broadway walk, where you put one foot behind someone else's and push their foot forwards. A slow drunken can-can. A falling upstairs.

Mademoiselle, he says, and I follow him in, past the gym kit on the floor, the heap of trainers. There are plates stacked on the coffee table. Sam immediately picks them up and takes them into the kitchen. The TV has been left on mute. I watch football players tackle each other, bright and blurred. While Sam washes up, I press the heels of my hands into my eyelids for a moment, to steady myself.

Now it's really Thanksgiving, Sam says, coming into the room and switching the TV off. His phone buzzes. He pulls it out of his pocket. Yup, he sighs. They're on their way back. Don't get me wrong, living with girls is great, but once they've started drinking . . .

He holds out his phone to show me the stream of gifs they've sent. A *South Park* character gobble gobble gobble. A girl in a Native American headdress mud-wrestles a pilgrim. A turkey bathes in a rush of gravy.

That's a lot, I say, pushing the phone back at him.

He laughs. You're telling me.

I follow him into his bedroom. I notice the spine of a Raymond Carver anthology on the floor. The window is steamed up. Thank god it's warm, I say.

He has opened two Lagunitas, which we do not drink. We leave them on the floor by his bed.

I need to lie down, I say. Just for ten minutes.

He wipes his hands on his jeans and says, Okay.

He lies down, and I curl into him, little spoon. Like this?

I nod. His shoulders are wider than mine. The curtains are cheap and can't keep the moon out. We hold hands, his circled around my waist. We lie there, for what feels like hours, but is less than five minutes. I feel him get hard against me, and stiffen, and squeeze his left hand, and ignore it.

Sorry, he says and doesn't move.

I do not want him to move. His sheets are navy blue and soft. I rub them between my fingers. Jersey cotton, he says. His arms enclose me entirely and my main concern is that I will fall asleep.

How much damage could it do?

He does not try to kiss me. His stubble grazes my ear. It is like discovering a new sense. I have only ever wanted Ezra. I try to place this feeling of terror and exhilaration, and remember the last time, three years ago, when Ezra was the one with someone else, and it was the two of us rushing upstairs, conspiratorial as children.

We hug. We cuddle. We keep our clothes on. And that is all it is really – a flip of the axis. I say I have to go. I don't move. I lie so still that it is almost movement itself, like I am exerting a downwards force, like gravity.

I am getting fuzzy by the time he touches my shoulder and says, Hey, are you going to feel weird if you don't wake up in your own bed?

He comes outside in his flip-flops in the snow to hail me a cab. When I look out of the back window, he has one hand in the air. I ask the driver to turn the radio off and keep my eyes on the moon.

Interlude

Iris:	I don't feel like myself any more. I don't want to ruin this as well. It has taken me two hours to get dressed and I'm wearing a tracksuit. I can't stop crying.	**17:34**
	And we haven't found a way to make the next bit work. I can't feel like this for two more years. I can't.	**17:35**
Ezra:	Well, it sounds like you're depressed so perhaps best to leave thinking about big problems which don't have an immediate resolution for another day? There's nothing I can do about the fact that I won't know my schedule for the next two years.	**17:37**
Iris:	I'm not asking for an apology.	**17:39**
Ezra:	I'm not apologising.	**17:39**
Iris:	Okay . . .	**17:39**
Ezra:	We've talked about this so many times. We've acknowledged countless times that this is as good a time as any for you to be away because I'm going to be away anyway. This isn't news.	**17:43**
Iris:	Thanks for the recap.	**17:43**
Ezra:	We're both doing what we want.	**17:43**
Iris:	But if I was there, I would be sitting around and waiting for you.	**17:43**
Ezra:	BUT YOU'RE NOT! AND YOU MADE THAT DECISION.	**17:43**
Iris:	Work will always come first for you. You can work	**17:50**

when I'm there. You work when you're here. You get
on with your life when we're apart.

It scares me how much I would give up for you.   **17:52**

I could spend my whole life following you around.

Ezra: I'm not asking you to give anything up.   **17:52**

I don't understand how you're still holding me
accountable for things that happened years ago.

Iris: But they did happen. Pain doesn't just disappear.   **17:52**

It flows to ground.

Ezra: Part of me thinks we should end this now. I'm   **17:56**

doing everything I can to keep you on your feet but
something tells me I'm being royally fucked over.

Iris: I love you.   **17:56**

Ezra: So, then there's the possibility of doing exactly   **18:05**

what you suggested, being apart, writing letters,
seeing other people if we want to, seeing each other
in the holidays and then resuming older and wiser in
two years' time. We could do that. We would end up
with a great collection of letters and probably have
fun, and at the very least a lot of great drama.

Iris: *. . . typing . . .*   **18:05**

Ezra: So maybe we should start seeing ourselves as   **18:07**

polyamorous?

Iris: Is that what you want?   **18:07**

Ezra: Or we need to break up, with or without an eye   **18:10**

towards getting back together when you're back.

Iris: Is that what you want?   **18:10**

Ezra: Whatever we do, something clearly has to change.   **18:15**

Your being in New York has started to feel like you
choosing to be away from me.

Iris:	If I was there, you would be away from me. Even when you're here, you're working all the time.	**18:17**
Ezra:	I recognise that destructive impulse to just cut loose, and start over again, alone, which I think stems from the feeling that things have gone wrong.	**18:20**
Iris:	If they have, is that undoable?	**18:20**
Iris:	Ignore that.	**18:20**
Iris:	Is that what you want?	**18:22**
Ezra:	If everything you've said about wanting space, and getting less dependent, and having other experiences is true – or if those are the main issues – then why does what I want matter?	**18:22**
Iris:	I don't know.	**18:22**
Ezra:	Unless all the things you've brought up are side issues and what you really want is proof that I love you. Which would, for the record, make me very, very angry. None of the things you've said seem fixable by me convincing you everything is fine the way it is/has been.	**18:22**
	Our relationship, or our emotional involvement is something more permanent than most people's relationships, I think.	**18:30**
Iris:	I'm so scared I'm so scared I'm so scared. Of the this of us replacing the that of us.	**18:30**
Ezra:	So yes, in a theoretical world . . . if we can just be happy with each other when we can, and immunise ourselves against other people, then eventually, the experience would make the problems other people have less intimidating (affairs etc.) because we'd	**18:34**

have experienced our love for each other as outlasting things of a similar nature.

| Iris: | *. . . typing . . .* | 18:34 |
| Ezra: | We would have to view other people as irrelevant, rather than a pro or a con. The thing which we both have to be committed to is being true to what the best part of each other would expect from one another. i.e. by all means live how you want to, but do your best not to hurt yourself, because that would hurt me too. | 18:41 |

II
L-O-V-E-L-E-S-S Generation

January–June 2017

1

On the morning of the Women's March, I lie in bed, wondering if Nance would believe that I'd slept through it. With NyQuil maybe, or a migraine? Trump has been president for thirteen hours. The TV is on, but muted. Twitter on, notifications off. These are my New Year resolutions, the compromises I am making with reality. I turn on Ezra's playlist as a reward for brushing my teeth.

Bob Dylan	It ain't me babe
Bob Dylan	To Ramona
Fleetwood Mac	Go your own way
Fleetwood Mac	Second hand news
Fleetwood Mac	Never going back again
Dr Dre	Bitches ain't shit

Ezra has changed. He is more affectionate, but it is the kind of affection that you offer a sick child. He is polite. It is as if he has moved out quietly, overnight. When he messages, it is to check if I am eating, whether I am getting enough sleep. When I mention anything to do with the future, he changes the subject. He tries to nudge me, gently, into the present, where I do not want to be. He spends most of January making cut-outs of samurai symbols which Max spray-paints onto the band van. There is talk of changing their name; Dolly doesn't think the label will be keen on knives or blades.

Ezra tells me on Christmas Eve that their two-week tour of

Europe will start before New Year's. I have forfeited my girl-friend rights. There are people Dolly wants them to meet and she thinks there's a publishing deal down the line. Ezra tells me this, shoving his Converse into his duffel bag like he is forcing them into another dimension. I say, This is all happening so quickly, and he says, It doesn't feel that way to me.

At the airport, I scroll through online articles about famous couples in open relationships:

1. Ashton Kutcher & Demi Moore. (Bruce Willis & Demi Moore.)
2. Will Smith & Jada Pinkett Smith
3. Tilda Swinton & John Byrne (& Sandro Kopp).
4. Simone de Beauvoir & Jean-Paul Sartre
5. Elizabeth Smart & George Barker

On landing, I send Ezra the list. He doesn't reply. Usually my lists are a filter; see x in terms of y. But they aren't holding things together any more, not even for me. I try changing the headings, but the problem isn't the form, it is the content. No one list can take everything into account. There are caveats and parentheses. I do not send Ezra these.

1. Do women suggest open relationships because they want to sleep with other people or because it's a way of renarrativising what their partners want? (Is Demi Moore non-monogamous or does she like non-monogamous men?)
2. Are open relationships different to ethical non-monogamy? If most people cheat anyway, why do we need another name for it?
3. Are open relationships different to polyamory? How many

people have the time and/or emotional bandwidth to love many people? Is *fuck who you want but don't fall in love* permission (encouragement?) to treat other women badly?

4. How do you know who is contingent? Or is it a question of duration (i.e. romance as an endurance sport)?

JPS: *What we have is an essential love; but it is a good idea for us also to experience contingent love affairs.*

SDB: *We were two of a kind and our relationship would endure as long as we did: but it could not make up entirely for the fleeting riches to be had from encounters with different people.*

Sartre had many lovers, de Beauvoir had few. She wrote jealous letters.

5. George Barker was married to someone else. He fathered fifteen children with four different women. *It is enough*, Elizabeth Smart wrote. *I do not accept it sadly or ruefully or wistfully.*

When I try to read, the words start moving like ants. For every ten minutes I persist with salt, I read the Trump Twitter archive for twenty. I sense a pattern forming, as if it will shift into focus after the next tweet. I search key terms. I paste tweets into thematically grouped documents on my desktop.

Aug 26, 2011 10:07:42 AM Why did @BarackObama and his family travel separately to Martha's Vineyard? They love to extravagantly spend on the taxpayers' dime.

Dec 14, 2011 11:45:55 AM I feel sorry for Rosie's new partner in love whose parents are devastated at the thought of their daughter being with @Rosie – a true loser.

Feb 14, 2012 2:45:58 PM @BarackObama's budget funds the "Arab Spring" with $800B and the Muslim Brotherhood in Egypt $1.3B in military aid. He loves radical Islam.

Nov 11, 2012 08:53:49 AM I am a very calm person but love tweeting about both scum and positive subjects. Whenever I tweet, some call it a tirade..totally dishonest!

Two hours go by. Nance sends a photo of her Free Melania sign on WhatsApp with a message:

Piers is reminiscing about the Anti-Nazi League rally.   **17:10**
He saw the Clash play in Victoria Park. He thinks he's
coming on the march. He wants to bring a picnic
blanket.

I close the archive and try to work. I never thought I could know a ceiling this well; the bumps in the paint, like expensive mould. The light from the window makes it look like it is reflecting water. I open the archive again and look for a tweet to send Nance.

May 7, 2013 7:04:21 PM 26,000 unreported sexual assaults in the military-only 238 convictions. What did these geniuses expect when they put men & women together?

Sep 10, 2013 4:48:46 PM Danger-Weiner is a free man at 12:01AM. He will be back sexting with a vengeance. All women remain on alert.

Jun 8, 2014 11:17:48 AM The Miss U.S.A. pageant will be amazing tonight. To be politically incorrect, the girls (women) are REALLY BEAUTIFUL. NBC at 8 PM.

Apr 21, 2015 3:52:29 PM .@JonahNRO You stated that I started "relentlessly tweeting like a 14-year-old girl..." Horrible insult to women. Resign now or later!

Dec 23, 2015 6:17:09 PM Hillary, when you complain about "a penchant for sexism," who are you referring to. I have great respect for women. BE CAREFUL!

I send Nance a photo of a sea of pink hats. I feel bad lying to her, but marching would make the futility seem louder. There's no point unless you want to hear yourself scream. Lisa is having a pink pussy hat party. I see people click Attending on Facebook, but I haven't been invited. Online, I have a bird's eye view. The galleries are being updated as I watch. I like the photos of small groups of friends, holding up their signs to the camera. I go through suggested Twitter accounts and curate my ideal marching band.

Tess on WhatsApp: Do some shouting for me! You're so lucky to be part of your generation. I scroll through Instagram and send her signs she might like: GET YOUR TINY HANDS OFF MY UTERUS. An Indian girl holds a sign saying NOT MY CHEETO. A cartoon Trump looks at the Statue of Liberty and says, EH, SHE'S A FOUR. A child with blonde ringlets holds up a sign covered in fridge magnet numbers: I COUNT. I get carried away. Trump as a peach (IMPEACH). RETWEET OTHERS HOW U WANT 2 BE TWEETED. An old woman holds up a sign saying

NOW YOU PISSED OFF GRANDMA. There are the more serious ones: FEMINISM IS THE RADICAL NOTION THAT WOMEN ARE PEOPLE. I put these in a folder for Nance. I will decide which one I carried later. I stay up until 2 am, finding my way in. I save 137 signs to my desktop. I can reconstruct everything about it. Why does it matter if I was there or not?

2

A Chinese proverb: As a daughter grows up she is like smuggled salt.

Tess was so set on not becoming her mother that she sometimes forgot I was a child. When I came home from school and declared myself starving, she'd say *How terrible* and look sympathetic but perplexed, as if I'd presented her with a problem beyond her grasp. The question – *What's for dinner?* – was met with: *Oh, I don't know. Fish-hooks and hammer handles?* Once I'd given up asking, she'd call *supper* in a faux-fifties way. When my friends came round, her response was a bright *What 'is' for dinner, Iris?* We ate whatever the confused pre-teen me assembled. I'd pick up a magazine and pretend not to notice, as if this was something all mothers did. In spite of myself, I grew bored of friends who didn't get Tess. She'd always been a kind of test you had to pass to prove you loved me.

Nance worships her though they've never met. She likes that Tess smokes Gauloises and will only drink San Pellegrino. Anyone who doesn't recognise that Tess is *fabulous* is a *boring bastard*. She pesters me for stories of Tess *flouting societal expectations* and *insisting on female autonomy*. I imitate the shudder this would elicit from my mother, but it only spurs Nance on.

That's cos she's iconic, she says. Like if Meryl Streep spoke five languages.

Tess speaks Hindi, Urdu, Gujrati, Burmese, Bengali. She doesn't count the European languages. *They're all the same*, she says, with a languid shrug. When I got a C on my French GCSE, all she said was, *Your father's genes expressing themselves . . .*

She mimed locking her mouth and throwing away the key.

Stable door, I said. She ignored me.

My father's genes also express themselves in my slovenliness, poor stamina and tendency towards – as Tess told me at nine years old – instant gratification. Her versions of Ray vary depending on the season, the radio and the state of the world.

Tess refers to Nance as my little friend. She has no interest in meeting her. I suspect if she did she'd think she drew the short straw, so I tell stories of Nance getting sick in the street.

Does she have to be quite so . . . over the top. If the top is here, Tess says, indicating a space a foot above her head, *she's over it.*

Summer mornings in our house were pure Gershwin. I woke too early, expected Tess too soon, and fell back into an uneasy sleep. Then she'd appear over the horizon of my duvet like some migratory bird just back from winter, a thousand times sweeter than she had been for months. Meals were an elaborate affair during the holidays. Picnics with linen napkins and cutlery, strawberries and thick slices of bread, lakes of golden honey. If there was rain, we ate on a picnic blanket in the living room. Tess, off-key and crooning, swaying to whatever hit wove through that summer, *If my mother could see us, Iris, you can't even imagine—* At home, Tess refers to Nana as Viceroy and Nani as Madam-Sir. Around them she was always Nishta. She wore the name sullenly, like a plastic nametag ruining her dress.

I used to cry in the bathroom when dusk set in because I was so scared of those summer days ending. *God, you're so sensitive. If a phobia of floors existed, you would have it. You'd demand I carry you around on my back – like a squaw.*

At least you can talk to yours, Nance says, glumly. Go to galleries and all that. My ma thinks yoga is mortal sin. A Hindu goddess attaching to the base of your spine – like the devil.

She sends me a link:

BISHOP OF WATERFORD WARNS AGAINST YOGA AND MINDFULNESS IN SCHOOLS.

Never mention yoga to Tess. Not all Indians—

The chance would be a fine thing, Nance crows. You won't let me get within an ass's roar of the woman.

I don't tell Nance that being Tess's daughter is like constantly failing a quiz.

⚐

On the Piccadilly line, the week before Christmas, I send Nance lists:

Iris: Allergies: air conditioning, pastry, American accents, cheap parmesan, portmanteaus, Bailey's (any kind of sweetened alcohol), people who describe themselves as sensitive, talking babies in adverts (see also: animals in clothes), sentimentality, imprecise use of adverbs (literally), eating on public transport, flashy labels, knock-off labels, leggings . . .

Nance: Cava?

Iris: Allergies cont.: stupid questions.
Cures: champagne (headaches), hot toddies (flu), fresh air (nerves), fresh air (self-obsession), exercise (aches and pains).

I dig up the jar at the bottom of the garden for the spare front door keys. I can't admit to Tess that I have left mine in New York. She has barely spoken to me since August. I dump my bag and dash out again for flowers. *How sharper than a serpent's tooth*, Tess says when I come home empty-handed. I'd been to three different shops, but nothing made the cut. She is bored of orange roses, pink lilies are *too sexual*. (How is a lily phallic? I grumbled to Nance on the phone. She means like a cunt, Nance hooted. I realise she's right. This annoys me. Tess is mine to understand.) White lilies, funerals. Yellow roses mean jealousy. Red ones *so cliché*. Tulips are out. Some blow-in friend asked Tess why she disliked them once and I winced. *Sylvia Plath*, Tess said, in the voice she reserves for the extremely slow. Then, at the look of incomprehension: *stillborn*. We were ten.

All the clothes in my cupboard are things I left behind on purpose. I raid Tess's room. I change into jeans and one of Tess's sweatshirts. I go downstairs to make chaat, but I can't open the tamarind jar. Tess raised me with the near-religious belief that one must never rely on a man to open anything. This involved banging jars in the hinges of doors, swearing, and colouring in the chipped paint with Sharpies. I grew up thrusting closed jars at men who happened to be passing through, saying, Quick! Loosen it!

I am worried that Tess will smell Liderman on me. The first time I got depressed, I was fifteen and my first boyfriend had broken up with me. He said I had a problem with boundaries. The next day, I couldn't get out of bed.

It's not that you can't, Tess said, *it's that you don't want to*.

I had crawled across my bedroom to go to the bathroom that morning and crawled back again. I remember Tess standing in the doorway. Her voice sounded very far away. When I peered out from under the duvet, she looked terrified.

Get up, she said. *We're going out to lunch.*

I have school, I said, listless.

Oh, I'm sorry, she said. *I mistakenly thought you were lying around feeling sorry for yourself. Up. Now.*

In the car, I cringed from the light but Tess refused to let me wear dark glasses.

You are neither a rock-star nor neuralgic, she said, and turned on the radio.

After that, she woke me up at 7 am every day by switching the light on. If I wasn't up by 7.30, I found myself steered through a day mysteriously crammed with urgent errands. She was a drill sergeant. I trudged after her on visits to galleries. She leaned in to scrutinise portraits and I looked listlessly at the frames. We walked around Battersea Park and Tess pointed out the worst-dressed couples. We had lunch at Fortnum and Mason; Tess flirted with the waiter, praising the cucumber sandwiches. I hated her.

When Tess gets home, she goes around the house switching on the lamps in every room, while I make salmon en papillote. Half of the furniture has gone. She has rearranged the kitchen and I have to open every drawer trying to find the brown paper, the string. I put a bottle of sauvignon blanc in the freezer.

She comes downstairs and moves around the kitchen shutting cupboards. She hugs me and her face is cold from being outside.

Your hair has grown, she says.

Hers is piled up on top of her head. She massages Parachute coconut oil into her scalp three times a week. Whenever I tell her she should wear hers down, she pinches her lips together. She thinks that wearing one's hair loose is for women under thirty.

I peel vegetables. Tess tells me that she's been rewatching episodes of *The West Wing* on DVD. She's working overtime at UNHCR because there aren't enough translators.

It feels like it did when I moved here and Thatcher's policies meant that nobody could give you a job if it could be filled by a 'true Brit', she says.

Somebody called her a paki in Tesco. Her eyes stay on the TV as she tells me this. The only acceptable reason to interrupt the news is to remark on which newsreader has gained weight.

After dinner, she hands me her iPad and I type Joni Mitchell into Spotify without thinking. 'A Case of You' comes on. I look out of the window, blinking back tears.

You've been unusually quiet about Ezra, Tess says, handing me a tissue.

Have I?

I blow my nose, noisily.

Attractive, she says.

Did you click on the link I sent you? Idle Blades have landed an advertising campaign. Some car. I forget which.

His parents must be thrilled. He's been back at home for what – two years now? She hesitates. Will we be seeing him at Christmas?

He's very busy.

She winces. Must you be so . . . devout? She clears her throat. Now that she sees me infrequently, she reins herself in. But your course is going well?

For a moment I can't remember what she means. She starts to

clear plates from the table, then sits down when I move to help her. I stack plates, gather cutlery, wipe the table down.

It's going okay, I say.

She rubs my fingerprints off the TV remote. I listen to her silent commentary, until she says, You know, T. S. Eliot was a bank clerk.

And J. K. Rowling wrote on napkins, I say. And you?

Tess wrinkles her nose. The odds of finding someone there's time to explain my entire life to are vanishingly small.

Presumably they'd have a life too.

She raises her glass as if I have proved her argument. Well exactly, and once we'd explained that to each other we'd both be pensioners – or dead.

We watch some murder mystery. A schoolgirl is found mangled in the boot of a car. I look away.

Iris, she says, disdainfully. Control yourself. You're emoting everywhere. She pats my head on her way out of the room. They can sense fear, you know, predators. I hear her open the fridge. On the other hand, she calls from the kitchen, it's good you still have a vulnerability about you. It's terrible, reality, but that's what men want.

She goes outside to smoke. There's something defiant in the way she fills the bird feeder with one hand, cigarette poised between her fingers. I want to run out barefoot and kiss her but tamp down my affection inch by inch. Must you make such a song and dance? she'd say.

The last father–daughter day at my primary school was also my tenth birthday, and I had no friends. I was scared, so I pretended to have a fever, and held my forehead to the radiator until it was all red and bumpy. Tess burst out laughing when she saw it and carried me to the freezer. She stuck her head in the freezer first, and then mine, and then our heads together. She called me a girl after her own heart. She let me cut a huge piece of the caterpillar birthday cake she'd made, with red orange yellow blue green segments. *He's going to turn into a butterfly in your tummy, Iris.* I closed my eyes while she transformed my face with loops and swirls of lilac and pink and gold, touching my nose whenever I tried to open my eyes. She turned on cartoons even though it was a Wednesday. I didn't notice her retreat upstairs. I was licking marzipan from my thumb when my mother came back in, dressed in shiny black shoes, tight black trousers and a white shirt. Her dark hair was loose and spilled down her back. She wore bright blue eyelashes. Curtseying, she asked whether she looked like a butterfly's father, and I said, *Yes*. Some of the mothers at the school gates stared, but all of the fathers thought she was wonderful. One of them said, *Fantastic, bloody fantastic*, and then their daughters thought I was fantastic too, and I was proud.

She comes back in and locks the door behind her. I can't believe you're still smoking, I say.

It's one a day. God knows I've earned it. It's different for my generation – we started before we knew it was bad for us.

Mine don't get to say that about anything.

I ask if I should blow the candles out and she shakes her head.

Those glasses don't go in the dishwasher, she says.

3

Whenever I want to Skype Ezra, I Skype Nance instead, even though she has started wearing silk scarves and peppering her sentences with *as it were*. She spent New Year in the Cotswolds, being fed blue cheese and quince by Piers, and reading Mayakovsky by the fire. His parents haven't met her, but they sent her a sourdough starter set for Christmas. It is from Fortnum and Mason, she tells me, swinging the mint-green bag in front of the screen.

Imagining the Talby-Brownes confronted with Nance is some consolation. She is singing along to 'Off to the Races' by Lana Del Rey. Her singing voice is like a bag of cats being stamped on. I have told her this, but she is unperturbed. She says she has the voice of an angel.

Things are going well with Piers then, I say.

She looks disgruntled. It would be great if you didn't attribute every shift in my mood to the men.

This stings. It is, I imagine, how she thinks my moods work.

Have you written a thank-you card yet?

I told them myself when we spoke on the phone, she says.

They sound like the kind of people who will expect a card.

Nance looks mulish. Says who.

They'll have put time into getting the house ready. Folding towels. It's just a way of recognising that, so they don't feel resentful later.

She frowns. Will you tell me what to write in it so.

What's his mother's name?

Guinevere, she says. And just don't.

Nance is usually lethargic, but she keeps flitting around. It is irritating. I type a few lines of innocuous text into an email and hit send.

Buy a nice card, I say. Look for a National Trust sticker. Or get one at a gallery.

Nance sings that she's a scarlet starlet, singing in the garden—

She pops a hip. I cannot stand it.

You know, when Lana straddles old men, they're Hells Angels. Can you imagine Lana on top of some B-list academic, *eating sourdough*.

Just because I have a boyfriend and you fucked things up with Ezra, she says.

I can tell she's been saving that one. I go into the bathroom and run my hands under hot water. They keep going numb, which Liderman says is psychosomatic. Pins and needles feels real though. It is so cold outside that my knuckles are splitting, but after a few minutes they are softer, I feel calmer. The lavender soap is wearing down. The faucet is bright and silver.

When I retake my seat in front of my laptop, Nance is putting on lip-liner.

There's a first time for everything, I say, as if it is touché.

She ignores me and pouts into the webcam. Piers took her shopping the other day and bought her a MAC lipstick called Oh, Sweetie.

✗

I am lying wrapped in a towel on the floor watching *Sex and the City*, the season one finale. *You told me to have faith, but I'm kind of losing mine*. I have been trying to read Jung's

Mysterium Coniunctionis but the words keep crawling. Jung says it's impossible to give an account of salt and its connections because it's really about the feminine principle of Eros, which brings everything into relation. I get to page five and give up. I open my Moleskine. On the fly leaf: In case of loss, please return to Ezra Munroe, 30 Camberwell Grove, SE5 8JA. I cross this out and write my own name, my own address in its place. It looks messy.

I take a shower, but I run out of energy halfway through. My hair is wet and matted with conditioner. I fantasise about paying someone to cut it off for me, but then I would have to talk to them. I get a cab to the Upper East Side, but the traffic is gridlocked so I get out. Dogs in snow-jackets prance over heaps of slush. Steam rises from grates in the sidewalk. Liderman's doorman doesn't greet me, but I have lost my sunglasses, so he probably doesn't recognise me. I look like I have been living underground. Liderman asks me how I'm sleeping, how much I'm drinking. I halve both numbers.

The sign in the frame today:

DO WHAT YOU'VE ALWAYS DONE.
GET WHAT YOU'VE ALWAYS GOT.

We have been doing this twice a week for three weeks now. I tell Liderman that the sleeping tablets are helping. I can end the day when I need to, and that motivates me to do basic things – strip the bed when I need to. I did that yesterday. When I tried to put on a new bottom sheet, it kept pinging back. I was too exhausted to fight it, so I made a nest out of the soft, rank sheets and threw a duvet over it.

Liderman does not share my triumph. She loops back to her main message: Lithium. It's a gentle drug. It takes its time, but it gets the job done.

I imagine little men with spades digging a hole in my brain.

It seems like a big commitment, I say.

Liderman gives me a long, hard look. I think you need to reconsider this. For now, I'm writing you another prescription for a drug called Effexor.

I bet it's very effective in cases such as mine.

She ignores me. It builds up over time; you won't even notice it, but you'll *notice* it, if you know what I mean. Just take it in the morning, have a coffee, and outta the door.

She gets up to feed the fish from a new bottle – the flakes are blue and green. The fish aren't interested and lurk at the bottom of the tank. The tank smells astringent and unclean.

There's a silver frame on Liderman's desk. While she's poking around in the tank, I reach for it. A freckled boy with chocolate ice cream all over his face grins at the camera. When Liderman turns around, rage flickers in her for a second and then it's as though she's been deflated. Her shoulders slump. I put the photo back, clumsily. I want to apologise, but when Liderman starts talking again her tone is brusque.

You take supplements, right? So if you had a weak immune system, you might take vitamin C. This is exactly the same. Are you getting enough iron, by the way? Most girls your age are anaemic.

I eat liver for breakfast every day, I say.

Liderman looks for her prescription pad and finds it inside *Glamour*.

Take it when you get up and don't think about it too much.

And whatever you do, don't Google it. There are always exceptions, but your presentation is typical. Trust me. I've been doing this for a long time.

When I tell her that I have never felt this bad before, that this has only ever lasted a week, maximum, she says, Really?

I don't know any more. There's an ad on TV for Zoloft where the world is black and white and then the actor takes a tablet and the room floods with Technicolor and everybody smiles. I mention this and Liderman smooths her prescription pad.

What you have to remember is that you don't have to want that. All you have to do is want to feel differently than you do right now.

She pushes the box of tissues towards me and places the prescription next to it on the table. She touches the back of my hand, and hers is cool, and softer than I expected.

⚘

Meet me at the Russian Tea Room at 7 pm, sharp, Lexi says.

She wants us to set goals for the year ahead. She has a new Comme des Garçons trench coat. It must be exhausting to be so put together. Lexi takes a packed lunch to work every day so that she can invest in what she calls key pieces.

Do you think anyone likes their colleagues? Do you think I enjoy going for drinks with Barbra? Find a quality that you can admire. If you don't feel it yet, that's fine. Act *as if*. Fake it till you make it.

Lexi has fallen for a married man called Fred. She brought him in as a lawyer on an equities deal. I try to say 'Fred' like Audrey does in *Breakfast at Tiffany's* but I am unsettled. Lexi is not meant to be the other woman. She only goes on dates on

141

weeknights. She has one drink. The man pays. He calls. Most of the time she declines, politely, with a response that she has saved in the Notes on her phone. Lexi says Fred's wife has excellent taste, which matters, because Lexi judges herself on the running average of her boyfriends' exes. We are judged, she reminds me, by the company we keep.

But so – Ezra is sleeping with other people, she says.

I look around for a waiter. I don't know, I say.

But . . . you have agreed that it is okay for you both to be sleeping with other people.

We have said that we are free to, I say. Have you ever had a sake Martini?

Lexi inspects the tackiness of her French manicure and waits for me to continue. I cannot bring myself to tell her how little we actually agreed.

There's a difference between monogamy and fidelity, I say.

The waiter materialises and asks us whether we like our Martinis sweet or dry.

You choose, I say.

I remember when Ezra tried to touch my foot, I kicked at his hand. I said, I mean it, whoever you fuck, keep her out of my world.

Lie to me. Please.

I said: What we do separately doesn't change who we are together.

Ezra put his napkin into the ashtray and set fire to it.

A person is a composite of their actions, he said.

Which means he cannot imagine me fucking anyone else.

He won't like it, you know, if you do, Lexi says. Which could be no bad thing.

She picks the toothpick from her Martini and removes the olive. Fred said I should cut back on giving unsolicited advice, she says, smiling ruefully.

I'm asking, I say.

Lexi sighs. Her blouse has a Victorian necktie. It is sheer and grey and makes her look like an elegant moth. Not for the first time, I think that if I looked like Lexi everything would be less complicated.

That night, I get an email from Ezra.

21.01.17 22:45
From: ezramunroe@gmail.com
To: irisirisiris@gmail.com
I suspect that your lack of communication means that you've found someone else :-(

Never mind . . .

I will win you back with songs.

See if you can figure out lyrics for the bridge? Do you think the first verse is a cliché? I don't mind if it's direct, so long as it's not indulgent.

Max's dad pulled some strings and got us onto Spotify's New Sounds playlist. 'Close By' has been streamed almost a million times! Even more exciting: the venue asked what we want on the rider. We got a bottle of tequila and a bottle of whiskey. No more hummus for us.

Remember not to open it in iTunes! Lucas would kill me. If you accidentally do, right click in iTunes and press delete, and if it gives you the option click delete permanently from your library.

https://dl.dropboxusercontent.com/u/269512/For%20
Iris%from20%L(0)TUSBordello.dmg

sleep well

p.s. Max tried to do the gig at the Shacklewell Arms in red trousers.
Please advise.

x

    I print off the email and stick it to my wall.

4

On Friday morning, I lie in bed watching newscasters arguing on CNN. A blonde woman in a lilac suit and a black man with square-framed glasses move their hands like marionettes. I make up alternative subtitles while I get dressed. Trump has issued an executive order banning travel to the US from seven predominantly Muslim countries. On the way to school, I buy a twist of hot nuts from a cart. My boots have started leaking.

We have two stories to workshop, Paul's and Tuyen's. In the computer room, Bassey is playing music on his phone, just loud enough to agitate everyone. Remi's talking to the room at large about exercising his right not to vote. Sam is trying to print Paul's story, but the printer keeps jamming. There are people knocking at the door, but Sam ignores them, thumping the printer.

That is some grade A bullshit, he says, under his breath.

Paul gets up from the sofa where he is reading *1984* and wedges the door open. Sam glowers at the back of Paul's head. We annotated my copy of Paul's story while drunk, so I have to reprint it too. I see Paul giving me side-eye and give him the thumbs up.

That tortilla chip casserole really nailed down the intentionality of the satire, I say.

Actually, that's an authentic Southern dish, Lisa says, flipping her scarf over her shoulder. She's reading tarot cards on the sofa, feeling maligned. The day before, she is telling us, again, that if she had known her dad voted Trump, she wouldn't have gone home for Christmas – He doesn't respect the experiences I've had *as a woman*, she'd said.

Bassey snapped, How you white women suffer.

By second semester, tit for tat has taken hold of our workshop. Paul gives single paragraphs of feedback with the opening sentences pasted week to week, so when it is his turn, nobody speaks. Bassey normally makes more of an effort than anyone, but he hasn't annotated it either. Sasha keeps up a fluent commentary, weaving together observations and referring back to principles. Eventually, she presses two fingers to her temples and says, Look. Let's take a moment to acknowledge that none of what's going on right now is normal. At the same time, we're in a classroom. So, I'm going to need you to at least *pretend* that what you're thinking about is contained in these four walls.

I've got two sides of handwritten notes but none of them are constructive, so I say nothing. Everyone knows Tuyen is the best in our class, except Tuyen, and Lisa, who says, Well sure, if you've got your subject ready-made.

Today Lisa wants to look good in comparison to Bassey – I really appreciated how visceral the mother–daughter relationship was, and the level of detail, like that little pink shirt.

Sure, Conrad says, but on a broader level it's emblematic of American foreign policy and the way it lays waste to these villages. The domestic scene is there, but the strength in this story is in its function as a political allegory.

Finn nods, reluctantly, like he is being compelled to speak: This shows skill in places, I guess. But how am I supposed to know where this village – Mui Ne – he sounds out the village's name in the most unlikely way – mah-wee-nay-ay—

I have to ask what American slang means, Tuyen interrupts.

The writer isn't meant to speak, but Sasha doesn't say anything. Tuyen lets her hair fall to cover her face.

Finn and Remi compete in using Sasha's phrases in front of her. Finn says, Yeah, I don't want to like, go on about it, but when you write a short story you kind of make a pact with the reader?

Sam interrupts, But this is a first-person narrative and if you're a hostage in someone's head, you'd articulate things from their perspective, right?

I haven't spoken to Sam since Thanksgiving. We sent a few emails back and forth over Christmas. He signed off each with a different name: Sammy-J, the great ST, Soudini, Sambo, Seinstein.

After workshop, we go to Dive Bar, because they do $3 beers on Fridays. Marcie comes along. She sits on a barstool drinking Michelob Light.

Lisa hands me a beer I haven't asked for. So, she says, slyly, how's it going with your beau?

Lisa never asks about my life unless the guys are around. While she explains my situation to the group at large, I drift over to the TV. MUSLIM BAN?

Bassey joins me. His eyes are fixed on the screen. Dude's backed by the fucking Ku Klux Klan and they voted him in. He's too stupid to stick to the GOP code and be all racially charged. Now it's out, anyone who reckons they're not racist because they don't go round calling us niggers is screwed. Same as everyone who acts like I'm exaggerating how many times I've been stopped – he throws Marcie a filthy look – unless people have direct experience, they don't believe it's real.

That's a general human problem, I say.

Maybe. Trump's face fills the screen and Bassey hoots. *Look* at this clown. I can't wait to watch this shit play out.

I hear Finn behind me, laughing, talking louder than he needs to – He's touring? Where, Slough? Probably for the best. If they hit the road, he'll have them queueing up round the block.

I order a round of shots. Marcie has two. We clink, and for a second I think she's not that bad. In workshop, we were paired up and she told me that she hasn't slept with her husband since the election. Then she starts imitating my accent.

Oh my God, she says, flapping her hands, Say aluminium again.

I oblige and the hilarity dies down. I drink the last two shots.

I'll get the next round, Sam says.

So, Marcie says, doesn't this guy sleeping with other people bother you?

I pretend I am Parisian. I twist my hair up in one hand, let it cascade down my back.

Declare: The human capacity for love is not finite.

Advise: Sex is one part of a relationship.

I gorge on the truth in private: I do not believe anyone else could satisfy him.

✶

The next day, I wake up hungover. I install an add-on on my laptop; it counts in milliseconds. In 248,000,000 seconds, I will be thirty. I toy with the idea of taking a cold shower. I turn on the air conditioning instead. I imagine a label tied around my toe. Jane Doe, 22. I turn it off again. I am meant to be talking to Ezra that afternoon. I check my email, but the only message is from Sam.

148

28.01.2017 15:51

From: sam.jogan@columbia.edu

To: irisirisiris@gmail.com

Hey, can you do me a favour? Can you look up *The Colbert Report* on Hulu? S09, EP52, way back in January 2013, when life was all raindrops on roses and kittens and . . . whiskers?

Spoiler alert: *George Saunders*. I know you're not a huge Colbert fan, and I get it, he's playing an intentionally antagonistic caricature of American journalism wherein he can push a whole lotta buttons in about 60 seconds . . . but he's silly and he's smart and it's the only talk show on cable television that's had fiction writers on live in the past 20 years . . . I hope that you're feeling better.

I put on a tracksuit and a hoodie over the leggings I've slept in and walk to Trader Joe's. When I get back, there is a sign in the lobby saying Your doorman is on a break and will return shortly. I stand with my arms crossed, shivering. A woman in a fur coat who I recognise from the building approaches. I don't know if she knows who I am. I started getting mistaken for Ray's mistress when I was fifteen. Last summer, Lexi and I were on the High Line, counting men with women half their age, and Lexi said, Isn't it crazy how one day we will be the women getting cheated on with girls like us?

I try to smile but my cheeks are stinging in the wind. I crouch to pet the woman's dog and it nips me.

She's just playing, the woman says. You're so very tall! Who did you say you belong to?

Nikolai comes hurrying back with a white polystyrene sack.

Rock salt. The road is a slip and slide.

When I get upstairs, I have a WhatsApp from Nance. There

are two screens full of stars and for a moment I think Piers has proposed. Then another screen: RECORD DEAL!

I go to get a glass of water and watch myself drink it in the mirror. When Ezra calls, I watch my phone vibrate across the marble before picking it up.

I can't believe it's actually happening, he said. *Laurence Bell.* Do you realise what this means? Of course you do, I haven't shut up about Domino for – fuck, years now. One sec – I can hear him closing doors and he lowers his voice – Nance is staying here for a few nights. She has to go to the British Library.

Okay.

I was going to take Darwin out later and call you then – can we Skype?

I'm out.

Later then. I told her not to tell you first. She's hammered. I wasn't sure if . . . you didn't say anything about the new name?

I have no idea what he's talking about, so I say nothing. I am mesmerised by the rage flowing through my reflection.

I knew you'd think it was lame, he says, but the fans love it. Lucas put it up on Instagram and they're going mad for it. God though, L(0)tus Bordello. But SEO wise, we're golden. He pauses, waiting for me to say something. Are you okay?

Yup, just getting home from a party, I say. There's so much snow.

Upstairs, I turn on speakerphone. Ezra is saying, We've started getting sent freebies, hair products, baseball caps, it's crazy – people want to pay us to wear their clothes, suddenly all of these people are involved – when I hear Nance shriek in the background – she was *so* not at a party.

I hang up. Nance and I have the same flaw – we make things

150

up. Daily life is not interesting enough. So we exaggerate. But my lies are splashes of colour, and to everyone except Ezra, they are easy to spot. Hers shift the parameters until truth and lie are close enough to seem a matter of perception.

When they call back, I hit accept, but I don't walk into the Skype frame. I watch them at an angle. Nance keeps glancing at the screen to check whether I have come back. There's no guarantee that Ezra knows how I feel, but Nance does. It is not the first time she's put herself between us.

May week, final year: Nance won the Stanford award, which meant full funding. She invited me to the scholars' feast as her plus one. She picked seats next to the Chinese students, and by the time the choir had sung grace, we had finished their wine. When Ezra slipped back into the hall and joined us, Nance pulled a face. She blamed him for my 2:1. I got obsessed with sugar roses and stayed up all night before my last exam making him a birthday cake. He needed to get Dolly the vocal line of the demo and he was wretched over it. I had been low for weeks, but that night I had so much energy, I couldn't have slept anyway, but Nance berated Ezra, like it had been his idea. He pointed out that he didn't even like cake.

Nance's family were sitting at high table. They had come from Galway for the prize-giving, and she kept looking over.

I will actually murder them in their beds if they show me up, she said.

She distracted herself by imitating me. Her accent was posher than mine though, lispier, girlish.

Ezra found it hilarious. A waiter refilled our water glasses, and Nance chimed, Thank you.

It's not that funny, I said. I drank more wine.

After dinner, Nance's mother told me how well I was looking.

Can you get Nancy out of these funeral clothes, she said, fingering the end of Nance's scarf. Nance knocked her hand away. Her family had booked the cheapest flight and had to head back to Nance's room to get their things.

You should go, I said. We'll wait for you.

I wanted to be alone with Ezra by the river. I sent him for wine and ice when Nance got back, but she was furious – Tonight was meant to be just us. We haven't spent proper time together since before finals, she said, sitting down on the grass.

I closed my eyes and pretended to doze. It was after midnight when Ezra appeared again.

I had to call Frank the booze man, everywhere's closed, he said. He drives an Audi. You would have thought he would upgrade, given the premium on this.

I lay with my head in Ezra's lap, while he systematically combed grass through my hair with his fingers. I had taken off my heels. I kept forgetting that my flats were in Nance's room, and wondering where they were.

They argue about abortion on and off. I wonder whether this is some kind of Catholic greeting, a way of sussing out the lapsed.

She died four years ago and defending the ideal which underpins a case you acknowledge as tragic makes no sense, Nance says. Giving the mother and the potential life as you call it equal rights is what killed Savita. That's the whole point of Repeal the Eighth. There's no way to establish the point at which a fertilised ovum becomes a person.

Ezra nods, vigorously. That's what *I*—

Nance interrupts: And if you're not sure whether something

is human it's better not to kill it, right? So, that makes it reasonable to be pro-life. But by the democratic principle, if you're in a state of irresolvable doubt – like you are about the ovum – then you don't have the right to tell another person what to do. The only person's body you can speak for is your own. Which makes it reasonable to be pro-choice.

Nance notes Ezra's silence with satisfaction and continues, So if you're sharp enough to handle a more complex way of thinking then you can believe that abortion is wrong and still defend a woman's right to choose.

Ezra pulls at the grass, sulkily. Ezra has no trouble with the morning after pill, I want to say, and Nance would never actually have an abortion, but I don't. I dig my toes into the mud. When Nance and Ezra argue, she holds back, and he, sensing that he is being patronised, speaks in clipped, outlandish statements. If either of them were only the person they are around each other, I would never have fallen in love. She is jealous, cruel, affected; he is arrogant, wilfully oblivious, selfish to the core. When I try and square their points of view, I disappear completely.

Are those porters over there, Nance says.

I haven't got my glasses, Ezra says. We should go though, it's getting light.

He tries to stand up and I roll over and snuggle into his leg. But the grass is so green, I say.

The grass is green in Nance's room. It's like a meadow in there. Don't you want to see it?

He helps me to my feet. They get up too, brushing the grass from their clothes. I walk ahead and Nance talks as if I'm not there – I cannot believe that worked.

Tricks of the trade, Ezra says.

Don't you find it boring, she says, having that much control.

Ezra laughs uneasily – She's probably cold. No shoes.

She's far too easy to manipulate, Nance says.

I turn and Ez holds out a hand. So green, he says.

5

It is late when Ray calls, wanting to pick up his golf clubs. I pause. Can I say no?

Fantastic, I'll leave work now, he said. Be with you shortly.

Okay. I might be out, so bring a key.

He makes a big show of stamping the snow off his boots and hanging up each layer. He goes into the kitchen and looks in the fridge. I have low-fat yogurt and white wine. The fridge door is lined with Absolut miniatures.

I haven't been cooking, I say.

I had lunch at Tamarind, he says. Superb eggplant dish. Your mother used to make one like it.

Client meeting? He nods, checking the label on the wine bottle. Nice life, I say.

He puts back the wine without comment – Lindsey has me on this 5:2 nightmare.

Does Tamarind know?

Dr Gerard says it's good for my blood pressure.

Oh?

Well, you know, when you get to this age – all the good things in life: wine, salt—

I flinch but Ray has no idea what I'm working on. When he asks, I say millennials.

He gets us both wine glasses. I imagine what Tess would say, *Feel free to collect your clubs, you know where they are*. Or, *How delightful, I didn't realise this was a social visit*. The sweet smell coming from the coat cupboard is suddenly very strong. I still don't know where to empty the bins and I have left it too long to ask. Now and again, I take carrier bags of trash to school, but the bags are still heaping up alongside Lindsey's furs.

Ray doesn't seem to notice. He sits down – How's Nance?

Good. She's dating a man your age actually.

The only thing my parents agree on is that they had me too young. By Tess's account, she gave up her career to become my mother. In Ray's, she got fired after going silent because what she was meant to be translating was *simply too stupid for words*. Ray got a promotion, then another.

Not that you weren't a delight, Tess insists. Like a fuzzy bear. But however fuzzy the bear is, darling, it's unlikely to be able to tell you anything you don't already know.

Other people's mothers—

Her interruption came out as almost a wail. You always wanted to talk about mermaids!

Ray wanted another child and Tess didn't. She told me this when I was thirteen, about to go to my first disco, in one of her dresses. We were standing in front of her mirror. She tipped her head to one side, and murmured, *beautiful*. She looked at me appraisingly. And your body really is suited to longer skirts. You have lovely elbows.

She sat down on her bed and started talking in her vague quiet way that means if I interrupt her, she'll leave the room. I started applying glittery purple eyeshadow.

You were about four and I just didn't want to. It hadn't occurred to me that could happen. And honestly, darling, twelve hours of labour. And you were born with *teeth*. She winces theatrically.

You've never told me that.

156

Tess stares fixedly at my eyelids. I glare back.

I had no idea you took such an interest in my reproductive health. Menopause?

I was five when Tess had an affair with someone at the golf club. He was called Danny. He had a scratch handicap. The indignity of this pisses Ray off more than anything – he plays off sixteen. I went through a phase of losing it in public, making myself a dead weight, screaming *But you had an affair*. Tess refused to engage and yanked me up, sharply. *There's more than one way of abandoning someone*, she said.

Ray looks pointedly at the news headlines as if he hasn't heard. In twenty-four hours, a petition to cancel Trump's state visit to the UK has topped one million signatures, passing the threshold for Parliament debate.

I turn the volume up and we watch in silence for a few minutes, then Ray asks, warily, whether Ezra will be visiting soon.

I shrug. Nance says dating a musician on tour is like having a lover in the circus.

Ray doesn't talk to me without an agenda. He's been calling once every two weeks to check on my progress in therapy, and he's worked his way around to Lexi, then Liderman. She thought it might be helpful for us all to meet together. I get up to get more wine.

She wants me to try a medication, I say. When you get to my age there's a lot to deal with; yearning, angst.

Ray smiles, awkwardly, to acknowledge the joke being made. Can't hurt, he says.

I stick my head in the fridge and point out that antidepressants can kill creativity. I list side effects.

It's only a few weeks, Ray says.

I imagine another few weeks without Ezra, which is twenty-one days which is five hundred and four hours, and it really is that many because lately, I miss him even when I'm dreaming.

Ray says, When you get to my age, a few weeks is a drop in the ocean. What have you got to lose?

I go to top up his wine glass too and he puts his hand over it – What's the plan otherwise? The highs are lower, the lows are higher. Welcome to adulthood.

What if I don't want that, I say.

It doesn't just affect you though. If you're sick, then not being medicated is going to put an undue burden on any partner. You have a responsibility to the people around you.

I'm tired, I say, and put my wine glass down. It leaves a ring on the counter.

§

On Monday, before school, I get an email from Ezra, blank except for the subject line: It's meant to sound like notes falling into each other.

There is an audio file attached. *You are a lightning child, how you flash and you boom but you burn his vision so blue.* Flash and boom your way through the subway. Blaze your way through class.

I call him and say, Thank you so much. I love it. Sometimes just a call though – a conversation—

I've been writing that song since Christmas. It's more than I'm ever going to be able to say on the phone, he says. Why isn't it enough?

Say, I'm in Duane Reade. I'm holding a tube of toothpaste. I go to pay, but the cashier cannot hear me, even though I'm

158

speaking at a normal volume. She looks confused, like I'm moving my mouth but all she can hear is a gurgling. *Ma'am are you okay.* The queue edges forward behind me. I hold out the toothpaste – Can I buy this please – but I cannot make myself heard. It is happening again. The lights are lurid and the toothpaste doesn't look real. My clothes start to feel like a costume and it is too tight or too itchy or too hot. The cashier gets irritated, or worse, pities me. I back away, knowing that all the things that have allowed me to pretend have been a lie. How silly it is to get dressed and undressed to make a bed and sleep in it to get dirty and wash. Because I have been like this all along. It never really left, I just forgot about it, like one forgets a bad dream, or the fact that one has a shadow.

With Ezra, I did not have to explain myself. Now, if I try and explain how bad it is, and if no one understands, then I will be alone inside the sadness forever. As long as I do not try to explain, there is hope that they might if I did. As long as I do not talk about it, there is a chance I might be rescued.

I fall asleep thinking *entropy* and wake up thinking *not again.*

♵

On the day my work is workshopped, it rains all morning. I watch it smear the windows. Sasha catches me by the water cooler. She likes the work I handed in on muses.

It has an energy to it, she says. Why aren't you writing about this?

I don't know anything about muses, I say to Sasha, not really.

How much do you care about the history of salt though? The economics of it, the geography? Eat salt. Salt the water when you're making pasta, throw it over your shoulder, go wild. Kick up your heels. Look, I'm not telling you what to write. But there are some really nice moments here.

Nice?

Sasha asks me into her office. I scan the bookshelves and notice *By Grand Central Station I Sat Down and Wept*.

George Barker, I say, like I'm saying death.

Sasha looks amused by this – You know Elizabeth Smart posed as a manuscript collector to get in touch with Barker. And when she paid for his ticket from Japan, she knew his wife was coming too.

Fifteen children though.

Sasha looks at me astutely. There are two sides to every story. Some people go seeking the conflict out.

Afterwards, in class, I pretend to write down the feedback and write out the facts I know.

In Madagascar, there was a demon who lived in a lake, so averse to salt that if anyone was carrying salt past the lake they had to call it something else or the demon would dissolve it.

In Finnish folklore, Ukko, the mighty God of the sky, struck fire in the heavens; a spark descended from this was received by the waves and became salt.

In some regions of the Caribbean, it is thought that demonic spirits masquerade as women during daylight hours, then discard their skin, flying around at night as balls of fire. To vanquish these demons their shed flesh must be sought out and salted. That way, they cannot re-disguise themselves as women in the morning.

The Dutch proverb Hij komt met het zout als het ei op finds its

160

French equivalent in the proverb Arriver comme les carabiniers, meaning to arrive too late. The literal translation is He brings the salt once the egg is eaten. It deals with the importance of offering help, or at the very least counsel, at the right moment.

Finn says, There's book-smart and there's, you know, life-smart. What's the take-away? It's just this girl talking about salt.

When I get home, I shake one of the capsules into my hand. It looks like a Lemsip, except each half is a different shade of blue; aqua and navy. I fill a glass with water from the bathroom sink and take one capsule – half a dose. I go to bed for the rest of the day. I expect to wake up with wings.

6

There is a horrible taste in my mouth, something chemical. Like I have been rubbing firelighters on my gums. I lie down on the sofa in the computer room. I check my calendar to confirm that it is February, that it is Tuesday. The lights nibble at my skin like tiny fish. I am nauseous, though I know I'm not going to be sick. It feels like I'm coming up, the same lurch behind the navel. I must not Google the side effects; that was part of the pact.

I can make you happy, Liderman said. You just have to let me help.

Being around other people is risky; I am not in control of what I am saying. Nice one, Paul. High five. Got any pecan pie, Paul?

In workshop, I share anecdotes. I know they're vaguely inappropriate, but nothing bad happens. Who has the time and patience for shibari, really. I conduct a straw poll.

Sasha congratulates me on being out there with my sexuality.

I take a cab back and tell Lindsey, who is outside, talking to the doorman, or inspecting the sidewalk, or whatever it is she does, that I have come home with a migraine. Nikolai has a hose. The pavement shines with water.

Ezra calls. He sounds like he is on a walkie-talkie. North Korea has tested a ballistic missile. I practise my horrified face in the mirror.

He starts telling me about barefoot running. He's made sandals, he says.

I impersonate Edvard Munch's *The Scream*.

I looked it up, he says. I bought this kit online, I'll send you the link.

He barely has time to talk. That's because he has become a cobbler. Why didn't I guess.

I turn on the TV. I imagine being locked in a cell with Trump's voice piped in twenty-four seven. Solitary confinement is designed to induce a state of learned helplessness. I Google how to survive it. Create structure. Impose systems. Live them with devotion. Walk the perimeter of your cell, counting steps, heel to toe. Visualise throwing a tennis ball and catching it. Would buying into every word Trump says help you cling to sanity?

I hear a key in the lock and jump out of my skin.

Lindsey looks startled and younger than usual. The concealer under her eyes is flaking. She's holding a measuring tape.

I didn't mean to bust in. She glances at the TV and winces. Do you mind muting that?

I oblige and stare at her dumbly. She puts her handbag on the coffee table and starts measuring the far wall, keeping one eye on the screen.

This'll take just a few minutes. I'll be right out of your hair. I want to get this place fitted with cabinets; I've gotten really into storage solutions, we've had them done in Chicago—

At Ray's—

She cuts me off. Our place, yes.

I watch her try to extend the tape measure vertically. It flops to the floor. I fetch a chair to help her and she looks taken aback.

Thanks. I don't know, what with all this . . . I get a stupid kick out of fixing things.

I stretch the tape measure up to the ceiling. She taps the measurement into her phone.

And your father isn't exactly Mr DIY.

No?

Lindsey blushes. She thinks I'm taking the piss.

He's in San Francisco this week. We must have enough air miles by now to fly to Barbados and back. She nods that I can let go. How's your head?

Still there.

Do you need anything?

I mumble that I'm going to have a nap and she looks relieved. She gives my shoulder an awkward squeeze on the way out. She bites her nails, which she sees me notice.

Yeah, I need to take care of that.

Sleep is like being chloroformed. What would it smell like, ether?

꙳

My second day on Effexor, I walk to school so that I can make eye contact with strangers. I am poignantly horny, in the way that gives your crotch a pulse and makes the sidewalks gleam.

Why do you make life so hard for yourself, Liderman asked. You have been walking around with a backpack full of rocks. It's time to take the backpack off.

At the Apple store all the Macs are showing Mitch McConnell defending his silencing of Elizabeth Warren. She was warned. She was given an explanation. Nevertheless, she persisted.

At the gates, I run into Sam. His beanie is pulled down over his eyebrows. He is eating an Egg McMuffin and holding a

164

coffee that he keeps spilling on himself. I hold it for him as we walk up to Dodge.

We could go to the park, he says.

The subway carriage stops underground. I panic, but Sam is there, standing behind me. I lean back and hear the blood pounding in my ears.

In the park, he points out mallards sheltering under the trees in rain, brides huddling under furs. He points out a baby in a bucket hat.

That kid is gonna be a superstar, he says.

We talk about Marcie, who has dropped out of the programme. She spent years saving up for the MFA, and she's gone back to being a nurse. I can't justify this any more, she said.

I didn't like her, but it was still a shock. I wish I wanted to help people.

Sam stops to get a hot dog, and fills my hand with salt sachets, which I drop. He hands the vendor $5 for two hot dogs. Want to talk about it?

No.

You know, I didn't go to Oxford but I can tell you that if you look at the floor less, you'll see more. The ground is probably pretty similar in England. So, there's a tree. Or is it a shrub? What is the difference between a tree and a shrub? Who knows? Not me, that's for sure. The great Soudini is not well versed in botany. Is it botany? Did you study it alongside Latin and what is it, etiquette?

Sam is the only person who has made me laugh properly – like my body has been taken by surprise – since I landed at JFK. His nonsense catches me off guard and my body capitulates. He makes a fool of himself for my entertainment – Look, you don't have to talk about it, and I'm not going to pester you, but I got your salt stuff from Finn. He threw it away actually. Don't feel badly about that, he's a dick – I'm glad he did. I'd love to read more. I pull a face and he says, It's got to be better than whatever bullshit casserole Paul has got for us next.

God, Paul. He just wouldn't exist in England. We walk in silence for a few moments. Did you see the 2012 British Olympic ceremony? I can't explain, but that's what I miss.

Sam scrunches up his face. Really? From where I was standing it was snooty as hell; a bunch of in-jokes designed to exclude everyone who didn't get it. He chuckles. You just don't like Americans.

That's not true.

Ah, go on. You think we're all loud, obnoxious, superficial—

I've never said that.

It's obvious though. I saw you flinch when we were watching the game in Dive Bar.

I was surprised! I didn't know the USA chant actually happened outside movies. It's more that I grew up thinking of America as an invader.

Because Britain has got a great track record on subjugating indigenous people, Sam says, then laughs and almost chokes on his hot dog. I thump him on the back. He coughs until his eyes water.

Seriously though, he says, wiping away tears. You gotta just write whatever you want, and not give a shit what anyone thinks.

⚔

Nance tells me the latest on WhatsApp. Sex makes Nance uncomfortable, which she covers by expertise in Judith Butler,

166

Eve Kosofsky Sedgwick, and diffusing her discomfort into other people. She's the Wife of Bath when we're talking about my sex life and the Virgin Mary when we talk about hers.

Nance:	You'd be bored by him in bed.	**14:05**
Iris:	?	**14:06**
Nance:	The problem with seeing a fetishist is that he displaces not just his own desire but your own character into objects.	**14:10**
Iris:	What did he actually do?	**14:11**
Nance:	Are you drunk?	**14:11**
Iris:	I'm in class.	**14:15**
Nance:	The question stands.	**14:15**
Iris:	I'm bored. And you always ask me.	**14:15**
Nance:	Are you expecting me to say *and then he had me over the bannisters*?	**14:17**
Iris:	The way you talk about P is aesthetically appealing.	**14:20**
Iris:	It's not that I want to join in.	**14:20**
Iris:	But I wouldn't mind being there.	**14:23**
Nance:	I wouldn't want it to be just the two of you though.	**14:24**
Iris:	No offence, but gross.	**14:24**
Iris:	Maya Angelou: jealousy in romance is like salt in food. A little can enhance the savour, but too much can spoil the pleasure.	**14:25**
Nance:	Or poison you.	**14:25**
Iris:	Who would you even be jealous of?	**14:26**
Iris:	Do you want me to reiterate how much I don't fancy Piers.	**14:28**
Nance:	You know that isn't what I mean.	**14:34**
Nance:	So, like in Amsterdam windows?	**14:37**

Iris:	Not exactly.	14:37
Iris:	I wouldn't mind being a lamp.	14:39
Nance:	I'll make a note of that one, shall I.	14:40
	Available: One lamp.	

I do not tell Nance about my sex life, though she asks constantly. I tell her it is private, but I imply more than I mean to, and Nance purses her lips and makes bold statements like BDSM enforces and enacts patriarchal oppression.

Iris:	Maybe if I have sex with someone other than Ezra, I won't have all the *these are my feelings* and *these are your feelings* problems. There won't be that blurring between inner and outer self.	14:44
Nance:	Try telling the men about the blurring between your inner and outer self and there'll be no problem I'd say.	14:44
Nance:	You're porous but you're not a fucking swamp.	14:49
Iris:	Thanks.	14:49
Nance:	It would be good for you to have some normal sex.	14:49
Iris:	Normal?	14:49
Nance:	Without the power differential. If one person feels bigger it's because the other person feels smaller.	14:50
Iris:	Or both people become infinite.	14:50
Nance:	You would give Panadol a headache.	14:55

Ezra calls to tell me that he's been reading *A Lover's Discourse*. Barthes says that the lover's fatal identity is to be waiting.

Sirens go wailing past. Say nothing. Fuck the fuckwit who told Ezra about Barthes. Suspect sabotage. Fuck Barthes.

He has never consciously lied to you. He never forgets to say, consciously. Which of you is the more selfish. Decide it is probably you.

⚹

There is only one fish in the tank. It moves like it's on Xanax. Its fin is trailing, pink, translucent, and I wonder whether it is an angelfish, whether angelfish and goldfish can breed.

Behind the desk, Liderman is getting very big and small again, like an ink-blob.

Gosh, Iris, she says. Do you mind if I graze? The day I've had, you would not believe. She opens the drawer under her desk and pulls out a half-eaten pastrami and mustard sandwich. Can you reach into that drawer and grab me a napkin?

The drawer is full of napkins from Subway. She holds out a hand to encourage me to talk, but my brain wobbles, like an egg in a glass of water. I remember reading about how if you slap the glass the egg won't break, but if you shake it, the egg will shatter. It was about babies' skulls.

All I manage to say is, Skulls.

The first few days can take some adjusting to, Liderman says. How do you feel?

She pulls an ornamental chopstick from her chignon and stabs it back through. I imagine her assassinating strangers on the street with it.

Not like myself, I say.

Fantastic. Any side effects? Nausea? Double vision? Headaches?

Nausea. Increased libido, I guess. And weird dreams. Like hallucinations, but with realistic detail. You know portkeys in *Harry Potter*?

If you ask me, our culture's fixation on magic is a blight to children, Liderman says.

Yeah. Well, it's a bit like that. I keep getting this thing like a body shudder, like my neurons are getting the tailwind from little zaps of electricity—

Brain zaps, Liderman says, triumphantly. That's good. I only gave you a sample because some people do have adverse reactions. Stay on this dosage till the end of the week, and then we'll double it.

Times Square is full of men dressed up as M&Ms and Elmo and Pikachu. I walk past a gym where sweaty people in lycra pedal furiously, going nowhere, concentrating on a man in spandex at the front. He wears a headset and is screaming them on. At the bodega, the cans of Diet Coke are gorgeous. I buy two and hold one in each fist. I begin to understand Lichtenstein. I listen to the *Tangled* soundtrack, repeatedly. I listen to 'Shake It Off'. I shimmy.

7

On Skype, Nance is folding paper napkins into fans. She is throwing a dinner party with Piers. He won't let her help with the cooking because she has broken too many wine glasses. She looks at me, jealously. I want a jelly bean now and I don't even like them, she says.

Sam got them for me.

Nance pulls a face. You've never mentioned a Sam before.

Of course I have.

Which one is he?

Nance is already clicking through Facebook.

Jesus Christ, she says, you have not mentioned this one.

I stare at the bouquet of yellow roses behind her. Duane Reade is full of heart-shaped chocolates in red foil, rose-shaped candles. A sign offers a service called Say it with bears.

Nance looks at me beadily. You don't seem like yourself, she says. Go on then. What's he like?

He's very . . . upbeat. He could play video games all day and be happy.

Sounds like a retard.

Isn't there something good in being happy?

Imagine it though, being happy all the time for no reason. Nance glances at me, then goes back to pleating her fan. I was reading an article on hereditary trauma and Mary Shelley. Trauma can change your DNA apparently, so it gets passed down as a legacy in families who have been through the Holocaust, or Partition – of feeling you have to earn your life. So you're never

171

happy with just being in the present.

Since I stupidly told Nance that my great-grandparents were murdered during Partition she keeps bringing it up faux-casually, like she's hoping for an inside scoop. But there's nothing to tell.

Tess says: not *everything* needs to be talked about.

I'm not sure anything bad has ever happened to Sam, I say.

Probably I wouldn't like him so, Nance says. Ask him about this business with Russia as he's got so many fascinating opinions. Did you see Michael Flynn resigned?

On Valentine's day, I sent Ezra *The Beauty of the Husband* with notes in the margins, and some notes on salt tucked in the back. For safe-keeping. I hoped that he would care about it until I could.

Piers's house is full of wooden crates from Sotheby's and Christie's.

His father gave him a Cornell box for his fortieth, Nance says. He's had it since the sixties. She frowns, clicking around her screen. They had so much art when he was growing up that the children weren't allowed to run in the house. People like that shouldn't be allowed to have art, it's criminal. I'd be a great rich person. I mean it wouldn't be wasted like.

She sends me jpeg images of her favourite boxes. They have glass fronts. Their insides are wallpapered with dark velvet, cut-out ballerinas, hotels Cornell had never been to. They are toy worlds, stuffed with Victorian dolls, birds, marbles, miniature trees. I sit on my hands to stop myself from forwarding Tilly Losch to Ezra. Nance's favourite box is the only one I don't like. It's called *Habitat Group for a Shooting Gallery*; the glass is shattered by a bullet, yet still intact; a cockatoo's head is lopped off in a spatter of blood. That one's horrible, I tell her. Cornell's ballerinas didn't learn to dance any more than his birds learned to fly, Nance says.

As I click through these images, I find it hard to breathe.

It was on loan to the Royal Academy for their *Wanderlust* exhibit two years ago. He hasn't unpacked it yet, Nance says, eyes shining, but he's going to and I get to pick where it goes.

He wants to read her notes. He suggests she reads more Kafka and thinks seriously about epistolary forms and futility, about how we invented letters, like railways and aeroplanes, to pretend that we can communicate, that we are not all alone. Nance knows what he means. It's like what Flaubert thought about railways. They permit more stupid people to move around, meet and be stupid together. When she hands in a chapter, Piers takes her to Bob Bob Ricard in Soho. They eat lobster macaroni and cheese. He gives her control of the Press for Champagne button.

He must have regretted that, I say. I am following her progress on Google maps, reading reviews, reading menus, picking out what I would have ordered.

I didn't drink that much because we were talking, she says. It's like a supervision.

I am worried that Nance will laugh at me, that she will realise I cannot keep up.

What else did you talk about, I say.

Caprice, she says. Shadow-boxing, aphasia, political morality, whether satire is possible in a hyper-saturated culture such as ours, whether Trump is impeachable.

She pulls a *TLS* from her bag and presses it to the screen.

Backwards, Nance.

What? Oh. I'll send you the PDF. I'm in his footnotes. He wrote down something I said at dinner and kept it on a napkin.

Ezra refuses to acknowledge the part I play in his creative process. We had an argument about this: I'm not your fluffer, I said, on hand until inspiration strikes.

Ezra went quiet for a few minutes then showed me the definition of fluffer on his phone. Is this what you meant to say?

Were I Nance I would have said, How stupid do you think I am, yes, I did, yes.

Men who like Nance do not like me. Men who like me do not like Nance. All who like either of us judge the other as manipulative or a bad influence.

Nance says this is because we only show them our softer sides and keep the worst of it for each other.

I have been on Effexor for three weeks. Liderman congratulates me. You're beginning to *thrive*.

I call Ezra and ask whether anything has come in the post.

They're winding up the EP and he can only talk in the ten-minute window it takes to walk from Max's house to his. They're negotiating copywriting contracts. Ezra has started saying *my* songs instead of *our*. He has a concussion. He hit his head on a hanging speaker.

It fucking hurt, Ezra says. Ndulu was dancing backwards. The usual. Such a retard. We had a full-on collision on stage. All he has to do is play bass and not fall over, and he can't even do that.

Whenever I check Spotify, he's listening to remixes. A few days later, I WhatsApp to ask again.

At 4 am, he replies: Got your book, no room in bag (touring) but I'll read it when I'm back. Thanx.

174

A photo of Ezra eating a vegan burger gets 1,732 likes on Instagram before I have showered.

Hang out with a girl who drinks vodka sodas. Drink vodka sodas.

Sit in a corner, muttering, *the art of losing isn't hard to master*. I cannot remember the rest.

For two nights, Ezra sends a flurry of WhatsApp updates which belong on the band's Twitter feed. His other messages are strangely scientific, as if he is reporting back the findings from his research.

A good way to let girls down easy is to send them an image of Maslow's hierarchy of needs.	00:36
It is a bad idea to sleep with girls more than once, otherwise they get clingy.	03:42

His texts are random and give the impression of being in the middle of a conversation we are having, will always be having. *He loves me, he loves me not*. Evidence of both. For the rest of that night he sends random details about groupies. There is the American girl who makes him into memes. The Irish girl who followed him from Croatia to Berlin. The freckled girl who haunts stage doors with a sign that says: Ezra PLEASE.

I order pad thai from Thai 72. They refuse to deliver because I am too close.

I tell them I will take my custom elsewhere. I order from a place on the LES called One More Thai. One of the reviewers says she hasn't had pad thai this good since the full moon party in Ko Pha-ngan. I order pad thai, deep-fried tofu with sweet and sour sauce, gado gado, soft-shell crab, coconut ice cream.

I give Nance a redacted account of these messages. She says, he's not fucking Sting, and I laugh because she can't think of anyone more impressive.

Iris:	He's working very hard.	18:21
Nance:	You have got to get over this idea that men's brilliance entitles them to behave badly.	18:21
Iris:	You do it with us.	18:24
Nance:	Yes, but we're revolutionaries.	18:24

I feel a rush of warmth in my stomach when she says *we*. To prove her point, Nance calls me on Skype. Piers is in the bed behind her. He is sleeping.

What the hell are you doing, I say, transfixed.

The creature in its natural habitat, she whispers. Then, Piers stretches so dramatically that I think he has been awake all along. He yawns and I can see his tonsils.

I'm looking forward to meeting you, he says. Since you two spend so much time on Skype anyway. He goes to take a shower and we talk, but Nance is sleepy. Piers sulks when she has to work late. She gets up after he's gone to sleep and works at his kitchen table. Nance looks annoyed at herself. She sends me a screenshot of her inbox to demonstrate that Piers messages her much more than she messages him.

There is nothing less attractive than being wanted, she says.

I ask her to change my Facebook password so that I can't stalk anyone. She changes it to I love Nance, then falls asleep.

Her hair is falling out at the centre of her head. There is an

176

uneven star of white there. She doesn't realise when she's pulling at it. I hate the idea of anyone else telling her.

I send a message for her to wake up to: Do you think there's such a thing as an emotional Madonna/Whore complex? His groupies are deluded enough to think they are more than fuck-mittens.

I place the laptop on the windowsill so that Nance can see the snow when she wakes up. I wake up to a message from her.

Welcome to the boat afloat a sea of shite. Keep all limbs away from the edge and you'll be fine. You are not a fuck-mitten. Bet you 100 euro he gets in touch before the end of the week. I'm not defending him now. I'd bash his head in with a shovel if it were me. But in his thick-skulled way, he might be trying to include you in his escapades. Maslow though, Jesus. I hate to point this out, but didn't you suggest the break? Honest truth though: When I saw him, I didn't think he was doing that well.

⚔

It is my first poly meet-up. The coffee shop is in Park Slope and has a self-help book section. We go around the circle, introducing ourselves and I am so busy grubbing around in other people's sex lives that I forget to speak when it's my turn. When I explain our Don't Ask Don't Tell policy there is palpable disapproval, which deepens when I express my growing unease about other girls, other girls with names and faces in particular. We're new to this, I say.

The woman opposite me has dark hair and quick nervous fingers. Marco, her boyfriend of six years, has taken a lover. They agreed to open the relationship, she says. They agreed she would be out for the evening. She went to a wine bar and played Candy

177

Crush and texted her sister. It wasn't so bad, she says. When she got back home, he had made the bed, which was unusual, and to her surprise they had incredible sex.

But afterwards, I was getting ready for bed, and there were three blonde hairs in my hairbrush.

I am reeling with the horror of this as the circle closes in.

So, your problem is that this girl used your brush?

If you have issues with personal space then you have to advocate for yourself.

One candle doesn't rob another of light.

She should be taking pleasure in his pleasure. Perhaps she isn't trying hard enough. After all, a woman says, you have something in common. You want the same man.

I take my headphones out of my bag. So this is not my tribe either.

I get the train back from Park Slope, which takes an hour. I read IMPORTANT ARTIFACTS AND PERSONAL PROPERTY FROM THE COLLECTION OF LENORE DOOLAN AND HAROLD MORRIS. A love story told through a catalogue of possessions, openly curated.

8

In March, Trump accuses Obama of wiretapping his phone before the election. At school, various people explain wiretapping. I am scrolling through old photos when I realise that I am the only one tagged. Ezra has deleted his Facebook account without telling me. I was getting too many messages from strangers. Anyone who needs to reach me has my number. He is in the studio and can't pick up his phone.

Ezra:	Why would I tell you that.	16:34
Iris:	None of the photos are of us now.	16:34
Ezra:	That's ridiculous.	16:34
Iris:	You have just erased swathes of our history.	16:35
Iris:	Why can't you see that?!	16:35
Ezra:	Swathes?	16:38
Iris:	Not the time to be cute.	16:38
Ezra:	Cute? Me?	16:41
Iris:	I'm really upset Ez.	16:41
Ezra:	I'm sorry if you're upset, but you're being silly. You know it's me. I know it's me. It didn't occur to me that you needed us to be tagged on a public forum.	16:45
Iris:	This is what would happen if you died. You're a ghost.	16:47
Ezra:	If I died then my account would stay active so that people could grieve.	17:02
Ezra:	It's actually a really interesting technological	17:02

Ezra: Iris? 17:30

One week later: The only person who wants to be here less than me is Ray. Liderman is raring to go. She told Ray she wanted to make the appointment at her larger practice and didn't mention it was in New Jersey until he said yes. She is wearing a peach shift dress without pantyhose. There are slashes of stubble around her ankles and her knees. Liderman is the woman who buys the summer edition of Venus razors in lemon-yellow.

Instead of the fish, there is a book called *How to Make Your Cat Instagram Famous* on a small brass stand. Above that, there is a framed meme of a fluffy white show cat, rolled into a piece of sushi, resting one paw on a slice of daikon and dunking the other in wasabi.

Ray looks very unhappy.

Sit here, Dad, I say.

Ray looks taken aback and takes the chair nearest Liderman. He picks up the frame. The sign says:

THE DARKEST NIGHTS PRODUCE THE BRIGHTEST STARS

Ray has not taken my scepticism about therapy seriously. He says that it's part of the process.

It's like working out, you're not supposed to enjoy it at the time.

Just so you know, she thinks two glasses of wine a night makes you an alcoholic.

Ray coughs and goes pale.

In Liderman's office, she gives Ray her diagnosis and explains that I refuse to accept it. Ray says that we have other words in England – emotional, highly strung, sensitive, even.

Liderman says that I am non-compliant, and that both Ray and I are ignoring a problem, which is dangerous, and because of which she can no longer work with me.

Ray senses a deal in the offing. What would have to change for you to review this opinion?

Before she stopped taking it, Iris was on a low dose of Effexor. We're aiming for the maximum dose at which she can tolerate the side effects. So, what we need to do is get her back on it and ratchet it up until she's stable.

Stable-ised, I think, neutral-ised. *Uh, I think we spell that with a z here.*

Liderman says if I really wanted to feel better I would take the medication. She is a doctor, not God. She has a referral suggestion, and she wishes me all the best. She looks at Ray's Italian loafers.

He's book-smart, sweater vests, Upper West Side, Liderman says.

On the way out, I turn the photo frame face down on the table and hope it cracks. Behind me, Liderman touches Ray's arm and says, I think your daughter might find it easier to listen to a man.

On the Jersey Turnpike, Ray turns on Moby while I stare out the window and pretend not to cry. McDonald's, outlet malls. We get stuck in traffic. Ray clears his throat.

He doesn't manage to speak until I am crying like I didn't know I could. One year ago, the whole world was beginning.

Now Ezra's world is expanding while mine contracts and soon it will vanish entirely. Out like a light.

If the pills are helping, Ray begins. But there is no reasoning with me.

It feels like I am fighting for my life. There is something very wrong and I don't have the words for it. It does not feel like there are any choices. Ball your fists up, drum them against your head. Act like a caged animal. Ray keeps his eyes on the road. We get home three hours later. It is the longest I have been in a car with my father since I was eight.

⚑

In May, Idle Blades have a gig at the Bowery and Ezra doesn't tell me. I find out from Ray, who sees it online and invites him to dinner the night before. I check Spotify. Ezra is listening to 'Diamonds and Rust'.

I decide to run with it and call him. You're going to be in New York, I say, brightly.

Ezra says he didn't want to tell me because this gig is a big deal and he won't be fun to be around.

I just want to see you, I say.

The Manchester attack has just happened and I'm hyper-aware of how much time Ezra spends in crowds. I tell him this, and when he answers his voice is softer.

I'm the one on stage, he says. I'm harder to get to.

The day before the gig, Ezra turns up at the flat two hours early. In bed, he tries to articulate something about flow states and beta waves, and I cover my ears and go *lalala* until he covers my mouth with his hand. His sweat drips onto my face. I move to lick it away, but Ezra rolls off.

182

That's embarrassing, he remarks, as if it is someone else's sweat all over me.

What's next, I say. Orange quarters? Water bottles?

Ezra takes a swig of his then lies back for a few minutes, before reaching for me again.

I feel like that Martin Amis character who craves his next cigarette when he's already smoking, he says.

Later, I suggest that we go to the lake in Central Park. Ezra says he doesn't have time to row me around.

I have to be careful. There's a lot riding on tonight. I can't risk getting a cold. The studio is booked by the hour. I have a responsibility to protect my voice.

All he wants to do is find Chinese take-away containers like the ones in *Friends*. He says he needs to keep Ndulu on side. I suggest we watch the last episode of *The Good Fight* which we agreed to save to watch together.

I'm in a van for at least four hours a day. Do you want me to be bored when you're not there?

I watch it by myself with headphones on while Ezra is working. In the evening, I tell him that I'm perfectly happy ghosting Ray, but he cannot bear the idea of doing this.

He regrets it later, when Ray appears with bags full of Tupperware containers, and hovers in the muggy kitchen, readying himself for conversation.

They appear to be competing in who can stand up straighter, and I decide it is best to sit down.

Ray loads crackers with smoked salmon and black pepper. 'Ain't Misbehavin'' swells through the open window.

I saw this Sri Lankan opera singer, really excellent. Tiny head, you wouldn't expect it, Ray says, munching salmon.

Ezra listens at the window. Hey, Fats Waller! It's because they have resonant skulls, he says.

I mess up Ezra's hair. It gets shorter with every photo shoot.

Ray looks away. He asks whether the band have started turning a profit.

Later, once Ray is gone, I tell Ezra that the way he drops things like that into conversation is one of the reasons I fell for him.

Nuzzling, he says: Yes. But everyone in the music industry thinks I'm strange.

Dream about those resonant skulls. Store them on luminous shelves.

9

Piers is five inches shorter than me, which I knew was going to be a problem, but I didn't appreciate the extent. He holds an umbrella open over himself and Nance. His shirt is dark blue and expensive-looking. He wears a corduroy jacket. I apologise for being late until I realise that he is either not listening or refusing to accept my apology. He keeps craning his neck as though he is looking for someone more important and smiling, vaguely. His face is very symmetrical. He looks like he gets high-end haircuts and I can imagine him paying to be shaved. He is better-looking than I expected, but I know his type. His swagger is academic; it relies on small colleges, swooning undergraduates, on being a man in a room full of children. Nance keeps looking up at him with a shyness, a deference I do not recognise. He looks down into her face and squeezes her hand. Little face, he says, *Little you.*

I look at some pigeons fighting to the death in a gutter. I should make my home among them.

We were just saying how lucky you are to get such fine British weather for your visit, Piers says.

The sky is grey and pissing it down.

She did live here, Nance says. Come on you, get under.

I try to keep in step with them, but I have to stoop to stay under the umbrella. I walk a few steps lopsided and then duck out.

Why don't you just take it – you're the tallest, Nance says.

Right, Piers says. I'll lead the way then, shall I?

He strides off down the street, at the end of which I can see the sign of the restaurant.

He is taking us out for dinner, Nance says, making a half-hearted effort to speed up. He can be a bit strange in restaurants, so don't take on.

Like rude to waiters or—

I don't want to hurry you, girls, Piers says, but we do have a 7 pm booking.

Piers takes us to the Bleeding Heart.

When we get to the restaurant he hangs his jacket inside out on the back of his chair. Nance strokes the silk lining, as if she cannot help it.

I look at the low ceilings, the burgundy walls, the dark wood panelling. There are ink sketches in thick black frames at regular intervals. There is a black fireplace that has never been used. The waiters move around like mercury.

They bring us bread, oil, a little dish of Maldon salt. Nance dips some bread in the oil, then takes a pinch of salt and grins at me. Piers coughs and taps the back of her hand with the silver spoon that came with it.

I am not able to see what is unmannerly or wrong with putting one's fingers into salt, I say. Elizabeth David. She didn't see the point of salt spoons.

Piers looks at me for a second and then puts the spoon back in its dish.

I enjoyed Cooper's biography of David, he says, though the delicacies she revels in are, by my standards, a bit rich. Have you read it?

Not yet.

It came out in 2011.

I try and see what Nance sees. His fingernails are pared neatly and clean. He has a natural cadence and it is easy to fall into his stories when you're not the scapegoat. When the waiter appears, he folds the menu and hands it back, ordering foie gras, steak tartare, gravlax, artichokes, and when Nance digs him in the ribs, grilled langoustine, which come spiny with their heads and little legs.

Like centipedes, Nance says, making one walk across the table at him.

Please don't be childish, he says.

We drink a bottle of wine between us and Piers sips on rhubarb vodka that comes in a small crystal glass. When he takes a sip, the dent above his lip deepens.

We are sitting under a low dome in which the murmur of other tables' conversations reverberates, so that it is difficult to hear beyond the hum of other people's lives. I try and watch Piers's lips to decipher what he's saying. He leans back in his chair and picks languidly at his foie gras with the wrong fork. He cuts the crusts off his miniature toasts.

I ask how his work on Nabokov is going, and he gives Nance a look like it's meant to be top secret.

As if I care. I've got your number, I want to say, I know that you call out your mother's name.

Nah – bok – ov, he says.

He finishes his pâté and smooths the napkin in his lap.

Actually, I'm working on a long piece about the performative masochism of Lana Del Rey, he says. I'm particularly interested in the way girls – forgive me, *ladies* in your generation – fetishise a certain kind of—

Sex?

I'm a little drunk. I drink instead of eating.

Piers puts a piece of bleeding meat into his mouth and swills it with Beaujolais. Did Nancy tell you about the little talk we went to see at the Soho House?

I have a mouth full of gravlax and am trying not to retch. Raw, and pink, and thickly cut. When Idle Blades got signed, Dolly took us to Soho House and Ezra did a double take when he saw what I was wearing. We were magnetic that night, though we couldn't afford a drink between us.

Just Soho House, I say. No *the*.

Nance kicks me.

Oh, Piers says, peeling away a petal of artichoke as if to demonstrate his prowess. Are you a member?

Then he dips the petal in butter and says to Nance, Open wide. She bats him away.

Yes, I am actually, I say.

Bit too *city* for me, he says, eating the artichoke himself. But they do have some interesting things from time to time.

I love it, Nance says. I stole a towel from the bathroom. It's monogrammed.

Piers closes his eyes with a pained expression. I want to squeeze her hand.

A waiter lights a candlestick on the piano. I am staring at the bit where the wax fountains have cracked, and Nance sees my face before she hears it.

The singer has a throat full of glass and so do I. The cutlery on plates around us scrapes and clatters. And I cannot help lifting myself a little to try and see the singer, though I know it isn't him. It is strange, still, how it hits me in waves, like a fainting fit. Or a poison.

188

Nance grabs a passing waiter's sleeve.

My friend here just got jilted at the altar. Do you think your man could play a different song?

Piers closes his eyes. Nance crosses hers.

Thank you, I mouth.

The bill arrives on a silver plate with edges like lace. Piers slides it across the table and then dabs at the corners of his mouth with his napkin. Nance is busy glaring at the singer.

I put my card on the tray and hand it to the waiter. Ray put an extra $500 in my account to show his concern. He has been avoiding me since Liderman.

Nance looks confused when the waiter asks for my PIN.

What's happening? Don't be ridiculous, we'll split it.

Iris wants to treat us, sweetheart.

He looks at me like a man wanting to put a pin through a butterfly.

The ballet, it turns out, is the all-male *Swan Lake*. Water drips through the corrugated steel we stand under. Nance spikes our Diet Cokes with vodka while Piers is in the powder room.

That was weird, I say, making light of it.

Well, he's been paying for everything, so. I'll pay you back.

The theatre is warm and the chairs are covered in plush red velvet. We are in the middle of the row. I imagine how we must look, the three of us processing down. Uncle and nieces out for a jaunt? Piers starts to explain Matthew Bourne's adaptation of the original narrative to the woman sitting next to him. Nance cranes her neck to see the orchestra.

I know I'm meant to be tapering off Effexor, but I want to be decisive about something for once. This, I have decided, is agency. I don't want to give myself the chance to go backwards, so I left the Effexor in New York and took the clonazepam to London as security. Without Effexor though, every detail of the world is garish, unexpected, hostile. Streets full of clowns. It takes me hours to adjust to fluorescent lights. Strangers' voices are monstrous. If nerves exist, then mine are being sandpapered. Liderman did say *take as needed*. All through the ballet, I eat clonazepam like Tic Tacs.

After the performance, Piers steps over the emptying seats in front, pushes his way down the row, then strides out of the theatre ahead of us. We wait our turn and when we reach the doors Nance runs out after him. I have never seen her run. She pulls on his sleeve, but I can't hear what she's saying. He bustles off again, his feet stuck out in first position.

How do you think I felt, Piers says, left on my own – what do you think people thought, a grown man trailing around after two young girls – but you don't think about how I feel, do you.

Nance says something, sharply.

Oh, and I'm expected to pay for dinner, is that it, he says. Have I not lived up to my role?

I catch up and thank him for giving me somewhere to crash.

He nods, curtly. As I can't evaporate, I stay where I am. Nance squints towards the end of the street.

And I suppose you'll want to get even more drunk now, is that it? A few lagers? Tequila slammers? Piers seems more drunk than either of us. He is red in the face. He paces off again and I follow him.

Have I done something to offend you?

No, no, not at all, he says. This evening has been *delightful*, listening to you and Nancy talk over each other and go on about men, as if we were animals. I am a man too, you know.

I'm sorry, I say. You're right, I've been monopolising her. We haven't seen each other in a while.

It isn't pleasant, you know, being made to feel like you don't exist.

Of course not. Let me buy you a drink.

We walk for a few minutes in silence. Nance is trailing us now, emanating fury, but Piers does not slow down. The streetlights are broken but for one. I watch the halo around it pulsing.

She talks about you constantly. All the time, I say.

I owe you an apology about dinner, he says, stiffly. You don't strike me as a pescatarian. Nancy hadn't mentioned it.

Behind us, the clouds are thick and strange, as if we have been smoking for hours in a tiny room. I don't know how to make him slow down. I consider sprawling on the pavement.

Has Nance spoken to you about her eyes, I ask.

Piers takes a deep, long-suffering sigh and looks at me for the first time. He slows his pace. He takes out a handkerchief to clean his glasses.

Because you're the only one allowed to know her, he says.

No. It's just that she needs to make appointments to see the specialists and she never wants to.

He is fascinated by the blueness of her eyes and disinterested in macular degeneration. It hits a nerve, his interest in what she reads, eats, wears, talks about, and total lack of engagement where she needs him.

I stop walking and start to explain how serious it is, how important it is that she makes the appointments, and even when Nance's fingers are digging into my arm I don't stop.

For the gynaecologist, I add, pointlessly.

Nance scowls at me, and then at the ground. I do not like to see her meek.

She paws at his arm. I stare up into the rain that seems to fall straight from a lamp-post. All around us, pubs are spilling out onto the pavement. I feel awake for the first time today, like energy is coming up through the soles of my feet.

To be young, and in love and in London. And here I am, with these two, wasting time. I imagine being back in New York, recounting our latest escapades, and hunt the pavements for lures. I look over at Nance and realise she is doing the same.

There, she says. You know them, don't you babe? Those two?

Piers perks up at that. When he spots the group of men smoking outside the pub, he smooths back his hair and tries for derision.

Oh, that lot, he says.

He knows *everyone* in London, Nance says.

She pulls me towards the pub, or am I pulling her, either way we are going. Piers looks pleased. When we step into the pub everything comes into colour. Amy Winehouse is playing, 'Rehab'. People are eating crisps and swarming at the bar. A man with a mullet is having the time of his life on the fruit machine. In my peripheral vision, I see the buttons are flaring, catching fire. There's a building pressure behind my forehead, like a band of steel. Every object in the room, even the silver polish on Nance's nails, even the fruit machines, will one day be destroyed or rot into mulch. Everything starts to shimmer, threatening to break apart into its constituent molecules. Two of the men recognise Piers and raise their pints. One of them looks me up and down from head to toe. At last, at last. It is like being filled in with a paintbrush. Flesh and blood, no girl cadaver.

Neither of the men is attractive. One, in fact, looks like a bear forced into clothes. But both think I'm pretty. They both know I'm here. They remember Nance and enquire after her dissertation, then start discussing a scandal I know nothing about. I pretend to be Nance's shadow, try and nod at the right moments. The bear in clothes asks me what I'm drinking. When I say vodka and cranberry juice he says that he hasn't heard that one in a while. I get out my Moleskine to write it down then leave my bag with Nance. When I get back, he is writing in my Moleskine. I snatch it from him and he laughs. He has written: You need to relax when we make out you'll enjoy it.

Nance pulls me away, hisses names I'm supposed to know, publishers and editors and owners of small presses. Someone makes a remark about Ireland and the Eighth Amendment and Nance is off. I am warm, overheating even. I'm all wrapped up in listening to her talk, how balanced her sentences are, how she blends pathos and fact, and then I see Piers start to get impatient. He exchanges a look with the bear in clothes over the top of Nance's head, and I want to kick him in the shins. Don't do that, I will hiss. It seems to give the bear courage, like he's got back-up against this twenty-two-year-old five-foot drunk loud talking girl.

You've got too much to say for yourself, the bear says.

Just as well. Because you haven't enough, Nance says.

There is a thrill in Nance behaving badly, it unleashes something in me. Piers looks appalled. The bear in clothes is, I gather, someone important. Men like him enjoy Nance's boldness until they feel threatened by it; I move closer to him and play with his beard. In front of Nance it is fun, winding men around my little finger. We order more drinks. We get a table. Piers tells a joke that's actually funny and for a moment I see what Nance means. He slips a hand around her waist and she rests her head on his shoulder. When I smile at him, he smiles back. We sit next to each other and he tells me stories about his worst students, who all sound like me and Nance. He does impressions. They're not good impressions, but as I laugh, he relaxes. He is pompous, vain, insecure, and trying hard to keep up the most flimsy of appearances. I can respect that. At least he thinks the effort is worth it, that there is a social ladder to climb, that there is someone he wants to be at the end of it.

We go pirouetting down alleyways while Piers strides ahead muttering.

Turn out! I say. Arabesque! Assemblée!

We stop at a chip shop on the way back to his house in Primrose Hill. Piers refuses to come in and stands outside, watching us through the window.

Nance gets a doner kebab. I get two portions of cheesy chips. We stumble along with the sky lightening into blue, licking our fingers, and take apart the people we have met this evening.

Mole man, I remember, I say.

Sam, she says, or David? Could he dance?

Did we dance?

You whirled around like Rose in *Titanic*, she says.

Oh yeah, I say.

Are you joking? Do you actually not remember that?

Of course I remember. It was mental. I span and span. Dervishes.

I sift through the loose-leaf memories of the last hours, flick through the images. I pummel my memory and locate only spinning and telling some man about how the real problem in

Casablanca is Rick's lack of communication, and the lurching in my stomach when Johnny Cash started playing and how the floor rushed up to meet me when I fell.

As soon as we're out of the pub, Piers keeps his distance and his vague contempt returns. I prefer to earn people's scorn. There is something jaunty in his step though and he taps the gleaming tip of his umbrella against the pavement. When we get to his front door, he turns and looks at Nance sternly.

Dove, he says, what's the rule?

I wonder if I am about to be entangled in some strange sex game. The thought neither appeals nor disgusts me. I am so bored. And as soon as the drink wears off, I know I will be bored again.

Please, Nance says. Just this once.

Her babyish voice sets my teeth on edge, and it doesn't work either. Piers stares at her until she closes the polystyrene carton, stomps to the bins and throws it in.

I stuff chips into my face and Piers watches me. I pull off strings of cheese. When I show no signs of stopping, he sighs in disgust and fumbles for his keys in the dark.

Nance picks the cheese off my chips.

That was brilliant, she says. But it'll only make him worse. Also, have you noticed how you're getting more like me?

Inside, Piers goes upstairs with a curt nod which I assume means goodnight. I turn on the tap and hand Nance a pint of water before filling a glass for myself. The moon throws panels of light on the kitchen floor. I stand in one and watch dust swirl in my glass. I miss the tap water from my bathroom in New York, it is warmer and easier to gulp without tasting. Here, I am agitated, and the water tastes alive.

The apartment is decorated like Piers has been studying the houses of North London intelligentsia for years. It also has what Tess would call a touch of the Home Counties; a White Company fur throw over the back of the black leather sofa, a spray of blue silk flowers in a vase. Piers's mother probably *rescued* them from the shrine of his childhood bedroom. I imagine the flowers stuffed in the back of the Merc. When I sit on the sofa-bed, it sags. The sheets folded at the end have a busy floral print and smell mossy. I look around for my handbag and one more clonazepam. I cannot imagine going to sleep. I can only focus on the bright things in the room – Nance's red handbag, the green velvet curtains and how they spill to the floor.

Don't go to bed yet, I say, pulling at Nance's hand. Stay down here. I'm scared.

She puts her knee on the sofa and peers into my hand.

Are they the ones that taste like strawberries? Can I have one?

Dove! Piers shouts down the stairs.

I don't want the night to end. I shake out one little pink pill, hold it out to Nance, and then eat it myself. I need it more than she does – I am full of static electricity. I am dangerous this way. Piers calls again and she heaves herself upright.

So unfair, she says.

She is so pretty barefoot.

After I hear his door close, I take a zopiclone and swear to myself that when I open my eyes it will be morning. But the house is full of sounds, like there are people moving in between the walls. If they're having sex, I can't hear it. I hold my breath and listen. I don't know how their sex would sound. Like laundry falling downstairs, presumably.

I try counting New York streets: Park, Lexington, Madison, Broadway, Columbus, Amsterdam. I have learnt no new streets by walking, which sickens me. My head is full of New York streets and green street signs but I can't focus on the print. Colours: try purple – royal, amethyst, lilac, indigo, prose. Birds: Raven, crow, sparrow, thrush, lark, nightingale. Types of salt: Maldon, kosher, table, Himalayan Pink, Black Hawaiian, Red Hawaiian, smoked, Kala Namak, fleur de sel.

One day I will be rich enough to buy a vial of fleur de sel. I will wear it around my neck on a long silver chain, like an amulet. The crystals are blue-grey. They come from the coast of Brittany, where they have to be skimmed from the surface of tidal pools, like cream from milk. They can only be harvested on dry, breezy days, and only with traditional wooden rakes. I imagine the rakes like balsa wood, light and malleable. There's a ticking that I think is my heart, but when I check my pulse is slow, sluggish. I follow the noise into the kitchen. There are varnished oars from the St John's rowing team on the wall. I read the fancy gilt writing on the handles and give up before I find Piers's name. The clock on the wall, the clock on the oven, and his watch laid neatly on the counter all show different times. Nance's fingerprints, everywhere. His watch is heavy and gold and cool when I slip it on. There's an old hardback book on the counter, all scuffed spine and illuminated script. I pick it up, expecting *Arabian Nights* or some other coffee-table treasure. When I open it though, I see Piers's laptop; it is an ornamental laptop case and not for carrying. Piers must have had it made.

I take the malbec left open for cooking and locate my copy of *Diary of a Call Girl* stuffed behind a bookshelf where Nance told me she hides things. I curl up against the arm of the sofa and wait for exhaustion to take me. Trying to chase sleep is its own unrequited love affair. When my eyelids start to drop, I catch myself from falling. I can't control this reflex; it has nothing to do with how much I want to be awake. I am stuck in between states. So, this is purgatory.

I dream of Ezra in a tangle of limbs, saying, This is what you wanted.

I wake up when the overhead light clicks on. It looks like someone is shining a torch straight down through the ceiling, the light doesn't reach the room's corners.

Make space, Nance says. I couldn't sleep. His Lordship is snoring. Got yourself a nice little den down here.

She throws herself down next to me.

My phone is by my head and the display shows 3.30 am, which according to Tess is the closest we come to dying in a twenty-four-hour cycle. Something to do with heart rates. The raw grey light slips its fingers around the paper blinds, the colour of dread. I cannot stand it, I cannot stand that I have had no break from all of this, that soon we will have to get up and it will begin again. I will have to do all of it again, washing, dressing, getting trains. And it is all pointless. And none of it will make you here or make you now. I wonder if I have slept at all, or if this is some drawn-out nightmare and my body is back in New York. It does not like to travel with me across the Atlantic.

You know what Dorothy Parker wanted on her gravestone?

If you can read this you've come too close, Nance says.

There is gravlax behind my teeth. I hook my finger and pick at it.

You're disgusting, Nance says.

Have you noticed how he has dandruff in his eyebrows?

Yep, she says. And stop freaking out – I can see you doing it

– I won't be dictated to. We'll sleep when we sleep and the day starts when we start it. Did you know that human skin literally burns goldfish? It burns away the protective layer. If you take a goldfish out of the water and hold it in your palm, you'll see it curling, in agonising pain, but as soon as you put them back in the water they forget. They go swimming around again, happy as you like, as if it never happened.

Whose fish have you been torturing?

Nance taps the side of her nose and hauls the duvet over to her side. She tells me how goldfish have tastebuds on their lips, how they have no stomachs, how if you leave a goldfish in a dark room for long enough it will go stone white.

They need the light for the goldness, you see. Pigment. Like melanin. You're looking quite peaky yourself there.

After a while I give up trying to sleep and we raid Piers's bar. It is a silver cocktail trolley in one corner of the kitchen. Highball glasses, evenly spaced. A decanter full of whiskey with a heavy crystal stopper, Angostura bitters, Campari, vermouth. Nance pulls open the freezer, then bashes an ice-cube tray against the counter. She flinches at the noise and catches my eye. Nance is genuinely surprised when she touches something sharp and there is blood. We both tense up, but she can't acknowledge that she cares about waking Piers, so she bashes the tray again. The ice cubes slide across the green stone counter, and I watch her chase them. They slip between her fingers.

We won't be wanting the whiskey, she says. He wanted me sober the first night we had the ride, so I said I was going to the bathroom and had a poke around. The whiskey is mostly water now. And it was Scotch, so.

Couldn't he smell it?

Like he was going to say something at that stage and give up getting the leg over. Slice us one of these.

She throws a lemon underarm. It lands on the sofa and we both freeze again, listening for movement upstairs.

You know, she says, he has a Chagall in the attic.

She seems comfortable in this flat, padding around. Her natural hair is breaking through the raven at the roots.

The only problem is, she says, that I've done the same every night since. And I didn't fill them up with water because we're adults now but then the bastard didn't replace them or throw them out. See? She brandishes an empty decanter at me. My laugh comes out as a murmur. It feels like someone has stuck a ratchet in my calves and turned, all my muscles are tight.

Shall we go out again, I say.

Better not. Everyone will have gone home.

Nance hands me a tumbler over the back of the couch and looks at me sceptically.

Are you feeling okay, she says. You've got that manic glint. Like a wolf.

I'm just restless. I want to do something, I say.

The sofa is softer than I expected and plumps up around me like an airbag when I throw myself down next to her. I roll my face against the cushions, hoping to smear them with kohl. I turn them over so that Piers won't find out till later. *IwasThereIamIamhere.*

I know what you mean, she says. I want to go dancing. I could never go with him, people would laugh.

Can't say I'd blame them.

Nance scratches the sole of her foot and says, casually, So. What did you think?

200

When I kiss her, she keeps one hand on my shoulder, holding me at a distance.

This isn't fair, she says, kissing me back.

Her breath is hot and fierce. She smells of cheap beer and Jo Malone perfume.

Nance has dated girls. She says being bisexual is a political action. I like girls as art objects. Nance says this is morally reprehensible. During Freshers' Week, I kissed her at a silent disco. I was trying to make Ezra jealous. It didn't work, but Nance turned up at my door a few nights later. Her hair was dripping wet. My dryer's blown a fuse, she said. She used mine and grumbled about all the posh twats she'd met. I opened wine, glad to be singled out. Before we slept together, we lay on my bedroom floor, making snow angels in the carpet. A week later, I started going out with Ezra, and Nance got over it. Since then we've made out a few times at the end of nights when we are drunk enough that there is little else to be done. I always freak out first. Nance has pointed out I am also the one who starts it. How can a person be so soft and firm. Yet as soon as she reciprocates, my interest dies. She is breathing hard.

She jumps back as if I have burned her. Piers is at the top of the stairs. I watch him begin to descend through half-closed eyes. King of the castle.

I could pretend to be asleep, but I want to see what he will do.

Nance is for some inexplicable reason turning the kettle on. I turn to the window and watch the moon. It is pale and sickly. It seems too close to the house. I lean back on the sofa and close my eyes for a moment, but still my pulse skitters along.

Do you remember with the lamp, I say to Nance, loud enough that she can't pretend she hasn't heard. There's a pause and then

201

I hear her murmuring to Piers. His voice at least is softer now. I turn my back to the window. I try and imagine what painting is behind the sheet in the corner and the colours blur.

You know we don't have to do this, Nance is saying.

She is pouring me water.

Still, this thing has its own momentum now and I started it. It is easier. And why not? I must want this. There is no reason not to. Why not expose myself to experiences while they cannot hurt me; like having surgery under anaesthetic.

I like the idea of making myself do things. This is agency. Try everything now.

We split the rest of the clonazepam and grind it in a heavy marble pestle and mortar. I hold the bowl straight while Nance wields the pestle. I tap the powder carefully into our drinks. I pour the most into mine and ask Piers to open some wine.

Are we doing this or not, he says.

There are no curtains in Piers's bedroom. The window is the old-fashioned kind, cut across with bars which send their shadow, or the shadow of their shadow, floating over the sheets.

She kisses me in front of him and it is strange, like we are mannequins being arranged, though Piers sits back and watches, leaning in every now and then to touch her breasts, my hair.

They start kissing and Piers has his hand inside her nightdress. His eyes are closed, but every few moments he pats her thigh, as if to reassure himself that she's there, and then opens one eye to confirm that I am too. I move to kiss her too and he puts a hand in between us. He does not let us kiss again. I lie face down. Then she is on top of me and he is on top of her. I pretend to be a rock. I pretend to be the girl in *Metamorphoses* mid turning into a tree. Their skins stick to each other and then

202

become unstuck. Their sex is like fish slapped on a counter. In and out and oh. Oh.

I am surprised at the force with which he moves into her. Nance does not make a sound except for a sort of sighing. I keep asking whether she's sure that he isn't fucking me.

You're fine, she says. It's fine.

You'd know if I were, *sweetheart*.

After, Nance clambers off me and blows her fringe from where it is stuck to her forehead. She looks flushed, unsure. She glances between us, but she does not look directly at Piers. Her eyes aren't quite focusing. She steadies herself on the bed and looks about to say something, but she hesitates. I'll be back in two minutes, she says. Then she pulls down her nightdress, grabs a towel and pats me on the arm. Her hand is shaking. She leaves me lying on Piers's futon, on top of the soft dark duvet, like a washed-up thing. I hear the bathroom door close. Piers is wearing a paisley silk dressing gown. It is emerald green and has a dark green tie. His eyes are caviar black.

I notice his hand on my knee and pretend not to, because if I close my eyes I can pretend it is Ezra. I put Nance and her anxiety about the two of us out of my mind. His goatee is bristlier than I imagined. His mouth is cold and his tongue is quick and darty – he is a cold water animal, I decide.

Do whatever you want to me, I say.

My voice is strange and drawling. My hands look like someone else's hands.

Piers makes a sound like he is choking.

The moon outside is sickly and pressed up against the window like it's trying to get in. I close my eyes and imagine myself a different animal. A goldfish, twirling, aflame, agonised, scales falling away, orange, quick as a beam of light, renewed. Starting over.

I don't notice the bathroom door open because my eyes are closed. Then, Nance, standing in the doorway, looking at me like I've crawled out from under a stone.

10

Sasha draws a pyramid on the board and we go around the class.

CONFLICT

RISING ACTION

CLIMAX

FALLING ACTION

DENOUEMENT

At 5 pm, everyone springs out of their chair. It is a Friday. I watch Lisa tapping at her phone, checking her route on City-mapper. I am scared of the weekend. Once I go back to the flat, there'll be no reason to leave until Kennedy's class, which is in five days. If I could give that time to someone who deserves it, some child with a terminal illness – or spend it unconscious – that would be ideal. Last night, Ezra made his activity feed and all of his playlists on Spotify private.

Sasha glances at me while she packs up her bag and wipes the board. She comes over to my desk. As I hand her the stack of printouts for next class, I catch the sharp scent of unwashed animal hanging around my body. Sasha doesn't comment. She puts the handouts in her bag.

Did you get my email? she asks. You're late on a few assignments.

It feels like everyone assumes there's a mechanism to stop the world falling apart, I say. Like everyone thinks the worst things won't be allowed to happen. Or at least – you know how in cartoons, if you fall off a cliff, you hit shelves of rock, and pinball all the way down. Your bones might shatter, but you at least slow down. Here, there's nothing.

Sasha interrupts, and her voice is kind, but firm. Iris, my daughter is waiting outside. She's nine. I'm going to switch off the lights when I leave. Go home, take a bath, get some rest.

After she has left, I sit in the back row, copying out Matthew 5:13 over and over.

You are the salt of the earth; but if salt has lost its taste, how shall its saltness be restored? It is no longer good for anything except to be thrown out and trodden under foot by men.

Lorde releases *Melodrama*. In an interview, Ezra is asked whether he is single and he says yes. I WhatsApp him to ask if there's anything he wants to tell me and he replies PR.

He does not call after the London Bridge attack or when Grenfell burns.

He only calls after 3 am when he is the kind of high where the world has receded to a single point which his addled mind locates between my thighs. I tell myself that I am where his mind goes when his defences are down. I take advantage of the state he's in and build on the fantasies he wants to rehash, but it is 8 am, and he is too high to get to the end of the sentence. He loses the connection, calls back. I want to be the only one he can talk to this way, but I could be anyone, and tomorrow he won't remember calling. Perhaps addicts are people looking for religious experiences in the wrong places, looking for God and finding a needle. But I do not want this degraded version of what we had.

✻

At school, Kennedy collars me by the water fountain. He says that he's still waiting on a reply to his email.

They must be going to spam—

He cuts me off. If a student misses three of my classes, that student flunks. Last week was four.

Kennedy saw me crying on an escalator in Barneys. For weeks, I convinced myself it wasn't Kennedy, he doesn't seem like the kind of man who buys his own clothes.

That wasn't me, I say, lifting my chin. I am terrified of escalators.

Kennedy looks at me, then appears to lose patience. End of the week, he says.

In workshop, my latest draft is torn apart. Half of the class is off sick and Sam is avoiding eye contact. I stare at my fingers while Lisa makes a feminist critique of my passive characters.

Does agency require action? Sasha asks.

The answer, uncertain and scattered but almost unanimous, Yes.

Sasha presses a finger to her temples. What about Jean Rhys? What about Maggie Nelson? What about all of these writers – does this mean that they lack agency?

Finn pipes up, It seems kind of pointless to be writing about salt given everything that's going on right now. Kind of selfish too.

But what if salt is the only place I can get a foothold? It is the surface on which everything relates. Without salt, nothing tastes.

I wait five minutes and leave. I do not go back. I put the history of salt down the garbage disposal, page by page.

A postcard from Ezra:

27 June 2017

Well, there's more rubbish on the Great Wall of China than you'd think. Also, more people selling water bottles for 34 yuan. We went the wrong way at first so we saw the same bit twice. We're staying in the DongChen district because that's where Mao Livehouse is. I used up all my storage taking photos of the Wall on the drive back – parts of it are so eroded that nobody is allowed near. People keep wanting photos with Ndulu. Dolly says they think he's Mo Farah, but seriously, what the fuck. It's very smoggy and everything is neon. I can't read the street signs. It took us fourteen hours to get to Beijing from Shanghai. The train-cart sold chicken feet and duck embryos. I ate four Snickers bars. We went to a speakeasy the night before. There was a topless girl on a stripper-pole but Dolly didn't seem phased. As we were leaving, I realised we were walking out of a ten-foot painting of a sexual organ, which I suppose means we walked into it too.

I throw it away. I have nothing new to tell him, nothing funny, nothing interesting. I take two capsules, the full adult dose, every morning with water. I don't see what there is left of myself to preserve. Why hold on to the wreckage.

III
Video Games

July–December 2017

1

Sober, on the walk to 1020, Sam tries not to look at people's faces. Most of the MFA have stayed in the city for the summer, and he isn't in the mood. He has been rewriting the same paragraph all day. He has a shitty air-con unit from Best Buy in the flat, but the whirring gets to him. He steps off the kerb and kids swarm past, flirting, screaming about new bands and new bars – it's like they don't even see him. He watches a Latina girl in tight jeans put on lipstick in someone's wing mirror. When she sees him looking, he kicks a Coke can and watches it go pinwheeling under a car. One Jameson and then he's heading downtown, somewhere loud.

He reaches the bar which if he'd been thinking straight he would have skipped – it's always full of talkers. There is a girl in the bouncer's arms, her neck and knees slung between his elbows. She moans and pastes her hands over her face.

Shh – shhhh, honey, you're going home, the bouncer says. Her friends said you were outside. You are Ezra. Right, friend?

Sam recognises the name before he recognises Iris. He has not heard from her since she dropped out. She stopped answering his calls months ago and then he upgraded his phone. He liked to think she had called and got no dial tone.

Ez, she mumbles.

Sam holds out his arms. Watching how the girl crumples into him, the bouncer relaxes.

Right, Sam says. He walks back into the hot night, looking down between steps into her smudged face.

Lynn and Tina are playing poker in the main room when Sam carries her through. This is what his roommates do after work, get drunk, play stupid games. Sam walks straight for his bedroom door, but Tina calls after him – Uh, you do know about statutory law, right, Sam?

Iris's head slips against his chest and Sam stops, cradles her closer.

Aw, Tina says, sweet. Can you ask this one not to leave her panties on the bathroom floor? I don't want to catch something.

Sam wants to say that Iris is a friend. He wants thicker walls and clean sheets. He doesn't know how long it has been since he spent a night sober. It makes it hard to talk.

You should give her some water, Tina says, as his bedroom door shuts.

Thanks, says Sam. I was thinking vodka. Straight.

For five minutes or so, she is conscious.

Hey, Sam says. Hey. Don't worry. I've got you. Your friends asked me to look after you—

Sam, she says, between splutters and gasps, retching into his sink.

Sam rips the sheets off his bed, then lays her down on the mattress. Iris mews. As she drifts, Sam smooths her hair and makes hushing sounds. She opens her eyes for a moment and looks so relieved that Sam feels recognised. Then she passes out.

He could have been anyone, Sam thinks, she got lucky. He cannot stop watching her trust. Her dress is red and too short; Sam spreads it out, fanning it out around her. He hears Tina and Lynn talking about him on the other side of the door.

There is something private and closed off in Iris's face. Even now, part of her is somewhere he can't get at. He wants to shake her; to grab one narrow shoulder, then the other; to listen and see if she rattles. Sam brushes the front of his fingers over the curve where her ribs become breasts. She does not move. It's hard to believe that this wasn't intentional on some level.

After they hooked up, Sam asked Iris out a few more times. She didn't say no, but she always had something more important to tell him, about Lisa's latest drama, about her theories of Paul's deviance, about Trump's latest on Twitter. Sam had nodded along.

In their last conversation, he said, You can delay all you want, it doesn't bother me. I'm playing the long game over here – and watched her swallow.

That's romantic, she said. Sam recognised the sarcasm but also sensed that she wanted to sleep with him anyway, that she wanted to be persuaded.

♟

Iris cannot find her socks in the dark. In her head, she lists the names of friends who have done this before, woken up with a man they don't know, but it does not help.

Dirty stop-out, Nance would say. Nance's worst prophecies about Iris are true.

Pipes yawn, juddering life into the network beneath the floorboards. Iris hears the man in bed yawn and she curls into a ball on the floor, wishing herself invisible. He raises one lazy arm and yanks the cord of the blind, which whips up to show the ash-grey sky.

Iris looks up at the bed, and her head pulses. Oh Jesus.

Your face, Sam says, laughing.

She hides her face in the sheet wrapped around her – Fuck. My head. Why. I'm so sorry.

She wishes it had been a stranger. Sam yawns again. When she looks up, he has closed his eyes. Do you have school, she says, dumbly.

Holidays. July.

Right. Without getting up, she starts edging towards the door. Good to see you then—

Come back to bed. Day hasn't started yet. My guess is you don't know the way home.

Sam pulls her in under his arm and lets the blind down. Iris feels his breath grow shallow and makes her own match it until he sleeps. Surely, she should be relieved. Sam, who thinks she hung the moon.

⟆

That night, Iris calls him, and on the sixth ring, Sam picks up.

Iris? He pauses. I'm hanging up if this isn't you.

Iris stands in her bathroom, tracing the taut patch of skin on her stomach. She found it, translucent, crusted around the well of her belly button, and protected it from the shower with her hand. Beneath that: a phone number written with a Sharpie.

It was a return if lost sort of deal, in case you're wondering, Sam says.

His voice is monotone, and Iris can't tell if he's joking.

You forgot to write a name, she says.

He can tell she's trying to make light of the situation, but he isn't ready to let her. He doesn't say anything. Iris's mouth feels glued shut. Her tongue is covered with little bumps. She shakes her head, quickly, reminding herself that she knows Sam and

214

there is no reason to feel helpless.

So, we met at the bar? she says.

No, kid. I just picked you up on the sidewalk. Do that a lot – let random men carry you home?

Fragments: licking salt and biting lime to the rind and headlights making diagonals. For a moment, Iris thinks Sam can see these images too, nauseous, floating between them.

You weren't random, she says.

Her stutter and his smirk meet strangely on the line.

I have to go, he says. Go back to sleep. Drink water. Don't go home with any more strange men.

2

On Saturday, Sam chooses Bunga's Den, off Union Square. They agree to meet at 2 pm. As he's heading out, he shoves his copy of *In Our Time* in his bag. He gets there early, to watch. The pages are covered with Iris's notes. They hung out all the time last year, and in class they were allies, but her coldness since then has been astonishing. Sam is not used to chasing. He has a second beer. Twenty minutes later, Iris arrives, holding a plastic bag to her chest. Spilling herself onto the counter, she asks the bartender questions and the urgency in her voice carries. Sam wishes he could hear how she describes him. He watches her poise collapse. One of the regulars joins the conversation and Sam watches as Iris is revitalised by a joke he cannot hear. Every word she hears plays out across her face. He watches as this nobody sipping seltzer becomes fascinating in her reactions.

It's you!

He hugs her back briefly, gets another beer, then walks back to the table, listening to Iris explain that she was worried he would have left already and how the 14th Street subway is such a nightmare. She's sorry, she says, she always does this.

Sam slides into their booth and waits as she slides in opposite. So, he says. Why do you think those men were talking to you?

Iris unfolds a paper napkin and puts it carefully in her lap – Not for the same reason you are, she says, with a hopeful smile. You have a thank-you present to retrieve. For looking after me.

She reaches into her bag and hands him a parcel. He tests its weight, then takes out a cardboard box printed with violet musical notes and lime-green electric guitars. She snatches the box back and tears it open. They're drumsticks, see! I saw some on your floor. Well, I crawled on them actually. I mean, these are just toys but—

They're great, he says.

Sam sips his drink and glances at the score on TV. Redskins vs Panthers. In the edge of his sight, he sees her fidgeting, and her whole body seems to lap at him. He tears the wrapper on a straw and blows it across the table. Iris begins shredding it.

Sam clears his throat, screwing up his face as if reaching for the particulars.

So, this one time, back home – it must have been sophomore year. There was a party. And afterwards, I threw up in one of my buddies' shoes, and in the morning he stood up and stuck his foot right in there.

Iris groans – Please tell me I didn't do that.

You have a prett-ee good aim actually, Sam says, grinning. Straight in the sink. Such a lady. You know, on some level, I reckon you knew it was me. He clears his throat as if he's sparing her modesty. Your behaviour was *cordial*, he says.

He has never seen her blush before. As he is thinking this, she looks up and scans his face. She has eyes like flash photography. Sam looks back to the TV screen with the uneasy sense that he is being caught in an unflattering light.

Are you angry with me? she says. Sam watches her unscrew the salt and pepper shakers and swap the lids.

Why would I be angry with you? he says.

I don't know. I can be awful when I drink.

This is my resting state these days. Sam chuckles, quietly, as if to himself. Trust me – you do not want to see me angry.

He begins experimenting with his present, pretending he is with his Pearl Export kit. Iris dances sitting down. After a few seconds, he puts the sticks down. Thanks. These are great.

He picks up his phone and stares at it, laughing at the messages he has missed.

That guy, he says. Those guys.

⚓

Tina and Lynn are in Cabo, drinking fishbowl margaritas and sending videos on Snapchat of them screaming Spring Break till we die! When Sam gets up to go to his desk in the morning, Iris stays in his bed. There is something serene in this, Sam thinks, like part of his life is taken care of. It makes him want to buy a typewriter and start listening to jazz. At some point in the morning, Iris moves to the sofa and reads there. She spends a lot of time staring into space, but when Sam asks if she is happy, she nods. He says she is like a cat and she says *prrr prrr*.

At 5 pm, he makes cocktails. He perfects his recipe for Old Fashioneds. He puts the tumblers in the freezer and shows her how to muddle bitters and bourbon. He hands her shot glasses to taste. She picks a different favourite recipe every time, but Sam doesn't tell her that. If he says, This is my favourite, but it's heavy on the bitters, so go easy, Iris will say it is her favourite too, though her mouth is puckering. He likes how easy her issues are to fix. She worries about things that have never occurred to him as problems, confessing Netflix binges as if a great weight is being lifted. He has never felt so competent. She tells him things she thinks are terrible and he nods, to show he is taking her seriously, then says – This calls for Doritos. Have you seen *Jersey Shore*?

After a week, Sam starts encouraging Iris to work when he does. One morning, he clears a space at Tina's desk and puts a carnation in an empty beer bottle. Iris sits down, reluctantly. Her presence makes him feel calm, though he doesn't get absorbed in his work again; he is too aware of her sulking, and, five minutes later, slipping back to the sofa. He pretends to work for a while and then suggests a cigarette break. She watches as he puts on his shoes, then puts her shoes next to her feet.

Hey, he says. You know what we should do later. Benihana.

You're kidding, right?

Who doesn't love Benihana.

Isn't it for kids?

Not the Benihana I go to. They have shrimp in hats. He starts doing up her laces. They have rice shaped like Mickey Mouse, he says.

You are a strange person, she says, patting his head.

Perhaps you didn't hear me. I said shrimp in *hats*.

It is like high school, Sam thinks, or a version of it he never had. Like a summer fling, but with books. When they're smoking, he tells her that he has finally finished *Lolita*.

Once you get past that Shit what if I'm a paedophile moment, it's actually pretty good. I got really into tracking his style around the allegory of America—

– Do you get why I was so upset when Marcie said that, as a *mother*, she couldn't read it? I would have thought that would be a reason to read it. Tess kept hiding it, which didn't work, obviously. I remember thinking that Lolita was exactly how I wanted to look.

Sam thinks the sudden contempt in Iris's voice is directed at him. He doesn't remember the *incident* as Iris recalls it; Marcie,

219

in front of the class, explaining that Iris had clearly misunderstood *Lolita* as a love story, whereas in fact Humbert was a rapist, and Lolita was a *child*. This last phrase, Iris recounts in a dumb American accent, a nasal twang. Sam doesn't like it. She switches back to her own voice and starts talking about empathy, taboo, erotic revulsion, puritanical Americans – as she jumps between unrelated topics, Sam notices the physicality of how she talks, how she moves her hands, exaggerates, widens her eyes to make her point, and he gets suspicious. He has the sense that she has done this, all of this, before.

On Friday, it gets more humid, like the sky is getting lower to the ground. They drank too much last night. They went to karaoke with a few of Sam's friends at Volume Up. Sam saw that she was nervous and went to the bar to get drinks. He was apprehensive when he saw Iris talking to Nick, but she was in her element, wearing red lipstick, telling how they met, how she'd been Such a mess. I'm telling you, huh? This guy, she said in her best Jersey impression.

As Sam had, Nick laughed, and Sam wished she would not always revert to this version. He didn't like the way Nick was looking at her. He put his arm around her shoulders.

She's just playing around. We go way back. We were on the same course.

Is that right? Nick said, clinking Coronas with her, and winking at Sam.

Now, everything hurts Sam's head. He sits at his desk and wonders how many brain cells he killed. At 4 pm, Iris kisses him on the cheek – I have to go and babysit. Wish me luck.

When Iris leaves, she takes his energy with her. Sam drinks a Red Bull and it tastes of chemicals. He starts mixing cocktails at 4 pm. It doesn't occur to him that she might not come back. The cocktails are too sweet but Sam drinks them anyway. He has used up all the bitters.

The next day, Tina and Lynn return with shitty souvenirs, and Sam moves back into his bedroom, where he stays all weekend, playing *Grand Theft Auto* in his boxers. He smokes out of the window and wedges the butts into a crack in the windowsill. The fifth time his avatar gets jumped by a hooker, he realises he's waiting for her to text, which is an amateur move.

Sunday, City Diner, 2 pm, he texts.

At the diner, Iris is floppy. She's wearing a tracksuit and her hair is wet. Sam doesn't know whether it is okay to kiss her, though they have been kissing all week. He hides his confusion by ordering grilled cheeses and a pitcher.

How's work, she says.

He scratches his head – Every time I figure out one part another goes cattywompus. So, it's Seinstein on the straight and narrow. No cigarettes, no booze. It's a good thing you ran out on me actually because there wouldn't be anywhere for you to sleep. There's dystopia *all over* the apartment – Iris is smiling, vaguely, so he amps it up – I'm like if Speedy Gonzales had a typewriter. Did you guys have Speedy Gonzales? I guess he's pretty offensive actually, the sombrero and all. He could be a little Trump mascot. Oh, and yeah, Don DeLillo called. He's getting jealous, but I told him – Don, I said – I know it's hard, man, but to make art you have to make sacrifices. Don, look at my left hand.

Sam holds it up like a claw. Iris pulls his hand to her mouth, presses her lips to it, then drops it to the table. Sam sits, stunned for a second, then sips at his beer. He doesn't understand what is happening and he doesn't know how to ask. She is a completely different person when she's naked. He wants to say, Hey, d'you know where this crazy British girl went, but he doesn't think it will land. The food arrives. They talk, unevenly. Iris takes a bite of her grilled cheese and then pushes her plate away. She asks more questions about his work, but Sam has the feeling they are pre-prepared.

Whoever taught you to bang ketchup at the top is an amateur. Give me your hand, he says.

Look. Sam rubs her hand against the ridged fifty-seven on the glass bottle. Feel that? Good. Tap there. Properly. Pretend you're playing with your toy sticks.

Iris stares as ketchup schlups onto her plate and oozes around the cheese.

They're your sticks. Haven't you used them?

So much so that my flatmates have been complaining. Jesus, I'm kidding. Don't look at me like that.

He takes in Iris's lost expression and almost joins her, there, before turning away. He digs in his pocket, taps at his phone, then hands it to her – on YouTube the Cookie Monster leads the muppets in protest against an orange Trump muppet. A smile passes over Iris's face, but it's not enough for Sam.

Do you ever stop thinking? he says, taking back his phone. It must be draining.

Mostly, I can't hear myself until I talk. My brain is full of white noise, like on planes. Iris follows Sam's gaze, to where a girl is bending over the pool table. How do you walk without falling over? Sam spits an ice cube back into his glass, laughs and wipes his mouth. Iris goes on talking.

You know when your mind empties? Runner's high, flow,

people have different words for it. But you dive, sink into a moment. You forget time exists . . . it's like dying, but you don't leave. You just keep going, without edges, but it doesn't mean you're not you. Just you, no props. Oblivion. Losing your ego. I think it's—

Ob – liv – i – on, Sam says, sliding into the drawl she expects from American men.

⚑

Before the interview on Friday, Iris Googled tutoring in New York then followed the advice and deleted everything except Oxford and Columbia from her CV. She wrote herself a reference from the O'Malley family. She had been working with them on and off for years, on a voluntary basis.

Specialises in highly intelligent children with behavioural difficulties.

The apartment was on the Upper East Side, straight across the park. It was hot and Iris wished she had dressed differently, but all of the clothes which were cool enough felt flimsy.

Melissa wanted a twice-a-week babysitter to take the pressure off. She wore beaded slippers which she referred to as indoor shoes.

We went for Navajo White for the carpets, she explained, leading Iris through the hallway. Iris tried not to think of how long it had been since she last washed her feet. She stood in the shower every few days but didn't have the energy for much else.

I want to get the kids settled before September starts and we're all crazy busy again.

Iris sat down on the cream sofa opposite her. Melissa made an unsettling amount of eye contact. Iris felt grubby, coated in

223

a thin film of sex and television. Sam wanted to eat vanilla ice cream off her stomach. Afterwards, he agreed it was overrated and made the sheets sticky. Your skin is too warm, he said. It sinks right through you.

Melissa is talking still. We had to fire the nanny. Such a sweet lady, she really was, but she didn't get what we're about as a family. She wasn't on brand. But that gives you room for manoeuvre. And we have a vacancy for a tutor too, so if the kids like you, who knows. I try and let them guide me. Melissa sipped at her iced tea, then placed it on a coaster – You need to know that I run this family like a business. You'd have to be ready to be part of the team.

Absolutely, Iris said.

Melissa smiled and Iris imagined her teeth in a glass of water by the bed. She asked about Iris's education, and looked pleased but doubtful – And now you're a babysitter?

It makes sense while I focus on my studies.

Good for *you*. You'll love the school. Wetherby-Pembridge. Very exclusive. There's a real emphasis on English manners and customs, which we love.

That evening, Iris gets an email from Ezra. She stares at the icon. Two months since she heard from him last. Does he have some kind of antennae, that he senses when her thoughts finally leave him? Does he feel a chill? Or is she more like a dog with a shock collar getting too near an electric fence.

She could be happy with Sam.

She deletes the email, then goes into the trash folder and moves it back to her inbox. Then she marks it as spam. Then she opens her spam folder.

From: ezramunroe@gmail.com

To: irisirisiris@gmail.com

Interesting thing: There have been some *mind-blowing* rainbows in London recently. Ndulu's sis showed me one a few days ago and it was probably the most serious rainbow I've ever seen i.e. I've never seen a double one before. Of course, theoretically speaking, all rainbows are double rainbows but the second bow usually isn't bright enough to be visible. So, rainbows always appear in the section of sky directly opposite where the sun is. Light refracts when entering each water droplet, then reflects off the inside of the droplet, and then refracts again on the way out. So the double refraction means each wavelength is refracted to a slightly different degree, and splits into a different colour.

In a double rainbow, the colours of the outer rainbow appear in the opposite order to the inner rainbow. The second ring is caused by the light rays being reflected TWICE by the inside walls of the water droplets . . . so it's like a mirror reflection of the smaller, inner rainbow.

Life thing: We played a random festival in Houston in a car park. It was extraordinarily hot. The whole thing was on a tiny stage that looked like it had been hammered together with spare bits of wood.

Iris takes a photo of the email, then deletes it from her inbox and empties her junk folder.

3

It's August. Sam is typing in corrections and taking breaks to play fantasy football. The keys of his laptop are filthy. Since his air-con gave up and he dumped it on the kerb, they have been working in a sports bar. It does bottomless coffee. When they walked in the first time, Sam fell to his knees – Heaven has air conditioning, he said.

Iris made a beeline for a table and sat down. Americans like Sam's stunts, women look over indulgently, men high-five him, but she is never sure what to do with them. She has started dreaming of salt again. She wants to start writing, but she is scared of trying and failing. She doesn't have any other books with her though – she flicked through Sam's, but nothing grabbed her, and she didn't want to go back to her flat. The more time she spends away, the emptier it gets. Sam sees her frowning at her notebook.

Hey, he says. Come back.

Iris looks so grateful that something inside him lurches. He moves around the table to sit alongside her.

You've got this, he says. Low stakes, right?

I've never had a cheerleader before.

I like to think I'm more of a coach. Those flippy skirts do nothing for my thighs.

Iris goes to the bathroom, and Sam looks, quickly, at her Moleskine. He doesn't get the point of her lists. The bartender switches on the news and Sam says, Buddy, do you mind turning that off for now? My girlfriend's feeling fragile.

226

No problem, it's all bad news anyway.

When Iris gets back, she grimaces like she's about to throw herself from a height and starts reading. Sam watches her read the same paragraph over and over again.

keeping the colours bright on boiled vegetables; making ice cream freeze; whipping cream rapidly; getting more heat out of boiled water; removing rust; cleaning bamboo furniture; sealing cracks; stiffening white organdie; removing spots on clothes; putting out grease fires; making candles dripless; keeping cut flowers fresh; killing poison ivy; and treating dyspepsia, sprains, sore throats and earaches.

Sam plays with his phone, talking to no one in particular – I'm so ready to go back to school. I cannot *wait* to rub Conrad's face in how badly he's losing. He's such a show-off. Like, look at this guy. Everyone knows he can't even score a four-pointer.

Iris pushes her notebook away. It's the air conditioning, she says. It gives me goosebumps.

He's about to suggest she reads something else, something that makes her feel good, when her phone pings. She picks it up to read the text. Her friend Lexi is back in town. She wants to get dinner this weekend.

Awesome, Sam says. I know exactly the place. Little bistro on the Lower West Side. Sophisticated, dishes with names no one can pronounce, those little candles you love.

It hasn't occurred to Iris that Sam would want to come. When she mentioned falling out with Nance, Sam had seemed hurt. You didn't tell me that, he said.

They have had various low-key arguments, on similar subjects, about how little of her life Iris shares, for example. When Sam mentioned that this bothered him, Iris laughed. She had apologised and explained away the laughter by saying that she was surprised, that it was an unusual complaint, but she didn't sound sorry at all, just amused, haughty. It happened again later that week, when Sam tagged her in a photo from Benihana and she rejected the request.

I look horrible, she said.

Are you kidding me? He pulled up the photograph again and zoomed in. You look adorable.

Can you not? Anyway, given everything that's going on, I'm not keen on giving Facebook even more data. I'd delete my account if I could.

Why don't you then.

Why don't *you*.

Sam had started laughing then. Their fights seem to come out of nowhere, so they are easy to forget. Like when he mentioned that he hadn't met any of her friends, and she snapped, What friends.

They have a truce on some subjects, but Sam's displeasure outlasts the conversations that cause it. Iris has started to think of this displeasure like a hangover manifesting itself in strange ways; tingling in the hands and feet, facial spasms.

Iris watches Sam joking around with the bartender, who is practising tricks with the bottles. She doesn't want to disappoint him.

She texts Lexi: Sam joining us if that's okay with you? I'm easy either way. I haven't mentioned Fred.

Lexi replies: Can't wait to meet him!

They spend ten minutes waiting on the corner of Great Christopher Street. Iris is wearing a floaty white dress and Sam can't keep his hands off her. When Iris spots Lexi, she untangles herself.

That's her, she says.

I figured, Sam says, watching Lexi cross the road. Don't get me wrong, she's attractive, but from the way you go on I was expecting Cameron Diaz.

Iris giggles and hushes him. Sam makes a mock-sombre face. When Lexi draws level, she kisses Sam on both cheeks. He offers to help with her bags.

Merci beaucoup, Lexi says.

So, Sam says, as they start walking, were the French as rude as ever?

Have you been? Iris says.

Oh, sure, Sam says, though his jaw tightens. He walks ahead of them, making a path through the pedestrians, addressing Lexi over his shoulder – I was young though, so I don't remember much. I was nuts about the Eiffel Tower.

I needed a break from New York, Lexi says. And with Brexit, who knows – she shakes her head – anyway, I barely checked my emails – once or twice a day, tops. I dropped in at Ladurée for you, Iris – rose and pistachio – they're in my bag. Iris hugs her, which slows down their walking – Parisian rudeness has a *quality*. I appreciated the history, the richness of the culture, so much more than before I moved here. Little things, like the attention given to ingredients. The wine. And the *bread*. So *un*-American. I stopped to buy milk on the way back from the airport, and all you can buy is a gallon. The human body does not need milk *by the gallon*.

We got through it quick enough growing up, Sam says. If you've got three or four kids you want to buy a gallon.

Lexi smiles politely. Do you have brothers?

Have you seen *Cheaper by the Dozen*? That's basically my family. *Cheaper by the Dozen does Texas.* Nah, I know what you mean with the bulk-buying – we're a pretty embarrassing country. Supersize Nation. Of course, bulk-buying saves time for things more interesting than trips to the store, but I guess there's not much romance in that.

We have exactly the same number of hours in the day as Barack Obama, Lexi says.

Lexi listens to a lot of podcasts, Iris says, reaching out and squeezing Sam's hand. He pulls it away, which Iris sees Lexi register.

Eh-oh, he says, we're running a little late. I don't want to lose the reservation, so I'm gonna walk on ahead, give you gals some time to catch up.

He puts his hand on Iris's waist and kisses her. Iris thinks he will look back, but he doesn't and she watches him get absorbed by the crowd, face hot with a mixture of pride and shame.

My, Lexi says. What a grown-up.

How old is Fred again?

Forty-three and in his prime, thank you very much.

Iris has spent most of the day trying not to imagine this evening, and she's quiet as they walk, listening to Lexi talk about how satisfying it was to do daily things with Fred, like drinking coffee in the morning. Iris wants to pour water on this, though she doesn't know why.

Right. I mean you couldn't do that together in real life, because his wife makes him breakfast—

We had a balcony, Lexi says, ignoring her. The only bad moment was when he called his kids to say goodnight. Which may not sound that bad, but it was every night. He's a good father.

Nope, Iris says. That sounds pretty bad.

All right, Lexi says, sharply. I'm not *proud* of it.

They don't talk again until just before the revolving doors, when Lexi catches Iris's arm – I locked myself in the bathroom and turned on the taps. I know how it sounds. But I'm not the married one. And I'm not naive about him. If it wasn't me, it would be somebody else.

When Lexi comes back from the bathroom, Sam hands her a menu with an easy smile, though Iris is hungry and irritable.

So, what's good here, he says.

The waiter comes over and starts reading out specials from a small notepad. Sam holds up a hand. What can you tell me about this wine?

He puts his finger on the menu and the waiter stoops to read it with evident disdain. Iris takes advantage of the moment and her own embarrassment to talk quietly to Lexi – Sorry. I wasn't trying to make you feel bad.

So, Lexi, Sam says. My dad was saying that it's been a tough few weeks for the markets. Though I cannot tell you what that means for all the gravy in the world.

Iris snorts into her water glass at this latest in Sam's series of Americanisms she hasn't heard.

Seinstein patented, Sam says, nodding to her, appeased. You're welcome.

His crudeness strikes Iris, again, and she is charmed by it. Lexi looks back and forth between them, smiling uncertainly.

231

Yeah so, Sam says, reaching for the bread basket. I'm trying to imagine your day-to-day at Goldman but I can't picture it. Iris and I are just sitting around writing or trying to write. I got as far as watching *Wolf of Wall Street* on Netflix. Where are the Quaaludes, that's what I want to know.

I'm not sure how helpful that film was for the industry, Lexi says. She tears a piece of bread in half and leaves the second half in the bread basket.

Oh, I didn't mean to be critical. That was a dumb comparison.

God, this bread is good, Iris says, they must make the butter, have you tried this? Lexi is used to it, right? People get pretty mad about her job. We lied about where she was working for a while.

It's not forever. I want to be able to send my kids to private school one day and pay for it myself, and I want to buy my dad a Porsche. That's it.

I respect that, Sam says.

He's always made a joke out of wanting a Porsche, but he's been making the same joke since I was seven, so you know. They worked their whole lives to pay for my education. It's an immigrant family thing – Lexi smiles, quickly, at Iris, and Sam looks confused – I know people think I sold my soul, but I don't have a vocation like you guys.

I'd sell my soul in a heartbeat if somebody wanted it, Sam says.

What are your plans after the MFA?

Sam has an agent, Iris says, quickly. He's all set.

My dad wants me to join the family business, Sam says to Lexi. He is aware that he hasn't mentioned this to Iris before, but if it bothers her, it doesn't show. She is refilling their water glasses, lifting the jug with both hands.

That's great, Lexi says, what industry?

Real estate, Sam says, making a face. My parents are pretty successful. I mean, my ma is the receptionist, but whatever, the family has done well. It's a heartless empire. He looks embarrassed. You don't want to listen to this sad little rich boy *nonsense*.

Before their food arrives, Iris excuses herself to the bathroom and steals a hand towel. She makes it as far as the door then turns back and folds it into the pile of unused towels. On her way back, she pauses next to the kitchen, watching their table, trying to imagine the impression she'd have if they were strangers. A champagne cork pops somewhere in the restaurant, and Lexi's first meeting with Ezra spills into her mind. When she returned to the table, Lexi had rolled her eyes – I'm glad you introduced us, it's not like our paths would have crossed otherwise, but seriously – look.

Ezra was trying to catch grapes in his mouth.

He's been doing that for five minutes. He has yet to catch one, Lexi said.

Grapes hit his nose. A few went rolling on the floor.

Sorry, he mouthed at other tables, Sorry. Look! he said, seeing Iris.

Lexi catches sight of Iris hovering in the doorway and waves. She looks more relaxed, their food has arrived, and Sam is refilling her wine glass.

When they hug goodbye Lexi says into Iris's ear – You deserve someone who knows how much you're worth. He's clearly besotted.

Iris thinks that she is about to add more, but then Sam hails a cab and holds the door open.

Au revoir, à bientôt, blowing kisses.

They wave until Lexi's cab is out of sight. Uber, m'lady?

I'm happy walking.

We don't want those legs getting tired.

I'm okay.

Iris looks up at Sam, so pleased with how it has gone. There is something unsettling in seeing Lexi managed so efficiently. She shakes the thought loose and slips her arm through his. They pass Washington Square Park and Iris points to a dark line of hedges – Isn't it that way to the station?

It is the first time she has known the way home. Sam takes a bow to the hedges, to a homeless man and says, High five! Ladies and gentlemen. She's getting it.

4

Two weeks before school is due to start again, the apartment is full of the smell of the hot-dog stand below the open window. Sam leans against the wall next to his desk. He stands there for a moment with both hands behind his head, like he's looking into the blueprint of the building. Then, he punches the wall. His knuckles make a sad cracking sound, and if Iris hadn't been watching she would not have heard. As it is, she cries out, and Sam doubles over, clasping his knuckles.

What the hell was that?

Sam doesn't answer her – he curls and uncurls his fist – it wasn't a full punch but he is pissed off by how much it hurts. Iris opens the freezer for ice and wraps it in a tea towel.

That's not going to help anything, she says, hurrying over.

No shit. He lets her hold it on his hand for a few seconds, then he pulls away – I need some air.

Give me a minute, I'll find my shoes.

By myself.

Are you sure?

Sam is tying his shoelaces like he's lynching his feet. Iris sits down on the floor next to him and touches his leg – Do you want to take the ice with you? What happened?

See for yourself, he says, lifting his chin in the direction of his laptop. He grabs his jacket on the way out.

Iris sits on the floor as dusk falls and reads the email. Sam's agent has rejected the extract he wants to send to Graywolf Press. You're fixating on the surface. This is all too writerly. Where's the energy of the first draft?

The apartment is dark all day but it gets the sunsets. It takes longer for Iris to get up than it should.

That evening, Iris suggests they watch *Good Will Hunting*, and makes herself cry in case Sam wants to, but he is expressionless, even when Robin Williams says, It's not your fault. He's silent as the credits roll. When he goes to brush his teeth, Iris runs her hand over the wall. It's only a faint mark, like it has been scuffed by moving furniture. She hears water rush into the sink and sits down again.

Sam's shirt is brushed cotton and it's soft against her face when he kisses her. He is sheepish and won't meet her eyes. They sit on the edge of his bed, and Iris rubs his shoulders and talks as if she could be talking about anything, and if he chooses to tell her that it is her problem, and telling her this helps him, she'll take it.

I know it's not where you want it to be yet, but I'd love to read your draft. I don't mind either way. But it would be good for me to use my brain. She moves to the knot beneath his shoulder blades. *Or*, if you need a reader with an English accent I might know the girl for the part.

He nods and she kisses his cheek. Sitting behind him, she wraps her legs around him – Right, she says, settling down, happily. Let's make a plan. What is the first thing you're going to do tomorrow.

She walks him through the day until he can see it. Once Sam is asleep, Iris checks her email. Nance hasn't spoken to her since Piers. Iris called once, but Nance hung up. In June, Nance sent her an article about the deal Theresa May struck with the DUP, but there was no reply. Iris assumed she was on one of Nance's mailing lists. She is still awake when Tina and Lynn stumble in at 2 am, drunk, dropping their keys, giggling and telling each other loudly to *be quiet*.

Sam is already at his desk when Iris gets up to make coffee. He has cut himself shaving, and something about the plaster, and his embarrassment when he sees her, pleases her. She tiptoes around the apartment, cleaning things that are already clean. She makes them tuna sandwiches for lunch. That afternoon, she wants to watch the VICE documentary about Charlottesville, but can't find her headphones, so she goes into Sam's bedroom to watch it on her laptop. She closes the door behind her and turns the volume down to one bar.

She's ten minutes in. White men are baying in the streets, some march holding torches. Jews will not replace us, they chant. Whose streets? Our streets.

Does it feel good then? Sam says.

Iris is transfixed by the crowds chanting White lives matter and Sam's tone is so even that for a moment she doesn't register it's directed towards her, that he's talking to her through the door. She hits the space key. Sam? Are you talking to me? There's no response, only the pipes banging.

Sam?

He doesn't turn around. He puts his pen down and repeats himself slowly, like they've been over this: Does – it – feel – good to have your theories about America proven right.

Iris studies the back of Sam's head and tries to configure the moments leading up to this. Her mind is blank. She watches herself pad over to him and wrap her arms around his neck. A different outfit would be better, a silk slip, a negligée, something soft.

I had some wonky views about Americans, she says, until I met my American. She strokes the back of his head, rhythmically.

After a moment his shoulders slump. Ah, man, sorry. I'm being a dick. School starts in two weeks. I should be further along. I can't screw this up. I don't want to be the guy who only has unfinished projects. And you're pretty distracting. Paul's going to be so smug – his piece of shit manuscript has been accepted. Conrad's going to be unbearable. All this Charlottesville stuff is a goldmine for him, fucking gonzo journalists.

You don't have to tell anyone how it's going. Why don't we go to the park for half an hour? Grab a hotdog?

Sam sighs. No. I have to focus.

Iris has been writing more lately, if only because when Sam takes breaks he says – So how's it coming along. She is just rereading notes, playing at working, but in the evenings she shows Sam the fragments and he reads them avidly, making suggestions in careful pencil. Sometimes when he's done reading he puts the work down and presses the heels of his hands into his eyes like he's trying to process her brilliance – Jeepers, he says. Have you *read* this?

She feels warm when he says things like this, like he recognises something living in her that she had long ago resigned to death. Where his own work is concerned, Sam gives into despair easily. Keeping him from it gives Iris's day an arc; tension and relief. It's not that he loses his temper. In a way it would be easier if he threw his tennis racket, like Nadal. It's more like there's a storm gathering, but that's all Iris knows. Like she's standing on a wide open plain, and she feels a shadow pass over. It's cooler, but otherwise barely perceptible. It's a shift between tectonic plates, a shift where normal conversation suddenly acquires a subtext and there is nothing safe to say. There are fault-lines on the floor. Keeping up with their shifting makes Iris feel awake, alert, vigilant. The only one who can defuse the suicide vest. More and more, she can anticipate what sets him off, and steer him, gently, away. For Iris, the hardest thing is Sam's helplessness within his moods; she can see his fear of their occurring. He has lakes of anger inside him. Mostly, he keeps them at bay, goofing around – he stays near the shore – but it is like a dripping tap, that has been dripping for generations. When it passes, he is exhausted, like he's been temporarily possessed by something darker, hardwired, which he cannot throw off by himself. He's in therapy, but it's not that effective because he cannot believe how gullible his therapist is.

It's okay, Iris says. Of course you're on edge. You have a deadline in two months. It's normal.

Thanks for reminding me.

Sorry, she says. He touches her shoulder to show he forgives her.

Sometimes, they joke around about it. They're sitting side by side on the couch watching TV and Iris clinks her beer against his – wouldn't it be great if a little sign appeared above your head when I'm pissing you off, like the blood-loss gauges on video games.

I'm not used to dealing with all these feelings, he says, half in self-parody, half not. I wasn't like this before I met you. You can ask around, I'll give you the phone numbers.

Iris likes this idea of herself, causer of tempests. She sits cross-legged on his sofa watching Sam move around the room, aware of the power she has to calm him down. She plants ideas in his head, she prompts him. She copies out extracts from books he hasn't read, so that he won't feel threatened by her having read them. Where before his confidence and direct way of talking were appealing, now he has hidden depths too. He has raw talent, but no sense of how to look after himself, no self-discipline, so when Iris drags him outside for a break and he feels better, he is amazed.

This whole fresh air and water idea is working out gangbusters, he says.

On the good days, Iris feels like the words filling Sam's laptop screen are hers.

Today, though, none of her tricks are working. She has hay fever. Her breathing is loud. Sam doesn't want to open the windows because of the stink of frying onions, but there isn't enough oxygen in the room.

Here, Sam says, handing her his headphones.

Thanks.

She sits on the sofa behind Sam and watches the documentary with subtitles. A bald man is telling the reporter about race. We're talking about whether white people are capable of violence, the journalist says and the man she's interviewing waves it away: I didn't say capable, he says. Of course we're capable. I carry a gun, I go to the gym all the time, I'm trying to make myself more capable of violence.

Iris watches the line of Sam's shoulders over the laptop. He isn't typing. He adjusts the brightness on his screen, scaling it up and down again. After twenty minutes, he goes outside to smoke and when he comes back in he is tense, as if daring her to comment. Iris frowns at her laptop. Just write something, she thinks, anything, write your name. Then she worries that he might hear her and tries to stop thinking too.

She checks her emails compulsively, but there's nothing from Ezra. All summer, he has sent emails with attachments and no messages: a film of a topless man pouring a mandala on the sidewalk in LA, a clipping of Calvin and Hobbes, a *Peanuts* cartoon. She didn't reply. Occasionally he sent a non-personal anecdote: Did you know that when Morrison went on the Ed Sullivan show, he was asked to change the lyric *you know we couldn't get much higher* to *you know we couldn't get much better*, and then during the performance he sang the original, and then the show's producer said the Doors would never do the Ed Sullivan show again, and Jim Morrison said, Hey man. We just did the Sullivan show.

Iris didn't reply to those either. Then, one Thursday, on WhatsApp:

Ezra:	We have a gig in Brooklyn tomorrow if you're free.	16:20
Ezra:	Or if you want to hang out the day after? Here till Sunday evening . . .	16:26
Iris:	I haven't just been sitting around waiting for you.	16:46
Ezra:	That's good.	16:48
Iris:	Why are you asking me the day before.	16:49
Ezra:	I didn't want to tell you in case it fell through.	16:50
Ezra:	So given how unlikely it is that you are free tomorrow on such short notice, then if this works out it must mean – what's the word you use?	16:51
Iris:	Kismet?	16:52
Iris:	Screw you.	18:00

That evening, Lexi invites her to a School of Life talk. The auditorium is warm, and Iris falls asleep while the speaker is talking.

Afterwards, the air has cooled a little. Women in twos and threes pour out of the building around them. As they walk down the steps, Iris pulls on her cardigan.

So, you liked Sam?

Mmmm, Lexi says, checking her phone. I like how happy he makes you. She sees Iris's face and puts her phone away – Don't get me wrong: he's charming and good-looking and attentive—

Okay, Iris says, pulling her sleeves over her hands.

But would you go out with him in London?

Would you have an affair with Fred in London?

Lexi goes a dull red, and Iris notes, with pleasure, that she isn't pretty when she's annoyed.

I just thought there was something phoney about him. Like, why is he trying that hard.

That's just the way he talks. He's trying because he really likes me.

He kept talking over you, Lexi says.

Iris is suddenly furious. Not once has she pointed out to Lexi what an almighty mess she is making.

I was quiet because I wanted you guys to get to know each other, which was obviously a mistake. I'm sorry he doesn't meet your standards.

Well, he wasn't actually invited so, Lexi says, then exhales deliberately. If he makes you happy, I'm happy.

I am happy.

They walk in silence for a few minutes, before Iris bursts out – I was *miserable* before Sam. I've started to feel like myself again. I don't know what the fuck I'm meant to be doing. Ezra keeps making offhand comments about me going on tour, and where we might live one day, as if we have this whole future together but never directly, never in a way I can hold on to. He hasn't even said he wants me to come home.

Okay, okay, Lexi says, softly. She points out a baby in a sun hat and both girls stare at it impassively before walking on.

So, Sam's okay with the whole Ezra situation?

Iris turns to wave at the baby though it isn't looking at her. I'm writing again, she says.

Writing isn't everything.

Yes, Iris says. It is. She brushes away tears, angrily – Christ, I'm hormonal. Did I tell you about this guy on the course who was obsessed with moon cycles? He had this app on his phone, like that one which tells you which song is playing. He'd say, we're in the sub-lunar phase, or whatever, and I'd be like, Bassey, every girl in the room is bleeding. We are literally the moon.

Lexi smiles but she doesn't take the bait. Iris isn't sure how to navigate away from the topic. For a spiteful moment she wants to ask about Fred, but then Lexi steers the conversation away from men.

After dinner, she fishes in her bag and then pulls out Midol and hands it to Iris.

It helps. You shouldn't take it while we're drinking though.

Iris pops four onto the tablecloth and hands back the strip. Lexi rolls her eyes but doesn't comment. They smirk at a first date at the next table where the girl is saying that is *so* interesting, that is so *interesting*, and running out of intonations. With one of her bursts of enthusiasm, Lexi starts telling Iris about her dream sabbatical in China, studying public spaces, communities – obviously the main reason the population is dropping is because increased feminism and aspirations for upward mobility don't leave much appetite for kids. I read this article which seemed pretty far-fetched, but still interesting, which drew out another thread – young people have no privacy. We think it's bad here, but in China the young people have nowhere to go. What do you think? What makes Europe different?

In general?

In terms of birth rates.

Alleyways?

Iris is joking, but Lexi nods, thoughtfully, as if this is a serious suggestion and Iris is relieved by the size of Lexi's world, and grateful to be at the edge of it. They finish eating and order a second bottle of wine. Lexi is flushed and looks more herself again.

You're a terrible influence, she says.

Honestly, my tolerance has gone up with the antidepressants. More alcohol required.

Lexi sips her wine – That's a very American way of looking at it. Uppers, downers.

Tell me another way.

Lexi takes a mouthful of food and then puts her cutlery down again – Goldman has these amazing policies where if you have a breakdown and you need to take time off, they pay you in full.

I didn't have a breakdown.

I'm just saying, some environments are conducive to poor mental health.

Iris takes a forkful of food off Lexi's plate – You know, people think artists aren't as ambitious as bankers, but we're worse.

Art collectors are the worst.

We worship different gods, that's all, Iris says, gulping wine. We make blood sacrifices. You have incentives. Sam's there all day tap-tap-tapping away, but then at least he has an agent. You know, Paul has sold a manuscript? *Paul!*

Later, on the sidewalk, when they have both lit cigarettes, Lexi brings up Liderman again. Iris takes a drag and looks up at the bridge they stand under.

Maybe it wouldn't do any harm to talk to someone else, Lexi says.

Yeah. I don't know. Sam pointed out that the pills were meant to be an interim measure – the side effects are pretty grim. And things are different now. I didn't have a proper support network before.

A train clatters over the bridge and Iris watches its shadows, then spits onto the street. Lexi waits until the echo of the tracks fades, then says, What did you just do.

My mouth tasted bad.

That is so unattractive.

Sam taught me.

You know, he likes it when other men find you unattractive.

Oh, come on.

It's true, Lexi says, evenly. In the same way, your getting fat means you're less likely to leave him, as one day, he already knows that you will.

When Iris tells Sam a version of this, later in bed, he grins and scratches his stomach like he's been caught watching porn. She stops what she is doing to stare at him – Are you serious?

That Lexi, he says. Oh, c'mon, you know she's just winding you up.

5

On Saturday, at 5 pm, Iris picks Ezra up from the subway outside the Lincoln Center. He doesn't kiss her, but he hugs her so hard she thinks her ribs might crack. They go to Vanguard. They talk on the way, but Iris cannot look at him. She woke up in Sam's bed, and though she went back to her flat in the afternoon and scrubbed herself with salt in the shower, she can feel the prints of Sam's hands, his mouth, so viscerally that she is sure Ezra will too. She imagines lipstick smudged on Ezra's stomach and it makes her defensive. They have both slept with other people. She is no better than him and no worse. Are they equal?

Ezra tells her that they have started taking the clocks down in the studio, like Fleetwood Mac.

You know, he says, perking up – when they were writing *Rumours*, there were two massive break-ups going on—

– and Stevie Nicks was furious because her ex Lindsey Buckingham sang that line about her wanting to shack up with him. Said it was all she wanted to do.

Ezra mouths the lyrics along with her and then says drily, Well, it's official. I've turned into my father. You've heard all my stories but I keep telling them anyway.

This slightly ironic way of talking suits him. They're sitting facing the bar, but he turns towards Iris, and begins to relax. Dolly has asked them to stop making things up in interviews because reporters don't realise when they are joking.

Ndulu is still pissed off about the name change, so he keeps calling us stupid names like L(0)tus Gigolo – Ezra draws lunulae in the air, like air quotes.

Do that again?

He repeats the sign, visibly relieved to be teased. Journalists, he says, shaking his head. Have you had a chance to listen to the new songs? You've probably been too busy, he adds, hastily.

They're great, Iris says, and feels him sink a little – No, honestly. They are. Your voice sounds different, that's all. Like it couldn't exist without technology.

Ezra pulls a face, embarrassed but dismissive too. It's sort of over-produced, he says, but it gets people dancing.

I'm so proud of you, she says, squeezing his arm. She apologises and blusters into her latest salt discovery, an Indian fairy tale. A king asks his seven daughters how much they love him. The eldest six say as much as sweetmeats. The youngest says like salt.

Ezra nods, but he looks preoccupied. Why are you apologising?

Iris watches the bartender shaking mojitos. She cannot look at him in case there is recognition there, in case this is something Ezra has been trying to tell her for years.

I think sometimes I talk in a way that can seem like I'm talking down to people, she says.

He looks perplexed for a moment, then shrugs.

For what it's worth, it's not something I've noticed, he says.

Iris asks about the new album, not really listening. When she tunes in, Ezra is talking about a new song, about the cryosphere – The cryosphere?

The cryosphere! From *kryos*, the frozen sphere of the earth; all of the frozen water, and the permafrost, which is the soil that has existed below freezing for extended periods of time. All the glaciers and nilas and floes.

You can't just make up words.

Keep up, he says, clicking his fingers, maddeningly. Why aren't you writing them down.

I'm taking a break from that, Iris says. She gathers her hair over her shoulder and inspects it for split ends.

It'll come back, Ezra says, briskly, and they're real words. I'll send some stuff to you.

Iris picks up the salt shaker and pours a little onto the counter. Ezra gets out his debit card and starts cutting lines of salt. She doesn't know if he realises what he is doing. They talk for an hour in an abstract way. She is mesmerised by the care he takes in making lines. It makes her think of Japanese rock gardens. She has the sensation that they are talking in a private way, which both understand implicitly; not everything can be said and incorporated in the moment, some things need to remain coded; then she notices how fluffy Ezra's hair is in the light of the bar, the few grey hairs. He looks tired.

Your tagline should be Iris, he says, quietly. Living life by adjacent possibilities.

Iris sees herself fragmented; one of her lying in the bath, blowing foam from Sam's chest; one helping Tess with dinner; one on Skype with Nance, drinking pink gin; one still at Oxford; and one where it has always been, with Ezra.

She tips back her head against the gravity of the tears. This isn't what I imagined, she says. Ezra sweeps the salt into his palm and pours it, carefully, into his empty glass.

It is still light outside. Iris hasn't checked her phone for three hours. As she is getting it out of her bag, Ezra fixes his gaze on the green street sign and says, I know it's complicated. But when the time is right, I'm confident that you'll fall in love with me again.

6

They had agreed to meet at 9 pm at Dive Bar, but Iris doesn't get there until 10 pm.

Sam has his laptop but all the chargers are taken with people's iPhones. He's been drinking all day, only beer, but he's tired. He has a crick in his neck from working on his bed. Iris didn't reply to his texts except to say sorry running late! When she turns up, she is glowing, like she has spent the afternoon in the sun. She kisses him like they haven't seen each other in months. She shows him her bag full of clean clothes and the $80 from babysitting.

I'll buy you something pretty, she teases. She asks a couple at the next table if they'd mind her charging her phone.

Sam says, Tina had some douchebag round last night. I was *this* close to banging on the wall.

Same guy?

How should I know. We didn't exactly share waffles in the morning.

Did you get what you needed to done?

I don't want to think about it right now. It's the weekend.

They talk for an hour or so, with Sam getting more drinks as they finish them. He tunes in and out of what Iris is saying. It doesn't seem to bother her that he doesn't talk much, like he's an extra in her movie. He checks his phone but that doesn't stop her either. He starts testing what he can do without stopping her talking and grows increasingly resentful. It's like she's having a conversation with herself and he's the pivot point. Like bouncing a ball against a wall. Iris to Iris and back again.

You know, I've been thinking about Nance a lot, and neither of us was blameless. I'd write to her, but she'd probably tear it up or send it back covered in menstrual blood or something. I want to say, Look, Nance, the fact is, no one came out of that night covered in glory—

Sam puts his arm around Iris's waist and gives her a little squeeze – Babe, has it occurred to you that Nance is bored of listening to you talk?

Iris freezes for a moment, then digs out the compact she carries in her purse and looks at it with a strange intensity, as if to check her reflection is there.

Sure, she says, voice bright. What were you drinking?

When she gets to the bar, she hesitates and then walks straight past it. The door onto the street is wedged open. It is almost midnight, and dark, but Sam can see her through the window, and she knows it. He watches her tap a stranger on the shoulder. After a few minutes, he hears her laugh, and her voice cuts through the traffic.

Can I light it myself? It's my favourite part.

Sam feels his insides contract. He can hear her voice get higher-class – she rings it like a bell. He should record it, he thinks, play it back to her. Sam gathers up his things and goes outside. The man talking to her is older, pale, telling a story about some loser in his office—

But at the end of the day, that's the quid pro quo of modern life. That's what I tell myself every day. We pick what to give up, is what I'm saying – the man glances at Iris, but she doesn't introduce Sam. Instead, she touches the man's arm and says, And then what happened?

For a minute or two, the man tries to regain his footing,

then yawns. I better be getting back. It's a school night. Nice talking, he says, nods to Sam and goes inside.

Cigarette? Iris says, sweetly.

You have my pack.

Iris lights one off hers and hands it to him. He smokes it while she leans against the wall, smirking. When they go back inside, the noise of the bar is draining away. Their table has been taken by a couple making out, so they hover by the bar. Sam looks up at the TV screen, thumbing his chin like he's trying to rub off dirt.

I don't think you realise how you come across, Sam says. It's embarrassing.

How do you mean?

It's embarrassing to be so visibly desperate. People feel sorry for you.

Iris flinches. She puts her arms around his neck and tries to make him look at her. Sam undoes her arms and pushes her away, and Iris stumbles a few steps back, catching her hand on the metal edge of the bar. She yelps and clutches it.

It's just the nail, she says.

Jes – us – Christ. Sam fishes ice from his glass and holds her hand in between his.

It was an accident, she says.

What can I do? I'm sorry. I've had too many beers. What do you need? Do you want Tylenol? Do you want a pony?

It is one of their bits, but Iris doesn't laugh. She watches the barman lining up clean glasses on the bar.

I know you're having a hard time, she says, stiffly, but you said you didn't want to talk about work. I was trying to dis-tract you.

What? Sam says. When?

He shakes his head like he's trying to follow, and she's moving too fast for him – I thought we were having a pretty nice time tonight, and then you're out there – he nods toward the window, and she turns to look, as if watching herself.

What do you want to drink?

I'm fine, she says. Thank you.

He comes back with a beer and a cocktail with a fancy straw which he puts down next to her. The couple leave and they reclaim their seats. Sam takes Iris's fingers and blows on them, then lifts her hand, to point at the screen. Trump again, with subtitles. There's a delay and his words appear beneath the newscaster. There was blame on both sides. I've condemned neo-Nazis. I've condemned many different groups. But not all of those people were neo-Nazis, believe me. Not all of those people were white supremacists by any stretch.

I wasn't flirting, Iris says, quietly. I'm sorry if I seemed to be. I didn't mean to.

Sam nods, but he doesn't say anything. For a few minutes they watch Trump, then her hand slips into his lap. It's late, she says. Let's go back to my flat.

I'll have to leave early, Sam says.

That's okay.

In her flat, Sam drops his bag and says in disbelief, You have air conditioning?

He laughs though, and they wrestle, briefly, then settle on Iris's bed, noses pressed to the window.

Sam is naming the constellations – Big Dipper, he says. North Star. Arcturus.

Iris wriggles beneath him, and he rests his chin on her head. They're still for a moment.

You've never asked me to stay at yours before, he says, quietly.

Yes, I did. You said *All my shit is at mine.*

Nice try. I'm on to you. You didn't want to share the air conditioning. They kiss for a while and then she pulls away – What?

Nothing, she says.

Tell me, he says.

She laughs into the sheets like she's trying to smother herself. I wish it could always be like this, that's all. With us.

And you're always like this? Sam says, digging his chin into her shoulder. Can you blame me for getting a little gun-shy?

She points her fingers into a gun and shoots down the North Star. Sam unwinds them, gently, and then less so, stretches their bodies into winged creatures. He pulls her knickers to one side and watches her face in the window.

⚹

A week later, on the afternoon of the eclipse, Iris stays in Sam's flat and pulls the thin curtains closed. He invited her to watch with people from school, but she didn't want to.

It's weird that it's not at night. I imagined it at night.

She messages Nance on WhatsApp: I know things have been weird since Piers, but I really need you right now.

It is her second day without Effexor. She is tapering properly this time. Sam watched her unscrew the capsules and tap half of the beads down the sink, then hugged her so tightly her toes left the floor. I'm so proud of you, he said. And it won't be that bad this time, I'll look after you. You're perfect the way you are, au naturel.

253

Iris tells herself the crash is only chemical. She sits on the floor in the middle of the room, so that she can see the door and all of the windows. She messages Ezra again and props her phone up against the wall, so that she can check the reality of his texts and the mark on the wall at once. It's become a habit, like checking the door is locked.

Ezra:	I haven't seen you like that for a long time,	14:45
	before realising it's you I mean. Across the square.	
	I saw you and felt something like transcendence.	
Iris:	When are you coming back?	14:45
Ezra:	I'll let you know as soon as I know. Remember	14:46
	your magic glasses!	
Iris:	I told you, I'm staying indoors. I won't be able to	14:46
	resist looking.	

Two minutes before the eclipse is due, she messages him again. Ez? You better hurry up. Because I think the world is ending.

7

September. Hurricane Irma is leaving reluctantly, dragging leaves across the sidewalk and pulling at the edges of skirts. Iris sits on a bench, watching children pelt around the playground near Wetherby-Pembridge. Two boys are competing in throwing rocks. Double Dutch is going on, but none of the girls can do it, they step into the centre of the swirling ropes, then someone gets hit and starts crying. The nannies have a way of telling when it's serious. When it is, one of them materialises and carries the screaming child to the benches that box in the playground. The other nannies don't talk to Iris. They sit in twos and threes and swap gossip about their bosses, eating out of tupperware containers hidden in bags from Tiffany's, from Saks.

A woman in a purple head-wrap with a bold pattern thrusts Jack at her. She doesn't look happy. You want to keep an eye on this one. Thinks he's a big man, bullying the girls.

Iris takes Jack's hand from her, coldly. Once they're out of earshot, she hisses at him. Where's your sister? When did you get out of class?

Hours and hours and hours ago, stupid.

That isn't nice, Jack, Iris says. She can't keep the hurt out of her voice.

Why isn't it nice?

Because.

Why?

I don't know.

Because you're so stupid, Jack says.

Go and get Lacey. Now.

She watches him amble towards the swings where Lacey is holding court and brushes away tears. He is six years old. She wants to clutch the hands of passers-by and ask – did I use to be like this? But nobody here knows. If Sam were there, he would goof around, make Iris laugh, win Jack over. Kids love Sam.

He has been back at school for two weeks. Iris only has to work on Fridays, so she drinks coffee with him in the morning, then dozes fitfully until she's ready to start work. He leaves her his debit card.

Get whatever you need, he says. There's this new vegan cupcake place that Lisa has not shut up about, he says, then he winces as if he has been insensitive. He kisses her forehead to make up for it and Iris submits; she doesn't know how to convey how little she cares about school.

You know, I've spent more time with the cast of *The Office* than with Lisa, she says.

British or American, he teases. I'm telling you, he says, ducking the pillow she throws at him – the only difference is yours are uglier and less satisfied.

Iris wishes, more than anything, that she could call Nance and hear what she would say about this, something sarcastic, something brutal.

Watching Lacey and Jack come running over feels good. They have to hold hands with Iris on the sidewalk and she tugs unnecessarily hard on their arms.

Keep up, she says.

Marie never made us walk too fast and Marie can make toe-rings, Lacey says. And Marie has a boyfriend.

Iris bites her tongue. Sometimes there are mummies and daddies and sometimes there are open relationships and then, Lacey, we get what grown-ups call a clusterfuck.

And Marie wasn't *stupid*, Jack says.

At 79th, Iris waits for the traffic lights to turn. She is dizzy. It's only the third day, she reminds herself. It's probably still in her blood.

This is the hardest bit, babe, Sam said. You're doing so well.

Now, looking at the determined figures crossing the road, Iris thinks, those children are too young to be out on their own, before realising they are hers, and let loose. She goes running after them.

On Monday, Iris gets woken up by Tina and Sam, bickering in the corridor.

She's not dying, Sam. It's not *leprosy*. She needs to see a doctor. And I don't know if you got the memo, but she's not paying rent.

Iris hears Sam's voice, and it sounds dangerous but quiet. She can't make out what he is saying. She looks at her phone – it's 7.30 pm. It's dark outside. She has slept all afternoon. Sam opens the door, swinging a paper bag, which he puts down to hug her.

There she is, he says.

His coat is cold from outside and Iris shivers.

There's a new Thai place on the corner, he says, switching the lights on.

Perfect, Iris says, blinking. She hasn't talked to anyone all day. Tina is slamming around the kitchen. Everything okay?

He pulls off his shoes and gets into bed, fully dressed – It is now. What are we watching?

Iris peels the lids from the food and places the containers between them. He hands her cutlery. They watch two episodes, eating. He warms his legs between hers. Iris gets sleepy, and protests when he gets up to go to the kitchen – you stay exactly where you are, he says. Iris watches the blunt figures move around the screen.

He comes back with two glasses of water, which he puts on the bedside table. He is looking at his phone, and Iris mistakes it for hers.

When were you planning on telling me? he says.

Her throat constricts before she realises he is teasing, and she has to tamp down her heartbeat as he continues – I heard someone in the area was getting a whole lot of poison out of their system and needed fro yo, stat.

He hands Iris his phone, and silently, she chooses white chocolate, strawberries, miniature mochi.

Atta girl, he says.

They watch another episode. When the buzzer goes, Tina yells, Not me, and Sam kisses Iris's forehead. He comes back with tubs and unwraps the plastic spoons.

On days when Sam doesn't have class, he writes by himself in a bar. He comes in around 11 pm, smelling of whiskey. There is a moment when, listening to his shoes clunk off in the hall, Iris experiences a rising dread, combined with irritation at being disturbed, though she is living in his bedroom. She hasn't told Sam that she has started writing again, it never seems the right time. Index cards covered in salt are singing under the bed. Even before he opens the door, she knows they are shaping up to have the same argument. She can tell by the way he takes off his shoes and by her own strange pitch

258

of vibration. She is fretful, though he hasn't done anything wrong.

Sam says he doesn't want Iris to go back to her flat during the day, that he wants her there, that he likes thinking of her there, in his bed, but then he doesn't seem pleased to see her. In the beginning, he asked if there was something wrong, but she was tearful, clingy, unable to explain her mood. Then he stopped asking. They ate the pizza he brought in bed and watched Netflix. She stayed quiet until he had time to unwind. If she could stick it out for an hour, Sam became himself again, and reached for her like a milk-drunk calf.

Whenever Iris didn't want to sleep with Sam, she stared at the pinprick of red light on the smoke alarm and pretended it was a camera. There was something in the heat of Sam's body, his shaves-twice-a-day testosterone, that took away second thoughts, that stilled their vibrating. He was fluent in filth and loud in his appreciation. He told her everything he loved about her body and how he was using it. She became a different kind of object at these times. He pumped her up against the headboard, and when he touched her, she came in a mechanical, shivering way that threatened to extinguish her. Sex, she realised then, is nothing to do with loving. Instead, a sickening rush of pleasure like cigarette smoke in the morning, and then she was gone. She was no one. She was nothing. Yes, she wanted it that way, she was glad it was happening, the slightest move from her made him groan. She observed her body like a rock on the floor. Not an object any more, a nonentity.

Watching it from high above, glistening, desirable, she admires it – she should win awards for these performances, and when she thinks of how good her performance is – she comes, over and over. It is like morphine, their fucking. It gives her a break from herself, then it gives her body back to her.

Oh Jesus, he says, clutching her. Oh God.

8

She's just come back from the library. It's 2 pm, and she wants to clean the apartment before the others get back. She opens her laptop to put on Ezra's latest song and sees an email from Nance. She sits down on the sofa in her coat to read it.

05.10.17 12:35
From: nancyomalley@magd.ox.ac.uk
To: irisirisiris@gmail.com

Btw — and I don't want to talk about it — but I finished with Piers.

I realised he'd been writing down everything I said for his stillborn second tome. He's totally washed up. Also, I found a book called *She Comes First* in his bedside locker. We both know that never happened.

Have you read this? I never trusted the man. But seems like the sort of thing that would happen to you. A business breakfast . . .

https://www.nytimes.com/2017/10/05/us/harvey-weinstein-harassment-allegations.html

Shakespeare in Love used to be one of Iris's favourite films. Nance will have remembered this. Iris writes a bitchy WhatsApp message about Nance's secret love of *Emma* then deletes it. She clicks on the link and reads the article about Harvey Weinstein. Then she reads it again, glares at the wall for a second and messages Nance.

| Iris: | Obviously, I'm doing something wrong. | 14:35 |
| Nance: | That's not what I meant. | 14:36 |

Iris reads the article again, bitterly. So this is what Nance thinks of her. What has Nance ever actually done? What has she risked? It's easy to have theories about people if you don't engage with them, if you move them around like chess pieces.

Yes it was, she types, and hits send.

Sam says there's no point in cleaning, but Iris wants to win Tina around. The other day when Tina was watching *Say Yes to the Dress*, she said a vase full of cabbages arranged to look like roses was cute. Iris went to Fairway's and bought a bunch, which she put in a vase, but the stems were too heavy and they toppled over. She closed her eyes for a moment then found a dustpan and brush. She swept up the broken glass, slowly.

All Tina ever says to Iris is, um, excuse me, like Iris is in the way no matter where she stands.

Iris is quickly disheartened by how squalid the flat is. Tina and Lynn work in events and most nights they eat out. Still, Iris thinks, Tina is pretty disgusting. Sam is careful in looking after his appearance, his clothes, but he doesn't clean. He sprays Febreze on his sheets, but he's frank about it. Tina has perfect nails, hair extensions, and is a secret slob.

Iris cleans the kitchen and the bathroom. She takes the cushions off the sofa, attacks it with the nozzle of the vacuum cleaner. She finds Special K, bottle tops, a few nickels, a pair of earrings without backs. She takes breaks to lie on the floor and listen to Björk instead of Ezra. When she goes to hit play, again, she has another email from Nance.

From: nancyomalley@magd.ox.ac.uk

To: irisirisiris@gmail.com

That wasn't what I meant, but I'm not sure what I did mean. Perhaps that I can imagine you being so embarrassed for the man in that situation, that you wouldn't say anything in the moment. Not that you'd actually enjoy the wanking, of course. But that having to acknowledge it would seem a further violation [of yourself].

I'm meant to be on my second draft, but all I can think about is tattoos. You know Dorothy Parker had a star on her elbow? Disappointing.

See below. Copyrighted to me, you understand. Try it on your forehead, so you'll see it in the mirror. Permanent marker recommended.

YOUR COMFORT MATTERS MORE THAN HIS DISCOMFORT

Iris writes it on her forearm with a Sharpie and takes a photo of her arm against the table. The photo is creepy, like a discarded limb. She writes a message, but there is too much context to explain. She sends the picture without it. She scrubs her arm in the kitchen sink. She eats cereal, standing up.

That evening, Iris curls up on the sofa with Sam. Tina has brought home leftover wine from an event, and the atmosphere is unusually light, chatty. Weinstein is all over CBS and Iris and Tina swap dire anecdotes in ironic tones until Sam wants attention and then Tina turns back to Lynn and her office drama. Tonight, Sam is letting Iris look at the first few pages of his novel. He sits next to her while she reads. When Nance pops up on Skype, Sam tickles her.

Shit, do the paparazzi know she's here? When Iris doesn't pick up the call, he says, What are you waiting for?

I won't be long, Iris says. She takes her laptop into Sam's bedroom and closes the door. She messages Nance on Skype.

Nance:	Word on the street is that the circus is in town.	19:21
	I had no idea you two were talking again.	
Iris:	Hi!	19:26
Iris:	I'm at Sam's right now so I can't really talk about it.	19:26
Nance:	You're on a screen, the man isn't psychic.	19:27
Nance:	Can we Skype like normal people? With video?	19:27
Iris:	The wifi is shit.	19:29
Nance:	FINE. Is it because you're still in your pyjamas?	19:29
Iris:	I haven't been well. Flu. Sam has been waiting on	19:31
	me hand and foot. He makes real hot chocolate	
	with a little whisk. Irish hot chocolate, obviously.	
Nance:	Do you remember that guy Jim on the undergrad?	19:31
Iris:	I don't know any Jims . . .	19:32
Nance:	Yeah you do . . . the feller whose ears were too big	19:32
	for his head. Pitch-black hair. Writes surrealist plays.	
Iris:	Oh, yeah. What about him?	19:33
Iris:	This is like Tess texting to tell me a celebrity has	19:33
	died. (Roger Moore, so sad, he's only 30 years	
	older than me.)	
Nance:	He's been accused by a singer – Kate something.	19:33
	She was in the year below, in choir, I thought Ezra	
	might know her.	
Iris:	of rape?	19:33
Nance:	Did you just type rape question mark?	19:34
Nance:	Everything but.	19:34

Iris:	Have you spoken to him?	**19:35**
Nance:	I hardly know the man. He's one of your arty literati.	**19:36**
	It's brilliant, everyone is talking about it. He got	
	asked to leave someone's birthday party.	
Iris:	Poor Jim.	**19:37**
Nance:	Praying for sarcasm, knowing there's no God.	**19:37**
Iris:	No, obviously if he did then that's awful.	**19:38**
Nance:	You are literally siding with a rapist.	**19:38**
Iris:	You said it wasn't rape?	**19:38**
Nance:	There's not a hierarchy of these things.	**19:38**
Iris:	Said no rape survivor ever.	**19:39**
Nance:	When you're correcting systemic violence, you	**19:42**
	use all the firepower you've got. Women have not	
	been believed for all of time. If a few innocent men	
	get kicked out of parties, so what.	
Iris:	Parties might not matter but sending innocent	**19:44**
	men to jail does. You can't punish people for things	
	they didn't do.	
Nance:	Only one third of rapes are reported to the police.	**19:44**
Nance:	In the US just 6% of rapists get arrested. Less than	**19:44**
	1% get a felony conviction.	
Iris:	But why would I believe a second- or third-hand	**19:47**
	anecdote from someone I don't know about a	
	friend that I do? Giving all the power to any one	
	group because they are in that group is just stupid.	
Nance:	In the UK 1 in every 10 rapes reported reaches trial.	**19:47**
Nance:	Can I see you please, this feels like msn.	**19:50**
Iris:	Ha! I love msn. If I never have to have a Skype	**19:52**
	conversation again, I'll be happy. I have to go –	
	Sam's made us dinner. Soon.	

Iris has started throwing the duvet on the floor, so that she's less likely to get back into bed. She is meant to be helping Lacey and Jack make Halloween costumes.

You're a creative, figure it out, Melissa said. We want something that represents our family's blend of diversity and personal style.

When, in the thrift store, Lacey said in horror, Are these dead people's clothes? Iris worried her thoughts had leaked through her skin. She scrubbed Lacey's hands with Purell. That night, she looked online for costume ideas and copied and pasted suggestions from Mumsnet to Melissa: Elsa from *Frozen*? Rapunzel? Dorothy from *The Wizard of Oz*?

I was thinking more like a sari, Melissa replied.

Iris sits on the sofa, watching YouTube videos on how to tie saris. Sometimes she goes to the St Agnes Library on Amsterdam. This isn't a secret, but she hasn't mentioned it to Sam yet. She doesn't know how to explain finding it. On days when he has workshop, she has started taking the subway to areas where nobody knows either her or Sam, and losing herself. She writes in Irish pubs, and drops what she writes at Ray's flat, and opens mail. If she writes at Sam's flat, she tears what she has written into little pieces and puts out the trash.

Sam's first workshop of term didn't go well. Iris found this out when he dumped the stack of annotated manuscripts in the bin. He pulled out a beer from the fridge and started telling her about it. She half-listened, and kept reading about Weinstein, scrolling with her little finger.

And then Finn said our society has evolved past satire. That the market for dystopian fiction is hyper-saturated. Can you believe that?

He opened a beer for her and put it on the table. Iris took a sip. It was ice cold, and she held it against her forehead. She hadn't realised how hot the flat had got, she had been inside all day. She thought of lobsters, boiling.

Can I open a window?

Sure, do what you want. I might hurl myself out of it, but whatever.

Iris stayed half out of the window for a moment, looking straight down into the street. The cars looked like toys. Sam came up behind her and put his hands on her hips – Hey there, he said. She ducked back through the window too quickly and cracked her head on the frame.

So, here's a question, she said, resting her hands on his chest, as if nothing had happened. Which fictional character do you most identify with?

Sam let go of her and retrieved his beer from the table, glancing at her laptop screen.

His films are so overrated. Have you ever tried to really watch *Pulp Fiction*? He sighs. Obviously, you've already decided who I am. So, go on.

That's the thing. I have no idea. Gatsby is the closest I can get and that's more to do with sales pitch than anything else.

I'll take that as a compliment.

It is, she said, quickly.

I guess that makes you Daisy.

Daisy is blonde though, right? She has to be. Iris blew down the neck of her beer and it made a low fluteish sound. Do you have a copy? I want to check. I'm not sure it's in the text.

Nerd alert, he said.

He got out his laptop and started working in a way that made it clear they were done talking. Iris followed suit, and after a while she stopped glancing up to check on him. After an hour, he said, I'm beat. I'm going to get an early night.

He came back into the room in his boxers and offered Iris the NyQuil pack – they tended to split the strip, but she shook her head.

Okay, but don't keep me up later, he said.

Now that he is snoring, Iris can think about what she will tell Nance. She combs their first extravagant dates for the details which will make Nance jealous. She wants Nance to be impressed by Sam but confused enough to keep her at a distance. He calls me Daisy, she will say. He goes to the gym every afternoon and drinks milk from the carton. He owns a big foam finger and collects baseball caps. I was going to start running again, and he said, You don't need to, you're already gorgeous.

Oh, and you'll love this. The other day, I had a meltdown because I couldn't get my hair untangled. A comb broke in it. I just couldn't. It was wet and matted and I kept thinking about dead people's hair in drains. So I got back into bed with it, dripping, which was bad enough, but then Sam got freaked out because I kept saying, *Like a corpse bride's hair*. He booked me into a salon a few blocks away and walked me there. He sat in the waiting area reading *GQ*. He bought me a conditioner with avocado in it.

What Iris will not tell Nance: how sometimes, in public, she floats up out of her body and notices how loud Sam's voice is. Or how, when he explains her behaviour, her motives are clearer than she has ever experienced them, but she does not recognise

268

herself. She admires the girl though, how she holds back to make other people do the work, how she manipulates people to get what she wants.

You do this when you're flirting, he says, imitating the way she holds herself. You do this when you are lying.

She tells Sam that Nance would make short work of him.

But she's so teeny, he says. I can handle her. Besides, I only like to get a rise out of you.

9

It's November when Sam finally gets the email from his agent. He has been waiting for it for weeks. It is so cold outside that the windows keep steaming up. Iris is cooking. She has bought lilies and groceries, fresh bread.

Sam puts his laptop down on the coffee table and says nothing for a few beats.

Guess which guy you're talking to, he says.

Iris tries to sound ironic, but her voice is too high. Might it be you?

The guy whose pages Graywolf *loved*.

As Sam gets up from the sofa, Iris marvels at the transformation, his expression taken over by a pure, fierce happiness. He stands behind her, hugging her, then puts his hands over hers and chops onions with her. There is a dent in his chest where her head fits when she tips it back against him.

So, do I get to read the whole thing now? I'm so proud of you.

Sam lets her go, and Iris curses herself inwardly. He opens the fridge and gazes into it. She is about to apologise when he says, Tell you what though, I'm exhausted.

But worth it, right?

Let's go out for dinner, he says.

While he gets ready, Iris covers bowls of ingredients with clingfilm. She says, into the fridge – hey, while I remember – I have to go home next weekend, to my flat I mean. I have a family thing.

Do what you gotta do, Sam calls back.

They go to Mel's Bar. Sam is doing the Brew Crew challenge – he's only got seven more beers to go – they stamp your card each time you try one and there are forty stamps to collect. Iris drinks vodka sodas and watches him drink pale ales and porters the colour of treacle. Sam goes up to get the drinks and comes back frowning, his eyes on the TV screen behind her. They're playing a montage: late-night show hosts and comedians talking about Louis CK.

Are we losing?

Oh, no, Sam says, sitting down. I've gotta say, I feel bad for the guy.

Iris glances at the screen and goes back to reading the menu, following it with her finger though she has the same salad every time. It's not that she has been avoiding talking about #MeToo exactly. Ray calls and brings it up after two minutes and thirty seconds, which is when he usually reveals the purpose of his call. He asked if a younger colleague wanted to share a cab and then issued a disclaimer, because you can't be too careful these days. He is keen to demonstrate his engagement.

You're not even on Twitter, she says.

I can still see accounts, he says, defensively. He seems unwilling to let it drop. I can't believe how many women have these stories, he says.

I'm surprised by the uproar. I thought everyone knew already.

I certainly didn't, Ray says.

Well, you wouldn't, she says. Would you.

Lexi got called into Human Resources because of an email Iris sent at 2 am:

I just read this thread where all these women are decrying #MeToo as victim mentality. As if acknowledging the shitty things that men are doing makes you a victim. Like being strong means literally how much you can take.

WHAT THE FUCK IS THAT?

WHAT THE FUCK IS THAT?

WHAT THE FUCK IS THAT?

Lexi asked her to delete that email address and use the Hotmail account that Iris knows she keeps specifically for her family in Slovenia, because otherwise they take up too much time when she's at work. Iris was ashamed. She started to tell Sam the story and then realised how out of control it made her look and diverted – I sent her a link to a lingerie website. It's pretty filthy.

Sam liked that. He had reacted badly to the subway incident last year, which Iris had only told him because Marcie overheard her telling Lisa.

I don't know where you girls are hanging out, but this is not a world I recognise, Marcie said, like they must have been mud-wrestling on the platform to provoke such a response. Iris had thought Sam would find this amusing, as she had, but he looked stricken.

Was it when I was with you? he said. Was I there?

No, of course not, Iris said. It probably wouldn't have happened if you had been.

I am so sorry you had to go through that, Sam said. I would have knocked him out.

Iris was taken aback by the vehemence in his voice. It disoriented her, irritated her, even.

272

Don't be silly. It wasn't a big deal.

Then she felt guilty, like she hadn't earned the apology – she hadn't mentioned her skirt, or the fact that she didn't move away, and if she did, then Sam might take it back.

Girl, you're a New Yorker now, was Lisa's response, before Marcie delivered her verdict. They were in the computer lab before class. They stayed idly checking emails, trading horror stories of middle-aged men who said Jailbait, until they drove Marcie out of the computer lab. One time, I was coming back from Coney Island late and there was only one guy in the carriage. And he fully dropped trow, Lisa said. Iris had felt lighter – the train was just another incident they shared and could laugh at, like getting catcalled or flashed or bullied at school. That day, Iris belonged.

Seriously though. It's getting out of control.

Iris followed Sam's gaze to the TV. Who do you feel bad for?

Louis CK. What he did is creepy, but it's not like he raped anyone.

Iris nods, slowly. I know what you mean. But it's a pretty low bar.

Sure. And it's weird that he's been doing it so long, and that nobody reported him, but it's also kind of pathetic. He's just this guy, getting his dick out.

Iris watches the waitress explaining Brew Crew to a table of men and tries to catch her eye. She isn't planning on saying anything, but tweets keep popping into her head. All Alyssa Milano's tweet said: If you've been sexually harassed or assaulted write 'me too' as a reply to this tweet. Half a million people responded within twenty-four hours.

How would you feel if a female writer asked you for coffee, and you went along, excited to be in her presence, thinking maybe she'd read your work, and then she started wanking, Iris says. She gives up on the waitress and turns back to Sam, who is grinning. Forget it.

Aw, c'mon, I'm kidding. It depends who it was. But sure, it'd be off-putting.

To be honest, there are loads of writers who could do that in front of me and I'd just sit there, Iris says, stabbing the lime in her drink.

In fairness, Louis CK did *ask*. He didn't just whack it on the table.

The waitress comes over, and they order and hand back their menus. Sam holds up his Brew Crew card and she smiles. You should do the Flower Power next, it's my favourite.

Sam looks at Iris, who drains her vodka soda and nods. She'll have that, Sam says, and I'll do another of these. He looks back to the TV. I'm just saying, this #MeToo stuff is pretty faddy.

I think it's been around for ages? Tarana Burke started it. In 2006, maybe?

I was reading about this guy, Brian Banks, who went to prison for five years because some girl at his school said he raped her. She got $1.5 million, and his life – Sam snaps his fingers – over.

How did he prove that he didn't?

That's the whole thing though, he couldn't. That's why she got away with it.

How did they prove she was lying though?

Oh, Sam says, dismissively. She confessed and he recorded it.

That's terrible. But it's so rare.

Their burgers arrive. Sam bites into his, looking sceptical. I know plenty of guys it's happened to.

Personally? As in girls have accused them of rape or actually pressed charges?

Sam chews for a moment, then grins, like he's just remembered – I meant to tell you earlier. So, Dad emails me this morning. Subject line: Consent. Message: Get in writing.

Iris doesn't smile. Sam sighs and puts down his burger. It's about due process. The fact is that there are some girls – and I'm not saying all of them – who set out to ruin the lives of innocent guys.

Iris picks up a French fry and then puts it down again. Maybe that's not the movement's fault, she says, hesitantly. Because it's a reaction to the problem, right? Not the problem itself. Like, if someone attacks you and you break their nose, the crime is still the attack.

Sam looks bored. He pulls an onion out of his burger. Pretty sure you would still get sued for that, he says.

Iris tries to let it go, but she can't. What gets me is the arrogance of Louis CK using his abuse as material and knowing that nothing would come of it. He had audiences of women laughing at the *sad man*; they were on his side.

Sam laughs but there's an edge to it. He puts his hands up as if she's pointing a gun at him. Okay, okay, he says. We don't have to watch his stuff on Netflix any more.

When they get home, Iris turns the kettle on and opens her laptop. Louis CK is trending. A twenty-one-year-old journalist has tweeted: So what if some innocent men go to jail in the process of dismantling the patriarchy? Totally a price I am willing to pay. Iris doesn't agree with that, but she scrolls through the replies, envying their conviction.

@ChrisStillon I bet you thought the Salem Witch trials were a hoot.

@USApatriot69 liberals = fascists

@NationalistMags What a MAN HATER. Somebody clearly has "daddy issues"

@Davedreson As a Black Man that knows the legacy of Emmett Till and countless other black males that we've lynched over an accusation, I implore you to reexamine your viewpoint.

@thislonelyroad You make Jesus cry

@TinyDeplorable Feminism is cancer. What's your husband's name so i can falsely accuse him

Iris promises herself she'll only scroll down to the end of the scroll bar twice more. At the bottom, there's an image. It seems like a natural stopping point and she clicks on it. It is a yellow poster with black letters: #himtoo.

She hears Sam yawning, and closes the browser. When she turns around, he is standing in front of the sofa, smiling at her.

You're looking pretty pleased with yourself, she says, turning off the desk lamp.

What can I say, it's been a good day, he says.

He leans back against the sofa and undoes his fly. She watches him, her eyes tired from reading. She isn't sure whether it is some kind of meta-joke, whether there's a punchline that she is missing. She notices the lillies, how heavy the pollen is, how Tess would have cut the stamens out.

See? he says, grinning. You could just walk away.

When Iris thinks about this later all she will remember is how he tasted sour and how her knees kept slipping on the floor.

10

God, I miss this, Iris thinks, watching him split a gram of MDMA between four bombs and twisting the Rizla paper carefully.

Rub this on your gums, Sam says. He wants her soaring. She was away for the weekend at some family thing and he had not expected to miss her as much as he did.

On the way to the gig, Iris finds eight lost treasures, as she calls them, and runs to catch up with Sam, to present him with her gifts. Sam just sees the pale pink tulle of her skirt before she jumps on his back. He tracks the beauty Iris sees, and in the fourth, a twig with winter buds so yellow, he feels himself coming up. He pockets a twisted piece of gum, toothmarks intact.

Thank you, he says.

Midsummer Night's Dream, Iris says, accelerating, meets Harajuku girl. Harajuku girl in a *Midsummer Night's Dream* forest.

In the line, Iris starts panting, and begs him to check her heartbeat – I feel like everyone's looking at me, she says. She looks at the bouncers. My pupils keep doubling or my eyes – shimmying – Sam, am I safe?

You're not what the police are after. It's the guys you'll attract they're looking for.

He pulls her chin up and looks at her eyes. She is wearing blue contacts, almost turquoise. He thought they would be creepy, but he likes it. She looks like an alien. As they walk past the bouncers, Sam feels himself getting bigger and bigger, his fingers more solid with hers, clammy, clutching. She trails after him, but people notice her first – she marks him out.

You're going to heaven, kid, he says. Just do what I do.

Rushing, she is jet-atom black and fleeting, she is velvet, she is Titania. She texts Nance to crown her Puck and Nance replies Puck goes at five miles per second.

When you realise everything is connected, you'll see the tissue, Sam. It can't be broken, only lived and played around – Iris would sing if she knew music sweet enough. They are on the same astral plane, she will reach down to him – Come, play! And next could be anything, always melding, breaking, but not shattering; no ending. New stories are not revisions are not endings. He played here too, Ez, you know Ez, do I? She shakes her head violently. But I'm not scared any more, no need, no need, because it never – Iris prances under Sam's arm – The third dimension, the poet said, Sam: God, space for more more more: that's you, the third dimension! And there is nothing he can do to stop her – nothing anyone can do because she is born to astonish, that kind of creature; marmalade eyes pixie-cropped kind of creature – the chrysalis of fake alive she's been trying to breathe in shattering—

Cold water sprays his jeans dark. Wrist firm, Sam holds her head under the faucet. She ground her jaw so hard, couldn't even hear him. Loud, so loud, he needs the noise to stop. She will be fine, just has to calm down, she is hysterical. He waits for bubbles, pulls her up and Iris comes up drowning. Gasp, dripping hands slap the edge of the sink wet. Gold chipped nails look more metallic, more mineral than the taps.

Iris, he says, I was worried, are you—

She slaps him away like one of those girls in those films she watches, those black-and-white ones, and he catches her wrists in his hands like he knows he should. Except she isn't like them, she claws. And it stings more than it should. Bitch. His Iris isn't this girl with her pupils flooded.

He seizes the back of her neck where the hair curls under – how he learnt to pick up kittens as a kid, won't hurt her. He turns up the faucet, and she shrieks as he pushes her under.

Sam, I'm sorry, she splutters, and he swears, pulls back as the water continues to spray, until he is soaked and she means it, I'msorryI'msosorry. Please, I'msorrySam.

Sam makes tea and takes it to his room. Iris is lying on his bed. She looks peaceful. He wishes that he could just sit there, for as long as he wants, while she stays sleeping. He can't tell how she will be feeling when she wakes up, or how that will make him feel. He covers her with the duvet and her phone falls out of her boot. He expects her to have a password, but she doesn't. He goes through the last few months, mechanically. He isn't surprised when he finds old photographs, new texts. Endless playlists.

Sam scrolls, the obviousness of it settling around him like a fog. He has never been able to hold the whole of her attention. He made himself chalk it up to her personality. He can imagine her laughing at him with Lexi – she has done everything in plain sight. She has made a fool of him, has had nothing but contempt for him from the start. He, the one who has been so good to her.

When she wakes up, she smiles at him sleepily – It's you.

Sam hands her the phone with Ezra's email open. Iris goes very still, then touches her cheek, where her jaw must be aching, she ground her teeth so hard. She says nothing for a moment.

Why did you look at my phone. It's private.

She says *private* like it's a curse, with all her breath behind it. Sam is surprised by the steel in her voice. He is expecting her to cry, the whole performance, some flaky explanation. Right on cue, she puts her head in her hands.

It's not that I love him more, she says quietly. It's that I loved him first.

𝚡

For the rest of November, Iris spends more time at her own flat, as if by leaving and coming back, she can push a reset button. Now, she wants him to come to dinner with Lexi. Now, she'd love to go to the party, whichever party. Now, let's go to the park.

Sam doesn't have a pretext for blowing up now because he doesn't need one. Whatever he says to her she sits very quiet and very still. The rest of the time, though, she is even clingier, like a dog that he keeps kicking. Sometimes he is disgusted at himself for these thoughts but mostly he is taken aback by their accuracy and writes them down. When he mentions that he's meeting up with Nick and the guys, she jumps at it.

I love those guys, she says.

You met them once. But sure. If you want to tag along, whatever.

At the party, Iris is less repentant, like having people watching gives her some kind of licence. She knows the people who work at the bar by name. She is acting single, people are buying her drinks. Sam watches people he has known for years spill their guts to her.

Hold on to this one, an ex-girlfriend says.

Your girlfriend is messy, Nick says.

After an hour, he pulls her to one side and says, Let's go.

She snatches her arm back – if you wanna talk about it, let's talk about it. We don't have anything to hide from our friends, right, Sam?

He opens his mouth to reply, and Iris runs outside. After a few minutes, Sam follows her and sits down next to her. Iris gives him a look that he cannot read. She goes back inside and all the girls who have ever been fucked over by a musician buy her a shot. Sam waits until she blacks out and carries her home.

Iris wakes up, refreshed, rolls over to kiss Sam. He sits at the end of the bed, already dressed. He has been watching her sleep. Water rises in Iris's eyes, ready to spill.

He'll let her wait, until she chooses to remember last night.

He hears her say, Sam? I'm sorry. I'm so sorry. He pushes her away and takes his time lacing up his shoes. Please don't be mad at me, she says.

It doesn't matter, he says. You were drunk. I need to get some air.

Whatever I said, I didn't mean—

Of course not. Because things just *happen* to you, right, Iris? Nothing is ever your choice.

Iris calls after him as the door bangs. She pulls on leggings, a sweater, and runs after him. An elderly couple turn to look. Sam slows down and stares at the sky.

Please, Iris says. Tell me what I did so I can fix this.

Iris:	Sorry I haven't been able to talk! It's been so busy. Sam has got a deadline soon. He's going to dedicate it to me :-)	21:55
Nance:	Don't worry about it. I have another chapter due on Wednesday.	21:55
Iris:	How is it going?	21:56
Nance:	I got the latest on your man.	21:56
Iris:	He is literally not my man.	21:56
Nance:	According to your man Jim, nothing happened. He tried to hook up with her and she kind of brushed him off but she seemed into it. There was a house party and they shared a bed, which was her idea. She has a boyfriend though, which she told him, but after she suggested the bed sharing, he tried it on again.	21:59
Iris:	Is that it?	22:00
Nance:	Isn't that enough?	22:01
Iris:	Well it's not rape is it.	22:01
Iris:	Also – if it's the crowd I think – that's a bit much. Trying to get with someone who doesn't express much interest is their modus operandi. Throwing Jim out of the circle isn't going to help.	22:02
Nance:	Why are you always protecting the men?	22:03
Iris:	I just hate hypocrites.	22:04
Iris:	Also, if persistence is assault then most of the men I know are rapists. So if anything is going to change we need a better model.	22:04
Nance:	We have laws against sex with children and every now and then someone is wrongfully accused. But, as a society, we rate maintaining the norm we've chosen as worth that sacrifice.	22:06

Iris:	But there's no right way of having sex with children.	22:06
Nance:	. . .	22:06
Iris:	I mean that it's an easier norm to maintain because it's a black-and-white area. Sex isn't. Two people can experience the same situation differently in a moment. People misjudge things when drunk. Mixed signals, ambivalence, etc. There's a lot more to take into account. I am *so sick* of everyone pretending complex things are simple. That's how you get to Trump.	22:09
Nance:	If I said to you, I'm going to make a cup of tea and you said um not sure, maybe, and I made you a cup of tea, and then said, Go on, you know you want the tea, I've made it now, it's getting cold, etc.	22:10
Iris:	That's a ridiculous analogy.	22:10
Nance:	It's not though.	22:10
Nance:	You still there?	22:17
Nance:	Can we try something if I promise to drop it afterwards.	22:20
Iris:	Cross your heart and hope to die?	22:20
Nance:	Daily.	22:21
Iris:	I can't sleep anyway. Sam isn't back yet. He has this thing about proper ice cubes, so he's probably stopping off.	22:25 22:26
Nance:	Have you ever had sex that you didn't want to have?	22:26
Iris:	. . . *typing* . . .	22:28
Nance:	?	22:30
Iris:	. . . *typing* . . .	22:31
Nance:	It's a yes or no.	22:32

283

Iris:	You're actually enjoying this.	22:32
Nance:	You should at least be honest with yourself.	22:33
Nance:	(1) Have you ever had sex that you have been too drunk to consent to?	22:34
Iris:	Y	22:34
Nance:	(2) Have you ever wanted to withdraw consent but gone along with it because you were worried about the reaction? (anger/resentment/ignoring)	22:35
Iris:	Yes.	22:36
Nance:	which?	22:36
Iris:	Yes. Yes. Yes.	22:38
Nance:	(3) Have you ever wanted to withdraw consent but gone along with it because you feel there's a point of no return and you have passed it, or because you didn't want to hurt somebody's feelings.	22:40
Iris:	Obviously.	22:40
Nance:	(4) Have you ever had non-verbal cues ignored by a sexual partner e.g. pushing away	22:41
Iris:	Yes.	22:45
Nance:	(5) Have you ever been groped, catcalled or masturbated towards in public	22:45
Iris:	Yes.	22:45
Nance:	(6) Have you ever had a direct no ignored	22:46
Iris:	Am I going to be a source for a study?	22:56
	Your ethnically-diverse-mentally-ill-would-stay-in-a-room-with-Weinstein friend.	22:59

It's 5 pm and Iris and Melissa have just picked up the children from Wetherby-Pembridge. It's getting dark. When they turn onto 81st, the sidewalk is full of people shoving them back the

284

way they came. Over their heads, Iris sees a group of men brawling in the road. She hears the slight rhythmic grunting they make, fighting, and the jeers of the men on the sidelines, egging them on. Police are blocking off Columbus with plastic barriers. A police car comes screaming through the gap and shoots straight past. Iris looks into the faces passing, but no one seems to know what is going on.

Let's go around, I don't want to get caught up in this, Melissa yells. She grabs Lacey's hand and hurries towards the barrier. Iris quickly loses sight of her. She picks up Jack and holds on to him tight. She cannot take her eyes off the heap of bodies or make herself walk past.

But it's a Tuesday afternoon, she says, dumbly.

It's going to be okay, Jack says.

He starts burbling about his day at school and Iris spins, slowly, around. She can't tell whether the people hurrying past are running away from the fight, or whether the panic is spreading like a gas. Jack starts crying with his mouth open, in a terrified animal way that scares Iris too.

It's getting pretty nasty, a man says, drawing level. There is a cut on his forehead. His shirt is covered in blood.

Iris's heart is thudding in her chest. Jack is so light. She could drop him. His skull would crack on the sidewalk. She turns and walks back towards Central Park.

We're going to take the long way back, okay, Jack, just to be sure.

Jack's chest is heaving. He clamps both hands over his mouth to stop himself crying. Iris tries to tell him that he doesn't need to, but he doesn't seem to hear her. She tells him to breathe.

She walks one block, then two, glancing over her shoulder

only once and seeing a man on the edge of the circle pulling back his foot to kick a man on the ground in the face.

Iris takes Jack for ice cream, though he is shivering. She doesn't know another way back and she's scared of running into another fight. They both get double vanilla cones, but Iris doesn't want to stop moving, so they walk round and around the same block. Jack's face is sticky. As he calms down, Iris does too, though her voice is still high and anxious. He listens, solemnly, to a senseless mishmash of all the salt stories she knows.

When she peers around the corner of 81st, the street is deserted. There is a dark patch of blood on the road, which Iris rubs with her shoe, to check that it's real.

Bad guys, Jack says.

It's five thirty when they get back to the flat, and Melissa is standing outside, clutching her keys. A vein pulses in her neck. Iris tries to put Jack down but he clings to her.

I'm sorry, Melissa. That was mayhem. I panicked. I thought it would be better—

Melissa takes Jack out of her arms and says, icily, Check your phone.

Iris does. Her hands are shaking. She has seven missed calls. Oh God, she says, I'm so sorry.

The journey up in the elevator is tense, in part because Lacey keeps stage-whispering things like, That was very naughty of Iris, wasn't it, Mommy.

Iris gets their shoes off and gives them animal crackers. She goes into the study, where Melissa is sitting on a Pilates ball at her desk. She doesn't look up.

There's $40 on the dresser in the hall.

I really am—

286

I had no idea where you were.

Melissa holds up a hand as if to say any more would be dangerous.

On the way out, Jack hands Iris her phone. He has written I love you in green glitter and stuck a gold star on the back. That evening Iris gets a text from Melissa's husband saying, We have talked about it and we think your strengths lie in other areas. We won't be needing your services any more.

☥

On the first day of December, Iris leaves Nance a voicemail. Nance listens to it twice, but she can't make sense of it because Iris is crying. Nance messages Iris, who denies calling at all.

Iris:	If it was me, it must be really old.	23:06
Nance:	If you were hammered obviously I'm not going to judge you but I'm worried about you.	23:06
Iris:	We're stuck in this vicious cycle where he gets angry, and then I get mean and then he gets angry at me for reacting to him being angry.	23:10
Iris:	I feel like I'm losing my mind.	23:10
Nance:	Skype. Now.	23:11

It is the first time they have been face to face since Piers's bedroom. On Skype, Iris feels Nance seeing the whole night in her face, over again. She mutters about needing water and slips offscreen, and at this, Nance begins talking determinedly about a grant she's applying for to study Edmund Wilson's letters at Yale's Beinecke Library, raising her voice to be heard over the tap, as if everything is normal.

It would be next summer. I'd have to make up some shit about wanting to see the letters but they'd pay for the flights and everything, she says.

Great, Iris says, sitting down again. That's great.

Nance watches her sip her water for a moment then says, What would you say if I turned up on Skype in your state.

That's different.

You can't discount every experience you have just because it's yours.

It wasn't like that. He pushed me over a counter and I didn't catch myself.

Has he shoved you before?

No.

Bit of the old rough and tumble? Nance says sarcastically.

It's not like that with him.

So he's a clumsy bastard then—

Iris interrupts – he's amazing most of the time. I'm probably imagining it. It's the way he looks at me sometimes. He said I love you months ago, but I'm not sure he likes my personality. Half a smile twists her mouth, as if she is joking. Sometimes I think he hates me.

Because of Ezra?

It seems fair enough, I'm not nuts about me either. But so. Do you think this is a problem.

Let's not pretend that you don't know that.

I'm not sure he realises, Iris says, meeting Nance's eyes for the first time. I don't think he's doing it on purpose. It's partly how I am around him. It's both of us. It's like a mechanical trap.

I don't give a fuck what's going on in his head either way, to be honest with you, Nance says.

288

IV
We All Go into the Dark

January 2018

1

I am in the flat, eating Rice Krispies, when I see the helicopter footage of the Women's March and realise how close it is. I hadn't planned to go, but I grab my phone and head to Central Park West. When I get to the barriers, I hesitate, but then I imagine merging with the crowd, becoming one of the colourful dots in the aerial view. Whose streets? Our streets. No Trump! No KKK! No fascist USA. The people! United! Will never be defeated. I imagine lying down, being trampled, disappearing in the rush of bodies. I zip the winter coat Ray bought me for Christmas all the way up, over my mouth. The half-dose of Effexor is working. I feel more like myself, except for the aphasia. Other bodies are so close it makes my fingers curl, but when someone asks how far I've travelled, I can't answer. Say It Loud, Say It Clear, Immigrants Are Welcome Here. My Body, My Choice. Show Me What Democracy Looks Like. This Is What Democracy Looks Like.

I don't know how long we walk for. Whatever the loudest person shouts, I shout back, exhilarated, as if shouting is enough. I am a face in the body of the movement. I haven't messaged Nance to let her know that I've given in and gone along, I haven't told Tess. I don't have a sign. I called Ezra as I headed out. He was in Berlin, somewhere loud. He talked me through my fears; a lorry driving into the crowds, someone asking what I thought of last year's march, or challenging me on feminist theory. Ezra listened, then said, Maybe it's more like the Haka, like demonstrating you're a force to be reckoned with.

I press my lips together to keep I love you from spilling out.

On Skype, I tell Nance that I have been invited on a Black Lives Matter march and she looks bored. Her indifference annoys me. For a moment I want to challenge it, but I don't know what to say. She is scrolling through an article.

I heard the march wasn't very good this year, she says. Have you read the piece in the *New York Times*?

Yeah, it's terrible, I say, grimacing.

Nance smirks to indicate that she knows I am lying. I have read the article, but I can't remember the details, and Nance will go through it point by point if I feign knowledge equal to hers. My brain is still spongy, only retaining rooms, moods, impressions. I want to ask whether saying yes when you mean yes and no when you mean no could count as a political action, but with Nance the power I had felt in this seems childish and insignificant.

Ezra is going to be here for the blue-moon eclipse, I say.

Nance frowns. On the 31st?

It's the first since 1983.

The irritation passes over Nance's face so quickly that I think I have imagined it. She is always grouchy after working in the archives. Over Christmas, I stayed in New York, and neither of us made much effort to keep in touch.

What's the face for? I say.

You hadn't mentioned that he was visiting.

I found out yesterday.

Nance mutters something that sounds like *snaps his fingers* and I glare at her.

All I mean is that you've worked so hard to feel better. And I don't want him to fuck it up, she says.

Why would he?

She is reading a message on her browser and does not meet my eyes. No reason, she says. Just don't be hurt if something comes up.

I let the subject drop. We are still recovering from the argument we had after she sent me the piece about Aziz Ansari.

On WhatsApp, I wrote: Maybe he's just bad at sex?

Then I wrote: Think of all the orgasms you faked with Piers.

Then I deleted it and sent: What terrifies me: I reckon that it's possible for a man to believe that he's having consensual sex when actually he's raping someone. But then, when I imagine what it takes to force part of your body into a body that doesn't want you . . . it makes less sense.

Nance's only answer was that it was typical that I took the article as yet another cue to try and understand *the men*. I was hurt by the way she dismissed my attempts to be articulate. I read an anonymous post in the comments section by a woman who I imagined to be Tess's age. It used to be that any time she had a man over after dinner, for coffee or a drink, whether he was a friend or a colleague, he would try and sleep with her. Because of this, she became adept in a kind of erotic ju-jitsu. At some point he would pin her to the sofa, and she would push, gently, against his chest, twice, and then duck out under his arm. He would get up, and it would be understood that the evening was over. There was a choreography to saying no, a physical communication of consent or non-consent which everyone understood. I knew Nance would say that making it sound like a ritual dance was dangerous, and conveniently left out rape, but it mattered to me – that there had been ways of men and women understanding each other. I wanted it for myself, though I wouldn't

293

want it for my daughter. But reading about #MeToo had made me think that Nance's absolutes weren't the only way of talking.

Iris:	What if our only weapon (collective experience) doesn't work? What if it's all out in the open and condemned and then nothing changes?	16:24
Nance:	Then nothing changes.	16:24
Iris:	But then the only explanation will be that either a lot of people don't care what women go through, or that they think it's what being a woman is. I'm not sure what it would be like if they always respected our boundaries. I don't know how sex would kick off.	16:25
Nance:	If you can't imagine being a woman without having to deal with this shit then you're more cynical than I am.	16:28
Iris:	Trump got voted in after the pussy-grabbing. I'm just being realistic. But also, I don't want to be presented with a permission slip. I want the messiness, and the back and forth. What about chemistry? What about lust?	16:30
Nance:	Can you not set yourself up as the crusader for Eros? It's a bit much.	16:31

♟

I have been going to see Dr Agarwal for a few months. His office is on the Upper West Side, near 96th Street. It is full of books.

I mentioned him to Tess on the phone without thinking and she said, Agarwal? Oh, perfect. An Indian man telling you what's wrong with you.

When I tell Nance this, she says, I would have thought Tess would be up for that, given that he's one of your own.

But Tess would hate Dr Agarwal's overtly Western-educated way of speaking, all flowery vocabulary and American twang, as well as the tasteful blend of Indian art and American furnishings in his office. He falls into the category she calls *the last colonials*; not Indian enough for an Agarwal, too Indian to be anything else.

He asked me to call him Rajinder in our first session. I continued to call him Dr Agarwal. He was small, quiet, unassuming, and wore gold-rimmed glasses. I asked him whether he was a Freudian or a Jungian and he said I'm a Joy-di-an. In my first session, I lay on the couch, closed my eyes and said nothing. He sat not looking at me, but paying attention, like a conversation had started.

He grew on me over those first weeks. He told me I was too smart for therapy, which I liked. He didn't want to rush to diagnosis, but continued, gently, to say that medication combined with psychotherapy was more effective than either one or the other.

It's like putting on waterproof clothing before going on a ten-mile hike, he said. You might not need it, but you might, and it'll make the whole process more comfortable.

I start rating my mood on a scale of 1–10, putting black marks in my diary for the lost days. Days in which I watch less than six hours of television are still progress. I try to explain to Dr Agarwal that the last thing I need is further sedation. I try to explain how driven I used to be.

I don't run any more. I used to get something out of feeling bad, from pushing against it, like I was overpowering something.

Being able to do that made me feel strong. If there's a life raft in a sea full of sharks, you'll swim to it.

Do you want to spend your life in a sea full of sharks?

If the choice is between that or floating in a sensory deprivation tank, like in *The Matrix*—

He raises his pen to remind me that he has not seen it. He claims immunity to all pop culture references. He says that it is interesting that I use external references as co-ordinates for my internal state.

Not particularly, I say.

It's one of the ways you mediate your anxiety, much like your reliance on humour to distract people.

Does it work?

Dr Agarwal smiles patiently. Suddenly, I want to shock him. I say, the real reason I'm here is that I don't get the big hullabaloo about vanilla sex.

He pauses. What is vanilla sex?

I gaze at a dying palm tree, regretting it. Not kinked sex, I say.

What is kinked?

Really? What about your clients. Patients. Whatever. Someone must have the same problem.

So, you think it's a problem?

I watch him pick up a small blue water bottle and spray the palm in a gentle mist. The fronds sway and shiver.

All I know is that the only guys who are attracted to me are sadists. Which is fine when it's conscious, but when it's not it's something else.

So, you think you only attract men who want to punish you?

I did not say that.

Now I am thinking of Ezra and the sweet-salt taste on my

296

tongue, my face stinging. I touched my lip and marvelled at my wet red finger.

Let me see, Ezra said, holding my lip like playing doctor. Oh God.

It's fine, I said. It's the bit that bleeds easily.

He sat me down like I might need stitches. I am so sorry, you know that was an accident. I would never—

I pouted, enjoying my swollen sulk. You've done worse, I said. He looked like I had just slapped him. I quite liked it, I muttered. I'm sorry if you scared yourself.

That afternoon, he wouldn't touch me, as if to prove the excruciating point that he didn't need to. He stood, an arm's length away from me, naked and hungry-looking. He told me to change position. I did. It went on for hours.

I have never felt an object of so much wanting, I say to Dr Agarwal, or closer to anyone.

Dr Agarwal clears his throat. I notice the fan whirring, a hundred other microscopic sounds that are normally invisible.

You have given a lot of power to a very private world.

2

Nance and I agree that we will meet at Grand Central station at noon. She has research to do at the New York Public Library and can't afford an Airbnb. I want to see her, but I am wary. It has been almost a year since I have seen her face to face. I have got used to curating reality for her; I edit my messages, I use filters on photos. Without her here, I keep all of it at a distance. I am nervous about the intimacy of being around her.

I turn the shower on but I can't bring myself to step into the water. Every day, I get a little closer. I wash my face. I wear a summer dress sprinkled with blue flowers. It is humid, and by the time I get to Grand Central it is damp. There are no chairs free and I consider salvaging a newspaper from a bin to sit on, but I know that Nance will appear as soon as I stick my hand in. I sit down on the floor to check my email. Nearby a group of teenagers sit around with backpacks. I can't tell how old they are. Every ten minutes, a boy pulls a girl's hair and she says Dylan, I – am – going – to *kill* – you, and they get up and run round and around the signs. I sip from the two-litre bottle of Diet Coke next to me.

I check my email. I refresh my browser, but there's only a political newsletter I receive weekly and never read. Still nothing from Ezra. In January, after we slept together, he told me he was going to India to visit the Indians. I didn't hear from him for three weeks. I messaged him on WhatsApp: How was India x o x.

He saw the message. It got the green tick. I felt a lurch of hope each time he appeared online.

A few days later, he replied: It's impossible to describe. The people are so warm. I felt at home there.

A week later:

Ezra: We're playing Coachella! We have a gig in New York soon and I could meet you after?

Iris: Kind of weird not to offer NY tickets . . .

Ezra: Oh no sorry!!!

Ezra: I just can't imagine anyone wanting to come to the smaller gigs any more. Same set list.

It's March now and there has been nothing since. I take another swig of Diet Coke. I check my phone. It is 12.27. Nance's phone won't work in America and I have left my charger at home. I panic for a moment, but we have a system. Nance stays where she is and I run around searching. I find her by the whispering wall, her eyes sweeping the hall and back again. She doesn't like to be seen first, so I bawl her name across the station.

Well, you took your time, she says.

I hug her. She doesn't hug me back. This close to her, I can smell my own animal scent and I let her go, hastily. She is carrying two huge suitcases, one of which I take from her.

Have you got a body in here, I say.

Got to stock up on essentials, she says. Duty-free is mad at Heathrow.

She is wearing a necklace with a blue stone that I sent her for Christmas and which she didn't acknowledge.

Right, she says. Where's the nearest shit Irish pub.

This way, I say, beaming.

On 43rd, the traffic lights aren't working. I say we should

walk further down the road, but Nance refuses. I've been on my feet for hours, she moans.

You've literally been on a plane, I say.

That was before you abandoned me. And then I was on my feet, all alone, searching high and low.

I watch the traffic, waiting for the man next to us on the sidewalk to cross first. Nance walks straight into the road and the traffic stops. The man follows her. A driver presses down his horn and Nance sticks two fingers up and keeps walking. I dash after her mouthing *Sorry, sorry* at the van driver.

Nance waits until I draw level, then says, What, were you waiting for an escort.

I have a stitch and clutch at my side. Human shield actually, I say.

Nance opens my jewellery box, rubs the fake flowers in the hallway. She takes photos of the view from the window and unpacks methodically. Then she herds me into the shower.

You're the one who's been on a plane, I say.

The state of you though – she hands me a shampoo bottle through the curtain – you realise it's the shampoo that lifts out the dirt.

Now I know what it'll be like for your kids, I say.

The shampoo smells of synthetic watermelon foam. I have run out of everything.

Lucky little fuckers, Nance says. She puts the lid down on the toilet and I hear her sit down.

Look – in London. You shat the bed on that one. But it worked out because I couldn't get back in it after that. And he was an awful bastard. So. Thanks for that.

*

At first, I go through the motions of being a functioning person, but there doesn't seem to be much point. Nance likes lying around reading and then going out drinking. She starts calling up boxes of loose-leaf letters on the NYPL website.

You missed my whole Diana Vreeland phase, she says. She had this column in *Harper's Bazaar* that made suggestions like Why don't you rinse your blonde child's hair in dead champagne to keep its gold?

She glances around the apartment as if I might have a bottle open.

Not happening, I say.

We could drink it after? she says, hopefully. According to Vreeland, pink is the navy blue of India.

When I worry about how I'm squandering my privilege, how much time we're wasting, Nance slows down. She talks about the commodification of leisure and my eyes glaze over.

She throws pillows at me. Whose else is it to spend?

Around 2 pm we start telling each other to have a shower. Four hours later, Nance rises: Six o'clock, she says, and not a child in the house washed!

We never find the same bar, restaurant or cinema twice. With Nance, all of the singular incidents that remained random, and terrifying because of that, become part of *us*, the New York edition. We collect strangers' phone numbers. We rehash every drink, gesture, conversation. Nance gets an affection for the word normcore.

I tell her about one of Lexi's friends recounting last night's date to an Uber driver. No mention of a name, or even if he was attractive. She basically itemised what he bought; oysters, oyster

Martinis. I was half expecting her to pull out receipts.

Nance picks up one of my lipsticks to look at the brand. Moll Flanders kept all the receipts. What the men paid minus what she spent catching them.

Have to spend money to make money, I say.

Balance at end of affair with Gentleman of Bath. Husband no. 4 includes value of diamond ring. The best are the lying-in charges after she turns to whoring.

Later, I use the word basic and Nance does not know what it means. This is a first.

Is that one of Lexi's words then, she says. Is *Lexi* basic.

We are getting ready for Conrad's birthday party. I am surprised to be invited, but his friends are the only people I have hung out with this year. Conrad makes an effort to include me, filling me in on the background, and in that context the details he grants feel generous. He is wearing a Radiohead T-shirt which is too small. He laughs and I notice his Adam's apple. It is the first time it has occurred to me that someone else might have found Columbia difficult.

Conrad smiles when I say this and opens another beer – Yeah, well. Being twenty-one and being thirty . . . I don't want to sound patronising, my kid sister keeps getting on me for *mansplaining.*

I actually like people explaining things when they know what they're talking about, I say to Nance. She is sitting on my bed, taking her make-up off and throwing the cotton wool on the floor.

You would, she says. That's not what Solnit meant though – it's supposed to be men explaining things that you already know, like the correct way to reverse park.

I point out that neither of us can drive, and Nance grumbles, You know what I mean. If you ask me, we'd be better off if they'd stopped explaining things altogether.

Nance only agreed to go to the party after hours of coaxing, and only then when I said she could wear my favourite black dress. It is too formal, but that doesn't bother her. She keeps swishing it from side to side.

Which shoes then, she says.

You'll have to stuff the toes, I say, handing her heels. I tell her that I am excited about her meeting Conrad, about her being a part of my life in New York. I try to say this phrase like it has substance.

Americans though, she says.

Just give them a chance. I go into the bathroom and then hesitate – Can you actually though? Like, don't go into it hating them.

Who said I did?

You know what I mean, I say.

I'm not going to pretend I like someone if I don't.

I have begun to feel close to Conrad. I like his girlfriend, their friends, their flat together. O'Hara wrote 'Having a Coke with You', not having a coke alone.

Promise me you'll just be less . . .

Less what, Nance says, meeting my eyes in the mirror. Less of myself, you mean.

Less in your face, I say, then correct myself. Just be *nice*.

We drink on the train. Nance reminisces about an August we spent in Dublin. About the lock-in at O'Donoghue's. The morning after, we dragged ourselves to the deli across the road to buy overpriced green juices from vegan girls who despised us. At lunchtime, we went to Cornucopia and bought heaping boxes of salad, then spent the afternoon working in Grogan's. I was writing a story about a girl who commits suicide after the Dewey Decimal System is put out of use. Nance was reading Emily Dickinson's letters. When old men talked to us, Nance was short with them, but they didn't seem to mind. She had that way about her. Once, when Nance was in the bathroom, I started explaining Indian independence to one of the regulars, who wore a khaki jacket and always sat in the corner. When Nance came back, a slight awkwardness came over her face, but she struck a jovial tone. Sure, she's a Catholic, she said. She doesn't fuckin' sound it, he said. He had a Belfast accent. India and Ireland have a lot in common though, I said, given that ten million people died in the Bengal famine, and given Gorta Mór.

Nance put her head in her hands. Then his wife called and he said, This posh bitch thinks she's telling me about independence. Nance pulled me into the street, hissing, you eejit, they were IRA. When I say *bad men*, you have to listen.

Nance goes on, digging up her most embarrassing stories, telling lewd jokes, reminding me of the time we ran into the boy she once loved, and how fat his new girlfriend was.

Wasn't she though, Nance says. Wasn't she practically obese.

I murmur vague assent, hoping Nance is getting this out of her system. We pour a small bottle of vodka into a big bottle of Diet Coke and I drink most of it.

Conrad's party is in a weird venue – an underground bar with low ceilings and the lights have a blueish tinge. He has booked a table and it takes me a while to find it among the other tables. Nance follows me, emanating resentment. I avoid eye contact.

Stay here, I say brightly. I'll get us drinks.

I find Conrad by the bar and fling my arms round his neck.

You made it! Did you bring Nancy?

I take Conrad's hand and drag him to meet her. She is standing by the door, making no effort to talk to anyone. He reaches out and shakes Nance's hand, and I see her take this in, and his chinos, and his shirt.

It's so great to meet you. Iris talks about you all the time, he says.

That's strange, I've not heard a thing about you.

Conrad's neck flushes a deep red, which satisfies Nance's need for dominance sufficiently for her to ask about his short story collection. She sets out from the view that humans are shit and to get what you want you have to keep people beneath you. Conrad is flattered to be asked, and by the intensity with which Nance listens, not knowing that from Nance this kind of attention is artificial and calculated to show how much she has to exert herself not to be bored.

Oh, really? Nance says, making her eyes very wide.

Yeah, Conrad says, it's crazy – I wince as he moves on to David Foster Wallace.

That's so original, Nance says, and I dive in, hastily – I meant to tell you this the other day actually, Conrad. So Foster Wallace said the first draft of *Infinite Jest* was like—

I can't find the word. I stare at the floor, which is dirty. I click my fingers softly at my side. I can feel the words clustering, vibrating behind my lips. Conrad leans in, thinking I have spoken quietly.

Nance sees my distress and interjects – Foster Wallace said the first draft of *Infinite Jest* was like a piece of glass, dropped from a great height.

305

Conrad rubs his hands together. I *love* that.

I haven't told Nance about the aphasia – it isn't noticeable when we are alone because she often finishes my sentences. I excuse myself to go to the bathroom. I run my hands under hot water and put more eyeliner on. When I get back, Nance has drunk our drinks and is waiting by the door.

We're leaving, she says.

I see Conrad by the table, watching us. He looks embarrassed. I make a what did you do sign, and he shrugs. I follow Nance out. It has started raining, drizzling.

What a cretin, she says.

What happened?

He was really rude about you.

I stop walking. Are you serious?

He went on and on about how drunk you are. You didn't hear how he said it.

I am pretty drunk, I say, uncertainly.

Go back if you want, Nance says. I can find the way home.

I can't leave her so I keep walking, but she isn't satisfied by our leaving – I know you think he's your friend, but he's a smug bastard. Typical Iris, making a show of herself, he said. I almost kicked off.

We argue all the way home. I say that maybe she misheard.

If you want to be friends with people who don't respect you, that's your funeral, Nance says.

She falls asleep soon after we get back. I watch *Friends* with my headphones on and think about the first day at Columbia, when Conrad read out someone's story in the bar.

At 2 am, Conrad texts.

Conrad:	Where did you go? Lisa just got here!	**02:04**
Iris:	If you're going to bitch about me to someone,	**02:09**
	maybe don't pick my best friend.	
Conrad:	?!	**02:10**

I stare at my phone for a few minutes then type: I told Nance you were my favourite person from the course. So the fact that you were horrible about me is pretty humiliating.

But I delete it, take a sleeping tablet, and send: Forget about it. Enjoy your party.

When I wake up, he has texted back: I'm sorry if I offended your friend? It was so loud in there I could barely hear. But all I said was that you seemed hammered. FYI, I was too.

I am not sure of the sequence of events. I remember eating pizza, for example, but not getting from the subway to the pizza place. Nance often picks up on things in people before I do. She says I have rose-tinted glasses, especially where *the men* are concerned. Whether or not Conrad meant to put me down, maybe the scorn was there, latent, in his words. He doesn't love you like I do, was what Nance said.

3

Nance is reading about aphasia. She starts leading me towards polysyllable words. When I tell her it's a side effect of Effexor, that the words will come back, she says, sarcastically, Not if you don't practise. No pain, no gain. She crows over the gaps in my memory. Sure, you've always been a goldfish, she says, switching to an American twang – We'll just have to *make more memories*. She relishes describing my reactions to films before they occur. I tell her that I wanted to lose my virginity to Kurt Cobain and she says, That's exactly what you said last time. We go out drinking and she drinks me under the table. I wake up and say, What happened, and she wraps herself in the duvet and fills me in – We were savages last night. You ate the entire block of cheese and then demanded another, she says. Even by my standards, it was quite unreasonable.

On Friday, I sit at a corner table in a bar near the library with a sip of merlot left in my glass, waiting for Nance. I am reading about alchemy, which I want to believe in. Salt was thought to be one of only three elements from which seven noble metals could be formed. Mercury epitomised the spirit, sulphur signified the soul and salt stood for the body. Mercury exemplified illumination, sulphur an act of union, or of coming together, and salt a state of cleansing or purification. I am trying to gather enough notes to convince Nance I am working.

Nance is half an hour late and she has my debit card so I can't get another drink. I'm eyeing an abandoned glass of wine when a man wearing a blue suit with wide lapels comes in. He looks like Tony Soprano. The place is empty, but he sits down at the table next to me, on the same couch. The bartender brings over an ice bucket with a bottle of white wine and the man pours a third of the bottle into a glass. I smile-grimace and project outwards that I do not want to talk.

He shoves the ice bucket towards me. Mind if I join you?

The bartender is drying glasses, flirting with a male-model type. There's a waitress somewhere, lighting tealights.

Sure, I say, and keep my eyes on the screen. Herrick in his *Hesperides* says, The body's salt the soule is.

What are you working on, he says.

A novel.

My mother wrote a novel, he says.

I count three mississippis and then say, with no enthusiasm, What was it about?

You're not from here, I can tell. I'm Karl, he says. I'm Dutch. He stares at my breasts openly. But it is more uncomfortable for me not to make conversation than it is to engage, and it's already too late to extricate myself. I can't leave anyway, because of Nance, and I can't move to another table. He hasn't done anything wrong.

So what was it about? I say.

What?

Your mother's book.

She's dead, Karl says.

That's awful. I'm sorry.

He signals to the bartender, who brings over a second wine glass.

That's okay, I say, half-heartedly. I have a friend coming.

Don't be silly, don't be silly, Karl says, pouring me a glass.

I feign an internal struggle and accept it, thinking gleefully what Nance will make of Karl. I scan the scene for details to message her so that she gets here faster. He's about six foot two, no wedding ring. Broad shoulders. He's not the sort of man I consider a sexual object, though he clearly thinks he is one.

They should write a book about me, he says. My life would make a great movie.

Who would play you?

Who do you think, he says, leering at me. I twirl my hair around my finger and pretend not to have heard. You see that building over there? He continues pointing, until I say, That one?

I own that.

All I can see is steel and plate glass. And it was a car park, I will tell Nance. It was a Starbucks.

You're not American. I can tell, he says.

You got me.

He's more drunk than I realised. You've got that exotic look, he says. I like Japanese girls.

If Nance were here she'd be on her second glass, she would goad him further and make him complicit in his own ridicule. I want him to say something so perverse that Nance will say *no fucking way. I cannot believe I missed that.*

We finish the bottle and the bartender brings another. The air conditioning is on too high and I can feel my nipples puckering. When I go back to reading, Karl's eyes slide down my body. He's the kind that wants to suckle. I wish he would ask me out so that I could say no and get it over with.

You see that building over there?

No, I say, under my breath, then, You own it?

He draws in the air with his finger – Tick. He fishes something out of his wine glass and looks at it on the end of his finger – all work and no play makes Jack a dull girl. I could keep you, you know. It'd be a nice life.

He's too ridiculous to be threatening, but his sudden swerves in mood unsettle me.

I'm going to read now, I say.

Oh, am I bothering you? I won't bother you, I won't bother you.

Five minutes later, he starts inching around the table. Surely he won't. Surely, if he knew how much he is embarrassing himself, he won't. He stares fixedly at the wall, as if to deny that he is moving. He cranes his neck to read my laptop screen. I change the zoom setting to 125 per cent. He moves closer. I change the zoom to 75 per cent. Then 50 per cent.

I like girls like you. You have cat eyes, Karl says.

By the time Nance arrives, I'm two glasses in. The bar has filled up around us with the after-work crowd. He tells me about his mother's funeral, which was last week. He filled the church with black roses which he says only grow in Turkey. As he drinks, he starts losing track of where he is in the story.

Are you an actress too, he says when Nance sits down. Her nose is sunburnt.

Oxford, she says. DPhil. She gives me her why do you get us into these situations look.

Clever girl, he says.

Nance allows this twice, then says – Sure we'll drink your booze but we are going to have a conversation—

We are? he says, dirtily.

311

Nance points, firmly, between me and her – *We* are.

Diddly dee, he says. Where were we where were we.

Your mother, I say, quickly.

Tick, he says.

Nance tells me about her day and I try not to give into hysterics. My lip keeps twitching.

Occasionally, Nance answers a direct question from Karl, or makes a sarcastic comment, or says something like, Didion didn't have to put up with this shit. She alternates between talking to him like a misbehaving child and insulting him in a deadpan way which he doesn't register. He makes no effort to contribute to the conversation, beside making occasional announcements about his prowess. When he repeats himself Nance says, That's two, Karl. That's three. We've caught ourselves one here, lads. When Karl feels he's not getting enough attention, he tries to tell us about his women, but he gets as far as a name and then forgets. I watch Nance run circles round him. She doesn't miss a beat.

He interrupts and points at me, like he's picked one.

Fuck's sake, Nance says.

Why aren't you being nice to me, he says.

He's looking at Nance in a way I don't like, but she has no sense of male danger. She has a furious self-worth which does not recede, even when it is not safe to have one.

We're not the cunting entertainment. We aren't paid to be nice to you, she says.

Thank you for the wine. We're going to head off now, I say.

Why should we? Weren't you here first, Nance says. She is flushed with anger.

I thought we were friends, Karl says, mulishly. Why aren't you being nice to me.

We have been playing, and he has not. Nance looks steadily at him. I have seen her throw drinks in men's faces before. I can't get out from the table without clambering over him.

Karl jabs a finger at Nance, suddenly suspicious. Is she your girlfriend?

I snort into my wine glass. If Nance is hurt, it doesn't show. She turns on Karl. Because how else could she resist a man such as yourself?

How long ago did you lose your mother, I say, to divert him.

Yesterday, he says.

Bollocks you did.

Nance, I hiss.

It feels like yesterday, Karl says.

Nance lets me drag her to another table but not to another bar. It's the principle of the thing, she says. She wants a burger and I get one too. I'm sitting with my back to the room, so I don't see Karl behind me, but I see Nance's face. He reaches out and touches my hair, wrapping a strand of it around his finger. I freeze, like there's an insect on my head. When he drops my hair, I realise I have stopped breathing, and then the back of his hand brushes my nipple, and Nance roars. I move to stop her standing up. If she slaps him, he will hit her, and then I will have to kill him. Everyone is staring. My head is full of blood pounding shame. My nipple is hard, visibly so.

Don't make a scene. Let's just go.

I'm making a scene, Nance says.

Lower your voice, I plead, which is a mistake.

We fight on the train. Nance says I'm pathetic.

You can't just go around threatening to stab people, I say.

It's a turn of phrase. Do you actually like old men feeling you up? Is that what this is about.

Nice, Nance. Really nice.

He assaulted you, she says.

I look around the carriage and hiss, Can you *stop* making me sound like such a victim. It wasn't assault. It was just disgusting – I try and cool my forehead on the metal rail. How did I let that happen? How I must have looked, flirting, for more than an hour, writing things down, questing and giddy with anticipating what might happen next, how we would talk about it.

I don't know where to start unpicking your notions, Nance says.

We should have just moved tables.

We had a right to be there, she says.

It's a bar, not a bus seat.

You didn't have to be polite to him, she said. Oh, I'm Iris. It's been a pleasure talking, why don't I just suck you off—

Why can't you accept that I deal with things differently than you.

I don't know how you get through the day thinking so much about how *the men* are feeling.

Reacting to everything would be exhausting. I don't want to walk around shouting at people.

Having agency, you mean, she scoffs.

Choosing not to let something affect you is power.

He groped you, she says, and I snap, I'm aware of that, thanks.

My nipple is burning, itching. I want to have a shower. I stare at an ad for American Apparel. A teenage girl in a leotard and knee socks and Converse scowls at the camera. Canal Street. Houston Street. Christopher Street. Sheridan Square. One day, I'm just going to flip. I'll be going down an escalator on the subway and some guy will leer at me and I'll start screaming THIS ISN'T FOR YOU.

Nance grunts but she still isn't talking to me. The model has a gap between her front teeth the size of a pound coin. Her nipples press against the leotard. But her breasts don't mean what mine mean, they don't send the same signals. I'm thinking that I need to start wearing a bra. I'm thinking about how I shouldn't have accepted the wine. How, even if there had been no wine, I wouldn't have known how to deter Karl without offending him. How urgent it felt not to offend, or embarrass, Karl. I let a stranger touch my nipple because I didn't want to embarrass him.

Nance puts her face close to mine and breathes heavily. You have cat eyes, she says.

Once I start laughing, it is hard to stop. Every time one of us stops the other starts again. I get the hiccups and holding my breath doesn't help.

Christ, Iris, stop causing a scene, Nance says, as people turn to watch us.

We run out of clothes, so we have to do laundry. While we are putting it away, Nance is going on about the abortion referendum, and then I hear Ezra's name and I stiffen.

When was this?

We had a coffee in January, she says, pulling at a thread in her tights. He had to pick up some guitar bit at Zed's. A ladder splits in her tights, but she doesn't stop playing with them – I told Ezra that Wittgenstein said the way to deal with a problem you perceive in life is to behave as though the problem does not exist. And he looked delighted, like that makes it right.

Makes what right?

And he said: No way! That's how I deal with everything.

I start pairing socks. I try and laugh, but it's a weak sound. So, this is why I have felt myself disappearing.

In my last class at Columbia, Sasha passed a basket of rocks around the class. We glared at whoever held it, like they were hogging the joint. There was a rock that looked like hardened lava, one full of minute holes, aerated by waves, a hunk of amethyst, a piece of fool's gold. I wanted to be sure I made the right choice. I picked a white smoothish pebble. It felt alien in my hand. I asked for the basket back and swapped it with another.

You can't do that, Lisa hissed.

Now, Sasha said. As long as you are writing, I want you to have that rock on your desk. Whichever rock you have chosen. The only rule is that when you give up, when you decide to do something else – and if you can, by all means you *should* – you have to throw the rock away.

At some point, in the next few weeks, the rock vanishes from my desk. It was on the back left corner. Sometimes, when I was sitting there and staring at the wall, I liked to put my hand on it, to shelter it. I never held it, but I held the space around it. It was mine.

I think that maybe Nance stole the rock but then I realise I have not seen it for a long time. I tear the flat apart looking for it. I look in the bins, behind sofa cushions, behind my books. I move pillows and haul the mattress from its frame. I look under the cupboards and in the pockets of everything I own, even though I have been wearing the same black jeans for weeks. I crawl around with my face pressed to the floor, nose level with the plug sockets.

That night, when I am crying in that gulping way which feels like drowning, Nance pads in and gets into bed with me. She does not like hugging, but she tries. Of course, she thinks that I am crying over Ezra, and I cannot explain that it is the rock, and all of it.

I didn't even notice, I say. I didn't even notice it was missing.

She curls herself around me. She is like a radiator, very warm and very still. I pretend to be asleep so that she won't feel obliged to, but she stays.

4

Ezra tells me that he'll visit after they play South by Southwest, at the end of the month. They'll be in New York for a few days. He tells me this on WhatsApp. I forget sometimes what it's like to be around you. I don't tell Nance. She is in a foul mood because she's been living in Oxford for four years and after eighteen months emigrants are not allowed to vote in the abortion referendum. We have been driving each other crazy this week. It is scorching outside. Nikolai shows me how to turn the air conditioning off, and I open all the windows. It is the first time there has been enough air in the flat. Nance hates it. She puts ice cubes down her top and lies on the sofa, moaning, Tell me when it's over.

She has been staying with me for two months. Her work isn't going well. She transcribed one of Margaret Fuller's letters weeks ago, but she forgot to record the details in her bibliography, and she can't find the original. She spends the afternoons poring over the NYPL catalogue and requesting boxes she's already looked through. She refuses to ask the librarians for help.

When I try to cheer her up, she says, Leave me be. You don't have a monopoly on being unhappy. I'm trying to work too, I say, and she gestures around the flat. Yeah, she says, in this place.

Nance has got used to me being like her – low-energy, cynical – but when Ezra texts, I change. She catches me smiling at myself in the mirror. While she is agonising over her bibliography, I get a pedicure; pink, glittery. Nance calls me Indian Barbie. I want to watch romantic comedies. She says we still haven't seen *Blue Is the Warmest Color*. We agree to work separately for a few days. Afterwards, we meet at Malachy's. Some girl at the library passed Nance her phone number on a catalogue card which Nance throws on the table between us.

Very nineties of her, I say.

Nance complains about how long it has been since she had the ride. I can't tell how much she actually cares because she says it like she is joking. She only ever tells me about being upset after the fact, when she is back on top, and can use it to show how she has prevailed.

Love only has to happen once, I say.

Nance has made a lot of vomit noises this week. I have missed this role, the ingenue. Nance's disapproval makes me more aware of it, which causes random surges of affection towards her.

After she leaves on Thursday morning, I gather up all of her stuff and throw it under the sink.

Ezra wants to meet in Times Square because it is near the studio. It will save on travel time, he says. I wait until Nance is safely at the library to message her.

| Iris: | The circus is in town. I'll message when you can come back. Work in a bar or something. | 11:14 |
| Nance: | Where are you meeting? | 11:31 |

It is so typical for her to want that detail. I reply Times Square and then turn my phone off. Ezra will have no signal in the studio anyway.

When Nance first arrived, I let her think that Ezra had been in touch; I picked up my phone and reread old WhatsApp messages. As the weeks passed, she started flinging out remarks when I was off guard, seeding doubt. She was in a black mood and reading obsessively about an Irish rape case involving some rugby players, flicking through TV channels trying to find coverage. I was trying to read about the use of salt in religious ceremonies, but Nance started ranting. Her eyes were blazing. The girl wanted to leave the party but he pulled down her pants. She was on her period. Paddy Jackson started it and Stuart Olding joined in. A woman opened the door and saw them, but the girl wasn't fighting back, so she closed it again.

When I left the room, Nance raised her voice. There's nowhere in the flat she isn't audible. So next morning, right, she told a friend she got raped and her friend suggested she go to the police and tell them what happened, and she said, I'm not going to the police. I'm not going up against Ulster Rugby. Yeah, because that'll work. I'd report it if I knew they'd get done but they won't. Oh, Nance said, and here's a text from one of the men:

We're all top shaggers. There was a bit of spit roasting going on last night fellas. It was like a merry go round at the carnival.

At the end of March, all four were acquitted. Nance squinted at the screen, uncomprehendingly, as she read it out. I opened my mouth to speak and she ran to the bathroom and threw up.

I started reading about the case too. Paddy Jackson said he'd sue anyone who called him a rapist. I sent Nance YouTube videos of the thousands taking to the streets in Belfast and Dublin chanting, Sue me Paddy! I sent a link when the players were all dropped from their teams. Nance didn't reply. She kept rereading the WhatsApp messages.

In the first week of April, she got an eye infection. I could tell it hurt her to read. I asked if she needed anything from the pharmacy, and she seemed bitter that I'd noticed the yellow discharge around her swollen lids. We were on the cross-town bus when she finished Mark Ford's *Six Children* and tossed the slim blue paperback in my direction.

The title comes from Whitman. He claimed he'd fathered six children all over the US. Of course he didn't, but does the premise remind you of anyone?

I tried to look indifferent. Ezra would never do that, I said.

He would, she crowed, Because *he'd create a universe of logic in which his behaviour was acceptable.*

Nance does this, hurts me and then acts like she's doing it for my own good, like she is educating me. So we avoid the subject of Ezra, warily, like politics, like there is a line we cannot cross.

Ezra is late. Times Square is a stupid place to meet. I turn on my phone and get Nance's WhatsApp from earlier: Romance. Ezra's mobile goes straight to voicemail and I feel sick. I had an egg and cheese roll this morning. I took out the cheese and the egg.

Times Square smells of hot tarmac and candy floss. I stand on the bench in the middle of the intersection. I am scanning the crowd when a man with a shaved head touches my foot and I kick at his hand before I recognise it.

Manners, Ezra says.

I jump down and fling my arms around him. I was looking for you with *hair*.

He doesn't kiss me. He converts my hug into a sort of head-lock. To hide my confusion, I wriggle free and skim my hand over the surface of his head.

Oh, I thought it would be prickly. It's soft.

I am wearing a black dress which clings to me like wet silk. Ezra looks at the traffic lights and I study his face, hungrily. The only time I have seen the top of his head so exposed is with his face in between my legs.

Did Nance know he'd shaved his head? It would be just like her not to say.

He's wearing a leather jacket and it's eighty degrees outside. He checks himself out in the window of the Verizon store, then turns and says, abruptly, You look nice.

He links his little finger with mine, and I say, Do you deliberately withhold compliments so that they become more powerful or are you naturally averse to saying nice things?

Ezra looks intrigued by this new information about himself and considers it for a moment.

Both probably, he says.

There is something different, but I can't work it out. It is like walking along next to a hologram.

I watch our reflection ripple across the windows we walk past.

I have six bookings all over town: Mexican, Italian, Chinese, Indian, a diner, a champagne bar. I mention two of the reservations and Ezra looks dismayed, then surreptitiously glances at his phone. Sorry, scheduled post. Part of the job. But did you cancel? So that they don't hold the reservation?

I'm exhausted and point at the sign. That place is great.

322

In One More Thai, we sit awkwardly on tall stools. There is a gold Buddha on a side table, which Ezra hasn't seen yet. He is engrossed in the History of the Gold Siam section of the menu. I tell a stupid hangover story and Ezra says, God, I miss proper hangovers. They mean that the body still values itself.

Shall we get prosecco?

He looks doubtful and turns over the menu. We have Lexi's tonight, right? You get some though.

I'm not going to drink a bottle of prosecco by myself, I say, wanting to.

When the waiter comes, I say I'll do an Old Fashioned and Ezra pulls a face. When did you start drinking whiskey?

About the same time you stopped drinking prosecco. The waiter deposits a basket of prawn crackers on the table. They are very pink, veiny.

Ezra peers at me and says, Did Nance do your make-up?

Nance wouldn't lower herself to make up anyone's face but her own.

You look glamorous. Like an expensive model.

I sip my water. How did you know Nance was here, by the way?

She's been giving me feedback on lyrics. You know Nance – she doesn't pull any punches.

Not if you deserve it.

She's a wrecking ball, he says, under his breath. I try and hide my pleasure as he picks up the laminated menu and studies it again. How's the salt going? Before I can respond he goes on: *Did you know* it's the only material that can be blessed by the Catholic church –

– Apart from water and oil, yes, Nance mentioned that.

Ezra looks peeved. She's a strange sort of Catholic, he declares.

I mean she isn't one, or if she is, she's the same kind as you.

Ezra snorts. I thought you said she was running around throwing away holy water.

Sabotaging. Replenishing her mother's half-empty bottles with tap water. That sort of thing. And Nance doesn't run. I cast around for any other subject. I'm focusing on my job right now, I say. It's mostly transcription, but soon there'll be plenty of opportunities for writing.

I don't tell him that it was the only work I could get because of my student visa. It pays $9 an hour.

Doesn't that take up too much time?

We can't all be rock stars, I say, touching my face. My fingers come away dusted with bronzer.

Hey, I got some good news this morning. I mean, these things often fall through . . . but they're going to use one of our new tracks in the remake of *What Women Want*. It's called *What Men Want*. Dolly reckons it's a done deal . . . who knows. You're the first person I've told – he pulls out his phone and nods. Yep – I mean, I had some acid in this church in Portland – the visuals were insane – but two months, no drugs.

He shows me an app with a virtual star chart, then puts his phone on the table and assumes a penitent tone.

So, this month, I put aside about $300 to give to Syria. And *then* I realised that I'd spent that much on coke in *March*.

As long as you're contributing to the economy, I quip.

Ezra puts his face in his hands and looks at me through his fingers. How long has it been since we've seen each other?

I shrug like I haven't been counting the days. I pick up my menu. For every wave of arousal, there is a counter-wave of resentment and hurt which I must not let him see. I have never had sex with someone who hasn't called. As I told Lexi, I am not that kind of girl.

Like all the other girls? Lexi said, with uncharacteristic bitterness.

But I have always liked that about Ezra, found it sexy even. I like to be the exception to every rule.

Well, I say. That depends on when you got back from tour.

Oh, he says, suddenly vague. A month or so. It's been mental. Interviews, photo shoots. I've had to really carve out time for my practice.

I got Lexi a negligée for her birthday, I say.

Great, he says. From both of us?

I pause, but he isn't looking at me. If you want, I say.

He notices my headphones on the table and starts untangling them. What do you *do* with these.

I want to suck on his fingers. Oh, I say. You know.

Ezra glances up from unpicking the knots in my headphones – I have no idea what you're thinking right now.

Well, that's the nature of heads, isn't it. Glass houses.

We bicker about *Lemonade*. I assert my view that it's a kind of collaboration, given that Jay-Z and Beyoncé are married and one way or another the album is a product of their relationship.

Ezra is more sceptical – Bear in mind that 'Hold Up' has fifteen different songwriter credits and three production credits. Not exactly a love letter.

Can't it be both? I say, trying for coy.

It's a business collaboration. Jay-Z's label, Tidal, had exclusive streaming and download rights when they released it, which pulled hits from Spotify, Apple Music, all of them, so they doubled down on profit.

Fine. If he wants to pretend we are normal people that's fine. Ezra Munroe and Iris Jones, sharing, what, a few prawn crackers? A catch-up? He hands me back my headphones. He hasn't got the knots out, just pushed them further down the wire. I put them in my bag.

How are things with Lucas?

Same old. Things are rough at the moment because they can't agree who came up with the bridge. It's the royalties thing all over again. I won't bore you with it.

You're not boring me.

At the end of the day, our lawyer is a good guy. I trust him. And let's face it, I'm in a strong position. Ultimately, I'm the one they can't do without. And they know it.

I hold up the basket for more prawn crackers, but I move too quickly and prawn cracker dust rains down on me. I think about the shards of dust and glass that get in people's lungs in factories and kill them over time.

So, you have a lawyer now, big shot, I say. For contracts?

Yeah, kind of, yeah. And you know, in the current climate, it's common sense.

In the current climate, I repeat.

He looks embarrassed. I don't know how to talk to him without teasing. We start talking about #MeToo. I tell him about radical empathy and his curiosity makes me ache. When I say how taken aback I have been by men's surprise at the outpouring of stories, he looks disdainful.

It's rubbish that men don't know, he says. We know.

Oh?

But there's a difference between knowing that something is wrong and there being a penalty system, like would you rob a bank if you knew you wouldn't get caught?

I wince, then murmur, I probably would rob a bank. Do you mean it's not socially enforced?

Ezra looks faintly amused at what he senses is a criticism. And he's looking at me in that vague way and I know what it means.

So, I say, thinking, not yet. What are you doing after the gig tomorrow?

He keeps looking at my mouth. He clears his throat, as if to spare me, and tells me he is going on a retreat.

Wow. Will you just chant for three days or—

No, he says, earnestly. No, that's a common misconception. There's no talking. It's about being present. There's no deduction, induction, postulation – it's all about experience. Maybe it wouldn't be as significant for you, because you're quite Zen anyway. I mean, your logic does sort of fly in the face of the intellectual point of view. But it's good for me to get out of my head.

I zone out while he is talking. I cannot stop looking at his hands. He has a new ring – silver, with a black stone. He is wearing a fine chain with a mandala around his neck that swings forward as he talks. Of course, he's saying, there's always the risk that self-examination could become a stand-in for self-awareness, but ultimately, what matters is compassion—

I laugh and he smiles uncertainly. What?

Do you remember the metronome? I say. Ezra used to say that part of our communication problem was that we lived in different time signatures. He gave me a metronome for my twenty-first birthday. You – he said and set the ticker so that it went tick-tick-tick, then stilled it with his finger. And me – he released it again, and it ticked along, at a more regular pace.

Are you sure that was me? Ezra says, pleased by this image of himself, but disbelieving. He thinks I'm making it up. Yet I remember his red scarf and that he smelt of pencil shavings.

What else are you learning from *Zen* apart from compassion? I hear the hostility in my voice and try to moderate it – It just seems quite anti-obsession, anti-appetite, I say, and bite back *anti-me*.

He went to a guru and she asked, What is the sound of one hand clapping? He has been trying to solve it for months.

It's about not absorbing what other people need from you, not getting trapped in the cycle of wanting all the time. In true self-expression there are no bad actions.

That kind of absolves you from how your behaviour affects anyone else, though, doesn't it?

When the waiter passes, I change my order. She writes it down. Ezra hands her both of our menus and says, Thank you, like he is apologising for me.

Neither of us has an umbrella and we're dripping wet when we reach the lobby. Ezra shakes his head like a dog and asks Nikolai if he has an Android charger.

I have iPhone chargers, Nikolai says.

I don't support Apple. They design their products to break, it's unethical.

Nikolai makes $10 an hour. Ezra is wearing Prada sunglasses.

I'll check, Nikolai says.

Ezra pulls his second Blackberry from his pocket and walks the perimeter of the lobby with one earbud in. He has three-minute interviews scheduled with radio stations in Eastern Europe.

That's right, he says. I know it's a cliché, but I'd have to say Dylan. He pauses, thoughtfully. Well, ha, it's funny you should ask.

My friend is still out?

Nikolai nods. He has taken a shine to Nance though it's unclear why. Whenever we come in, she sweeps past him saying things like, Nikolai, I could get used to this. When he takes her coat, she groans, Nikolai, I'm taking you back in my suitcase.

Ezra picks up another call and mouths *one minute* to me.

Yep. Can you hear me now? Yep, I'm here. Well, ha. It's funny you should ask.

And still, I start to sweat in the elevator. My body starts to hum.

We get into missionary and still he does not meet my eyes. He looks at the wall about two inches up and to the right of my head. I put one hand either side of his face. If I can keep him here for long enough, I can bring him back from wherever it is he is gone. I braid my fingers behind his head.

Either fuck me or don't. Either be here or don't.

And then he does.

I am sitting on the edge of the bed, trying to put on tights, when he says, Nagarjuna says there is pleasure when a sore is scratched, but to be without sores is more pleasurable still. So, there are pleasures in worldly desires, but to be without desires is the ideal state.

Isn't that from that stopping smoking book?

No, says Ezra. Well, there's the bit about the sore you're inflicting on yourself and how every cigarette deepens it.

329

So Naga whatever is talking about addiction?

Kind of, Ezra says, as though I am dragging him off course. Over-attachment to any external thing.

Including romantic love?

He doesn't say, Ezra says.

I pick at the dry skin on my heel for a moment – If you're doing less coke then that's great. But conflating two kinds of wanting seems dangerous.

I don't think the part of me that wants is a very good part, he says.

We get to the restaurant drunk and talking too loud. Lexi is already there and nervous. Ezra wants to sign the card, which throws me, so I write Iris & . He seals the envelope before I can see what he's written.

The party is full of people who I didn't know were in New York. A blonde girl from our year squeals when she sees us and hugs us both. I haven't seen her since I was nineteen.

You guys finally figured it out!

I look at Ezra and he smiles ruefully. He can't remember her name either.

We're not together, I say.

Really? she says, looking searchingly into my face. But you look so—

I tuck my hair behind my ears. Ezra is staring at Lexi, who is snuggling into Fred, who is wearing a suit. He came straight from work. Lexi didn't think he was going to show. I have never seen her look so happy, and I am glad, though worried for her.

Actually, I'm meeting my girlfriend after this, Ezra says. We're going to a retreat.

330

5

I wake up on Lexi's floor, smelling of sick. She has covered me in a duvet.

There's nothing he can do to help you now, Lexi says, firmly. Make a list of everything you hate about him. Be brutal. Be precise.

The Uber driver wants to talk.

If you screw up a piece of paper and throw it away, it's worthless. He picks a receipt from the dashboard and demonstrates. But, if you write £100 on it, suddenly it has value.

I ooh and aaah and watch glossy cars slide past me. That's not how money works, I think.

Salt used to be called white gold. That's how rare it was, I say. It's everywhere now, but we still attach the same significance to it. I catch sight of his expression. Sorry, I mutter. I'm hungover.

He looks relieved. You should be, it's the weekend.

After we establish he is relating to me as a daughter rather than as prey it's okay. He plays me a song called 'I've Been to Paradise But I've Never Been to Me'.

What does he do then, your feller, he says.

He's in a band.

Aren't they all.

He tells me stories of his youth. In these stories, he is a Lothario who has been round the block and realised the error of his ways.

My girlfriend is in Ukraine, he says.

That's nice, I say.

She has cancer. I drive this Uber for her. I send money every week. She's twenty-two, would you believe it, he says.

Still, in this Uber, I am the fool.

When I get back, Nance is blow-drying her hair. I sit on the sofa and wring mine out with a towel.

Nance turns the hairdryer off and stands in the bathroom doorway, watching me.

You didn't come back last night, she says. I waited.

I scroll through Netflix and choose *An Affair to Remember*. Nance glances between me and the screen. I skip ahead in the movie. Cary Grant is making Deborah Kerr a promise.

So, you knew about the girl, I say, casually.

Deborah Kerr is running, she has decided on him, she will be there.

Nance goes on brushing her hair. Knowing is not the same as endorsing. And you were with Sam so. We'd only just started talking again.

Right.

There is something in her face like two opposing impulses wrestling. I hate her for doing this. She knows that I will not be able to control my asking. She holds up her tights to the light to look for ladders.

Jesus, you'd think an elephant had been wearing these, she says.

What did he tell you.

I stare at her until she says, Nothing. I was thinking about something else.

332

Tess must never find out, because otherwise when Ezra and I get back together, she won't let him visit. I look at photos of Lexi's party on Facebook. I choose the back of someone's head; long dark hair. It could be me. I do not remember much of the evening.

I WhatsApp it to Tess: You know me. Camera shy. What am I like?

I text Ray and tell him I need money.

He replies: I'm in town in a few weeks. Let's have dinner.

Nance finds reasons to walk past me. She gathers glasses, turns on lamps. I'm going to work here today, she announces. The library is full of perverts.

Do what you like, I say.

I think that this time it might have been intentional. That he wanted to let me go, cruel to be kind, wanted to stop me clinging round ankles. I used to sit on Ray's foot when he was heading back to Lindsey, wrap my arms round his leg, half joking. He would laugh along for a minute or two, then get irritated and try and shake me off without hurting me.

My pig-headed love. You're so stubborn, Tess said.

I used to piss all over the floor when he left. Somehow that was part of my stubbornness too.

Over the next few days, I tell Nance fragments of what happened. I don't mean to, but they are jagged, and cut through normal conversation.

Is it terrible that I shouted?

Depends on what you want, she says.

You were talking to him.

Not much, she says. I did tell you to be careful.

I shake this off. He would have told me if it was serious. Ezra doesn't lie to me.

333

Already a Catholic wife married to a philanderer, Nance says. *I am the one he comes home to.*

I'm not sure which of us Nance has more contempt for. She makes me laugh in violent bursts which hurt my chest.

I break a glass and drop to the floor after it. I am surprised to see blood, how red it is.

Careful, Nance urges.

Stay back, I say.

For an hour, I gather splinters of glass with a dustpan and brush and Nance stands on a chair, pointing out those I have missed with a broom.

I call Ezra, compulsively. The second of pressing the call button is a catharsis, I feel fierce and pure, like things could still go my way. When Nance confiscates my phone, I steal hers and charge into the elevator. Sometimes Ezra picks up and I have nothing to say. Sometimes I make airy conversation.

What about that Stormy Daniels, I say.

I don't think this is healthy, he says.

He says that he is sorry. That he didn't want to hurt me. That we agreed don't ask, don't tell. That he doesn't want to make promises he can't keep. That he hopes we can be friends.

We were never friends, Ezra, I say, bitterly.

He is so quiet that I hold the phone away from my face, to see the seconds counting up.

What if I had come home? What then?

You shouldn't come home because of me, he says.

I crouch down on the sidewalk. I adopt the brace position. In my peripheral vision, Nikolai comes running.

I was wrong, I say. I was wrong about everything.

What would your closest friend do? Fake her own death and send him an invitation to the funeral. White lilies, an announcement in the newspaper. Find the other girl and ruin her life. Send her an anonymous note, warning her of syphilis. Stand outside her bedroom window with a sign, like T. S. Eliot's wife. Tell him she's pregnant. Tell her that he doesn't want her to keep it. Become famous and then pretend never to have known him. Become fragile and mothlike. Make him jealous with someone older, richer, better-looking. Call him every hour, on the hour, and read aloud from Emily Dickinson. Use the fan-blogs to start a malicious rape rumour. Pretend to have cancer. Get drunk, get sick in the street. Get engaged in the next year. Launch a start-up. Get obscenely hot. Make it so that when you come up in conversation all Ezra ever hears is people whispering *is he crazy* or *maybe he's gay*. Start a new life in Paris. Join a cabaret in Berlin. Know that these things are never really over. Rise above it. Have dignity. Take control of the narrative. *Your girl is beautiful, Hubbell.*

Fundamentally he doesn't love me as much as I love him, I say.

Or respect you, Nance calls from the other room, unwilling to let me retreat to those delusions.

I am surprised by my friends' vitriol. They are the furies.

When I start crying again, Nance is exasperated.

She's not the first, you know, she says, quietly.

Don't, I say. I blow my nose on my sleeve. Go on.

And so she tells me about the ex-girlfriend who followed them to Coachella last summer. He snorted coke off her stomach.

I am not even surprised. I know which girl it will have been, and how affronted Ezra would be by my knowing. His ex-girl-friends have a habit of getting themselves unconscious and throwing themselves into his path. He finds this outrageous. He never forgives the women who tempt him.

He tied someone up and lost the key. Lucas still isn't talking to him because the roadies kicked up such a fuss. He checked into a brothel in Amsterdam and said it was to see what it was like when it's legal.

I get a lurch of pleasure and sickness in hearing these things. It doesn't matter if they're true, because he has gone beyond being someone I can imagine.

What do you call a religion that no longer rings true?

Dogma, you might say, or blind faith.

I met the girl, Nance says, finally. She studies my face, like she's calculating the final incision to make the carcass fall apart.

I went to this stupid party he had. I thought there would be celebrities. I was so bored that I drank six cans of Stella. He put me to bed under a pile of coats.

What Ezra told Nance: that he has never felt this way, that he has never loved anyone more.

ALCOHOL DOESN'T SOLVE ANYTHING BUT NEITHER DOES MILK.

I start to make a will online but there are too many forms. The will people call. I am early in the process, but the cogs are in motion. When I specify armfuls of peonies, lilacs, forget-me-nots, the woman on the phone snaps, That's not what we do.

When Nance gets back from the library, I am lying on the floor.

She sits down next to me and says, reluctantly, That Christmas, after you opened up the relationship, he was in bits.

336

He didn't say anything.

Would it have made a difference?

I don't answer. Nance sighs, He's obsessed with *Thoreau* at the moment. Living deliberately. Such an undergraduate.

Thoreau went to dinner at his mother's house every Sunday, I say. And the cabin was only a mile out of town.

That's right, Nance says, encouragingly. *And* she did his laundry. She gets up in disgust. I don't understand why you're not more angry. You should be raging.

He hasn't technically done anything wrong, I say.

He – made – you – think – it – was – back – on, she says.

Let me. He let me.

If you give someone a river when they mention a thirst, do not be surprised when they drown.

✗

In the third week, Nance starts to insist. The lights have to stay on. The blinds have to stay open. When she is in the bathroom, I cut the strings to the blinds, higher than she can reach.

Dr Agarwal doesn't produce a prescription until I ask, but he has already written it. Just until you get some ground beneath your feet, he says. If you have a good reaction, we can talk about increasing it gradually. There's a serious risk of inducing mania if you move too fast.

Liderman ruled out bipolar, I say, resentfully. She said my highs were too few and far between.

Dr Agarwal smiles vaguely at his desk. Diagnoses are just ways of explaining patterns of symptoms, he says, eventually. They can't tell the whole story, particularly in complex cases. And the experience of mania isn't exclusive to those with bipolar disorder, not once chemical catalysts are involved.

I tuck this crystal away in my mind, for later. I imagine relief; fever dreams instead of stagnation. My heart starts beating faster.

I notice Dr Agarwal studying my expression intently, as if he suspects me imagining these possibilities. I try to look bored.

Manic episodes are extremely dangerous, Iris, he says, slowly. They can be fatal. So, any changes in speech or sleep patterns, energy levels, any grandiose plans or reckless behaviour, any euphoria—

It seems strange to take them for pain, I say, distracting him. Like taking morphine for grief.

Sometimes you need morphine, he says.

When I get home, Nance runs me a bath and says, Get in. She sits on the toilet lid and talks to me. Did he give you anything fun?

Yeah, antidepressants. Real laugh a minute.

Can I see the box?

I threw it away.

Nance looks at me reproachfully. I dunk under the water. I come up when I have to, for air.

Those pamphlets all list the same side effects. I don't need to read them again.

Nance bites her lip. Did the doctor tell you anything to be aware of though?

I start to slide under and Nance decides to let it go. So, there was this girl right, who reported her friend to the police.

Was it for squatting in her apartment? I comb my wet fringe over my forehead.

Nance ignores me. So, these two Northern Irish girls were living together, and one of them opened the bin to find . . . a foetus. *No bin liner.* It had tiny fingernails and teeth. She called the police, and the one who'd ordered abortion pills online because she couldn't afford to go to England was sent to prison.

Nance hauls herself up to rest on the sink. Now, obviously your one is an irredeemable whore for calling the police but imagine the shock.

I do not say anything. I am thinking of tiny fingernails.

I'd make you bury it for me, Nance announces.

You know I'd do it anyway. If you asked. And came with me.

Tiny fingernails. And tiny teeth, Nance says, baring her fangs.

⚓

We take the F train to Coney Island–Stillwell Avenue. The ferry isn't running. The train back is full of young families. I watch an exhausted-looking man quiz his children.

Does it live in a hot country?

No! says the boy, sick with excitement.

Is it a polar bear?

No!

Daddy, wails the sister, you're doing it wrong.

If Ezra were this child's father, he would say: What would make sense here is to start off with the largest categories. The category of hot countries isn't a bad start, but it would make more sense to choose binaries first. To rule out the greatest number of possible outcomes. Which, if you think about it, is the whole reason for our way of naming. Genus, species, *Caretta caretta*, etc. So, *Is it north of the equator* would make sense, for example, or, *Is it a mammal.*

I don't realise I am talking aloud until Nance swivels towards me. Would you ever just shut up. He isn't here.

I sit in mutinous silence, until two stops later she says, *Caretta caretta*, etc. What a thunderous cunt.

The little girl pipes up, Is it a thunderous cunt?

When we get back, I have an email from Ezra. The attachment is a song he wrote about me four years ago. He has taken out the love words and replaced them with Vedic vowels.

The message says: Thought you might want to hear this.

Scenario 1

A. He does not know what he wants. He is conflicted.

B. He wants me to hear a song like you want a friend to see a new top.

C. It is an apology song.

D. He is reminding me that creativity is our refuge. *We'll always have Paris.*

E. He wants to be pen-pals.

F. He misses reading my work & is too shy to ask.

G. His girlfriend hates music. His girlfriend is dead.

H. It is a metaphorical lighthouse. A sign that he is still there.

I. He is high.

J. He has not thought about it at all.

Scenario 2

A. He does not know the pain he is causing (exoneration).

B. He does and takes pleasure in it (sadism).

C. (ambivalence).

Nance looks grim about the mouth as if this settles it. She opens Facebook and shows me a photo of the girl.

Okay, I say, dully. Got it. Happy?

✗

I ask Dr Agarwal, Is it possible to die of a broken heart?

The way he makes his eyes twinkle, he really does think he's Santa Claus.

When I was a graduate, I went to this tiny town in Alaska, a fishing village really. I was a student, not much older than you, and scared of what the world would bring. Did I go to the library? No, I did not. We stayed up drinking this clear spirit, a vodka that tasted more like rakia, which they brewed in great big vats. There were only a few hours of daylight in this town and a high suicide rate because of that. I set my alarm, determined to be productive the next day, to do what I thought I was there to do. Day after day, I'd wake up and curse myself. I'd rush to the window and see the pink disk of the sun dissolving into blue. And I'd watch, helpless, *freezing*, because I never did shut the window. And then someone would say, Hey Danny, are you coming to the pub, and I'd say, Well, this day is already done for. But I felt so guilty. Looking back though, those were some of the best – not the happiest – but the most important times in my life. I was waking up.

Your friends call you *Danny?* I say.

6

I worry that Nance is catching my sadness. She sits next to me in bed, watching *Frasier*, as the sun comes up and goes down behind the blind. I let her turn on the air conditioning. She goes to the door to get whatever food we are having delivered.

This can't be good for us, I say. I haul myself out of bed.

You know I've never liked going outside, she says. It's alright for you half-castes.

For every time I was cast as Pocahontas, Nance was Snow White. She lists this among life's great injustices. Jasmine is sexier than Snow White and that's an end to it, she says.

Jasmine is from Agrabah, I say. Disney made an Indian princess two years ago, but they decided the world wasn't ready because of what happened with Princess Tiana.

Esmeralda, Nance says, triumphantly, she's a ride.

Try saying that wearing a gypsy skirt and carrying a tambourine, I say. Come on. We're going to be late.

That night, we go to see Lydia and Simon. They have PhDs and are both working on their second collections of poems. His title: *Despair*. Hers: *Eudaemonia*.

Since graduating, they have begun to accumulate objects like teapots and coat racks. There are postcards from New Directions and Milkweed Editions on the wall. There is a red tablecloth on which they have set out crackers and jars of pickles collected on their travels. Giardiniera from Italy, red peppers, zucchini, smushed in garlic and olive oil. Purple kimchi. Pickled herrings, their silver stomachs pressed up against the glass, which we do not go near.

Would you happen to have any wine about the place, Nance says.

I do not know Lydia well, though we used to go to the same parties. She has sharp brown eyes. She wears high-waisted trousers and brogues. Since they got together, Lydia has become more taut and Simon has started to go soft around the edges. She speaks Russian, French and German, and when Simon brings this up, she smiles indulgently at him.

Not well, she says, moving swiftly around the kitchen.

Nance is studying the room, and I can tell she's assessing what she would take and what she wouldn't. Nance has developed her magpie style this way – she curates her taste by taking the best of everyone she meets.

I ask who has made the flat so beautiful, and Lydia raises a hand. Guilty, she says.

The Simon I know has been fined seven times for being drunk in possession of a bicycle. He tends towards mania and reciting Whitman. But he has mellowed, since Lydia. He points out their stack of vintage board games. They have a meet-up on the first Sunday of the month. He is growing vegetables, he tells me.

Ezra wanted an allotment, I say. And I am off, counting my grievances, when Lydia interrupts. She met Ezra once at a party, but all he said was, *I'm so high*.

She straightens one of her curls between her fingers and studies it. So why do you still love him?

By Nance's account, I am in love with a bad man. But how to gesture at this room, their domesticity, and say, I never wanted this.

343

The heart wants what it wants, Nance says.

Lydia flushes, knowing the source. Nance and Lydia clashed over politics during undergrad. Nance has the upper hand because she has worked a few summers in the car factory where everyone in her town works, and all of Lydia's campaigning for Corbyn can't compensate for that.

Lydia starts railing against developments in robotics taking away factory jobs.

Nance cuts her off. Jobs that degrade humans are better off done by robots, she says. We'll adapt.

I try to drive conversation onto other topics, but I have no news that isn't from nineties sitcoms and it slips back to our hometowns. Lydia went to St Paul's but grew up in Dalston.

My parents bought the house before the area got gentrified, she says.

I have no problem with privilege, Nance says, sharply. I have a problem with hypocrisy. I'm a champagne socialist, but I don't pretend not to be. I'll always want the nice things, but I do the work so that other people don't have the injustice. If you come from money, you can't understand.

Well then surely we have to learn from each other, Lydia begins.

Nance interrupts, Take Iris for example. Did she tell you about her two-month babysitting career? Not a dollar made since.

I don't want to talk about this.

Oh, go on, it's hilarious, Nance says. I glare at her and she mouths, *What?*

Simon starts reading aloud from *Despair* and I close my eyes. We leave soon after dinner. On the stairs, Simon kisses me clumsily. Don't take Lydia too seriously, she's very German, he says.

We sit sour-mouthed and rancid on the 2 uptown.

Do you have to bring up the factory every time? If Lydia saw the way you carry on with Nikolai—

I gave him $20 the other day, what have you ever given him?

He gets paid, I say, sulkily.

Nance interrupts – It's like what Ashbery said about O'Hara. I'm *caught between two opposing power blocs – too hip for the squares and too square for the hips*. Half of Oxford still act like my working-class ways are going to scuff their polish. Then there's Lydia's lot, who take their experiences for granted and refuse to acknowledge the advantage they have. She reckons she's earned everything she's got and still judges me for wanting what she was born with.

I envy Nance's patter with Nikolai. I dread walking past him and weigh it as a factor before leaving the building.

Most of them haven't realised that being woke is a currency yet and the ones that have are so greedy that they want all of that too, Nance says.

When we get back to the flat, I make margaritas.

These are the business, Nance yells, over the blender.

I add too much lime. Nance frosts the rims of our glasses in salt, rolling them carefully on the counter. I turn on one of my playlists which Ezra says makes no sense – La Roux, Aretha Franklin, Destiny's Child, Carly Simon. We dance our way around the flat, stopping only to pick up tangents abandoned earlier. Nance vogues her hands in front of her face, I twirl round and around her. We end up in Lindsey's cupboard. I go for the eighties exercise gear, Nance goes for the Manolos. We find a salsa outfit and argue over whether you can cha-cha to any song. I demonstrate too violently and knock down a shelf of shoes. 'When Doves Cry' comes on and Nance squawks and goes hobbling down the corridor.

One sec!

I lie on the floor to catch my breath and listen to Nance clattering around. She comes back with a mess of paper, handouts from a class she taught on tears in January. She puts our glasses on the shelf and sits down too, watching me arrange the handouts around us: Tennyson, 'Tears, Idle Tears'; Beckett, an extract from *Ill Seen Ill Said*; Barthes, 'Dark Glasses' and 'In Praise of Tears' from *A Lover's Discourse*.

Thought it'd be helpful for the salt, she says. I came up with the class after you left that voicemail. Depressives only stop crying when they've abandoned all hope, so I took it as a good omen. You sounded like you were singing. She pauses. I wasn't sure you wanted me involved till then.

I don't remember.

Ah well. It's like Schlegel said. Words, what are they? One tear will say more than any of them.

✗

Dr Agarwal tells me another story, of a man who was stranded in the middle of the ocean for six months. When I ask why, he looks intently at the bookshelves.

Luxury shipping disaster, he says. Anyway, this gentleman played second violin in the orchestra.

Like in *Titanic*, I said.

And when he was rescued—

What did he eat?

Oh, you know. Bread, fish. And when he was rescued, people

kept saying, How did you live? And he said, It's very simple. I washed my face in the morning. I drank the air. In the evening, I dressed for dinner, took out my violin and played.

This man dressed in black tie, I say. In a rowing boat.

Or it may have been on a raft, I forget, Dr Agarwal said, but yes. Why not?

♟

The first time Nance drags herself to the library, Lexi visits. I wonder if she has been staking out the apartment. I imagine her there with a matcha latte and the latest Esther Perel. I open the door for her, turn around and go back to bed. Lexi clicks into my bedroom after me. She sees the empty Jameson bottle on the windowsill.

I knew it, she says, grimly, like she's busted a drug cartel. She inhales sharply through her nose and then sits down on the bed. I stick my head under the pillow.

Okay. We can deal with this. Tell me. How long has it been, she says.

Too long since my last confession, oh Lord.

I can't stand you when you're like this, she says, like her.

It's not like you've been around lately, I say.

She's enabling you. She is an enabler.

Lexi is quiet for an uncharacteristically long time. I peek out from under the pillow. I can see the Jameson bottle, the label shredded like someone has clawed at it. Tissues covered in mascara litter the floor. Lexi measures her foot up against Nance's ankle boot, flung in the corner. She peels her foot to the floor in alignment with it.

I'm not asking you two to hang out. But she's here, and needs a place to stay, I say.

347

Doesn't it bother you? she says.

What?

Lexi keeps her eyes fixed carefully on the floor while she puts the boot back. I just think she wants to skin you and wear you as a coat, she says.

I laugh and it's an odd, cracking feeling. I am that brittle. It is like laughing in school when you're not supposed to, the same giddiness. Perhaps Lexi remembers too, because she smiles. Then she shakes her head, as if she has remembered somewhere important to be, and gathers up her handbag. She pats my head. I feel her recoil at the grease.

Call me when she's gone, she says. And we'll do something *fun*.

7

On the same day that Trump meets with Kim Jong-un, Ray finds that I am no longer a student at Columbia. It is Lindsey's fault. Ray would have gone on telling people about his daughter's MFA for years, but Lindsey wanted to come to my graduation. *Lindsey* wanted to take photographs. Ray likes the image of himself as a competent father. On the phone, he struggles to moderate his volume, which rises gradually, then shoots up, so that he is shouting for a word or two, before he gets it under control.

I, Iris, told him that tickets for graduation were sold out. Correct? So: he asked me a direct question and I gave him a direct answer. Correct? Am I aware that the telephone number for the Office of Student Affairs is listed on Columbia's website? Perhaps I am also aware that Lindsey called said Office of Student Affairs to make enquiries about tickets? And, if I know *so* much, is it possible that I also know – mysteriously, given that this is the first he is hearing about it, despite the fact that he has funded this entire endeavour so might have assumed it would come up – that I am no longer enrolled at the School of the Arts?

I hold the phone away from my ear. Fortunately, Columbia couldn't tell Lindsey I dropped out a year ago because of data protection. I can hear her coaching Ray through the rage. Ask her to explain her thought process to you, honey. Listen to what she's saying. Breathe.

If you think you're getting an allowance if you're not studying, you have another thing coming. Did you discuss this *decision* with Dr Agarwal?

*

That evening, Lindsey calls to explain that my dad is having a rough week. They're fine, it's all fine, totally normal, perfectly fine, reg – u – lar. She encourages me to talk to the school, enrol in a few classes, work up extra credit. If I need help finding a summer job, she has plenty of friends who would love for me to tutor. She offers me their phone numbers. Have you got a pen? Uhuh, I say, as she recites various numbers, Uhuh, I say, writing none of it down.

Nance is more upset than I am by this turn of events. She spent most of her grant in the first week. She is in her overdraft and still choosing the most expensive version of everything in Trader Joe's – organic hummus, artisan cheese. I start putting things back and she sulks. Paying for things makes me feel better about being such shit company, like I am contributing something to the friendship. She looks up the dresses Sam bought me online and recites the price tags with a sort of satisfaction. She unscrews new jars of moisturiser like they contain myrrh.

Having money hasn't saved me, though sometimes I thought it might. It lets me hijack my malfunctioning reward system. Spending alters my mood without demanding that I exert effort for which there is no pay-off – washing my hair does not make me feel better. So, I purchase relief an hour at a time: Seamless; booze; the occasional splurge on make-up which I don't have the energy to take off; anything to give myself *a pep, a lift, to treat myself.* It makes depression soft enough to smother myself in, like one of those people who eat themselves to death. Nance says those people are disgusting but I sympathise; it doesn't seem different from our drinking, or Lexi fucking Fred. Ezra, taking tiny bumps of coke to make his bag last. He used to open it at the edges and flatten it out, staring at it as if daring himself, before sucking on the plastic. I pretended to be asleep.

I do not tell Nance this, but I do try, haltingly, to make the argument that we all have a tendency to turn to whatever there is for comfort. She says, somewhere out there an obese woman is judging you.

We go on an online shopping spree, choosing garments in strange materials and the wrong sizes. I leave the parcels by the door. I have no interest in opening them and the post office seems an insurmountable challenge. I feel worse every time I see the bags, so I stuff them in the cupboard in the corridor. The morning after the return period ends, Nance points out that they are still around. I know she didn't forget either, but I like watching Nance lie around in jewel-coloured tones. It makes me feel less guilty. It makes her eyes more blue.

Simon sends me a message to ask if I am okay. He expresses the view that Nance is a Bad Influence. I tell him how delighted she would be.

I cash in Ray's various stashes of international currencies, which lasts us two weeks. I consider Airbnb, but I don't want to test Nikolai's loyalty. When the money runs out, I take more transcription work and tell Nance we have to stop going out. I consider a guy on Craigslist who says he'll pay $200 to rub some pretty feet.

I show Nance the post. We could sell your knickers online, I say.

Or we could just get on Twitter and abuse the *cashpigs*, Nance says.

A few days before, we'd listened to a podcast about men

seeking financial domination online and how the number has quadrupled since the 2008 crash.

Like how people got into leather and SAS boots after the Nazis, Nance said. I forced myself not to react while she Googled it, reading aloud with glee. The pervs hand over their bank details on command. *Definitely* that rather than the knickers.

Sounds more your scene, I mutter.

Nance looks thoughtful. I've too much self-respect is the problem. I'd probably bankrupt the fuckers. She reads for a while longer then closes the laptop, looking disgusted. Could you not give your dad a ring and explain about your visa and everything.

Nope, I say.

I am done asking anyone for help.

Dr Agarwal refuses to look at Ezra's social media accounts. He claims they are irrelevant. Instead, he makes me describe the photos: how, without me, Ezra looks mellow, self-assured, how his shyness has been discarded. He is part of a crowd who wear their glamour with ease, at parties full of ironic waifs and vapid pixies, where I cannot imagine myself. Not long ago, he would have pulled me towards him and whispered, *What do I say to these people.*

Every time I say *not long ago*, Dr Agarwal says, *how long ago*, as if the slip from denial to reason is one of the tongue. I loathe his neutrality.

I hate that he won't just say: Of course, photographs represent a curated version of reality; or,

Part of Ezra's job is presenting an image; or,

Perhaps it's time to take a break from social media.

He insists on talking to me as if I am an intelligent, rational human, which makes me want to howl and rend my clothes and smear my face with ash.

Dr Agarwal nods as I describe the photos, as though we are critiquing a piece of art on the wall – I have not had the pleasure of meeting Ezra. I do not know him. But from the little I can glean I suspect that he is setting up problems for himself in the future. People addicted to cocaine tend towards narcissism, which has its own fatalities.

I sit up, quick, furious – Sorry that you didn't get the memo, but most people experiment with drugs at my age. Maybe you didn't get invited to the right parties.

Agarwal taps his glasses on the arm of his chair, like he wants to let a few beats of time pass.

If you do something at regular intervals, say, monthly, or weekly, is it an experiment?

Before I can spit the venom in my mouth, Agarwal goes on – Ezra will not be able to outrun himself forever. Until he works out who he is, and what he wants, it would behove you to focus on doing the same. After all, we don't want you to become his Penelope.

I think about what Tess would say about Indian men who reference classical myths and say things like *behove*.

Dr Agarwal reminds me that it is a good thing to keep feeling, that my capacity for love is a boon.

Were I in a wheelchair, Dr Agarwal would say, *Look how speedy you are*.

I thrust my phone at him. Whatever Ezra is doing that allows him to stand there looking like that – whatever Zen shit he's pulling – I want *that*.

Dr Agarwal does not respond until I lower my phone – Your ability to keep feeling means that you will live a richer life, one full of learning, without which all of life would be less—

– muddled? Dizzied? Desolate?

I am panting. Dr Agarwal pauses for a moment and puts his glasses back on.

Narrower, he says.

I look at Craigslist and save jobs to my bookmark bar which I never look at again. Video captioning. Life model. My transcription work pays enough for food and drink. I become obsessed with the idea that careful record-keeping shores up reality, constitutes objective truth, where none otherwise exists. If taking note of the time and date of conversations could end a presidential career, I reason, it could save my life. I start keeping obsessive journals, cataloguing what I eat, wear, drink. I would catalogue my thoughts but my mind is a shuddering whiteness. Nance asks me to stop saying objective truth, but I have only had the word used against me before, and I am enjoying the weight of it. If I can believe in the principle of accuracy, that memos are proof of a conversation, it will be easier to get out of bed. Also, I like seeing money going into my account.

In the evening, while I tap away, Nance sits next to me reading aloud from articles. He's keeping children in cages, Iris, she says. *Cages.*

When I do not react sufficiently, she shows me the photos. I push her phone away. Take a break for a bit. Seriously. What good is refreshing going to do?

Because it's *happening*. You're part of the world, Iris. You have to be part of the conversation.

Yeah, but if the conversation is you talking to another person who already agrees with you . . . Obviously, it makes me feel sick. But if you can't do anything useful with it—

Says who? Nance snaps her laptop shut.

Oh right, I'm sure those kids would be much better off with a profound understanding of epistolary style.

I regret this the moment I say it. Nance's lip quivers.

You know if I could think of a single right thing to do then I'd do it.

I hug her, praying that I would too, praying that my numbness to it all is survival rather than not giving a fuck about anything.

L(0)tus Bordello tweet their disgust at the separation of parents and children on the Mexican border alongside a protest emoji. Ezra started changing the skin tone of his emojis a few months ago, which, at the time, I ignored.

Typical Ezra, I say, showing Nance, trying to reconcile. Right up his alley. Emojis as activism.

The words taste strange and bitter in my mouth. Nance nods, approvingly. She takes any negative comment I make about Ezra as a sign of improvement. She has started telling me things without my asking. She is careful about it, injecting venom by the milligram, as if by subjecting me to enough cruelty she can make me immune.

Late one Thursday afternoon, she catches me looking at photos of Ezra on Facebook and listening to Nick Cave. I see some resolve set in. I can feel her steeling herself to fight me, but there is no need. I know it is true as soon as she starts talking.

After the party, when she slept under a pile of coats – all other beds being taken – it was not surprising that Ezra would crawl under them too. That he would tell Nance his sexual escapades out of vanity, and curiosity as to her reaction, that he would want to test his logic against her morality and it would not occur to him that in doing so he was exposing me too. It was not surprising that in the act of telling Nance about his conquests, Ezra would get turned on, and that the vulgarity of her condemnation would rile him further. That Ezra was high and Nance was drunk: predictable. Less expected was that seeing the shame Nance could provoke in Ezra gave her a rush of power. So did rubbing salt in the wound. They got off on each other's talking, which Ezra explained didn't count – they did not touch each other, only themselves – and to Nance, blearily, in the moment, under all the coats, it didn't seem like *that* big a deal, didn't seem – she said this bit quickly – *that* different from the other thing we – she and I – had done.

I reached for my drink but the mixer had separated. Yeah, I said. Yeah, he does that.

Later, Nance is acting like a martyr. She makes me toast and puts it down on the table next to me.

I didn't want to hurt you, and I didn't know which would be worse, the knowing or the not. It hasn't been easy for me.

I force a smile and turn it on her – Honestly, it's fine, but I don't want to talk about it.

She looks at my bared teeth mistrustfully. I don't want things to be weird between us, she says.

Let's not make a big deal of it, okay?

She expects my sympathy. I want to shake her until her teeth rattle loose. You think that counts? That you even make the top ten? How smug she must have been when Ezra behaved exactly as she prophesied, how satisfied in her supremacy. I triple my dose of Effexor and walk around in a haze.

At night, I lie awake, stringing the beads of our memories in a row. The luminous ones. I do this every night, and soon it is all there is. An ornament too precious to be worn in public. I do not trust Nance not to smash it or smear it with dirt. She cannot take this away from me. I will not let her.

8

At 6 pm, I turn up at Lexi's flat with the take-out which she ordered from Pokéworks, which I picked up en route. Lexi shares a flat on St Christopher Street with two other girls who work seventy-hour weeks in the city. They're sitting in the kitchen – there's a freckled girl wearing an oversized T-shirt that says Namaste Betches. The other is in exercise gear, reading *Tatler*. She has a pore strip on her nose.

I pluck at the soy sauce on my sweatshirt. I've met Lexi's flatmates before, but I don't remember their names. Lexi always introduces me as Iris-her-friend-from-school.

Pore strip excuses herself. Freckles has Soul Cycle at half past and says she'll head out with her. Sure, see you later, Lexi says, a few beats too late.

I watch her unpack seaweed salad and distribute dim sum between two bowls. There's a copy of *The Life-changing Magic of Tidying* on the table and I pick it up, waiting for her to set the tone. We are in the autopsy stage of Fred, whose name she will no longer say out loud. Lexi notices the book in my hands and recovers some of her enthusiasm – Gigi says it's changed her life. Before you throw any object away, you have to ask yourself: Does it spark joy?

I want to ask which one Gigi is but my head is a landslide of all the objects that I will have to throw away. I go to the bathroom to check whether I'm passing as sane. My brain is queasy. I've spent the last few days browsing Tinder, pondering how many more bodies it will take to block Ezra's out. James's profile caught my eye. His torso could sell aftershave. He's looking for a Sugar Baby. I swiped right because he'd disgust Nance. I open the cabinet behind the mirror, but there are three shelves and I can't tell which products belong to who – they use the same brands and the same shade of powder. I leave fingerprints all over the mirror.

We sit on the roof and drink Brinjevec – a gift from Lexi's grandmother. She resents Lexi's parents for getting out of Slovenia before the Communists started allowing other political parties. The Brinjevec is the first present they have given her, but I open it anyway. It burns my throat. I make a show of admiring the view, but Lexi doesn't respond. When she hands me a bowl, I smell juniper and something dark, smoky, leathery. I associate Lexi with floral tones.

Nice perfume, I say.

Thanks. She holds out her wrist, mechanically, for me to smell – Cuir de Russie. Chanel made it in the 1920s for the first women who smoked. I stopped wearing it for him.

Not a fan?

It's part of being a good mistress. No lipstick, no phone calls, no receipts, no reservations under his name, she says, counting them off blankly – don't send him home smelling of you.

Don't fall in love would have been top of my list. Don't upstage the wife, stick to the role of mistress, pursue various modes of self-erasure.

He liked this hotel called CitizenM because you check in at an electronic kiosk, Lexi says.

She takes a mouthful of her food, then puts her bowl down on the roof. I want to know more. To stop myself from prying,

I talk about Nance. I want Lexi to criticise her, but I can't tell her what happened because that would mean acknowledging it.

When I got home this morning, Nance was dressed, ready for the library and sitting by the door. I wanted to make sure you were safe, she said, primly, and left. She feels politically compelled to pretend to be okay with my sleeping around. After she left, I messaged James. As far as Tinder is concerned, he's an upgrade. At least he has the sincere arrogance to say he wants something transactional; at least I'll get something back. Last night, my date arrived wearing a parka and a dour expression. He bought me drinks and got emotional about how Bernie Sanders was cheated out of the nomination. He tried to express his feelings to a female colleague, but he didn't feel heard. I spent two hours saying *how did that make you feel*. When I hesitated about going back to his, he sulked. In bed, he spat on his fingers because I wasn't wet enough.

Lexi furrows her brow like she's waiting for me to figure out the obvious. I widen my eyes to indicate that I refuse.

She opens her mouth to speak, then closes it and shakes her head. She sighs. Obviously, Nancy loves drama. That's why you like her.

This irritates me but I don't want to argue with Lexi too. I stare at a line of ants that have somehow made it nine floors up.

You know, Lexi says, in a few years, there's not going to be any snow left.

She gets up to retrieve the flowerpot filled with cigarette butts from the edge of the roof and stubs her toe. I move to comfort her, but she waves me away, so I stay put. I have never seen Lexi cry before. I'm not sure where to look. I watch the ants, evenly spaced, like a dotted line.

It's fine, she says, breathing through her nose. I'm fine.

I started envying Lexi's body when we were thirteen but looking at her now I am worried by how fragile she seems.

Shall we head in? I say.

Lexi smiles, foolishly, and shakes her head. We sit in silence for a few minutes, listening to the street. Lexi pulls a tissue from her pocket and blows her nose and the sound coincides with a furious blare of traffic, like there's a head-on collision down there, a pile-up.

Schätze, she says. I thought he was poetry.

⚐

I start to feel good. I slip out of bed at 5 am and dig my trainers out of the cupboard. I start running again, down the river, slicing through a haze of heat. The tarmac is already sticky. Men turn to stare at me. I watch the water glittering.

Nobody in Barneys is walking fast enough. I walk past rails and rails of dresses. I am drawn towards the dress I'm looking for, a sheath of merlot, a siren song. I leave my heaped basket by the changing rooms and walk out wearing it. Nobody stops me. All the traffic lights turn green. When I walk into Dive 75, *the men* stop talking. I order two margaritas for $6. A man with a buzzcut asks to borrow my pen – though I'm writing about him – then can't think what to do with it. Call me Ra, the Sun God, he says.

Next, Lexi says. Next!

Smell isn't like sound and light – it doesn't act at a distance, if you smell something, it means the atoms are inside you. I know, intuitively, what to wear, where to wear it. I wait in bars and let

361

the men sniff me out. It doesn't take long. Scent pours out of me.

Dante fucks like a wind-up toy. He uses a line about falling from heaven, and in the mirror I am a hot mess, like I ruptured all the clouds in plummeting.

I Google how to make money in New York on a student visa. Babysitting, tutoring, dogsitting, housesitting, life modelling, any modelling, phone sex operating, hawking other people's stuff on eBay, standing in queues for other people, helping other people move, organising their closets, rewriting their dating profiles, taking surveys, passing out fliers, secret shopping, being an extra, being a bike messenger, selling your hair, donating eggs, going on dates for money. All the adrenaline, straight to my brain. Ding ding ding.

I make coffee. I wash my hair. Sun streams through the blinds. My veins are singing with chlorophyll; my body is making energy light. I make a spreadsheet of sugar-dating websites and eliminate those with pop-up ads. I settle on Seeking Arrangements, which promises a Relationship on Your Terms. The homepage is like a perfume ad. A Clooneyish man sits on a bar stool. He has designer stubble. Her back is to the camera. She wears a black gown, a diamond necklace glints through her hair. Where beautiful, successful people find mutually beneficial relationships. Twenty million members worldwide. Men list their locations, professions, income bracket, asset bracket, whether they want to do gifts or pay an allowance. I read blogs written by Sugar Babies who post Mayfair-filtered selfies from hotel bathrooms.

When I'm with my Daddy, I get to step into a world where money simplifies everything. Doormen take my coat. My food is delivered with beautiful silver cutlery. Service is always impeccable, and no luxury is trop cher.

Be proud of yourself for finally stepping out of your comfort zone and for not settling for less than you deserve. Commodify your knowledge of your needs. Your needs are your power. Express them to get what you want or withhold the information to draw out mystery. Do whatever's necessary to be the best version of yourself and remember, you don't need the approval of others to have a sense of self-worth.

Lexi spends $130 a month on Pure Gym. She says it is an investment – but I think what you're talking about is something else, she says.

She is brisk, pulled together. She walks around the Goldman building three times on her lunch breaks. I am glittery and full of potential. I explain my idea.

You're talking too fast, she says, slow down. I stuff my fist into my mouth while she talks. We've all thought about doing it, she says. As long as you're not sleeping with them then in theory it's fine, but there's the stigma to think of, and the future.

I laugh at the idea of having a future and Lexi interjects in hushed tones. I meant to tell you this the other day. We were booking a holiday and I realised that none of the women were paying. Like, when we go out to dinner as a group, if I'm with a guy, we're the only couple paying fifty–fifty. I asked a few questions in the Ladies and apparently the guys pay for everything.

Like a beauty tax? Or that article about wives on the Upper East Side getting bonuses when the kids get As?

Lexi is scandalised. What I want to know is if the women want to get a manicure, or have dinner with friends, do they ask for money then? Or is it that when they're with the men, the men pay.

I mull this. Do you think it's because if Goldman guys only dated women who make what they make the pool would be pretty small?

I'd rather have no money than be that dependent, Lexi says.

Lucky you're one of the rich ones then, I say.

Lexi's voice gets serious. I can tell she's near the end of the third lap: That aside, there's a difference between fantasy and actually doing it. If you're serious, then you have to *promise* me, the most important thing, the golden rule: you *cannot* sleep with anyone. Because that's when it gets quid pro quo.

I promise and cross my fingers behind my back. I will do every single thing that Ezra could not imagine me doing.

⚑

That evening, Nance and I are sitting on the couch, eating ramen. Eating feels strange after a few mouthfuls, like I have too much blood. Nance chops red and green peppers and they shine like broken insects. She bitches about the archiving system at the library, and I fork ramen into my mouth. I try not to make sudden movements and swap to chopsticks. Nance is observing me. I try and affect tranquillity, but my mind goes fizzing elsewhere. When she runs out of complaints, she asks how I am. She eats as I talk, saying nothing, stopping only to get up, stiffly, to get some salt, though the ramen are drenched in soy.

It's literally getting paid to go out to dinner, I say. Isn't it crazy that we could be making good money from doing things we have to do anyway? Wouldn't it be empowering to be rewarded for conforming to beauty standards rather than punished for failing to meet them? Why have I been paying to go on dates with people who I know I won't fall in love with? Wouldn't it be *subversive*? I notice that my chopsticks are shaking and grip them tighter – The average girl makes $3,000 a month. In a year, that's over $20,000 more than a student working full-time at minimum wage. Some of them make $5,000, $6,000, $9,000 a month!

Nance goes into my bedroom while I'm talking and sits on my bed. I begin to clear our plates and she calls – Sure, they're paying for more than your company though. Do you follow that Twitter account Humans of Late Capitalism?

See, that's what I thought, I say, earnestly, but it's a common misconception.

I clamber onto the bed next to her and show her the articles saved to my desktop. I show her a blog post written by a Sugar Baby with over thirty thousand followers. Remember: You are not obligated to have sex with your Sugar Daddy. Sex is never a requirement, just an aspiration. I show her a video from the SA summit: seven hundred girls paid $200 each to attend panel talks on personal style, feminism, #MeToo, internet safety, and a fund-management session hosted by a former Republican campaign staffer. You see? I show her another video. A Harvard graduate with a *Pulp Fiction* bob says, If you walk into the conversation knowing the gender pay gap is real, that it's happening to millions of women across the country, then it's a lot easier to smile and ask someone for $1,000. Brandon Wade, the CEO, reminds everyone that sex is not part of the deal; that would be illegal. For the record, though, Wade's advice is to hold out as long as possible – when you have sex you give away all your power.

I close the browser window and open another: in *Vice*, a feminist who identifies as a sugar cunt compares her work and hours to that of her friends who are lawyers, consultants and entrepreneurs, ironically, the top three professions amongst her clients – capitalism makes whores of us all. On her blog she has a reading list: Zora Neale Hurston, Sara Ahmed, Roxane Gay, Chimamanda Ngozi Adichie, Sheila Heti, Audre Lorde. There are too many windows open and I move them around, searching for the essay on radical feminism which I want Nance to see – It's here somewhere, I say. Also, membership is free for students because so many men want to help out with education specifically. There's even a student section on their menu. Hang on, I'll find it. You know I'd make more money in one hour as a stripper than in a week as a waitress?

Nance scowls. Fair play, those being the only options available to you, she says. She pulls the laptop out of my hands and puts it away from us, like it might detonate. You get that this is all curated, right? The men won't look like your man here.

Have you ever been on a Tinder date?

Since Nance's revelation, being in close proximity to her repulses me. She smells like cheap vanilla. I commando-roll off the bed and explain my new theory from the bathroom – There's something to be said for the Outright Bastard. Part of the reason for all this agony – I have taken to doing this, talking as if I were Tess, mocking my teenage self – all this *agony*, I say, wringing my hands – is that my expectations were unrealistic.

When I go back in, Nance is tapping purposefully at her phone. I have a premonition that she's telling Ezra. I snatch the phone from her hands. She is searching Side effects of Effexor 150mg + clonazepam + diazepam + Zopiclone.

I chuck the phone on the bed. She thinks she's so clever and she doesn't even have the right dosages.

What was her last tirade? You can't love a person like an element or a colour. Because then you're in love with a potential or an idea, she said. What people do matters. How they treat you *matters*.

Nance doesn't get to tell me what to do any more. The next day, when she's at the library, I upload a photo and screw around with the pixels until I do not recognise myself. I sit on the floor kneading the cramp from my calves. We excrete over 90 per cent of salt through urine and sweat. Salt deficiency through too much of either causes cramps; it is a sign. I must drink less water, so that I do not lose whatever blood mineral is making me feel so good; I must eat more salt. When my profile is confirmed, I punch the air, fruit machines ringing triple dollar bills. I make a soundtrack: 'Pretty Woman', 'Material Girl', *Moulin Rouge!*. The songs I want appear on Spotify like magic. On *Let's Talk Sugar* I read blogs by Sugar Babies who have made it.

Investing everything you have in your appearance pays serious dividends. So get out the armoury of sunscreen and Botox. Go to the gym like it's your job, because looking good IS your job. It is your responsibility as a Sugar Baby to boost your Sugar Daddy's self-esteem by looking fabulous, always.

I text Nance about how interesting it is to construct yourself as a symbol and she replies So as a writer what you choose to signify is abstract male desire. I turn my phone off. There is a category of experience to which Nance will never have access. However glamorous Ezra's life is, he won't have this either. These are mine alone only. Mine mine mine mine mine.

That evening, Nance brings home drugstore flowers – carnations, baby's breath.

You shouldn't have, I say.

I cook pasta and she sticks to safe topics. We laugh at other people. My fingers tingle and I flex them while she's talking. I complain about the knots in my shoulders and she digs her thumbs into the crook by my collar bone. When we try to watch *Sex and the City* the episode keeps buffering. We watch the blue bar struggling to fill itself. When Nance dozes off, I keep reading.

MYTH #1: SUGAR DADDIES ARE PLAYERS

These guys have fifty different girls that they rotate on a daily basis. They throw around cash like it's Monopoly money. Both wrong (though we wish the second were true, right ladies?).

Let's be real: Some guys are players. But loads of businessmen are just too busy to invest in a serious relationship. So, why not have a Sugar Baby who understands that you're only looking for something casual? When you think about it, it's actually more respectful that they're not engaging in a relationship where the girl is waiting around and hoping for more. Being a Sugar Baby is about setting realistic expectations and boundaries. It's all about mutual respect. Your allowance amount is how much you are worth. You decide.

Asking a stranger for money is the part that terrifies me. These girls hustle, they post budgets. I study them. I create a folder called Sugar on my desktop and in that folder there are other folders. When Nance wakes up the clock on my laptop shows 3.43 am. I am wired and pleased to see her. I plump up the pillow behind her so that she can sit up – I want to talk strategy.

Nance is sleepy and confused – Have you been awake this whole time?

You have to see this. Guys on Tinder have leopards – this guy has a *snow leopard*.

I thrust the laptop at her. Nance puts her arm across her face. She rolls over and doesn't respond when I say her name, or when I push the books off her bedside table. I prep to be ready for her next wave of arguments, and over the next few days, I am cool, and smug when she asks.

What if they're married? What if they have children?

If you think sleeping with a married man with kids is worse than a married man, then you're valuing the woman for her womb instead of her personhood.

She keeps needling me. Eventually I lash out. What does it matter if I'm not with Ezra? Why do you have to ruin everything?

MASTER THE ART OF NOT CARING.

When meeting your potential Sugar Daddy, live in the moment and stop worrying about whether he's gonna call the next day or how things will work out in the future. The more emotionally attached you are to him, the more power he has over you. It's human nature that we always want things we cannot have.

369

What a Sugar Daddy really wants is to have a strong and confident drama-free Sugar Baby who knows her place. A jealous woman is never attractive, so save the petty what are we or who is she questions and never put your Sugar Daddy in an uncomfortable situation where he has to put up with your crazy-girlfriend attitude.

9

On Nance's last weekend in New York it rains the whole time. We have agreed to go to dinner with Ray, but I hope he will cancel. When I am getting ready, Nance appears behind me in the mirror wearing a pencil skirt and a #believeallwomen T-shirt.

It'll be a nice restaurant, I say.

I've got a cardigan, so. When she sees my face she grumbles, All my other clothes are in the wash. She goes into my bedroom and comes back wearing the Fuck the Republicans T-shirt she's been sleeping in.

I wouldn't wear a pro-choice T-shirt to dinner with your mother, I say.

I wouldn't care if you did, it'd be a talking point. I won't undo the cardigan.

Didn't you once pretend to everyone at a party that you'd been raped by a priest.

What's your point, she says, coolly.

I continue curling my eyelashes.

I apologised to everyone in the morning, she says. That's a pretty trivial thing to bring up. You know I'm ashamed of it. You're playing right into the *she cried rape* bullshit – that wasn't an allegation, it's not included in any statistics. That was being drunk and talking shite.

You started it, I mutter.

I was trying to make you laugh so. Will you lighten up.

I stare at myself in the mirror until my pupils blur.

Ray takes us to some swanky restaurant on the Upper East Side. I have been dreading his meeting Nance but she is coy – It's so good to finally meet you, she says.

Ray puffs up his chest. When he goes to the bathroom, she says, Your dad's a ride. You want to see mine. He looks like Danny DeVito.

Yeah well. I don't see him much.

Before dinner, I drink two vodka gimlets. Nance nurses a Jameson and tells sad stories about her childhood. Ray hangs on her every word. I jangle my ice cubes and look for the waiter, but he's nowhere to be seen.

I mention an article I was reading about how at Brown University students voted to stock poison tablets in the infirmary, so that if it came to it they could choose suicide instead of death by nuclear fallout. That wouldn't work now. Imagine how many times a day you'd risk biting down on a cyanide tooth if you had one.

Well, your grandparents were certain that I wouldn't be born, if that's what you mean. Everyone thought nuclear war was imminent.

Did it feel like this, Nance says. We both turn to look at him.

Ray chews. No, but then we didn't think about every moment in the same way. If anything, my grandparents were probably less scared than you are. He moves on to the bread basket – I told them to take this away, he says, glancing at my glass. Perhaps we can order some food while you're at it. He tells Nance to order whatever she likes. You can always take it home, he says.

They talk about growing up poor. Nance tells Ray about having to man the calving jack on the farm. It feels like there's a hummingbird in my throat, a blur of wings, quivering. Ray is telling Nance that the greatest thing about having means, aside from supporting his family of course, is being able to throw things away.

Nance tells him about our New Year's Eve in London in 2016. Ray had invested in the hotel, so we stayed there for free. Ray preens hearing about it, though he is uncomfortable when Nance repeats the comment the bellboy made about dykes when he delivered room service. After years of travelling with Tess, I stormed down to the lobby and unleashed hell. The manager promised everything in the hope that I didn't, as I threatened, call the *Guardian*. They gave us dinner and drinks on the house. Nance ordered: Beef bourguignon; camembert with redcurrant sauce; steak with peppercorn sauce, asparagus, pommes allumettes; a dark chocolate fondant; a bottle of pink champagne. She fell asleep before it arrived and I watched the food congeal and grow lurid on the sheets. I watched two episodes of *Sex and the City* in a haze of passive aggression and then shook Nance awake. She got me to fill two champagne glasses and take photographs of her lounging near the tray. Then she got back into bed – I only wanted to order it, she said. That's the best bit.

I put the tray out in the corridor covered in shame.

That's my girl, Ray says, looking proud. Nancy, I can't tell you how great it's been to see Iris so happy. You must come again.

Nance looks to me for affirmation and I scowl – Hey sourpuss, she says, in a jaunty tone.

I try to kick her and miss.

We have creme brûlée for dessert and I crack it with the back of my teaspoon.

It's almost too pretty to eat, Nance says. Though I notice she has no trouble. I leave a spoonful in mine, pointedly, but the waiter takes it away before it has time to make an impact.

Nance and I argue in the Ladies. I can see us reflected in every surface, I am multiplied. My thoughts are racing between trivial observations – Can you give it a rest?

Is it my fault I don't have a father?

You didn't come from a bloody stork.

I like being spoiled. It's not like I can take him away from you.

I know.

I've never been to a place like this, she says. Why can't you share?

Oh, be my guest. If you want him, you take him, I say.

My fury rises when she says Yes please to Ray's cab money and when she says That will be all to Nikolai, who smiles gamely. In the flat, she puts her #believeallwomen T-shirt back on.

I throw her a filthy look and she pounces on it – Are you weird about this because you're worried someone will accuse Ezra?

All the blood rushes to my head and roars behind my eyes. What? she says, defensively. I'm not saying he's a predator, I'm saying when you're having sex with that many people when you're *that* high, and given his predilections – I walk away from her and she calls after me – Why so repressed?

As soon as I'm in the corridor I start screaming into my bed-room, with my back pressed up against the wall. I say that I know what she's implying and No, I am not worried that Ezra is a rapist. That just because Nance can tell the most compelling version of something doesn't mean it's true and that wanking in a bed next to him doesn't give her the right. That the fact that she still can't tell the difference between consensual BDSM and sexual violence just means she's ignorant, and so has to belittle

374

it, like she does with everything else. I tell her that I say yes to Ezra and I say no to Ezra and Ezra gives me what I want. I tell her that slut-shaming me isn't a feminist action and that my sexuality is not her domain – Nance looks taken aback, like she thought she was just playing with matches and touch-paper – Do you just store up everything I tell you, and play with it, until it's the darkest, most contorted version of itself? Sit there fucking sharpening it on a rock, saying look at this blade flash—

I stop talking because my mouth is dry. My skin prickles like it's being brushed with thousands of lit metal wires. I take my laptop into the bathroom and lock the door. I give up halfway through *When Harry Met Sally* and go to bed. Nance is still reading, but I turn off the lights. I get up to soak a flannel in cold water and put it on my forehead, but I don't wring it out properly and it soaks the pillow.

Ben is sitting in the bar of the Savoy. I step into *Pretty Woman*, but he's wearing a short-sleeved shirt which ruins it. I'm wearing a black dress and a vintage faux-leopard coat. I have taken every piece of advice: Straight hair, French nails, nude lips; feminine, conservative. Up-to-date, but not opinionated. I checked the headlines for current events before I left the flat.

June 24: Saudi Arabia's King Salman lifts the ban on women driving. Parking spaces are painted pink.

Ben takes me in, sourly. What's with the grunge chic?

Quite Kate Moss, no? I ball the coat up and put it under my chair.

Membership costs $100 a month, you know that?

He tells me that he doesn't need to pay for it and I say, Of course you don't.

He grunts – you might as well sit down – and I feel a thrill of achievement. He orders two glasses of Riesling. I drink mine too quickly and talk about being a student. He sits back and assesses me, like fruit that's spoiling before his eyes.

He tells me that he had a Hyderabadi girlfriend and that I'm fair too.

You've got a great ass, he adds. I noticed it. But I expected a six and you're a low five.

On the way out, I panic in the revolving door and consider going around again. Turn and turn about. Would they call the police eventually, the fire brigade? I go around four times hoping to get drunk on the dizziness. When I step out, I paw ineffectually at Ben's chest and he brushes my hand away in disgust and takes the next cab.

I get back with blisters, blood buzzing. As soon as I hear Nance moving around, I endeavour to enjoy the evening retroactively. Earlier, she went snooping on my laptop and saw my username cocoprincess and said I was exploiting my heritage. I couldn't bear her condescension. I was tired of explaining myself – it hadn't occurred to her that, to me, Coco would mean Chanel. I decided I'd rather be a whore than a victim. I found an article suggesting the name exoticivyleague and showed it to her. I'm cornering the market, I said. I did not show Nance the multiple messages saying I've never had sex with an Indian girl nor the one from finerthings6996 asking how dark I was, and if I could go darker, and how dark *could* I go, nor the one from ranchowner694u that said wanna play slaves?

Nance comes into the bathroom and sits on the side of the bath watching me take off my make-up. She is wearing my burgundy silk slip. It makes her skin like milk.

He wanted to fuck me, but I wasn't in the mood, I say, languidly. He wasn't happy about it.

No surprises there, she says. You can't rebel against the patriarchy and expect approval for not conforming.

I wasn't . . . whatever. If I was about to have sex and then at the last minute they said, Oh, sorry, I don't fancy it, I wouldn't like it.

Nance narrows her eyes. So, when you say *it's not okay* what you mean is that the men don't like it.

Until that moment, I hadn't realised how much easier it is for Nance to have her theories. She never puts herself in situations which test them.

I've had some pretty great sex that I wasn't sure I wanted at the start, I say, pouting at myself.

Stop it, she says in disgust.

What?

Nance puts out her hands as if she wants to shake me, then turns me to face her, and kisses me. Her mouth is so warm. Her hands move to my waist and I pull away. She stares at the taps. She is pale except for the colour flooding her cheeks.

Stop thinking the men are the same as you, she says, bitterly. They're animals. When they don't get what they want they don't feel bad about it, or *sad*, they just get pissed off, like it is their due.

I don't know if it is *the men* or Nance's view of them that makes me more desolate. I pretend to yawn, but my teeth are chattering – Did you turn the air conditioning on?

It's roasting in here, Nance says.

I ignore the way she's looking at me because she has looked at Ezra that way too. I gargle with Listerine and spit out mint-green – I have to show you this other guy. He's Russian.

Nance turns on the faucet too hard and water sprays every-where. She scrubs her hands.

You're not doing it again, she says, and it isn't a question.

I comb my hair, gaily. Why wouldn't I?

She makes a big show of packing her bag, though we both know she can't afford to get an earlier flight.

10

After Nance left, I stayed up night after night reading blogs by Sugar Babies. When I woke up, I read until I got hungry and then headed out. It was late July. The sidewalk was full of tourists who knew no better than fighting the heat. I spent my afternoons lying in the shade in Central Park, letting my thoughts bleed into the sky so I could see their colours. Nance had a way of showing me the single fact about a person that would poison the rest. She said that Lexi was fundamentally boring and needed a kooky friend in her portfolio, that Conrad made fun of me behind my back, that Ezra would have cheated while I had a child in the womb. I could not stand any more of her pity.

I emailed Dr Agarwal to say that I was going to Ibiza to get some sun. Or Mykonos. Or Cancún. He called and I didn't pick up. He left a voicemail, urging me to make an appointment, which I deleted. I had found the prescription that worked. I wouldn't have cared if it was poison. I couldn't risk him taking it away. I counted up what I saved from Liderman and what Agarwal gave me; enough for two months.

I went to Soul Cycle with energy coursing through me. I went double-time. I heard the girls behind me whispering in awe and picked up the pace.

I knew that I wasn't well, but in America I had never been well. I had been miserable for months. We kill animals in less pain and call it mercy. After so many wasted hours, days and

379

weeks doing nothing, and making nothing, how much better to be electric. I performed star jumps for each depressed day I had lived through. I tied my hair in a messy topknot, like a supermodel. Make-up took an hour. I took hundreds of photos of my mannequin self. I scrolled through and watched myself fast-forward. I liked the idea that I could record this process and hone it until each take was identical.

YoungDrivenNoFakersPlz, late 40s. Grand Central Station, Food Court.
27 July: *The longest lunar eclipse of the 21st century.*
Balance: $137. Compensation: $50
Receipt: $12 *(Tsingtao x 2)*

I had assumed the Oyster Bar; I'm wearing a yellow silk dress, slit to the navel.

Tyler hands me an envelope; he doesn't want this to *feel transactional*. He attempts a wink but it looks like a tic. Where are your parents from exactly? He takes a swig of his beer, adding casually, Were they strict?

Very. Where my mother comes from, you get married at sixteen. That's probably why I wanted to do this.

Tyler swallows hard and moves on hastily, telling me about the girl he supported through school, about shopping sprees. He wants cum-company, he says. A little intimacy. In-tim-a-cee. Macy's. A glowball of spit hits the table and stays where it lands.

I pin the receipt to my bedroom wall, with the others; I keep my records alongside my research. I take off my make-up with care and apply papaya enzyme. I remember how careful Ezra was to look after his voice, and practise my accents; little-girlish, husky. I will be one of those who demand $1,000 to show up. I am smarter than the others and my eyes are full of glow. I hunger through comment sections.

Midwestern wife: If you give head for money then you're a hooker
Twinkle: You suck dick for free though, right?
PrettyInPink: A wife is just a whore with a long-term contract
Midwestern wife: Whores get herpes, not husbands.

If one gives me $3,000 a month for dinner once a week, which is what, three hours tops? $3,000 divided by 4 is $750 divided by 3 is $250 an hour. Is that enough?

I only go out at night to run along the river. When I return, Nikolai is watching the security cameras. You should be careful out so late, Miss. I skip around the desk and throw my arms around him. Nikolai pulls away, adjusting his uniform. As the elevator doors close, I feel him eyeing me, warily.

Days pass. I text Dr Agarwal asking him to send my prescription to the pharmacy; a friend will FedEx it to Ibiza. He calls again. When I don't answer, he texts: he is concerned I am exhibiting symptoms of mania. He urges me to call him ASAP. I start covering the windows with Post-it notes – pink for dos, blue for don'ts. The humidity breaks and I lie on the bed with the windows open, smelling the rain. I do not need to sleep. I pace the flat like a tiger. I throw the salt index cards away and order ten new packets on Amazon Prime.

1 August: President Trump calls for the Russia investigation to end and accuses Special Counsel Robert Mueller of being 'totally conflicted'.

Balance: -$45. **Compensation:** $100. **Gift:** *Godiva chocolate.*
Receipt: $289 *(Dover sole, braised greens, Daniel-Etienne Defaix, Côte de Lechet 2005)*

Chris stands to kiss my cheek. I'm not drinking, but you can if you like. I'm thrown off by his being British. It's part of my armour, I need it. We can tell my friends we met on Tinder, ha. How different is it from any other dating site, really?

I shrug. The men are more successful. More alpha. Ding ding.

He has tried dating women his age, but they're a suspicious lot. He doesn't know what it is, but girls on SA tend to be more open to disparate experiences, more excited about life, more like *he* is. He tells me about his last social enterprise. Mahatma Gandhi once said *be* the change you want to see.

I try to look at him like he invented words.

He tells me about dinner the other night. Lovely young thing. Hair down to here – he brushes my arm with his index finger and my whole body shudders – good listener. But when I asked about her passions, what *drove* her – he tries to get the waiter's attention without appearing to exert himself. I order a glass of wine and he looks relieved.

Go on then, make it a bottle. Anyway, I made it clear that I didn't want to waste her time. God knows, it's taken me years, but I know myself. So I told her I couldn't see it working. She balled up her napkin, like this – I notice the hair on his knuckles.

And she said, do you have any idea how much money I've spent getting *ready* for *you*? It was a revelation; she viewed me as an investment; getting your hair done, nails, the rest. It was all a bit . . . Essex. If I wanted a call girl I'd pay for one. Whereas you are so exotic.

When I look up the hunger in his face is frightening. He texted earlier: I don't like to discuss these matters over dinner, but there's $500 if you'd like to stay over.

Chris kisses me like I am deep-sea diving equipment.

You have such big eyes, he says. So honest. Like a frightened deer.

I have targets to meet. On the way back to his apartment, I drop pins.

You should, he says, noticing. You *should* check in with your friends, I'd want Abigail to. He shakes his head violently, as if these two thoughts are warring species. He stops on the sidewalk to show me photos. His daughter has just got her first braces, pink and blue.

Back at mine, I Google: Define exotic.

People also ask: What does exotic mean sexually? Foreign, exciting; typically submissive. Is this what Tess calls *making the most of what I have*? I watch a make-up tutorial and line my eyes with kohl. The girl recommends hair extensions and bold jewellery, featuring beads, feathers and natural stones. Her bindi is diamante. Carefully, I draw one on with gold eyeliner. I take a selfie to send to Nance, captioned Indian Barbie. The buzzer goes and I answer the door without thinking. Nikolai stares for a second then thrusts my handbag at me.

You left it in the lobby.

My heart is hammering at my chest. I delete the photo but it's not enough, I want to undo this. I turn off the lights. I wash my face with soap and water. I scrub the bindi off with my toothbrush and nail-polish remover.

WealthyDemocratEntreFunEur, 34. Spyglass Rooftop Bar.
6 August: Boris Johnson writes in the Daily Telegraph that women in burkas look like letter boxes.
Balance: *$684*. **Compensation:** *$500*. **Gift:** *lingerie (estimate $300)*.
Receipt: *$142 (espresso Martinis x 6, tuna tartare x 2)*.

A queer sultry summer *Bell Jar* kind of day. We drink espresso Martinis. He mentions that he has booked a hotel room at the W.

You're talking too fast, slow down, he says, amused at first. Suddenly, he gets suspicious. He glances at my phone, like it might be recording. What is this, an interview?

It's not an interview, it's a room with a view, I purr.

What?

A hotel room is like whatever because you're here today, gone tomorrow.

I am struggling to hold our conversation together. I don't remember the last full sentence I said.

But it doesn't matter because my body is pulsing with the kind of wanting that makes his face pixelate. And why not. Why not.

After that, it is easy.

I let their gaze go through me. I imagine a force field so thin that it cannot be seen or felt except for a slight vibrating, if you are paying attention to the edges of the person in front of you, which these men never are. I become a receptacle to pour worries into, knowing they are safe, that they will not be judged, that I am capable only of taking. I only ask questions which they've already answered, which they want to answer again.

I send Nance a postcard of a woman drinking absinthe at a street cafe.

I only regret the drinks I do not remember.

I start writing the men down in earnest after one, Canadian, refers to his job at PriceWaterhouse Cooper as the love of his life. I mean, money can't keep me warm at night, but it doesn't demand children, or try to change who I am. Even if his preppy parents would think I'm a catch – Oxford, gentle-seeming, racially ambiguous but-not-black – to him I'm less than human. He smells like amaretto and shoe polish. We have a lingering disdain for each other. The sex is indifferent. I run out of wall space. I label a shoebox *Men Tell Me I'm Exotic* and start putting index cards in that.

AdventureCapitalist, 42.
10 August: Announcement of confirmation hearings for Brett Kavanaugh to be held in September.
Balance: *$2,213.* **Compensation:** *$200*
Receipt: *$280 (Del Maguey Pechuga Mezcal, small plates)*

We go to some place around the corner from his flat in Meatpacking. They serve small glasses of mezcal and wild boar and wilted greens and beads of pink velouté, as bright as coral. Antoine closes his knees around one of mine and puts down his fork, speaks coaxingly – But you are a nice girl. You don't want some old guy, saggy balls in your face, scrotum, fuckin', heart monitor – beep – beep – he makes a noise like he's flatlining, then reaches for his water because he's laughing so hard.

He has a lithe body, it reminds me of those feral cats that feed on scraps.

His apartment is vast, hotel-sparse. He offers me a drink, then kisses me suddenly, near biting, and I spill red wine on his white couch. I stare at the stain spreading.

You can make it up to me, he says.

He treats me like a rag doll and I go floppy. Part of the walls and the floor, I am everywhere, like God is. At 3 am he barks, I have to go to work in two hours and you haven't even made me come.

Seekingliterarypartnerincrime, The Empire Hotel.
21 August: Michael Cohen pleads guilty to eight federal charges of fraud.
Balance: $6,000 (spree of PPM). Compensation: $200. Gift: Delta of Venus, second-hand
Receipt: Kept for VAT purposes (gin and tonics x 4, bottle sauvignon blanc x 2)

My hands are shaking so I let Casey pour the wine. He keeps his wedding ring on. I tell him that Kate Moss had her wedding ring designed after Zelda Fitzgerald, isn't that tragic? Perchance, I add, I'll market a tooth floss after Kate Moss called Must Floss Moss.

Casey asks if I am feeling okay and says that I seem agitated. He clears his throat. My wife has mental health problems. We see a very good – very tough – but very good therapist.

His phone starts playing 'Here Comes the Bride'. He walks to the bar, mouthing *two more*. He sits down, explaining, It calms her, knowing that I'll pick up.

I notice that hair dye has stained his scalp.

So, you're listed as forty-something online, I say, playfully.

He pulls me closer. Well, I had to, otherwise the algorithm would have screwed me and we would never have met.

So, you're what, fifty? Sixty?

Do sixty-year-olds kiss like this?

His lips are cold. His phone goes off again. He picks up, getting increasingly irritable. I drink the second bottle of wine without noticing. When I bring up cash, he says he's not sure he wants to *monetise* this per se, but he'd be happy to act as a mentor. On the way out, he pulls me into the fire exit. He kisses in a rhythmic persistent way that makes my legs go jelly. We go on kissing in the lobby, on the sidewalk, on the subway platform. I see a man further down recognise him and detach myself, but there's no time to warn Casey.

Aren't you going to introduce me to your friend?

I extend my hand. Casey meets my eyes with no recognition. I don't know her, he says.

When the train pulls in, I climb on and press my face into the corner. They climb on after me. At 59th, I stamp, deliberately, on Casey's foot, grinding my heel in.

My last index card: Oliver. Grey eyes, wry smile. A lawyer who wanted to be a writer. He realises I'm writing him down, but he takes it well, as if he's commissioned me to make a statue. He tells me about the first time he masturbated. With each detail, he looks at me, hopefully. I feel so bad for him that I pretend to be taking notes on my phone. Wait, he says, wait. I can do better.

*

After Oliver, the men started blurring. One told me about all the girls he'd been conned by, including a French student who insisted her baggie full of crystal meth contained sequins. One, whose wife had given him a threesome for his fortieth, drank malbec, while she sat twisting her pearls around her fingers, her eyes begging me to decline. One put Saran wrap over his sheets because he was washing them too much and his girlfriend was getting suspicious, or was that the one who wanted to wrap me in it, who told me to wear it under my dress at dinner.

And finally, I stopped being able to write. I couldn't tell them apart. Instead: amber shadows running around the bottom of whiskey glasses. Instead, cascades: hotel rooms, service providers, wedding rings on bedside tables, trembling fingers, flabby backs, the base notes of expensive cologne; vetiver, erosion, stubble burn.

I scrolled through my WhatsApp thread with Nance.

Nance: Text me when you get home.
Iris: I got $200 for a pretty disgusting kiss and drinking a bottle of wine.
Nance: When are you going to get it. You're worth more than that.
Nance: There's no shame in coming home.

I called Dr Agarwal and told him that I was experiencing some negative side effects; I was working again – that's good, he replied – but I couldn't tell whether the connections I was making were real. I told him that I couldn't sleep and couldn't eat and that alcohol seemed like kerosene. Dr Agarwal answered that Ibiza had rung alarm bells. He had to hang up because there was an emergency – one of his patients had threatened a family member with a knife during an episode. I tell you this by way of example, he went on, because the majority of fatalities occur when patients stop taking their medication. It's crucial that you reduce the dosage gradually, rather than coming off entirely. We booked an appointment for the next day. Later, he texted: Please bear in mind that although you feel bad now, if you come off it might be even worse. By then, I knew that it would. I tapered gradually to a low dose, so low that Liderman had said any effect must be a placebo. I didn't care if it was. Moods can be disordered but they can also be tidal. As long as the moon is there, there will be a high tide and a low.

I spent a few days in bed listening to *Harry Potter* audiobooks. I dragged myself out to run, but my energy was watery. When I got back, I didn't recognise my window. It was full of Post-its, hundreds of them, covered with my signature. I had had the idea, I remembered, of leaving the men calling cards. The water in the coffee machine was rancid. The fridge was full of yoghurts with bright foil tops and the little boxes of sugary cereal children eat. My bookmark bar was full of tabs about sugar, but the granular kind, and the obesity epidemic, and the sugar trade, and how to treat raw sugar cane. I started piecing things together. I toyed with the idea of booking other dates, for the material. Various men texted and I pasted the same reply: I enjoyed our time together but I am not interested in pursuing this. Casey texted and I told him to go fuck himself. Antoine sent me a dick pic and I screenshotted it and considered blackmailing him, striking one at the heart of the men, and then I deleted it and went back to work.

I rewatched videos from SA's annual conference. I had been

looking at the girls before, like in adverts, but now I looked at the buyers. When I looked through the stories I'd pinned as important – the time I went to a 7-star hotel in Dubai and walked into a mirrored wall, my sexual liberation – I realised they were all advertisements, put out by Seeking Arrangements.

I started gathering the stories without glossy websites. I sent Nance another postcard: zjesc z kims beczkę soli: Polish friendship proverb, meaning to have eaten a cask of salt with someone. (I worry that I am too much, even for you.)

Sugar Dating is a small book about sex and capitalism. Shifting the focus from the objectification – and de facto commodification, and in the author's case, exoticisation – of women, the book asks whether sugaring is a legitimate means by which women can transform erotic capital into capital. In the #MeToo era, can those savvy to their market value profit from it? Or, does the jargon of the sugar industry merely provide young women with a sense of shallow professionalism and false promise of agency? Interviews with former Sugar Daddies and Sugar Babies sit alongside conversations with current CEOs from the Sugar industry. Part memoir, part cultural commentary, the book shines a light on the prevalence of sugaring in popular culture and asks Who was Holly Golightly if not a Sugar Baby?

I only remembered sending the email when the agent replied to it. She wanted to meet. She suggested lunch. I forwarded this to Nance without a message. Nance didn't reply to the email, but I got a postcard from her a few days later which she had sent in reply to mine: I love you. Why otherwise?

On the last weekend in August, I returned all the clothes – paisley, diamante, leopard print, shoes half the size of my feet, shoes with feathers. The receipts were in the bags. I hadn't even opened them. Ray called about settling Dr Agarwal's bill. Dr Agarwal suggested the three of us could talk things over. I told him that wasn't necessary. Ray seemed ambivalent about this. I told him I was going to go home before my visa ran out. He was silent for a moment, then said, If that's what you think is best. I didn't tell him about the agent. We met for coffee. He told me that he had lost his job. His ex-colleagues kept sending him bonsai trees for luck – *Pachira aquatica*, money trees – they're supposed to bring prosperity, he said, gloomily, but I've drowned five. I had $3,000 from the men in an envelope in my pocket – I had wanted to give it to Ray – I hadn't wanted to owe him. I kept my hand on it, as we made small talk, and then I said I had to get back to work. Every time I spent more than a few hours away from my manuscript I felt physically uncomfortable, prickly. As we were leaving, Ray looked at me curiously and said, You seem more yourself, and I said, Yes, I am, yes. That evening, I bought my own plane ticket home.

27.10.19

It's Ndulu's twenty-fifth birthday party. It's 3 am. They're in the woods behind Max's house. The bonfire has been burning for hours and flares up at random moments. Ndulu and Lucas are poised in sprint-starts a few metres away. They have been watching Persian fire-jumping festivals on YouTube. Iris watches them pelt forwards, as if they are going to jump it. At the last second, Ndulu swerves, and Lucas goes stumbling into the embers.

It's not funny, you guys, Max calls, watching proceedings from a deckchair.

Ndulu is running laps in the dark. He runs behind the trees, throwing his voice and laughing, eerily, and heads turn as he passes.

They're back from tour. Max's parents are away. He is the only one living at home now. The group has migrated a few times, to the kitchen and back, for more booze, to put Ndulu's laptop in rice, to get the next round of emergency chargers. Iris watches Max gather a few cups into a bin liner and then return to his drums. He plays with a grace that surprises her, like the drumsticks are supple, an extension of his arms. Lucas is still scanning the trees for a flash of Ndulu when he hears his guitar and realises they're playing without him. When they start again, there is a bit of heckling, a few whoops. Mainly there are all the other parties, and other nights, reverberating.

Nance and Iris are sitting on the perimeter with Nance's girlfriend, Alice. They're out of breath from dancing. Iris doesn't recognise most of the people here. The fire makes everyone outside their circle of light look silver and foxish. Every now and then someone shields their eyes and peers in at them. Nance points out the drum-guards on Max's arms to Alice, who nods.

He used to be such a flimsy bastard, but now look at him, Nance says.

Alice is a painter and smells like turpentine. She has blonde hair down to her waist. She listens to Nance with intense attention; she doesn't seem phased by the people dressed in glitter and coats or the drugs being passed around on plates.

I'm going to make s'mores, Alice says, pulling herself to her feet. Nance watches as she gets closer to the fire. She retrieves a bag of marshmallows from her pocket and Nance claps a hand to her forehead.

I'm only with her for her body, she says.

Metallic pink sparks burst over the dark field and everyone goes *oooh*. There's a wave of derisive laughter, but a second later a cluster of blue stars explodes and everyone goes *ahhh*. Iris checks her phone. Tess is in Greece with a man called Duncan she refuses to talk about. He started a WhatsApp group and added Iris. He posts photos of Tess posing in front of various sun-scorched walls. Tess screenshots an Anne Carson book open on the breakfast table. And kneeling at the edge of the transparent sea I shall shape for myself a new heart from salt and mud.

Alice returns by herself and drops down to sit beside Iris. They watch the flames lick at the branches of the silver birch. Max runs over with a bucket of water and Alice grimaces.

Iris laughs. You have no idea how many times this place has nearly gone up in flames.

Ezra has stuck near the fire all evening, claiming to keep an eye on it, feeding it twigs. They watch as he tries to strike up

393

conversation with Nance, who is skewering marshmallows. He points out the surrounding trees. Nance drops her s'more into the fire and swears loudly. Iris watches her kicking up embers, hurling fury into the night. She can't tell if the tirade is directed at Ezra, the s'more that never was or the flames that stole it. Nance stomps over with a few charred s'mores on a plate, rolling her eyes at Ezra, who follows, looking sheepish.

Alice accepts a s'more and a kiss from Nance. Ezra prods the grass, gingerly, checking if it's wet, before sitting down. Did you hear the fireflies exploding?

The wood probably wasn't dry, Iris says.

There's a crackling and Ezra gazes at the fire, as if through sheer concentration he can ignore the shower of golden sparks overhead. God, I hate Halloween.

When Iris doesn't turn to him, Ezra clears his throat and fiddles with his phone.

It's Diwali, actually, she says.

Nance interrupts. Does anyone want a fucking s'more or have I scorched my eyebrows for nothing.

Alice crams one into her mouth. Iris copies her. Nance looks at Ezra stonily, then thrusts out her pack of cigarettes.

He hesitates. No thanks. Every time I want one, I just have a line of coke instead.

Iris bursts out laughing. Ezra brushes his nose on the back of his hand. Iris picks up a twig and snaps it. Did you hear that Labour are supporting a second referendum now?

They've been doing that for ages, Ezra says.

Well, there were outliers who wanted a second one, but Corbyn ruled it out – now the leadership are in line too. He's only tolerant of the idea now because it's a way of avoiding No

Deal. Before the vote, he rated his Remain enthusiasm as a seven or a seven and a half out of ten. Not exactly a ringing endorsement, is it?

Politics penalty, Nance says loudly. That'll be a fiver.

Ezra shrugs. Not much point in putting it off.

You know we can only stockpile enough insulin for fourteen weeks, right? Iris says. And your phone won't work when you're touring.

It'd be good to disconnect. Ezra leans back on his elbows. The people voted. Democracy means respecting the majority opinion.

Iris pulls at the grass. If we had more citizens' assemblies, right, where people could deliberate over time and vote in a way that means something—

Imagine how much you'd hate having to make all those decisions, Ezra smirks.

Iris looks at him coolly. Ezra has never seemed small to her before. Now, the parts of him that always seemed to be changing are fixed. She can imagine who he will be in five years, or ten. She looks away.

Nance sits up, looking murderous. The next person to ask me about the backstop will be found in a ditch.

Iris mouths *you love it*. Nance mouths back *fuck off*. Nance tucks Alice's hair behind her ear.

Nance says that you're on a Stendhal kick. *On Love*? Iris says. Alice looks pleased. Do you know it? I've been reading his stuff on Racine.

I used to be obsessed with Stendhal. You know that bit when he talks about the process of crystallisation of projected ideals around the loved one. In the salt mines of Salzburg.

Ezra interrupts. When were you reading about that?

When I was writing about salt.

Wait, are the salt mines real? They exist in physical space?

Alice nods and pulls out her phone to find him a picture.

If you throw something in, the most meagre detail, a twig, even, salt crystallises around it – Iris cups her hands to show him – after a few months, the twig is transformed. Then, over time, it falls away.

Only Max is playing now, the kind of percussion that forms an acoustic haze. Ndulu is dancing like he's trying to start a Mexican wave. Lucas is a few metres from the fire, pawing the ground, sizing up his chances of making it over.

There's another bang from the fire and Nance widens her eyes.

This forest is full of noises, she whispers.

Alice shivers. So, when is the party over?

Ezra points to the first streaks of pink in the sky, like a wine stain that hasn't yet washed out.

Oh lads. Nance groans. I have to be at work in the morning.

Iris begins to detach herself from the warm heap of bodies. Her skin feels raw and dirty. Her hair smells like burning leaves. Don't tell me what time it is, she says, putting her thumb over the clock on her phone as she checks it. Got an early flight. Duncan has food poisoning. You'd think he was the sole survivor of a war. I've told him to write an aria. Will you be out all night? The birds sound crazed and there's a headache starting behind her eyes.

Acknowledgements

This book is indebted to *Salt: A World History*, by Mark Kurlansky.

My greatest thanks go to my editor Emmie Francis and to everyone at Faber. For her guidance and grace, I am extremely grateful for my agent, Emma Paterson.

To the London Library, for the Emerging Writers Programme and for the Carlyle membership. To Anne Stillman, for telling me about the saltmines.

I am lucky to have had many teachers/guides but I count my collisions with Joy Williams, Jenny Offill, Deborah Eisenberg and Rebecca Godfrey (anti-heroines!) as kismet. Thank you to Rob Spillman and the extraordinary team at Tin House. Most of all, my thanks go to Elissa Schappell, for making me feel sane and for telling me I needed an editor.

For their faith, generosity and support, my eternal thanks goes to my family and to Georgia Bird, Olivia Jones, Georgia Haseldine, Paula Petkova and to Jessica Lambert, for her reactions and for having patience while I learn to pose.

Thank you to my teachers and fellow writers at Columbia, who poured their time into my short stories, the fragments of which became *Wild Pets*.

Thank you to my readers Pete Target, for your steadfast attention, and Etienne Berges, for your elegance and for insisting on the existence of so many worlds.

Above all, thank you to Joanne O'Leary – miniature tyrant and muse incarnate – without whom *Wild Pets* would not exist.